The Boys of Hawkhouse School;

OR,
ADVENTURES ON SEA AND LAND.

I0691133

"'IS IT POSSIBLE THAT I KILLED HIM?' GROANED THE YOUNG MAN."

No. 1.

PRICE ONE HALFPENNY.

[PUBLISHED EVERY MONDAY.]

THE
BOYS OF HAWKHOUSE SCHOOL;
OR,
Adventures on Sea and Land.

———————

CHAPTER I.

HAWKHOUSE SCHOOL—THE NEW BOY—JACK FIREBRACE AND OLD FLICK HAVE A
STRANGE ADVENTURE.

"What is your name?"

"Jack Firebrace."

"Your age?"

"Sixteen."

"Know the classics?"

"A little; hope to learn a good deal more here."

"Then, I'm afraid you will be disappointed," replied the questioner, and then, after whistling softly, he renewed his inquiries.

"Can you fight?"

"A little."

"What's your fighting weight?"

"Don't know, but willing to try with anyone here," was the quick reply.

The inquirer nodded approval of this, but took no further notice of the speech.

"What is your father?"

"Dead."

"Mother?"

"Is also dead."

"Sorry to hear it. Give me your hand and let us be friends; but as I have asked you all these questions, and you have answered me straightforwardly and fairly, I think I ought to let you know as much about me—don't you?"

"Well, it would be fair. Still, I will not press the point if you do not wish it," replied Jack.

"Oh, I have no secrets. All the fellows know me thoroughly; my name is Felix Flitter. I am rising sixteen; know little Latin and less Greek. Can fight like an angel when occasion requires. Am an orphan, which I regret; shall come into a pretty good fortune when I am twenty-one, which I do not regret; and that is all about me."

"Since you have been so candid, Mr. Flitter—"

"Oh, hang the Mister business! call me Flitter; I shall call you Jack. I would ask you to call me Felix, for I like the cut of your jib, but it is such a mouthful; besides, it comes down at last to Flix."

"Why not call it at once old Flick?"

"That will do; and now, Jack, fire away with your question," said old Flick, as we shall now call him.

"Well, since you have been so candid about yourself, perhaps you would not mind telling me what sort of place this school is?"

"A mystery. Old Ebenezer Gruesome, the proprietor of the establishment, you have seen, so I need not say much about him. From his wandering propensities, both by night and day, but especially the former, we have named him the 'old Ghost.'"

"Rather complimentary to the headmaster of Hawkhouse," laughed Jack.

"Then there is Mr. Percy Pliant, better known amongst us as 'Supplejack,' for you can turn and twist him about just as you like; but he is a good, kind, daring fellow. I think you will like him."

"I am glad to hear that," said Jack.

"But mind, he is only tutor No. 2. Tutor No. 1 disappeared suddenly."

"Indeed! I should like to know how

that was?" said Jack Firebrace. "I love a mystery."

"Then you will have plenty of them here, I can assure you," returned old Flick.

"So it would appear. But go on with your story."

"Well, here it is, old boy. One night when we boys were in the dormitory, we heard such a row going on. It seemed to me that at least fifty men were rowing. Well, next morning old·Ghost—that's Gruesome, you know—said, in his acid manner, 'Boys, Mr. Willit got tipsy last night, and I had to turn him out of the house; he shall never enter here again. Mind, if you meet him, don't speak to him; if you do, it will be the worse for you,' and then he stalked out of the room."

"And have you ever seen him again?" demanded Jack Firebrace.

"Never; but Tomkins over there swears he has seen his ghost in the long room."

"Oh; but Tomkins is always seeing ghosts," chorussed the other boys, for the conversation took place in the school-room at Hawkhouse, and all the scholars had assembled together to find out what they could of their new school friend, Jack Firebrace.

"We will hear about the ghosts another time; now let us get on with the school," said Jack.

"Let me see—we left off at Pliant. Well, then, we will go to the house-keeper," continued Flitter.

"Always an interesting person in a boys' school," said Jack Firebrace.

"This is a very interesting party," grinned old Flick, "but you won't get round her in a hurry. Her name is Drusilla Drysdale, commonly called the 'Vampire.' Her nature is cruel, her delight evil. She is as dry as tinder. She has a son called Jim, nicknamed 'Goblin Jim,' for very good reasons. In the first place, he is always gobbling up something eatable or drinkable, and in the second, he is so fantastic and impish, that we doubt whether he is not the familiar imp or demon to the Vampire."

"Well, you really seem to have a nice family party here."

"So you will find out in a little time. As for Hawkhouse—a castle, for, really and truly, this is a castle—you had

better come with us and see what you can of it. But first learn this, the place is haunted! I have not actually seen a ghost, but I have seen strange lights, and as to the noises, they are sometimes terrible."

"Can you not account for them?" asked Jack Firebrace.

"In no way but one, and that is— ghosts! But come along, and let us search the castle."

Instead of accompanying the boys in their travels round Hawkhouse, we will take a rapid glance at that strange building, both inside and outside.

Hawkhouse had been built in the twelfth century, and had been strengthened by its successive owners, until it had become a place of considerable strength.

It stood upon a rocky headland, jutting out into the sea, its massive square stone tower frowning down upon the golden sands of a small bay.

The crumbling walls were ivy-grown, and out of the chinks grew the wild sea-daisy, and rich lichens clothed the stone embrasures.

From the distant village, which lay down in a valley, a broad road ran up to the castle, and, from this road, several footpaths led down to the sea-shore, whilst on the other side of the road were sheep-walks, leading off to the distant crags.

One part of the castle had been patched up so as to make a kind of mansion; modern doors and windows had been fitted into it, and several small out-houses added on to it, and what had once been the great dining-hall served now as the schoolroom.

A cheerless, dreary old place, filled with strange niches and corners; having queer, dark passages leading to staircases which led up to doors that opened on nothing, the rooms to which they led having fallen away.

A terrible place for a rough night, for there the sea sent in its heavy breakers, dashing and foaming against the rugged cliffs. The winds howled round the battlements, and shook the old tower as though they were the ghosts of the old warriors who had been slain in attacking this castle, now on its wings, trying to wreak their vengeance on the walls, and lay them low in the dust, even as they themselves had been laid.

In the deep winter months, when the snow lay thick on the ground, Hawkhouse was as dreary a place as one could wish, or, rather, was far more dreary than anyone would have desired it to be, unless the individual had a desire to go melancholy mad.

Such was Hawkhouse School, wherein is placed our story.

"Look here, Jack, old man," said Flitter, as he, Jack Firebrace, and Tomkins entered a dismal, stone-paved building; "this is the chapel. The stones which form the pavement are all gravestones. Can you read any of the names if I strike a light?"

"I don't know if I can, but if you strike a light I will try."

Flitter produced a flint and steel, for matches were not invented in the time of our story, and presently a few sparks fell upon the tinder, and old Flick began to blow it into flame.

As the red light from the tinder came and went, the old chapel looked very ghostly.

Suddenly a terrific yell echoed through the vaults, and an impish shadow appeared to fall from one of the crossbeams nearly upon the boy Tomkins's head.

Uttering the most dismal yells, the little impish form bounded and rolled about the floor.

Screaming with fright poor Tomkins rushed off, leaving Jack Firebrace and old Flick.

"What the deuce can that be?" said Jack. "This is some trick."

"Trick!" replied old Flick, in surprise. "Who do you think would venture here alone?"

"That I cannot say," said Jack. "I own the creature, whoever it was, alarmed me at first; but it must be one of the schoolboys."

"Nonsense! No boy would venture here alone, and I'm off," said old Flick, making towards the door.

"Stay!" cried Jack Firebrace, suddenly. "Did you not speak about a boy called Goblin Jim?"

"Certainly; but I do not think that Goblin Jim would venture here alone."

"Nonsense," said Jack Firebrace; "it is my belief that that young gentleman has much of this ghost business to answer for. Come, old Flick, blow up the flame whilst I watch the door. Goblin Jim shall not pass me, though he be a real goblin."

"All right, old man," and taking heart at his friend's words, old Flick once more bent him to his task.

The tinder caught; a stick dipped in phosphorus was applied to it, and ignited at once.

Flicker then produced an old rope's end, well tarred, which soon was on fire, and made an excellent torch.

"Now to seek for this Goblin Jim. If we find him, he shall pay dearly for his goblin tricks."

Vainly they turned over the lumber that choked up the aisles; not a creature could they find save rats and beetles, that walked leisurely away as if in no fear of the presence of man.

"You see," said Felix Flitter, "no one is here. Now, how can you account for these things?"

"By the presence of Master Jim the Goblin," said Jack, quietly; "and I propose we go together to find him out, and, when we do find him out, go as far as we can to make a ghost of him in earnest."

"With all my heart; for if these noises and sights be caused by man or goblin I do not know, but I should like to find out."

"There is another reason, Flick," said Jack. "It strikes me that this school will be a precious dull affair; so I am determined to make as much fun as I can for myself. Now, I can see no end of a spree to be had out of this."

"Can you? Then I should think you are the sort of chap who would see fun in a funeral."

"Come, things are not so bad," said Jack, laughing.

"Oh! you may laugh, old fellow, but you do not know this school," replied the other.

"But I soon shall, and I guess those who try to play tricks upon me will find they are rather mistaken in their customer. We will fancy ourselves knights-errant, who, in search of adventure, have come to this haunted castle, and have sworn to lay the spirits, or to perish in the attempt."

"It will be a jolly spree if we do lay the ghosts; but if they lay us instead — ha! old boy."

"Never fear that. Now to resume our search."

"Forbear!" cried a hollow voice close by them. "Touch not the tombs of the dead."

Flick started back.

Not so Jack Firebrace. Rushing at a heap of rubbish, from which the sounds appeared to come, he scattered it far and wide, but, to his astonishment, nothing could he find to lead him to the conclusion that anyone had been hiding there.

"That ghost came nearer to settling us than we did to settling him," said old Flick.

"That is right, Flick, old fellow," said Jack. "Laugh, and fear will never touch you."

"Oh, I don't mind fear touching me if nothing else does," laughed Flitter. "But what the deuce have you got hold of there pulling so hard?"

This last exclamation was caused by Jack uttering a cry of surprise, falling on his knees, and pulling violently at an iron ring which appeared fixed in the ground.

"Look here, old chum, this is a trap-door," cried Jack, excitedly. "You see we have discovered something."

"Trap-door? nonsense! As if they put trap-doors to tombs," laughed Flitter.

"I tell you what, old Flick," said Jack; "you are enough to make one mad. You say that you don't believe in ghosts, and you now seem to disbelieve that these sights and sounds are made by mortal creatures. Perhaps you will tell me what you do believe."

"I believe we shall catch cold if we stop here in this damp chapel. Just listen to the row the waves and the wind are kicking up outside. It is enough to make one shiver to death."

"Never mind that; you come and give me a helping hand."

"But who will hold the torch?" demanded old Flick.

"Stick it up yonder in the crack of the wall," replied Jack. "Do make haste."

Flick did what he was told, and soon returned to Jack.

"Look here, old Flick," said Jack. "This must be a trap-door, for here are the hinges."

"By Jove, Jack, you are right!" said old Flick. "Now for a long pull, and a strong pull, and a pull altogether."

The trap yielded to the boys' united efforts and slowly opened, discovering what at first looked like a deep well, but on closer examination Jack saw there was a spiral stone staircase, which descended far down into the darkness.

"Hark!"

Drip! drip! drip! they could here the water falling on the stone steps from the reeking walls.

"Well, Jack, now we have found this very pretty thing, perhaps you can tell me what we are to do with it."

"We must descend into the abyss, and examine it carefully."

"Phew! and is this what you call a spree?" demanded old Flick, with a grimace. "Oh, this is not at all nice."

"What! is my bold companion in arms afraid?" demanded Jack.

"Well, not exactly afraid; but I don't think that that place looks inviting. It's not the sort of place you would like to give a Christmas party in."

"No; but to the bold heart danger always looks inviting," said Jack, in mock heroic tones.

"Then I must say, the boldness of my heart does not quite come up to that standard."

"As you like; but I said I would find out the mystery of the castle, and I will; so if you don't choose to accompany me, old Flick, I will go alone."

So saying, Jack lowered himself down the trap and began the descent.

"Do you really mean to go down that wretched hole?" demanded old Flick.

"I do," replied Firebrace. "I am not afraid."

"I suppose I must follow you," sighed old Flick; "but if ghosts live there no wonder they are so jolly miserable."

Slowly, and, truth to tell, unwillingly, old Flick descended the slippery steps with Jack.

His head had scarcely descended a foot below the level of the chapel-floor when the stone-trap fell with a crash, dashing the torch (which Felix had held aloft to show a better light) out of his hand, and extinguishing it.

As the trap fell, both the lads heard a burst of shrill, fiendish laughter.

"Oh, lor'! they're at it again," exclaimed old Flick.

"Back to the trap!" shouted Jack. "Force it open."

Both the lads rushed to the trap, but they could not move it.

"We're in for it now, old man," said Flick.

Vainly they used their utmost power.

The trap seemed locked, or to have a heavy weight upon it.

At last, exhausted by their endeavours, they sank down upon the steps.

All around was dark, damp, and chill, even as the grave.

"Flitter," whispered Jack, for somehow he seemed almost afraid of the sound his own voice made in this miserable place; "Flitter, I have led you into this dreadful scrape—will you forgive me?"

"It's not your fault, Jack," replied Flitter, in the same tone.

"No; but it was foolhardy on my part to have done it."

"Well, I need not have followed you unless I had pleased," returned Flitter, kindly.

"You are a regular brick, old Flick," cried Jack, feeling inclined to embrace his newly-made friend; "and, if ever I get out of this, you may depend on me through life to death."

"We are both orphans," said old Flick, as he squeezed his companion's hand. "I have no friends in the world, you must be my brother. Let us, Jack, in this silent place, make that compact."

"Willingly, for I have not a friend in the world except Mr. Grindwell, and I scarce can call him one. It is true he has brought me up, but, at the same time, he has always seemed to hate the very sight of me. My father and mother were drowned at sea, and I should have shared their fate, but the ship in which Mr. Grindwell sailed happened in some strange way to save me and one, Owen Salter, a rough old sailor, who now serves Mr. Grindwell."

"So you scarcely know who you are?" said Flitter.

"Oh, I know my name, and that is all," replied Firebrace. "Mr. Grindwell adopted me."

"I can't bear Grindwell," said old Flick; "he's a humbug, I know. Whenever he comes on a visit to Mr. Gruesome the ghosts, or whatever they may be, kick up such a row that I verily believe there must be evil spirits who give a party to welcome him."

"He comes here pretty often then?" asked Jack Firebrace, in no little surprise.

"Often! I should rather think he does. Phew! I hate the old curmudgeon."

"Come, we must not waste time," said Jack, springing to his feet; "we must try the trap again."

"I am ready, Jack."

They used all their strength, but to no avail.

They could not move the trap.

Neither of them spoke, for they felt that to attempt to comfort each other would be useless.

They seated themselves down on the steps in gloomy silence to await their fate.

Silence and darkness around them.

"Hark! what noise is that?"

"Help, help! Murder, murder, murder! Oh! spare me! spare me! Oh, Heaven! I die!"

Jack and his friend suddenly sprang to their feet.

There was no mistaking the agonised tone of that cry.

It was the cry of a strong man, struggling for his life, and feeling that his murderers were gaining in the struggle.

One long, piercing scream, fraught with such agony and terror, that the two lads knew it was that of death, and then all was still again.

"Jack!" said Flitter, in an awestruck whisper, "what can we do? we cannot fly."

"Fly!" replied Jack, in a low tone; "no. That was no ghostly cry. That was the scream of a strong man in his last agony, and it came from the bottom of the well."

"But that makes it all the more dreadful," said Flitter. "What creature can live down at the bottom of this well? I tell you, Jack, that until now I have never believed in ghosts, although I have seen many strange things here, but now I knock under."

"Tut, my dear fellow! we are in the well, they are in the well. Why not one human creature as well as another? That cry—dreadful as it was—has given me fresh hope, for it tells me that most likely there will be a way out of this dreadful place at the bottom of these stairs. We cannot raise the trap. Someone has fastened it on the outside; therefore, we must descend cautiously and feel the walls as we go to find some passage which may lead us out of this dreadful place."

"Dreadful place it is, true enough," replied Flick, with a shudder. "Spirits may haunt it, for it has taken all spirit out of me. But you are right, and so let us be off at once. Come what may, Jack, old boy, we'll stick together."

"That is spoken like a trump; give me your hand. Do not speak. If I squeeze your hand stop, for it will be a sign that I wish to speak to you, or that I have heard something. Now come on."

Cautiously they crept down the stairs, but heard no sound save the dripping of water.

At last a cool wind blew upon the lads, making their hearts beat with joy.

"Don't speak; keep silent," whispered Jack.

Quickening their steps they soon arrived at a small loop-hole cut in the rock.

Through this they pushed their way, and found themselves on a part of the cliff which jutted out a few feet from the face of the cliff.

Up, far above them, rose the battlements of the castle, whilst some forty to fifty feet below them they could, in the darkness of the night, make out a narrow strip of land, and beyond the white foam of the tempest-tossed sea.

The hurricane was at its height.

The rain fell in torrents.

The wind howled and beat in gusts against the cliffs.

The thunder rolled almost incessantly, and the lightning's brilliant flash lit up the scene so vividly, that Jack could see it all after he had closed his eyes.

"We cannot escape from here," said Jack; "the cliff above us and below us is quite perpendicular."

"Still, we are better here than in that ghostly hole," returned old Flick."

"That is true; I don't want to die like a rat in a hole. Take care, old Flick, or the wind will carry us off. Let us lie down here; we shall not feel the force of the storm so much."

They crouched down on the rock and gazed out at sea.

Scarcely had they done so, than the same wild, despairing cry they had heard once before that night rose high up above the storm, chilling their young blood.

A brilliant flash of lightning, and by its lurid light the two boys beheld a man, dressed in black, with a long, black cloak hanging loosely round his shoulders, standing down by the hedge of the sea, his face turned to the cliff.

They saw the face but one moment, but both felt that they would never forget its livid hue, and the features working with agony and despair.

The man stood on the shore with arms upraised, his clenched hands pointing to heaven.

A flash and report of a pistol, the lightning gone, and all dark and still save the howling of the storm.

Again the lightning flash—but the figure was not there.

"Jack," whispered Flitter, "these are but ghosts, who act over and over again the terrible last scene which closed the drama of life."

"It is most strange," said Jack.

"Old fellow," whispered Flitter, "don't you know that, according to the legends of this part of the country, this castle was once inhabited by a band of wreckers, who, when they had wrecked the ships on the shore on such nights as these, killed the crew, and threw the dead bodies into the sea?"

"Well?" replied Jack, pretending not to see the meaning of his companion's words.

"Do you not see that there is no wreck here, no ship or boat cast on the shore?"

"Yes; but I do not understand what that has to do with it."

"How could that strange man have come here without a boat? Besides, we have no wreckers here now. No, no, Jack, those figures we saw are but the dead, acting the dreadful scenes which they played in their lives over again."

What he had beheld and heard was so inexplicable that Jack could make no reply.

"Let us return to the secret passage; who knows but that the trap was only fastened down by spiritual agency, and that, now the ghosts have vanished, we may be able to raise it again."

" We must try it," said Jack.

They had just reached the narrow embrasure, when they were startled by hearing hurried footsteps coming up the stairs.

The lads drew back, and crouched down on the rock, just keeping their heads sufficiently forward to watch if anything passed the window.

A bright flash of lightning lit up the whole scene, and by its lurid light the lads saw a tall man, wrapped in a thick pilot-jacket, and wearing heavy sea-boots, rush pass the opening up the steps.

His face seemed covered with hair from the eyes downwards, whilst his slouched hat covered completely the upper part.

Boom—crash !

Again came the fearful thunder, and, in an instant, all was dark.

" Come, old Flick," whispered Jack, " we must make our way after that ugly man. If he gets out, so can we also."

" Jack, Jack, old fellow, do be careful ! " called Flick, in a low voice; " if it be a man he will kill us."

But Jack had reached the steps, and was hurrying up them as fast as he could.

" I can't be left here alone," groaned old Flick. " This is my first, and I fear it will be my last adventure."

" Hurrah ! "

They reached the trap; it yielded at once to their efforts, and the boys once more stood safe and sound in the old ghostly chapel.

" What shall we do now ? " asked old Flick ; " the supper bell will sound soon, and I feel dreadfully shaky."

" Then the best thing we can do is to hurry upstairs and change our wet clothes for dry ones. The adventure has made me terribly hungry ; so come along, old Flick, and at bed-time we'll talk over our ghostly adventure. Come along."

CHAPTER II.

WHAT HAPPENED AT THE " GOAT INN"—THE MURDER IN THE CAVE—UNDER THE THUMB—PETER PIGWELLAN, THE DEFORMED FISHERMAN.

LEAVING our hero and his friend to change their wet clothes, we must go back a few hours before the time our story commenced.

We have already described the night as exceedingly dark and stormy, and one on which it was anything but pleasant to travel; yet on this night a tall gentleman arrived at the " Goat Inn," the ale-house of the village, and inquired his way up to the castle.

" It's a nasty bit of ground to travel," said the landlord, eyeing the stranger somewhat suspiciously.

" I cannot help that," replied the stranger. " I must reach Hawkhouse to-night."

" For my own part, I shouldn't like to go near Hawkhouse at all," said the landlord, quietly.

" Grant me patience, man," exclaimed the traveller, stamping his foot. " Who asked you to go up to the house ? I wish to know my way to it; I do not ask you to accompany me ! "

This sudden burst of temper surprised the honest landlord not a little, and caused him to take especial notice of the young man.

He was tall, thin, very pale, and more aristocratic than handsome.

His eyes were filled with a strange fire.

He had a habit of contracting his brows until the expression of his face was actually forbidding.

He was clad in a complete suit of black, and a long, black cloak hung from his shoulders.

In his hand he carried a small valise, fastened with a strong lock.

" You might ask me as much as you liked to go with you," growled the landlord, " but I should not think of going. I ain't fond of ghosts, and such like. How the poor brats can live up there in that castle I can't say; I know I could not do so."

The young fellow drank up the tankard of ale he had ordered, and fixing his hat tightly on his head, so that it should not be blown away by the storm, was about to leave the inn without his question being answered, when an old labourer stopped him.

"Don't be offended, young man," he said, "but, truth to tell, Hawkhouse does bear a queer kind of a name hereabouts. Some folks a' been sore scart o' a night as they passed along the road by the crag's foot by sights as they have seen. I ain't seen anything myself, but I have heard others say what others have told them, and that be near enough."

"Old man, I have no belief in those things; even if they exist, I have no fear of them."

"Lor' now—only to hear the like of that now!" ejaculated the landlady, raising her hand and eyes.

"Indeed," said the traveller, with a queer smile, "if such things as ghosts do exist at the castle I shall be very happy to see them. Therefore, if you can tell me how I am to get up the hill, I should be glad to know it. If not, I must find my own way."

"A wilful man must have his own way," said the old labourer. "Keep down the road until you come to a forked road, take the one that turns off to the left, and mind you keep to the broad road. The narrow ones will lead you down on to the coast by Peter Pigwellan's hut, and that is a more fearsome place than the other."

The stranger hurried away, and was soon lost in the darkness of the night.

"He be a queer chap," said the landlord to the labourer, who stood at the door of the ale-house, peering into the darkness so as to see the last of the stranger.

"It looked to me," said a man, who, up to the present time, had sat quietly smoking his pipe in a corner, and appearing not to notice a thing, "it looked more to me as if he had committed a murder, and was vainly trying to fly from his own conscience."

Having delivered himself of this speech, the man, who, by his dress, was evidently a sailor, relapsed into silence once more.

"Ah! Master Sidecraft," said the old labourer, "you always judge so hard of your fellow-men."

"I judge them as they have judged me," said the fellow, roughly, as he got up and shook himself much like a dog when leaving the water. "I have sailed the wide ocean for well nigh forty year now, and I have seen deeds done that would freeze the blood of old or young."

"Nay, Master Sidecraft, you have only been here three months, and, by dropping such words as these, you have become almost as terrible in the eyes of the people as Peter Pigwellan."

"I would like to see this Peter Pigwellan," said the old sailor. "I may know him, for I have sailed all over the world, and know many mariners."

"Ay! but it is no easy matter to find this Peter Pigwellan," said the landlord.

"I thought just now you said he had a hut, or cabin, down by the sea?"

"Yes; and there he keeps himself hidden. He takes to his boat at night, and fishes alone. Rough or smooth, it is all the same to Peter; that is, I think he likes the storm most. Oh! he has got something more than natural about him."

"Well, landlord," said Sidecraft, "I shall not be back to-night. I shall return to-morrow, and so good night."

The landlord bade Sidecraft good night.

Three months ago old Silas Sidecraft had walked into the village and taken up his abode at the "Goat."

No one knew him.

He soon became liked, but everyone noticed that Silas, idle as he appeared to be, had a purpose in view.

Buttoning his coat up to his chin, Silas leant his head down and fought his way against the violent wind that shot the sharp rain into his face.

He turned down a cutting in the cliff leading to the sea.

Here he had to cling close to the cliff to keep him from being dashed to the earth by the violence of the wind.

Still he struggled onward, now and then pausing to watch the foam-crested sea as the livid lightning lit up this terrible scene.

"Ho, hillo, hilloa, hilloa!"

The old man paused suddenly, and raised his hand to his ear to listen.

"Yes," he muttered, "that was a man's cry. If the time has come, well shall I be repaid."

Once more he forced on his way, and once more he heard the wild shout.

"It is his voice. Oh, I know its hard sound—those cruel tones. Now I will drag him to justice; he shall no longer escape my vengeance."

As he spoke he raised his clenched fists towards the inky sky.

Keeping close by the cliff, so as to feel the violence of the wind as little as possible, he crept slowly along, keeping a sharp look-out all round him.

As he turned a large point of rock which jutted out some feet from the cliff, he came suddenly on a narrow opening in the rock forming the mouth to a cave.

From this opening a light came.

"So, so," muttered Silas, "it is the same game as ever. I must be cautious."

He crept slowly into the opening, which widened as he proceeded, until it opened into a chamber some thirty feet deep by twenty wide, and of considerable height.

This cave was lighted up by a torch fixed in a cleft in the rock.

The old man had scarcely time to observe these things before he was felled to the earth by a violent blow on the back of his head.

"Confusion!" muttered a fellow, holding a boat's stretcher in his hand, with which he had just felled Silas Sidecraft; "who would have thought that there would have been anyone on the sands at this time of night; it ain't a Johnny* neither."

As he spoke he rolled the old sailor over with his foot.

No sooner did the light fall upon the old man's face than his assailant staggered back with a cry of horror.

"Silas Sidecraft! by all that is horrible! And here we are at Hawkhouse School!" he exclaimed. "What strange mystery is this?"

At the same moment Silas recovered his senses, and rose slowly to his feet.

"Yes, Richard Randulph, it is Silas Sidecraft who stands before you. For years I have pursued you through this world. I had but one hope, and that

* Johnny—slang name for preventive service men.

was to bring you to justice. Where is my old master, his beautiful wife, and their sweet babe?"

"Where I thought and hoped you were, Master Silas," replied the fellow, coolly—"at the bottom of the sea."

"I knew you could as little turn from blood as the tiger. I have travelled everywhere where I heard that wrecking or piracy went on. I knew that I should find you at last."

"Well, old man, and now you have found me, what do you mean to do?"

"Denounce you to the law, so that you may meet the reward of your crimes."

"You forget you aided and abetted me," laughed Richard Randulph.

"I?"

"Yes, you! Oh, do not stare so; you told me of the immense wealth your master was about to take home with him from the West Indies. You described to me the jewels and diamonds, and deplored the fact that he would sail in an unarmed vessel. Ho, ho, ho! how I laughed when I heard all this! It was fine to think that I should soon have all the wealth. Your ship, the 'Ocean Queen,' sailed in the morning; an hour afterwards my ship, the 'Sea Hawk,' sailed also. Before midnight the 'Ocean Queen' was mine, and every soul on board of her perished but you. How you escaped, old man, I know not."

"Heaven helped me. I was picked up by a ship bound for the coast of Guinea, a slaver, who laughed at my story of the pirates, and landed me on the coast of Africa to live or die, they cared not; they were too much in the same line to interfere with you."

"Honest fellows! You had better have joined with them, Silas," laughed Randulph.

"No, the angel of vengeance called upon me to follow you. I have found you at last."

"And your own death at the same time. Silas, you shall never leave this cave alive!"

"I scorn your threat," cried the old man; "and will drag you to justice."

He sprang forward, but Richard Randulph was far more powerful than Silas Sidecraft.

He grasped the old man by the throat, and dashed him on to the floor of the cave, and knelt on his chest.

"Now, Silas Sidecraft," he said, between his clenched teeth, whilst his eyes shot forth a strange, wild fire, "your time is short. Fool! you might have known that Red Randulph never allowed an enemy to escape. Oh! you may struggle! I like to see you writhe in my grasp. I enjoy your suffering. Silas, you had a son; you lost him years ago; that son is in my power. Ho, ho, ho! he is a coward, Silas, or I would have made something more of him than what he is; but he still must and shall work my wicked will!"

Silas Sidecraft attempted to throw off his antagonist, but the pirate was too strong for him.

With a deep groan the old man closed his eyes, and resigned himself to his fate.

The next moment the pirate drove a dagger into the old man's back.

A cry—a wild scream of horror, but not from the old sailor.

Richard Randulph sprang to his feet and faced the entrance to the cave.

Standing motionless with horror, his hands stretched forward, was the strange man who had inquired his way to Hawkhouse.

Presently the young fellow's face became livid and convulsed.

Foam flew from his lips; he staggered forward and fell over the murdered man in a fit.

For a few minutes even the pirate seemed lost in horror and amazement; but he soon recovered that, and burst out into a loud laugh.

"I think the devil must be hard at work to-night. Who could have dreamed of a meeting like this?"

He turned the young fellow, who was still in a fit, on to his back, and looked at his face.

"Yes, by Heaven, it is young Sidney Morrison," he said, and he chuckled to himself, until the veins on his forehead swelled out like whipcords, and the scar became a deep blue. "To think that he should come at this time," he added. "I'll make him help me to bury the body; more, I will make out that he is the murderer; his hands and clothes are stained with blood. Quick—his knife!"

Kneeling by the insensible young man, the wretch quickly drew from his pocket a clasp-knife.

"Good!" he exclaimed, as he examined the knife; "his name is on the haft, 'Sidney Morrison.'"

He opened the blade, and thrust it into the wound in old Silas's heart.

"His knife is much bigger than mine, so they will think it made the wound."

He then carefully washed his own hands free of all blood-stains, and removed all marks of a struggle.

This done, he seated himself at the mouth of the cave and watched Sidney, who was now recovering.

"Where am I?" said the young fellow, as he looked around.

"In a pretty mess, I should think," growled Richard Randulph. "Have you satisfied your vengeance? Are you often taken that way?"

Sidney sprang to his feet, and, seeing the corpse, remembered all.

"Wretch!" he cried, turning to Randulph, "why did you murder that old man?"

"I murder him?" laughed Randulph; "well, I like that. Don't you come any of those games with me, youngster; it won't quite do. Hang me! I don't believe you had a fit at all, but only put it on to cover your diabolical purpose."

The young fellow passed his hand over his brow, as if unable to recall what had happened.

"I put on the fit to cover my diabolical purpose? You cannot—dare not say I murdered the old man?"

"I do, though. If you don't believe me, look at the knife."

Sidney stooped down and looked at the knife.

"My knife—my knife!" he screamed in tones of heartrending agony. "Oh! I must be mad."

"Well, I hope you can prove that you have fits sometimes, for it is the only thing that excuses such a crime," said Randulph.

"But I saw you strike the death-blow," replied Sidney, now quite dazed.

"Come, stow that! I ain't a good-tempered fellow," cried Randulph, springing up, "and I am not one to have my neck thrust into a halter to please other people. You rushed in here, where this old man and myself had taken shelter, and you send your knife into him, and then go off into a fit. I don't know what folks fancy they see when they are in fits, as I never had one. Maybe you fancied you saw me strike the blow, and rushed forward to save him; but, being all abroad, down you fall and kill him. That's all I know about it."

"Can it be possible that I did it?" groaned the young fellow.

Then, overcome by the passion in his breast, he seemed to lose all control over himself.

"Come," said Randulph, "it's no good going on in that manner. I don't want to be hard upon you. I sha'n't say a word about this. You are the new tutor at Hawkhouse?"

"How do you know that?" demanded Sidney, in surprise.

"That don't matter. I do know it. Now, mark me. My business is smuggling. I shall want a friend in that old Hawkhouse yonder. You must be that friend. As long as you obey me you will be safe. If not, I'll have you denounced as the murderer of this old man."

Sidney Morrison moaned aloud, and leant against the wall, covering his eyes with his hands.

"Come, lend a hand here, and I will help you bury him," said Randulph.

The young man did not move.

Randulph then scooped up the sand to some depth, and threw in the old man's body.

"Take away the knife," said Sidney, with a shudder. "I dare not touch it."

"By your leave, we will let the knife remain where it is," said Randulph, turning the body over so that the knife was underneath. "It is a good witness on my side should we disagree at all."

"As you will," replied Sidney, "but I cannot yet believe I have done this deed. Oh! would I had died before this."

"That does no good at all. You have killed the fellow, so that is settled. You will now have to serve me. Do it well, and you are safe. Do you see that ring on the murdered man's hand?"

Sidney looked, and beheld on the dead sailor's hand a massive silver ring, made in the shape of two snakes twisting together, their heads up as if in anger, and about to strike.

"We won't touch the ring," said Randulph. "It will be better to leave

that until the time we want to identify the body. There! Now we will cover him nicely, and leave him alone in his glory."

Silently, almost as one in a dream, Sidney Morrison looked on. Randulph soon covered the murdered man over with sand, and piled boulders of rock over him.

"Now I think he looks comfortable," said Randulph, with a grin so horrible that young Sidney drew back.

"Come, none of that work with me," said the other, quickly. "I will have none of these put up airs. You are now a criminal. One word of mine, and you swing; and, if you dare to draw back in the slightest manner, you shall too. So look out for squalls, my hearty."

"What would you have me do?" demanded the young fellow, nervously.

"Keep quiet, go to the school, and carry out your duties as master well. Keep from this cave, for here, at times, I run in my cargo of moonbeams and flash.* When you receive a token from me it will come with a messenger. Whatever my messenger commands you to do you must do at once, and without compunction. If you fail, the 'Sea Hawk' will no sooner have her anchor atrip than she will make for the nearest port, leave a letter with a magistrate, and, before many hours are over, you will be safe in prison for murder. Do you understand me?"

"I do. May Heaven help me!" groaned Sidney Morrison.

"Tush! Cease that rot! Don't trust to anyone but yourself, for you hold your life in your own hands. Now go, and remember, boy, you have committed murder."

"Murder! murder!" shrieked Sidney, throwing up his arms.

"Silence!" cried Randulph, in a hoarse tone. "Do you wish to call people down to see what you have done? Remember I have a stake in the little business now. So, if you have any respect for your life, keep quiet."

"Murderer, avaunt! avaunt!" cried Sidney. "You must be the devil in human shape!"

"And, if I be, you have to obey me. See that you do so, or beware! **Your** life is in my hands."

---

* Gin and brandy.

Sidney sprang from him, and rushed out of the cave, screaming—

"Murder! murder!"

Quickly drawing a pistol Randulph fired, and Sidney fell.

"Confound the fool!" growled Randulph. "I did not mean to hit him. He was too valuable to me. I did not aim at him. He must be in another fit."

He drew the young fellow up to the shelter of the cave, and examined him.

"No! he is not hurt."

"You have not killed him, master," croaked a voice close by him.

Randulph started, and looked round.

At his elbow stood Peter Pigwellan, the deformed fisherman.

"Who sent for you, man?" demanded Randulph, in sharp tones.

"No one. But I heard a pistol fired, and came at the signal."

"True; I had almost forgotten that I gave the signal," growled Randulph. "So many strange things have happened to-night that even I scarcely know what I am doing."

"Something very terrible must have happened for you to be put out," said Peter Pigwellan, in half-sneering tones. "You, who have seen so much blood—"

"Blood!" cried Randulph, springing to his feet. "Who spoke of blood?"

"No one. No one spoke of particular blood; but I fancy I can smell it."

"Silence! man. Now, look. You see this young fellow. Take him to your hut, and tend well to him. When he recovers, say that you found him stretched upon the sand, and fancied he must have been cast ashore from some wreck. Take him, and go."

The deformed fisherman seized Sidney Morrison up in his arms, and bore him away to his hut.

Crawling through a small hole at the back of the cave, Randulph ascended a flight of stairs which had been cut in the solid rock.

Up, up, up he went. The staircase twisted round and round as if in a well.

Once, as he approached a narrow embrasure in the wall, he fancied he heard voices.

He glanced swiftly out, but could not see anything, so pushed on, and reached Hawkhouse chapel, where we will leave him, and return to Sidney Morrison and the deformed fisherman.

When Sidney opened his eyes he found himself stretched in a hammock slung to the thick beams which supported the roof of the hut.

This hut was part of a ship that had been wrecked on the inhospitable coast, and, having been turned keel uppermost, served as part of Peter Pigwellan's mansion.

The hut was built of massive timbers, strongly fastened together so as to bear the stress of the frequent storms for which the coast is noted.

The furniture was of diverse kinds, consisting of a table, several sea-chests, a telescope, rifle, gun and pistols, together with sails, masts, oars, and so forth, belonging to a fishing boat.

When Sidney looked up, he beheld the fisherman reading at a table.

The back of the old man was towards Sidney, so that the wretched young fellow at first thought that he was still under Richard Randulph's power.

"Where am I?" gasped Sidney Morrison. "Who are you?"

Slowly Peter Pigwellan rose from his chair, raised the lamp from the table, and then turned quickly round.

The sight which he showed to Sidney Morrison was indeed horrible.

Peter Pigwellan was built for a giant.

His head, hands, and feet were immense, his body large and heavy, with the breadth of shoulders of a Hercules; but Peter's legs had either been born crooked or had gone astray when young.

Thus Peter lost a good deal of his stature, whilst his long arms appeared to be hideously out of proportion.

His huge head appeared to be fixed on his shoulders at once, for neck he seemed not to have any.

On the top of his head the old fisherman wore a red night-cap.

Even when he put his tarpaulin hat on he always had the red night-cap beneath it, for his head was as devoid of hair as a cannon-ball.

His complexion was a dull blue.

This he accounted for by saying he had been blown up by gunpowder, which had destroyed the roots of his hair, so that he had not even eyebrows or eye-lashes, changed his complexion, and twisted his legs into the terrible deformity we have described.

His eyes looked dead and glazed, his

nose had been smashed flat to his face, a thin gash formed his mouth; but here again, as if nature had not made the man ugly enough, accident of battle had helped her, for a sabre-cut had laid both his lips wide open, so that, having never been sewn together properly, they hung open and showed his blackened tusks beneath.

"Did you call?" he croaked, in a voice which seemed to come from between his nose and mouth.

"Great Heaven! who are you? Where am I?" exclaimed Sidney Morrison.

"Safe—saved by me. What makes you look so scared? I'm not a beauty—everyone tells me that. Poor Peter is obliged to hide his ugly face from his brother-men, for they would kill him. I say brother-men, for I am a man in spite of my ugliness. I have a heart of a man, could love like one, if they would let me. But no, that they would not have; they have left me but one chance, and that is, to hate like a man."

"Pardon me for starting so. I have been ill and am still weak."

"Yes, very ill; I found you by the sea. Had I not come in time, you would have been drowned."

"I thank you greatly," said Sidney. "I must have had a fit. I"—then suddenly remembering all that had occurred, he exclaimed—"Oh, Heaven! why did you save me? Would that I had been drowned!"

"A strange wish for one so young," snarled Peter Pigwellan. "Here, lad, take some of this."

As he spoke he poured from a case-bottle a small quantity of brandy into a glass, and handed it to Sidney.

The young fellow took it and drank it off at once.

"Ha!" he said, as a glow came to his hollow cheek, "that warms the heart. I feel better now."

"Ay," muttered Peter, as he put up the case-bottle, "he wants the devil's courage, poor wretch!"

Sidney arose from the hammock, but found his legs were still so weak that he could not stand.

"I fear I must trespass on your kindness to let me stop the night," said Sidney. "I feel so weak, that I fear I shall topple over the cliff on my way to Hawkhouse."

"Hawkhouse!" exclaimed Peter, as if in surprise; then added to himself, "Better do that than reach it."

"You know Hawkhouse?" asked Sidney Morrison.

"Oh! ay; I know it," he growled. "Who can help knowing anything that has a bad name? It is only your virtuous, good creatures and things that go unnoticed. A bad man and a haunted house are known for miles around."

"Is Hawkhouse so very bad then?"

"I don't know—they say it's haunted; but I don't see any fault in that. I am haunted in this hut, haunted in my boat out at sea; always haunted. But I'm none the worse for that."

"No, but—"

"But me no buts; I don't like talk. There is the hammock; if you want rest, go to it, and sleep. If you don't want to rest, go to Hawkhouse. I want to read; that is enough."

Seizing his book and the lamp, Peter hurried into the back room, and disappeared, kindly, however, placing the light so that Sidney might see how to tumble into the hammock, which he soon did, and, in spite of the trying scenes he had gone through, he was so tired that he fell into a deep sleep.

Then Peter crept back into the room, and gazed at the sleeper.

"Poor lad—poor lad!" he muttered. "Another victim—yet another! When will his time come?"

CHAPTER III.

JACK AND FLICK BEGIN SCHOOL—THE PLAGUE OF FLIES—MR. GRUESOME INTRODUCES THE NEW USHER.

THE morning after the storm was as clear and beautiful as one could wish, and, as Jack Firebrace and his companion looked out at sea, it seemed difficult to think that the merry, dancing waters which smiled so sweetly in the glorious sunlight could ever have looked so dark and wrathful.

"Hark! there goes the school-bell, Jack," cried Flick. "Come along, old fellow. The only thing that Supplejack—that's Mr. Pliant—won't stand is people being late at school."

"He will have to stand a good deal, I fancy, before we have done with him," said Jack.

"I wonder what the new tutor will be like?" said old Flick. "He may be a hard nut to crack."

"Perhaps he won't turn up at all," replied Jack; "he did not show up yesterday."

"No; and how black old Grindwell looked. I wonder what he has to do with the school?"

"I can't say. Old Ghost—that is Gruesome — seemed quite under his thumb."

"Quite. But here comes Supple-john."

The boys bent over their lesson books, and pretended to be deeply engaged studying, when Mr. Percy Pliant strutted into the room.

He was a little man, about forty, with a pale, platter face, a snub nose, and blue spectacles.

His little, fat body was clad in a suit of seedy black.

Mr. Pliant advanced to his desk, struck thereon three times with his cane, and blew his nose violently.

"Silence—silence!" he cried.

Then he took his seat, rubbed his hands slowly over his bald head as if he were greasing an imaginary load of hair, and then called up the boys to lessons.

"What have you in your desk there, Thomson?" asked old Flick of a boy who kept on opening his desk in order that he might peep at something inside it.

Jack leaned over, and found that Thomson had a box with a glass lid to it in his desk.

"They are butterflies," said the boy. "I don't know what to feed them on; I've tried butter."

"You had better try flies next," laughed Jack. "What are you going to do with the little beggars?"

"I don't know."

"I'll buy them for a penny."

"Done!" cried the lad, and he handed over his butterflies to Jack.

"And now, what are you going to do with them?" asked the boy.

"That's my business! you have your money, so be contented."

Jack then entered into a long discussion with old Flick, and learned that Mr. Pliant sometimes fell asleep in school-hours.

"All right," said Jack; "then I will give him a little sport."

They had not long to wait before Mr. Pliant had one of his dreamy fits upon him.

Then Jack stole to an open window, and plucked some clematis and honeysuckle which grew outside this part of the old house, being away from the sea, and protected from the storms.

Having accomplished this, Jack quietly lowered the blinds over all the windows, save the one which was behind Mr. Pliant's chair, so that the room was darkened except at the end where sat the master.

He then placed the flowers behind Mr. Pliant and let out all the butterflies.

Still Mr. Pliant slumbered on.

Slowly the butterflies crawled about the flowers and shook their wings, evidently greatly delighted at having their freedom once again.

They then tried their wings and fluttered about, much to the delight of the whole school, who watched them with far greater attention than they had ever paid to their lessons; and now the butterflies became jubilant.

They flew high up in the air, and flitted round the tutor's bald head as if it were a flower.

"Oh, don't I wish they were blue-bottles," said one of the lads, in a whisper.

"I'll go down and get some," said old Flick; "I know there are lots in the kitchen."

"Here's the butterfly-box, old Flick," said Jack; "and get some treacle. We will have fun."

Flick crept from the room, but as he closed the door he made a noise, and Mr. Pliant arose with a start.

"Silence, boys," he cried, knocking his desk with his cane, and glancing around him. "Tomkins, bring up—

THE BOYS OF HAWKHOUSE SCHOOL.

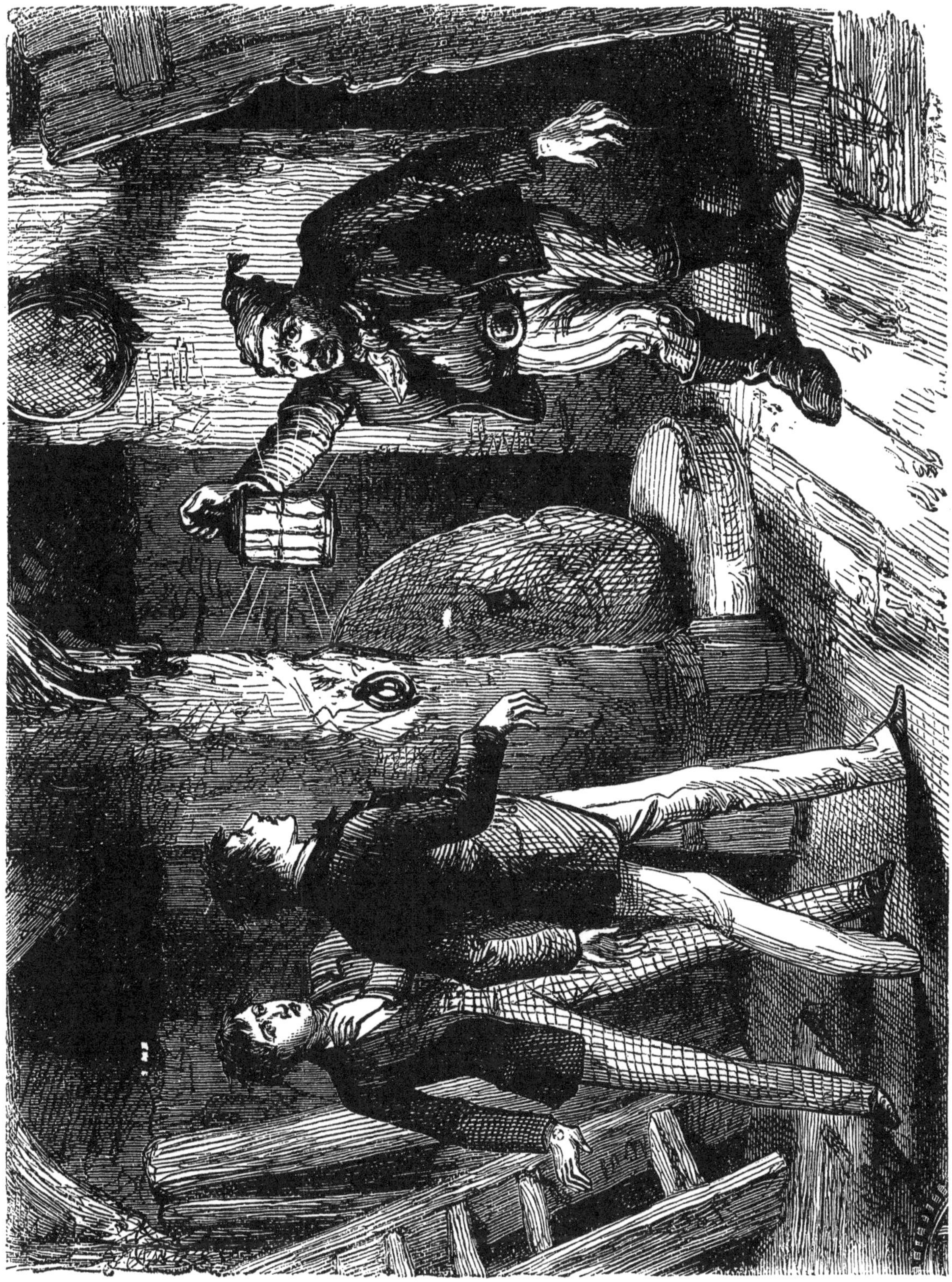

"A HIDEOUS CREATURE STOOD BEFORE THEM. BOTH BOYS SPRANG BACK."

2.

PRICE ONE HALFPENNY.

[Published Every Monday.]

bother these butterflies ! Why, it can't be possible."

He gazed over his head at the butterflies circling around him, seeming, as he watched their pretty antics, to be actually afraid of the pretty little creatures.

" Well, I never did see anything like this before, never. the ancients used to consider the butterfly as symbolical of the soul, and many averred that when a man was about to die his soul hovered above him in the shape of a butterfly. Dear me; I really hope that nothing serious is going to happen to me."

This thought evidently rather alarmed Mr. Pliant.

" Shoo—get away ! " he cried, as he waved his handkerchief about violently.

But if Mr. Pliant did not like the butterflies, the butterflies evidently liked him.

They perched on the back of his head, and crawled quietly up on to his bald patch, now and then putting out their long noses to sip at the pores of the skin. But, evidently not liking the flavour, they would flutter away and dance merrily up and down before the alarmed tutor, who leaned back in his chair waving his handkerchief backwards and forwards in a vague, and idiotic manner.

" If you please, sir," said Jack, springing to his feet, " I think those butterflies annoy you."

" Annoy me ! " exclaimed Mr. Pliant, who seemed as much astonished at the mildness of the expression as he was at the butterflies ; " they will drive me mad. That is all they will do."

" If you will allow me to go down to the kitchen, sir, and ask the housekeeper, in your name, for something to catch the butterflies, I think I could soon have them all."

" Good boy—sharp lad ! " said Mr. Pliant. " Go at once and get the stuff."

Jack wanted no second permission, but was off like a shot.

On his way downstairs he met old Flick returning.

" Halloa ! old fellow, have you got the critters ? " he demanded.

" Oh, yes," said old Flick, holding the box up, and showing it actually filled with bluebottles.

" Why, how on earth did you manage to get all those ? " asked Jack, in amazement.

" Easily enough. A sheep died, and we pulled him into a small cave, to keep him there for gentles to bait with. The flies are there by the million—no difficulty in getting them ; the only difficulty is to prevent their getting you."

" And the treacle ? " cried Jack, rubbing his hands with delight.

" Can't get near the jar ; the old Ghost is there, watching it like a she dragon."

" Never mind, old Flick. I can manage that ; you wait for me."

" You ! " exclaimed Flitter, quite overpowered with the other's daring.

" Yes."

" Well, you have got cheek. But fire away, old fellow, and get the treacle."

Down-stairs bolted Jack, and, walking up to Mrs. Drusilla Drysdale, asked for some treacle for Mr. Pliant.

" And what does he want treacle for ? " demanded Mrs. Drysdale, who was, in face and figure, the picture of a shrivelled-up old witch.

" To catch some butterflies," said Jack, putting on a very simple air.

" Oh, bother the flies ! "

" That's just what he has been saying over and over again," said Jack.

" I never heard of such fearful extravagance," said the crone, as she poured out a little treacle in a cup. " There, take that to him, and mind, I shall ask him if he has had it, and if I find that you have so much as touched it, so as to lick your fingers afterwards, I'll half kill you."

" But I don't like treacle, young lady," said Jack.

" Go along do," growled the old woman.

" Thank you, young lady," said Jack ; and then, as he left the kitchen, he said—

" If I don't serve you out for that, my name is not what it is."

" Come along, old fellow," whispered Jack to Flick ; " don't let out a fly until I tell you."

They entered the schoolroom, Flitter creeping to his seat, whilst Jack walked up to Mr. Pliant, who was still busily engaged with the butterflies.

" If you will keep still, I think I can send them all off directly," said Jack.

"Sharp boy—clever boy! evidently has a knowledge of natural history," said Mr. Pliant, bending down his head, and allowing the mischievous Jack to daub the back part of his hair with treacle, now and then giving a slight smear on the bald part.

"It's rather sticky, but it will keep off butterflies; there, look how they fly out of window from it."

As he spoke Jack threw up the window, and, naturally, the butterflies flew out into the open air.

At the same time he took the opportunity of throwing out the flowers.

"Yes, they have gone. Very strange —ver-ry singular indeed!"

"Junior geography class come up!"

Jack shut down the window, and retired to his seat.

Mr. Pliant knocked his desk with his cane, as he always did when he wanted to look very important, and stood up to examine the boys.

"What is an island?" he demanded, glaring through his blue spectacles at a little boy.

"If you please, sir, an island is a—"

"Booze-wooze woo—buz-z-z!"

At a sign from Jack Flick had let loose a dozen or two bluebottles.

"Dear me! this is very strange," said Mr. Pliant, looking about him in amazement. "But never mind the flies; go on."

"An island is a piece of land surrounded by water."

"Good! What is a promontory, Jackson?"

"A promontory—"

"Booze-ee-wooze woo! Buz-z-z-z! Booze-ee-wooze-woo!"

This time Jack had passed the box down to Tomkins, at the end of the form, and he had let out nearly all the flies at once.

"Well, sir, a promontory. What is a promontory?" demanded Mr. Pliant, pretending not to notice the flies.

"A promontory is—a lot of bluebottles!" continued the lad, staring about at the flies.

"Is a. what, sir?" demanded Mr. Pliant, in tones of thunder.

"I mean, sir, a promontory is—oh, my, what a lot!" exclaimed the poor lad, quite overcome with the buzzing of the bluebottles, for now all the bluebottles were free.

Many of the merriest of the flies had flown straight to the window behind Mr. Pliant's chair, that being, as we have already stated, the only light one, and, turning their backs to the panes, buzzed and beat away their loudest, as they kicked their legs out at the usher as if in defiance.

Mr. Pliant watched the insects with a queer look, as if he were asking them where the deuce they came from; but after a while he turned a stern look at the boys, and said—

"Never mind these poor household flies; they are quite harmless, quite. Go on with your lessons."

Lifting the book up close to his eyes, being short-sighted, Mr. Pliant began to search for his place.

Before he could find it a large bluebottle came buzzing under his nose, as if it were reading the book also.

"Dear me," thought the tutor, "this bluebottle seems searching after knowledge."

Still the fly kept wandering over the pages.

"Confound the flies! where can they come from? I never saw anything like it before in all my life!"

Here the usher attempted to smash one which was enjoying a treacle dinner on his bald head.

The fly was quicker than the usher, and consequently got away, whilst Mr. Pliant smacked his own head, much to the amusement of all the boys, who tittered with delight.

"Silence, boys!" said the usher. "I think—oh, confound it! these flies will eat my poor head up."

In truth, a number of flies had now settled all over the tutor's head.

They danced before his eyes, they invaded his mouth, they nestled in his hair.

Driven mad by the intolerable nuisance, Mr. Pliant clutched the cane and waved it aloft.

Quickly the class dispersed, and sought their forms.

Swish—swish—swish! went the cane in Mr. Pliant's frantic endeavours to drive off the flies, but to no purpose; the little torments stuck to him hard and fast.

Crash!

He had smashed one of the window-panes.

But bluebottles are not like butter-flies; they don't care about the open air and flowers, they rather preferred Mr. Pliant's bald pate and indoors.

Driven beyond the power of endurance, Mr. Pliant sprang from his desk.

"Silence, boys!" he shouted, as a titter went round the school.

He tied his silk pocket-handkerchief round his head, then, with his cane, prepared for war.

Anyone having seen Mr. Pliant's rotund person in repose would never have thought that he could have shown so much agility.

His little legs, cased in their black cotton stockings, actually seemed to wrinkle as he ran.

He waved his arms about in such a manner that the boys ducked down behind their desks to avoid him, a thing which they did not always succeed in doing, for many a heavy blow, directed with all the strength of hate at a blue-bottle, fell on a boy's shoulders.

Yells of agony, mingled with roars of laughter, arose from the boys.

The bluebottles still seemed determined to indulge in the sweets of the tutor's head, and he, finding that it was im-possible to attack all the bluebottles at the same time, singled out a fine, fat one, and pursued him with fury.

He had him within his reach, the cane descended, but as it did so the door opened, and it fell right upon the head of Griffiths Grindwell, Esq., the patron of the school, knocking that gentleman's wig to the back of his head, a compli-ment he returned by knocking Mr. Pliant flat on his back in the middle of the school-room floor.

"Perdition! Mr. Pliant," cried old Ebenezer Gruesome, hurrying forward. "What is the meaning of this? Here is Mr. Griffiths Grindwell come to intro-duce his young *protégé*, our chief tutor, Mr. Sidney Morrison, and you to have the school in this state!"

But no one paid any attention to Mr. Gruesome or Mr. Pliant; all eyes were fixed on the new usher, who stood with staring eyes, one hand pressed on his heart, and the other pointing to a blue scar in ugly Grindwell's forehead, which, his wig being pushed back, was exposed for the first time.

"Look! look!" gasped the usher; "the mark—the scar!"

The next moment he flung up his arms, gave a fearful yell, and fell forward senseless.

"He will soon revive," said Griffith Grindwell, hastily re-arranging his wigs; "he's subject to fits; has been from a boy. Undo his neckcloth. Quick!"

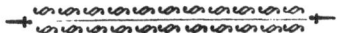

CHAPTER IV.

A SHEEP IN WOLF'S CLOTHING—THE MASK THROWN OFF—THE USHER SELLS HIS LIBERTY.

THE unfortunate usher was raised off the floor and placed on a form.

Mr. Grindwell to all appearance was a man of about fifty, tall, and strongly made.

His features were harsh, and were de-cidedly not improved by the way in which he wore his wig, namely, so as to cover his forehead almost entirely.

His clothes were of the glossiest broadcloth, and his walk was that of a staid city merchant.

"Ah! Firebrace," he said, in a low, soft voice, as he nodded to Jack; "I hope this is none of your plots."

Jack turned very red and looked down, but made no answer.

"Well, well, boys will be boys," said Griffiths Grindwell, in the self-same soft voice; but he raised his eyelids and shot a glance of such unmistakable anger at Jack that the lad involuntarily drew back.

"Dear me, this is very strange con-duct," said Mr. Gruesome, who was a thin, withered, pale-faced man, with long silvery white hair.

He was dressed in a long gown or gaberdine, girt round at the waist with a leather belt of considerable breadth and thickness.

With this belt his long, claw-like hands were always nervously playing.

Sometimes he would snatch the black silk skull-cap from off his silver locks, and thrust it nervously into his girdle; then after wearing it there a bit, would pluck it forth again, and hastily place it on his head, then mutter " Gold, gold," as he walked.

This strange conduct had procured for him the nickname of the old Ghost amongst the boys, and certainly when met suddenly at night in one of the moonlit chambers of the castle, he looked more like the apparition of an old miser than anything else.

" Yes," sighed Mr. Grindwell; " it is very sad; but we must be kind and gentle unto this poor young tutor it has pleased Heaven to afflict. Ah! it is sad --very."

Mr. Pliant, who had been industriously rubbing his bald head with his silk hand-kerchief, thereby making it look much like a batter pudding smeared with treacle, muttered gently—

" Good man—kind-hearted man!"

" Nay, Mr. Pliant, you are too good, far too good," said Grindwell. " But how are you now, Mr. Morrison?"

" Do not touch me, man—keep back! Oh, heaven! that I should meet you again."

" Ah! he is still a little queer from the fit. I will take him to his room; he will be better soon. These fits come on several times in a week, or a month, and then he has no more of them for a year."

" No, no! Stand off!" gasped Sidney Morrison. " I cannot go with you."

" Dear me!" exclaimed Mr. Gruesome; " the young man must be dreaming. This is your kind friend, Griffiths Grindwell, of Austin Friars, London, merchant and shipowner; he recommended you to me. You must thank him that you have got this place."

Sidney still struggled to release himself from Grindwell's grasp, but that gentleman, although appearing not to move a muscle, held him with a hand of iron.

Signing for the others to remain where they were, Grindwell led the usher away.

" Keep still, you fool," he hissed in the young fellow's ear, when they were too far away from the others to be over-heard; " be still, or I will crush your arm in my grasp. You are in my power. Remember the murder in the cave; be wise, and come at once with me."

Being weak and faint Sidney was obliged to yield himself prisoner, and Grindwell, or Randulph the Smuggler as he was known to the old sailor, led him to his bedroom, which was an old-fashioned apartment, with sombre furniture.

The large four-post bedstead, with its heavy hangings and dark plumes at the corner, made Sidney shudder, for it set him in mind of a hearse.

At one end of the room was a dark oak wardrobe, with grim carvings of the " Dance of Death" upon the panels.

No sooner had they reached the room than Grindwell threw Sidney on the bed, and, closing the door, double locked it, and put the key into his pocket.

" Now, lad, be warned. Let me have no more of this sham illness," he said, in a fierce, rough voice; " or perchance I may find the means of curing you altogether."

As he spoke his eyelids were no longer drooped, but raised, and his fierce red eyes shot forth a terrible fire at Sidney.

" Terrible creature," said the young usher, " who art thou?"

" At present I am Griffiths Grindwell, a merchant of the City of London, and your patron."

" Stop. I was, when a boy, told that my father had perished at sea."

" It is true; he perished by the sea," said Grindwell, carelessly.

" And that out of friendship to my father you would take care of me," continued Sidney.

" I promised it," replied Grindwell; " and I have kept my word."

" I grant it, for I know you by name," said Sidney Morrison, sadly; " but last night in the cave—the murder of that old seaman?"

" As for that, the murder, you must remember, is more your affair than mine," sneered Grindwell.

" But your disguise!" cried Sidney, as he rose from the bed; " you whom I had looked upon as the soul of kindness —to find you disguised, wearing a false beard and moustache to hide your face! What am I to think of you? Are you a good man or a villain?"

"Think what you like; I care not," laughed the strange and fearful man, scornfully. "But I will tell you a little piece of my past history, a history of hate, death, and revenge."

"Go on," said the young man, with a shudder; "I'll listen."

"Well, then, when I first started in life I was poor, very poor. I worked hard; bought a small ship, and under your father's advice became a smuggler. Oh, we worked well, and made plenty of money. He was my first mate, and we lived together like brothers, until one day a dispute arose—a quarrel was purposely put upon me. Led by your father, the crew mutinied.

"You see this pretty scar?" he continued, as he raised his wig and showed the blue mark; "that was your father's blow. I was put on shore and left, whilst your worthy parent sailed away as captain of my ship. Think you that I bore this without hoping for revenge?

"No; I gave information to the Government officers. We pursued them; they resisted. I trained a gun upon the place where I knew they kept the powder stored. One crash; a fearful report, and a large column of fire rose up to the sky. It vanished, and its place was taken by a thick cloud of smoke. In a few seconds pieces of wreck and dead bodies were falling all around. We had conquered. I had my revenge; the ship had blown up, and not a soul escaped."

"Horrible!" exclaimed Sidney, shuddering.

"Justice!" retorted Grindwell, fiercely. "I have kept a great part of my gains hidden away; I did not spend my money in dissipation. Well, I fitted out another ship, and became a privateer. That paid wonderfully. Then I traded in the China Seas. Fortune favoured me in everything. I became a well-to-do merchant, and sent other men to sail my ships.

"But this blow—this sabre-cut your father gave me, injured my brain. I see blood constantly before me; I am restless; I cannot sleep but what I dream of daring deeds done in action, and I long once more to be on board a swift schooner, skimming the waves like a seagull. To me the roar of the waves and the rush of the storm is music, and the clashing steel, the boom of the cannon, the crash of the ball as it hits the vessel's side and sends the splinters flying far and wide, is happiness."

As Grindwell spoke his bosom heaved; he drew himself up to his full height, threw back his head; his eyes gleamed with the baneful fire already described, and the scar on his forehead became purple.

It was a fearful sight.

"And you became an outlaw?" demanded Sidney.

"No; not quite that. But I did become a smuggler again. Listen to me, Sidney. I took you as a child—the child of the man who had tried to ruin—to kill me. I have treated you well—almost as a father. I tell you now that I delight in these rash adventures of smuggling. You must and shall aid me in them; it is the only return you can make for your father's crimes."

"What!" exclaimed Sidney; "to become a smuggler? to sink so low—"

"Silence, boy!" cried Grindwell. "It well becomes the son of a traitor and a murderer—ay, and a murderer himself—to use these terms to me, without whose assistance he would have died in the gutter."

"I a murderer—a murderer!" groaned Sidney.

"Ay, a murderer!" laughed Grindwell. "It little matters to me whether you did it in sudden anger, or if you had a spite against the old man. At first I thought you wished to kill me, having recognised me, but now I have come to the conclusion that the thirst for blood runs in your family, and, tiger-like, you rushed on your victim only for the pleasure to kill."

"You cannot prove this murder. I did not strike the blow. With my own eyes I saw you kill the man; I—"

"Boy, have a care!" exclaimed Grindwell; "the witness of your guilt lies in the grave—your knife! Think not that I fear you; I have you in my grasp, can crush you when I like. Hark you! supposing I did kill this man, you cannot prove it. I can prove I was not near the spot when the murder happened. The body is dug up, your knife is found all covered with blood-stains. Do you think they will believe your story about the respectable Griffiths Grindwell? No, no; it would but seal your fate, and send you with more ignominy to the gallows."

"Have you no mercy?" groaned the unfortunate young man.

"None! Man's hand has been against me, and my hand shall be against him. I declare war. All things are fair in war, so I will wear a mask, that I may the better work my will on men.

"Oh! it is fine to see them bow and cringe to me when they think I am the highly respectable city merchant. How I laugh in my sleeve when his majesty's revenue officers deign to consult me upon the astonishing way in which lace and tobacco have been smuggled into England! Ha, ha, ha! they consult me! ho, ho, ho!"

The wretch seemed to enjoy the idea of having wrought so much mischief.

Sidney Morrison was a clever scholar; indeed, too much study had ruined his health and caused that terrible curse, epilepsy. His nerves were shattered, and at times his brain had seemed affected.

He had no will of his own.

He shrank from pain as a child would have done.

He was broken in health and mind, the very instrument for such a man as Griffiths Grindwell.

"I must obey you," he moaned; "I have no choice; I am only your slave."

"Ah, that sounds better," laughed Grindwell, his eyes gleaming with triumph; "I have educated you carefully for this. Now sit down here. Take this pen and write what I dictate. Address the letter from here, and put the date at the top."

Sidney Morrison took the pen, and, having headed the paper, waited for Grindwell to dictate.

"'I, Sidney Morrison, of Hawkhouse School,'" dictated Grindwell, as Sidney wrote, "do hereby freely, and without any force, confess that I killed an old sailor in the cave which is at the foot of the Hawk's Rock, and buried the unfortunate man there. I had no reason for committing the crime, as I do not remember ever having seen the old man before, and can only account for it as a fit of madness.' Have you written that?"

"I have," said Sidney.

"Then sign it in full," said Griffiths Grindwell.

With the look of a demon Grindwell gloated over Sidney as he signed the paper.

"Ha, ha!" he screamed, as he seized the document when the unfortunate young man had signed it; "you are mine now, mine, both body and soul."

Livid with horror, Sidney watched Grindwell fold up the document and put it carefully into a pocket-book, for the wretched tutor truly believed that he had sold himself to the spirit of evil.

"Oh, you need not fear me," said Grindwell; "I am not the dread spirit you think. I almost wish I were. But you shall be taken care of now. Here is gold for you," and as he spoke he threw a heavy purse of gold on the table: "eat, drink, and be merry. Fill out that spare body, or, if you still love books, study until your eyes become dim and your body bent.

"But mark this! when you receive my token, it must be obeyed, come what will. In the meantime practise different handwriting. Mark me, this must be done. If you want gold, write to me, and you shall have more. Now, farewell."

He was gone, and the agonised tutor dashed himself on to his bed, weeping bitterly.

"Lost! lost! lost!" he cried. "All is lost to me for ever!"

CHAPTER V.

THE GAME OF HUNT THE HARE—THE MISHAP AT THE MILL—JACK FIREBRACE
AND HIS FRIEND HAVE A STRANGE ADVENTURE WITH PETER PIGWELLAN.

WHEN the disguised Mr. Grindwell had borne the usher away, Gruesome, who seemed quite overcome by the scene he had just witnessed, gave orders that Mr. Pliant should at once take the boys out for a walk.

Mr. Pliant, having been relieved from the flies, forgot all about the treacle, and, having put on his hat, in his absence of mind quite forgetting to remove his handkerchief from his head, sallied forth, with the boys at his heels.

No sooner were the boys free from the school-grounds than Mr. Pliant gave them permission to run wherever they liked, and amuse themselves.

"Jack, old man," whispered old Flick to his companion, "what do you say to make our way down to the beach?"

"I was thinking of going into the village," replied Jack, "for I feel jolly hungry, and should like to have a go in at some cakes and tarts."

"Cakes and tarts!" replied his companion. "You won't get any there. The only place to buy tarts in the village is at a general shop, where they sell bacon, cheese, blacking, tobacco, twine, fishing-nets, sealing-wax, herrings, and salts and senna."

"Oh, lor'! don't make a fellow sick. What a beast of a hole!"

"Ah, but the tarts; they look like discs of putty, with a dab of red paint in the middle."

"Enough, enough! I am not hungry in that style. Let us go to the coast."

"You'd better not. If you do I'll tell mother, and she'll tell Mr. Gruesome; and won't you catch it hot!"

Jack turned round, and beheld Goblin Jim at his elbow.

Goblin Jim was a small lad of about fourteen, but with a figure that would have been little for a boy of ten, whilst his face would have suited any age from fifteen to fifty.

It was long, thin, and narrow, with two bead-like eyes, black as sloes and bright as a bird's; a nose that twitched from side to side as he spoke, a mouth that always smiled, and showed a terrible row of green and black stumps (one could not call them teeth), and a chin half as long as the rest of his face, and as sharp as a shoehorn.

This little monster was an acrobat by nature.

He could pout out his chest until he looked like a pouter pigeon, or draw it in and curve his spine, making himself a humpback.

Bones he did not seem to possess. He could touch the ground with the back of his head whilst he stood on his feet, tie himself into a knot, make himself into a ball—in fact, do anything but walk properly like an ordinary mortal.

That he could not do. He danced along with a hop, kick, and a jump, generally managing to let the kick fall upon one of the boys' shins.

He had an insane love of hopping on one leg, and even preferred walking on his hands to the somewhat commonplace but highly patronised method of progression on the feet.

Spiteful, mischievous, impish, a sneak, a glutton, and a liar, Jim was treated with fear by most of the boys, for they dreaded his power to bring them into trouble.

"Tell your mother, you young imp!" replied Jack Firebrace, sharply. "What do I care for her?"

"Oh, all right, Master Firebrace. You are a big pot, you are," replied Goblin Jim. "We shall precious soon see if you are as great as you think yourself, that's all."

"Don't quarrel with that little wretch," whispered Felix. "He will cause you no end of trouble."

"Let him do what he likes. I don't care," said Jack. "It is my belief it was that little imp who fastened the door upon us when we were in the well, or secret passage in the chapel."

"Ho, ho, ho!" screamed the little fiend; "you are the lads who were in the chapel, are you? That's about the best thing I have heard yet. He, he, he! Now I have another hold over you. If I were to tell Mr. Gruesome that," he continued, the expression of his face changing to the deepest malice, " he would cut your life out with his cane. Ho, ho! your life out!"

So evil did the little wretch look that Jack for a moment actually shrank from him.

"You little whelp!" he cried, catching hold of Goblin Jim's ears, and pulling them; "you little whelp! dare you threaten me like that?"

"Leave my ears alone, can't yer?" yelled Goblin Jim. "Oh, won't I tell my mother! Oh, oh, oh!"

"If you do, you may as well tell her at the same time that I intend pulling your ears on each occasion you mention my name to her. So take that as an earnest of my kindly intentions."

As Jack spoke he turned Goblin Jim round and bestowed a hearty kick on him, which nearly sent that unaimiable young gentleman on his nose.

"Jack, old boy, that kick will cost you dear," said old Flick, as they strolled away.

"I don't care what it costs me," said Jack Firebrace. "I do not intend to let a little brute like that hector over me. I think it much the best to begin as I intend going on, and I have done so."

"Well, anyway, we are in for it now; and in for a penny in for a pound. So we will make it hot for the young imp."

"I say, Felix," cried Tomkins, making his way up to Flitter, "we want you to come and play hare to our hounds; and Firebrace can be the huntsman."

"That's not a bad idea," said Jack; "but where's Mr. Pliant?"

" Old Pliant has gone across Boulder's meadows on to Jenkins's Farm; so we can make our way across the hills, round by the old mill, across the stream, and so on to Jenkins's, where we can get lots of milk, and it will make a capital run."

" All right. I am on," said Flick. " Call the lads together, and we will start from here."

This was soon done, and old Flick, having taken some fifty yards lead, started off full pace over the country.

"Yoicks!" cried Jack, and set off at a good rate, followed closely by the other boys.

Perhaps no game is so healthy as that known amongst boys as hunt the hare.

The open air and the good exercise to the limbs tend to make it so. But the country round Hawkhouse was not an easy one to run over.

There were wide ditches, high hedges, and numerous streams. But in this case the hare, huntsman, and hounds were all of the right sort of stuff, and away they went, making the air ring with their boyhood shouts.

They were now fast approaching the old mill; the windows were all boarded up, and the door padlocked on the outside, showing that the place was uninhabited.

Beneath this desolate building flowed the swift mill-stream.

A bridge had at one time crossed this river close by the mill, but this had been broken away, its place being supplied by a narrow plank thrown carelessly across.

For this plank old Flick ran as fast as he could, for Jack was close upon him.

"Yoicks, yoicks!" yelled Jack, to encourage his hounds, who were lagging behind, for the rough country and great pace they had been running began to tell upon them.

This shout told Felix how close his pursuers were, and he made a gallant spurt to reach the plank.

Jack could almost touch Flick, but that youth made a sudden jump on to the plank, and as he did so, the treacherous bridge slipped, and fell with the lad into the swift and deep stream below.

One loud scream of terror, and Jack saw his friend struggling with the waters, which swept him on to the dark arch beneath the mill.

For a moment Jack paused in horror, but in that moment he thought he heard a fiendish laugh, and, glancing in the direction from which it came, he was just able to see a face disappear behind the mill, round which it had been peeping.

Goblin Jim!

Turning quickly round, Firebrace shouted to his schoolfellows for help, and then plunged into the stream to save his friend, for he could plainly see that Flitter could not swim.

"Keep up, old fellow! do keep up!" cried Jack. "Don't clutch hold of me, or we shall both be drowned. For Heaven's sake, Flick, be cool and quiet; it is our only chance."

Vainly did Jack fight against the stream; the current carried them beneath the mill.

Here all was darkness, for the stream curved so that the light from the entrance of the tunnel was shut out from them, whilst only a thin line of light showed where the water rushed away, the wall on that side of the mill having for some purpose been made so as nearly to touch the water.

Luckily Jack managed to catch hold of some woodwork. Clammy as the woodwork was, Jack was only too glad to have hold of it.

"Wake up, old Flick," he said, in as cheery a voice as he could assume.

"I—I am all right," gasped Felix; "but I can't keep up much longer."

"Just cling on to this, there's a good fellow, or we shall both go down in this deep river."

"How are we to get out of this place?" said Felix, who had now managed to get hold of the woodwork. "How slimy this is!"

"Keep still until help comes. I shouted to the fellows, and they are sure to get assistance. Try to crawl up here," continued Jack; "this seems a sort of ladder."

"Yes; but a precious slippery one. Where can those fellows be? We shall be drowned, Jack: I cannot hold on much longer."

"Don't be impatient, old fellow; the time seems long to us in this position," said Jack, cheerily.

"It does indeed," said Felix, in dismal tones. "It does seem an awfully long time."

Jack did not say a word—he had enough to do to keep himself and Felix from sinking.

"Jack!" shouted Felix, suddenly; "there are rats in this place."

"I should think that very likely," replied Jack, trying to laugh.

"But they are crawling on me. Why don't the fellows make haste? Help! help! help!"

"Confound the boobies! where can they be?" cried Jack, quite losing patience; "they must be mad to leave us here. Great Heaven! what shall we do? Hold up, old Flick."

"Jack, they must believe that we are drowned," said Flick, who began to feel very miserable. "I feel that there is no escape for us."

"Nonsense, old man; they must make some search for us," said Jack.

"I don't know so much about that. I cannot hold out much longer, Jack."

"How did the plank come to fall?" asked Jack, wishing to keep Flick's mind engaged.

"I don't know; I think it must have been shifted by someone."

"I expect so," thought Jack; but he did not speak.

"It will soon be all over with me, Jack; I shall not be able to hold out," said Felix.

"Nonsense; you must cling on. I will crawl up this ladder, or whatever it is, and see if there be not some way of getting into the mill. This woodwork was in all probability built so that the miller might descend into this hole to repair the mill-wheel. Hold on, old fellow; I believe we shall yet be safe."

Jack raised himself up as far as he could, and, stretching forth his arm, was pleased to feel that there was a bar above his head.

This he grasped, and pulled himself up so that he was now able to seat himself upon the wooden bar on which he had been clinging.

Having done this, he helped old Flick into the same position.

"You can hold on now, Flick, can't you?" said Jack, in a tone of encouragement.

"Oh, yes; this is not so dangerous as the last position was."

"Well, I am going to try a step higher," said Jack.

He raised himself up cautiously, but before he had gone a foot he struck his head rather forcibly on the top of the arch.

"Phew!" he exclaimed, "that was rather a nasty blow."

"Are you hurt, Jack?" cried old Flick.

"Well, one don't knock his head about in that manner and not hurt himself," responded Jack Firebrace;

" but I have made discoveries by this accident."

" Indeed ! " cried old Flick eagerly.

" Yes, old Flick," said our hero, cheerfully ; " either we are under a trap-door which leads to the mill, or the flooring is so rotten that we shall be easily able to smash it through. So come along, old fellow ; take my hand and climb up here. Take care how you get up."

" Never fear that," said old Flick, whose spirits began to revive ; " I shall take every care, for I can't swim, and in this dark no one could help me."

Cautiously the lad clambered up until he stood by Jack Firebrace's side.

" Now," said Jack, " place your left arm over your head so as to form a kind of cushion, and straighten your back. Mind we both make the effort at the same time, or it will be of no use, and will waste our strength. Now, are you ready ? "

" Ready," replied old Flick.

" Good. When I count three go at it with all your might. One, two, three."

Both lads, it is needless to say, pushed with all their might, for their lives depended on their being able to escape this way, for no other seemed possible.

The veins of their brows were swollen like whipcord, and they were nearly exhausted when the trap-door gave way.

They heard something roll over on to the floor above as the trap-door flew up.

The next moment they had scrambled into the mill ; but everything was pitch dark.

" The first thing we must do is to close the trap," said Jack, " or in this dark place we may fall through it into the mill-stream again, and a little of a bath of that sort goes a long way. So down goes the trap."

With that he slammed down the trap, making the echoes ring again through the silent mill.

As if by magic, a bright light shot through the darkness, and a hideous creature stood before them.

Both boys sprang back in horror, but the first to recover himself was Flitter, who exclaimed—

" Why, it's Peter Pigwellan, the boatman of the Hawk's Crag Rock."

" Yes," snarled the deformed boatman, " I am Peter Pigwellan ; and who are you ? "

Jack Firebrace could scarcely believe that the creature was mortal, it was so terribly hideous, and appeared so mysterious, especially in conjunction with the lantern of green glass it held in its hand and the horribly livid light around.

" Don't you know me, Peter Pigwellan ? " said Felix ; " I am one of the lads at Hawkhouse School. I have often seen you put out in your boat when no other fisherman could be persuaded to go out—no, not even from the Long Sands ; and yet you venture out from Hawk's Crag Cove, the most dangerous spot on all the coast."

" Danger ! " exclaimed the fisherman, with a horrible grin. " Why should I, a deformed, lonely wretch, hideous to look upon, unloved and scorned, why should I shun danger ? Answer me that."

" My friend," said Jack, " you judge other people's temper too harshly."

" Do I ? " cried the deformed boatman, turning upon our hero with a snap as if he would bite him.

" Assuredly you must. No one would scorn you for what is not your fault."

" Away with such cant ! " exclaimed Peter, stamping his foot in rage. " If it be ever your fate to get twisted and scarred like I am, you will curse the day that you escaped from that mill-stream—you will long for death."

Jack Firebrace and his companion could not help shuddering at this.

" Oh, the people round must pity you," said Jack, soothingly.

" Pity me ! " screamed Peter ; " I want not their pity. Pity, forsooth, pity ! "

" Surely he must have something on his mind," whispered Jack to his companion.

Softly as this had been said, the deformed boatman overheard it.

" There ; there is your pity ! You take the scarred and hideous face as an index to the scarred and blackened soul within. Oh ! you are all alike. If I go to the castle they buy my fish out of charity—at half price. If I go to the village, the housewives will not touch it. They declare I catch the finny creatures of the deep by the black art. The fellows of my own craft refuse to drink with me, and the boys hound and hoot me. Oh! but one day I will have a deep and great revenge."

"Yours must indeed be a sad existence," said Jack, kindly.

"Ah! I have times of joy, though," continued the deformed wretch, seeming to have forgotten the presence of the boys, and to be talking to himself; "it is when the storm spirits come riding up on the little dark drift-clouds and cluster together until the sky is like a huge slate and the sea inky and still.

"Then a low murmur comes slowly up from where a white line appears on the horizon. Louder and louder it comes until, with a terrific roar, the tempest bawls upon us.

"The demons deep down beneath the sea toss up the waves till they froth like yeast; the wind is fraught with pale spectres who fly hither and thither shrieking and moaning, trying to avoid the sharp, forked lightning as it darts its fiery tongues out of the angry heavens at them.

"Oh! then I spread my sail and fly over the sea, swift as the drifting scud. The pale spectres of the wind, the fierce fiends of the ocean, try to tear me out of the boat; but I laugh them to scorn. They dare not kill me. Life is my torture. Death could bring me no further pains. Ha, ha, ha, ha!"

As Peter concluded this speech he threw his arms aloft, and, shrieking with laughter, would have fallen, had not Jack sprung forward and caught him, then, with his wet pocket-handkerchief —he had no reason to fetch water, being soaked through, as the reader knows— bathed the poor creatures brow and wiped the foam from his lips.

Presently he opened his eyes, staggered to his feet, and gazed vacantly around.

"Where am I?" he muttered.

"You are quite safe in the old mill, and with friends," said Jack.

Peter gazed vacantly at the speaker, and muttered the word "Friends?"

"Yes, friends," repeated Jack. "We had the misfortune to get into the mill-stream, and were carried, by the force of the current, under the mill. Luckily we found this trap, and managed to open it. Don't you remember? It is lucky you recovered, or I should have called for help."

"Help! No one could hear you in this place."

"This is a queer place," said old Flick. "What a lot of barrels there are here!"

"Hush, hush!" said the old fisherman, quickly glancing round, as if he were in fear of being overheard. "These barrels were for flour, you know. The miller used to ship flour. He is dead, and the mill fell into the hands of the owner of Hawkhouse. He closed it up, and gave me orders to look at it now and then, to keep it in order, and to see no one damages or steals anything."

"Well, you need not fear us. We are pupils at Hawkhouse," said Jack.

"My orders were positive to lock up anyone I found here. But you have been kind. I don't wish to hurt you. Promise me that you will not say that you have been in the mill, or that you have seen me, and I will let you out by a secret way of my own."

"There can be no harm in our doing that," said Jack. "Besides, it will cast an air of mystery about our adventure; and I do so like mystery. Then everything about this place seems mysterious."

"Do you both promise?" demanded Peter Pigwellan.

"We do," replied the youths together.

"I can trust you," he said, after he had examined both the lads' faces carefully by the aid of his lantern. "I feel that. But, if you betray me, boys, you will be in more danger than when you were beneath this mill. Now, follow me."

He led the way from the room, turned down a long, dark passage, at the end of which he knelt down and undid a bolt.

He then cautioned the boys to be quiet, and, above all, to be secret.

When they had renewed their promises he opened a little trap of about a foot and a half square, and flush with the ground.

The lads crawled out, and found themselves standing in a thick plantation of trees.

The next moment the trap was closed and bolted.

"This is a strange adventure, old

Flick," said Jack. "What is to be done now?"

"I think we had better make our way back to Hawkhouse, and change our clothes."

"All right. Come along, old fellow. I am nearly frozen."

And so the two boys scampered back to the school as fast as they could.

CHAPTER VI.

JACK FIREBRACE GIVES GOBLIN JIM A LESSON, AND SHOWS THE OTHERS HOW TO CURE FITS—THE COMPACT.

JACK FIREBRACE and his companion managed to make their way into the dormitory unnoticed.

"By Jove! Jack, but that was a lucky escape," said Felix, as he stripped off his clothes.

"Yes; it was indeed."

"I say, old Peter Pigwellan ain't a bad sort," said Flitter.

"I don't say that he is," replied our hero; "but answer me one question."

"Fire away, old fellow; only don't be prosy."

"All right. Now, can you tell me how that plank fell into the water?"

"Why, no sooner did I touch it than the end farther from me slipped off the bank, and in I went."

"Very good. You have, I suppose, often crossed that plank before?"

"Constantly. I see; you think some-one moved the plank, in order that I might have the pleasure of falling in?"

"I do. Now, can you think of any-one likely to do such a thing?"

"N—no, I can't," said Flitter, shaking his head. "Stay! I know one who is quite capable of all that, and much worse. But then that little wretch was not there."

"But you have not told me what little wretch you mean. Out with his name, old Flick," said Jack.

"Well, then, he is known as Goblin Jim."

"And he was the very one who did it, too," cried Jack Firebrace.

"Come, come, Jack, we have no proof of this, you know," said Flitter.

"Yes, I have," replied Jack. "I saw the little wretch peep round the mill as you fell in."

"The deuce you did!"

"Of course, he would swear that he had never been near the spot. So the best thing that we can do is to wait quietly for some good chance to serve him out, and then do it."

"It will be difficult to face the little wretch," replied Flitter. "I shall so want to pitch into him."

"All in good time, old Flick. But at present we had better make our way back to the farm. You know the fellows must have missed us."

"Come on. I know a short cut."

The two lads bounded away back towards the mill.

They had just run across a field, and were entering on a willow copse, when they heard the sounds of voices proceeding therefrom.

In an instant Jack placed his hand upon his companion's arm, at the same time motioning him to crouch down behind a hedge.

"He can't be here," said little Tomkins, the ghost-seer. "I saw him plunge into the mill-stream with my own eyes."

"Ho, ho! ho, ho!" croaked a voice they knew to be Goblin Jim's. "What made him plunge into a mill-stream with your eyes, I should like to know? I have often heard of 'swimming' eyes. Are yours of that sort, eh?"

"Hold your tongue, you brute!" said Tomkins; "here are two good fellows lost, and you are jesting."

"Why should I not? I did not care for them. I never do care for anyone but myself. Ho, ho! ho, ho!"

Here the little wretch actually danced and laughed with glee, thinking Jack and Flitter drowned.

"I know I saw Firebrace spring into the stream," said Tomkins again; "I shall go back there."

"Go back there!" screamed Goblin Jim. "I tell you it is my idea that that fellow Firebrace has tempted Flitter to run away with him. If they have there will be such a hunt the hare as was never heard in these parts before. They will have the hue-and-cry after them. Oh, won't it be fine sport! The dark dungeon in the Wizard's Tower when they come back; their fare, bread and water; their companions, rats and bats; and, oh! won't it be delicious to hear them squeal when flogged!"

Jack uttered a most unearthly yell, then groaned, and, as he rose, slowly pointing at Goblin Jim, he exclaimed—

"Murderer; my blood be upon thy head."

All the lads were struck dumb with amazement, but Goblin Jim screamed, and fainted dead off.

"Don't be frightened, lads," cried Jack, as he and Flitter sprang over the hedge; "we are all alive."

"And kicking," added old Flick, illustrating his argument by kicking Goblin Jim.

"Oh!" groaned Goblin Jim, "their spirits have come back out of the water."

"You hear that, lads?" said Jack Firebrace; "he knew we fell into the water, and yet he leads you here."

"That he did," said Tomkins; "he declared he had seen both of you hide in this wood."

"Yes, we heard him say it," cried the lads; "we heard him say you were going to run away."

"Oh, oh! I shall die! Fetch my mother—keep the spirits from me—I am dying!"

All these exclamations came from Goblin Jim, who had at first believed that Jack and old Flick were two returned spirits, come from their watery grave to haunt him.

But as soon as he discovered that they were alive he pretended to be ill.

"Poor fellow!" said Jack, as he cut a good thick willow switch, and trimmed it with a knife; "he must be attended to. A little of this applied outwardly will perhaps do him good."

Before administering the remedy, Jack Firebrace took Jim's wrist, and felt his pulse.

"Dear me! this is a very sad case; he must be carried home. Here, old Flick, you are the strongest; carry him pick-back."

But Goblin Jim was determined to carry on his pretended illness to the last.

Therefore, he would not cling on in the way desired.

"Poor fellow, he must be weak," said Jack. "Tomkins, you take hold of his wrists, and hold them over Flitter's shoulders. You, Flitter, take great care you hold his legs tightly. That's it, lads. Now hold him fast, gentlemen."

This last part of the speech had the effect of opening Goblin Jim's eyes in more ways than one.

"No-o-o-o-o!" he roared, vainly struggling to get off Flitter's back, at the same time gazing in terror behind him.

But he was too late.

The pliant willow switch bit sharply across his unprotected back, and for some moments, as Flicker expressed it, the following conversation went on between Goblin Jim and the willow switch:

"That's" — whack! — "enough" — swish! — "oh! my" — whack! — "I ain't"—swish!--"ill"—whack!—"oh! let me go!"—whack, whack, whack!

"There," said Jack, coolly, as he tossed away the willow switch, "we have had enough of that sport. I am quite tired of it, and I am sure our young friend the Goblin is. But it has done us both good. It was capital exercise for me after my cold bath, and it has sent the Goblin's blood flowing through his veins until he feels quite happy."

This joke made all the other boys laugh; but not so Goblin Jim, who was twirling about in very much the same way one would think the celebrated fox did who is said to have had a wound, but did not know where.

"Do you feel better now, my pretty Goblin?" demanded Jack Firebrace, laughing.

"I—I feel so much—I mean—I mean," answered Jim, suppressing his sobs, "I mean that I don't feel half so bad as you will do when I have my revenge, John Firebrace—and have it I will. You have lashed my skin; I will lash your heart to pieces in return; so look out, John Firebrace!"

Jack made a step forward to seize the impertinent little wretch; but in a moment the Goblin proved himself worthy of his name, for he dived headforemost through a bush, and vanished.

"The little wretch is slippery as an eel," laughed Jack.

"Yes, and as venomous as a snake," said Tomkins, in rather a doleful voice.

"Bah! you do not fear him, I am sure," said Jack Firebrace.

"Fear him! No, I should think I did not," replied Tomkins; "but this is how the matter stands, Jack. The little brute will not fight one of us; he knows much better than that. If anyone offends him he goes to his mother, 'the ghoul,' and complains to her. She first cuts off that boy's rations, with no mercy."

"Well, I have heard it said that it is sweet to see the mother fight for its young," laughed Jack; "but what will be his next little move?"

"I think that Goblin Jim is right when he says you will get the worst of it, for I never felt such stingers as the doctor manages to give."

"And does he never thrash Goblin Jim?" demanded Jack Firebrace.

"Never!" replied all the boys, in a chorus.

"Well, then, all I can say is this," continued Jack; "if the doctor thrashes us, we will thrash Goblin Jim. Th[at] squares matters, boys."

"Ah, yes; but then look here," sai[d] another of the lads, "see how hot w[e] get it."

"Well, the hotter we get it, th[e] hotter the Goblin shall get it. The[y] dare not murder us."

At that moment Jack started.

Was it a vision, or did Jack Firebra[ce] catch a glimpse of someone watchin[g] him through the leaves of the trees.

Whatever it was it vanished in a mo[ment,] and so quietly that Jack could n[ot] trust his eyes.

"Holloa, Jack!" cried old Flick[?] "have you seen a ghost, you look s[o] startled?"

"Oh, there are lots of ghosts to b[e] seen hereabout," said Tomkins. "[I] have seen awful ones."

"Well, never mind the ghosts jus[t] now," said Jack. "We had bette[r] g[et] on as fast as we can, and see Mr. Plian[t.] Where did you leave him?"

"We did not leave him anywhere," replied Tomkins; "but he promised u[s] that he would be in Farmer Jenkins' field reading, and told us not to be late."

"Which I rather fancy we must be," said Jack, "so let us be up and away[.] But, before we go, are we sworn t[o] stand together?"

"We are!" shouted all the boys.

"We are not! I'll have my re[-] venge!" yelled an imp-like voice, whic[h] everyone knew must be Goblin Jim.

But they could not see him, so wen[t] on their way.

["The Boys of Hawkhouse School."

Given away with ... [

From out of the well came two little boots, soles uppermost.

"'WHY DO YOU ILL-USE ME THUS?' EXCLAIMED THE UNFORTUNATE BEING."

PRICE ONE HALFPENNY.

[Published Every Monday.]

CHAPTER VII.

MR. PLIANT MEETS MORE MISFORTUNES —THE ATTACK IN THE LANE—A BRAVE
GIRL—THE COWARDLY BLOW.

AWAY bounded the lads, as merry as could be.

They were young, and put care at defiance.

They soon came within view of Mr. Pliant.

"We need not have been in such a hurry to get back," said Jack, "for old Pliant is fast asleep."

"Asleep?" cried the others; "oh, what a spree! He won't know when we came back."

"I know something better than that," said Jack, with a laugh, "only you must not tell."

"What is it?" said the others, in eager whispers.

"Keep quiet, and you will see," replied our hero, who dearly loved a bit of mischief.

Mr. Pliant was sleeping calmly on a bank, with his head resting against a thick hedge.

Beyond this hedge was Farmer Jenkins's flower-garden, and doubtless the smell of the honeysuckle, which had crept over the blackthorn hedge, and the soft breeze, had wooed the usher to slumber, for his hat had fallen off.

The handkerchief which he had left by mistake on his head now fluttered on a bramble, having been blown thereon by a sudden gust of wind.

Jack Firebrace approached the tutor softly, and, taking the slumberer's watch from his waistcoat pocket, put the hands back a couple of hours.

Having done that, he slipped it back into its owner's pocket.

Gently as he had performed this trick, he still had disturbed the sleeper.

Mr. Pliant grunted, yawned, stretched forth his legs, and, with another prodigious yawn, awoke.

"If you please, Mr. Pliant, can you tell me the time?" asked Flitter, stepping towards the usher.

"Time—time?" replied Mr. Pliant, drawing his watch forth in a sleepy way. "I almost fancy I slept."

"That was just it, sir," said Jack. "We did not like to wake you, and yet dreaded the time."

"Been asleep—nonsense!" said Mr. Pliant, who, like many other people, would never admit that he slumbered. "I had merely closed my eyes; the sun is so bright."

Here he drew out his watch, looked at it, held it to his ear to make certain it was going, and then said, triumphantly—

"I told you I had only just closed my eyes. It is only twelve. Sleep, indeed! Quite absurd."

Mr. Pliant put up his watch, seized his pocket-handkerchief, and clapped his hat on his head; but scarcely had he done so before his pupils came to the conclusion he had gone mad.

First, he threw his silk handkerchief on the ground and danced on it, at the same time sucking his thumb.

The boys could not conceal their laughter, and Mr. Pliant glared at them like a hungry ogre.

Suddenly he paused, and, screwing his eyes and mouth up, bent his knees and shivered, looking, as Flick graphically described it, like a monkey with the stomach-ache.

Then he grasped the brim of his hat with both hands, and, dashing it upon the ground, recommenced his Indian dance, but this time using his hat instead of his handkerchief as a platform; and now all the boys understood the mystery.

The hat and handkerchief were full of wasps, which had been attracted by the honey.

"Boo-hoo! boo-hoo!" yelled the unfortunate man, as he danced about on his hat and smacked his bald pate at the same time. "Boo-hoo! Oh, the imps —yah! there's another sting."

"This is too bad!" cried Jack Firebrace, laughing. "Quick, quick, sir; it is your only chance. Run to the pond and put your head under water. Do make haste."

Mr. Pliant quite understood what was meant, and at once acted on the suggestion.

Away he scampered as hard as he could run to a pond in the corner of the field, the boys following him, only taking care to keep as much to windward of him as they could, knowing that wasps and bees cannot fly fast against a breeze.

The pond was not an inviting one; its banks were thick with black mud, whilst the water was covered over with a bright green duckweed; but Mr. Pliant had other things to think about than cleanliness at that moment.

In he rushed, taking a sensation header.

Down went his head, but—oh, horror!—it did not come up again; only a pair of short trousers bottoms, some six inches of blue worsted stockings, and a pair of high-low boots, remained visible, moving quickly backwards and forwards, as if some idiot were making a vain endeavour to walk on the sky.

"Merciful heaven! he has stuck head foremost in the mud; the man will be suffocated!" cried Jack Firebrace, in horror.

"Well, zur, I should not wonder if he were," replied a voice just behind him; "that pond be over foive feet deep in mud, I'ze thinking, and he's gone down head first."

The speaker was a thick-set country lad, with a shock of red hair, a good-natured, but somewhat flat face.

Jack did not look at the fellow much; he only noticed that he had a rope, or, rather, two ropes hung over his shoulders, which had evidently served for reins to drive the plough.

Jack never said a word, but seized these ropes, tied them together, made a slip knot at one end, and the next moment had lassoed one of Mr. Pliant's feet.

"Here! what d'ye mean by taking ov my lines?" cried the country lad; but when he saw the rope fly round the usher's foot, and remain fast to it, he paused in admiration, and exclaimed—

"Wal, dang my buttons! but that is a good plan to pull the man oot o' it. Here, I'll lend a hand, and willing."

"Now then, lads! a good pull, and a strong pull, and a pull altogether!" cried Jack.

"Pull ahoy! pull ahoy! pull a—"
Flop!

The mud gave way suddenly, and Mr. Pliant flew on to the turf, but those who were pulling at him also fell back, tumbling one over the other, for they had pulled so hard, and met with so little resistance, that over head and heels they went at once.

They were soon on their feet again, and, hurrying to the usher, found him stretched on the ground, spitting out vast quantities of black mud, whilst a thick coating of the same nauseous stuff covered his face and shoulders completely.

"Oh, crikey! he be in a state, and no mistake," said the country lad, grinning all over his face.

"Don't stand grinning there," said Jack, passionately; "but go to the farm and get help!"

"Oh, my! be you my maister, young cock-sparrer?" returned the country lad, grinning.

"If you don't do what I tell you, I will show you if I am a 'sparrer' or not."

"Oh, I ain't afeared!" replied the lad; "I can wait until you have cleaned down your schoolmeaster. Oh, oh! he do smell nice."

With that he sat himself down coolly, watching the schoolboys as they attended on Mr. Pliant.

This the lads did with such good will, that in a little time the unfortunate usher could open his eyes, and sit up and breathe.

"Where am I?" he gasped. "Oh, that wretched pond! Oh, those horrid wasps!"

"You will soon be better, I trust," said Jack, kindly. "Don't you think you can walk to the farm?"

"I don't know, Firebrace. What could have made the beastly bees bite me? It must be the honey I have on my head."

"Ho, ho, ho, ho!" roared the country lad; "well, I'll be danged if that bean't a good one. Why, yer mun be off your nut for to go and call that stinking mud honey! They be queer bees that would coom for such sweetstuff as that, I think. Ho, ho, ho, ho!"

"Hold your tongue, you unfeeling lout!" cried Jack, losing his temper.

"Coom, coom, my lad, none of that! I coom of a breed that doan't take insult quiet."

"When I am at leisure I will attend to you," said Jack.

"All right," replied the fellow, getting on his feet, and walking slowly away, "I'll be waiting for you in yonder lane. If you coom I'll gie ye as fine a drubbing as ever yer had, and if yer don't coom, why, I'll drub ye the first time as I catch hold of yer."

Pulling up the sides of his smock-frock, so that he might be able to thrust his hands into his trousers pockets with more ease, the fellow went off, whistling a low country air.

By this time Jack and his friends had managed to get the usher on his feet, and were leading him slowly up to the farm, one or two of the boys having been sent on in advance to beg the farmer to receive the unfortunate usher.

Farmer Jenkins was a burly, good-natured man, and, after having a good laugh at poor Pliant's expense, agreed to let him stay, and soon some of the farm-labourers were hard at work scrubbing the usher down, whilst the boys were despatched to the school to inform Mr. Gruesome of the accident which had overtaken his second master.

Jack and old Flick had forgotten all about the country lad, and were hurrying down the lane at the head of their companions, when, turning round a corner by a lone house, they came upon some dozen country lads of about the same build as the one who had made fun of Mr. Pliant.

"So you be coomed at last, my young cock-sparrer," said the fellow, striding up to Jack. "I was nigh coming to fetch you."

"If you had, you may depend I should not have come until I felt inclined."

"Well, we'll soon see if you can foight, then. That! for you and your school," said the country bully; and he made a tremendous blow at our hero's head.

Now the fellow, whose name, by the way, was Collin Clout, was a very powerful lad, but fortunately for our hero, and unfortunately for himself, he had not learnt the "noble art of self-defence"; consequently, he struck

round as if he were practising round-hand bowling at cricket.

Jack saw this, and, using both his right and left arms to guard, rushed in close up to his enemy, and immediately shot out a straightforward blow from his left shoulder, closing up Master Clout's right eye, and stretching him on his back.

"Boo-hoo-hoo!" roared Collin, who seemed quite beaten by this one blow; "boo-hoo-hoo! he's been and gone and knocked my eye out, that's what he's been and gone and done!"

"It is your own fault, you cowardly lout!" exclaimed Jack Firebrace, whose temper was now fully aroused; "you thought because you were bigger than me you could knock me about as you liked.

"You know the difference now, and I advise you not to try it on again. Get up!"

Blubbering like a great baby Collin obeyed, and Jack soon learned to his cost that it was astonishment and not fear which had caused the youth to remain so long prostrate.

No sooner had the countryman regained his feet than he rushed suddenly on our hero, and, dealing him a heavy blow on the head, sent him reeling into a ditch.

"You great coward, that's unfair!" shouted old Flick, as he sprang forward to rescue his companion from the polite attentions of Clout, who, having got Jack down, thought it was prudent to keep him there, and also that it would be a first-rate chance of pommeling him without the slightest danger to himself, and for that purpose had flung himself on our hero before he could rise; but Flick's interference was either mistaken by the yokels, or looked upon as an act of aggression, for no sooner did he dart forward than they all rushed upon the schoolboys, and a general fight ensued.

"Give it um, Giles—bravo, lads! don't give way to the bumpkins—'it un 'ard—stand firm, lads, don't yield an inch!—let the schoolboys have it."

Such were the cries that were shouted out by the combatants as they struck out furiously at each other.

Black eyes were plentiful, faces were swollen, and blood flowed freely, whilst, owing to the country boys' way of fighting—namely, catching hold of their antagonists by the hair with one hand whilst they pommeled with the other—a great quantity of hair was flying about.

Jack and his friend old Flick fought manfully, keeping back to back, and dealing out their blows straight from their shoulders; but all their skill was of little avail against the country lads' superior weight and strength, which told fearfully in an up-and-down fight like this.

Jack Firebrace saw this, and began to think how best to act, when assistance arrived in a way no one there ever expected.

The door of the lone house was thrown suddenly open, and a pailful of dirty water was shot over the combatants, causing both sides to withdraw a little and suspend the fight.

Before they could resume it again a young girl of about fifteen, but tall and strongly built for her age, wielding a mop, the head of which dripped with water, rushed between the combatants.

"Shame upon you," she cried, "to be kicking and scratching away in that style! Stand back, you thick-headed Collin Clout."

Here she thrust her dirty mop full into the face of Jack's enemy.

Sore and bruised as Jack was, he could not help laughing at this, and watching the girl with no little curiosity.

Her figure was extremely graceful and lithesome.

She was rather under the middle height, but, nevertheless, carried her head with the air of an empress.

Her face was round, but it gave a merrier look to her rosy lips and roguish hazel eyes.

Her complexion was perfect; her hair was a rich dark auburn, and her teeth small and pearly white.

She was dressed in a tight-fitting jacket of blue cloth, a short red petticoat, which showed a neatly turned ankle, and a small, well-arched foot encased in a well-fitting shoe, with buckles on the instep.

"Keep back!" she cried. "The first one who attempts to renew the fight I will punish with this."

To prove she meant what she said,

she gave one of the country lads a tap over the head with her mop, making him draw back very quickly.

"Vell, I'm blowed! there's muscle—there's a simetery for you. Wait a moment, miss, and I'll be by your side in two twos. I don't know vich side as you are on, but that's my side vichever it is."

All turned to see who was the speaker, and beheld a smart fellow dressed half as stable-boy and half as gentleman's groom.

This strange-looking creature got over the hedge in some way, and, having reached the girl's side, took off his hat to her, and made a bow with such a flourish that she could not help laughing.

"That's it, mum; keep your spirits up—never say die. 'Ere's a reg'lar gal'axy of talent—beauty, bravery, mirth, and virtue. Tell me who you want knocked down, and I'll do it. Lor' bless yer bright eyes, just you say the word, and I'll knock the whole biling on 'em into the middle o' next week in the twinkling of a bedpost."

As he spoke the word the fellow threw himself into a fighting attitude, and one which plainly showed that he, at all events, knew how to box.

"I don't want anyone hurt," replied the girl, half-annoyed, half-amused. "I wished to stop their fighting, that was all."

"Oh, I see! a case of armed neutrality. You've said the word, miss, and peace it shall be. Now, mind, all you fellows, I'm for peace, so the fust one as strikes a blow I'll knock down, or my name ain't Rob Rackstraw."

"You must permit me to thank you for your kindly assistance, miss," said Jack, stepping forward.

"Keep your place—keep back!" cried Rob, dancing up to Jack, "or I'll give you such a oner."

"Come here!" cried the girl, impatiently striking the ground with her foot. "I will not have you meddle."

"You've said the word, mum, and I kennel," exclaimed Rob Rackstraw, dropping his fists directly.

"You seem gentlemen," said the girl to Jack and his companions. "Tell me, what is the meaning of this wretched brawl? You must be to blame, for you are educated, and ought to know better."

"Pardon me," said Jack; "this fellow chose to laugh at a gentleman who had the misfortune to tumble into a pond and was nearly drowned. I rebuked him, and he threatened me. As we were returning home to Hawk-house School, these fellows set upon us, and hence the cause of the disturbance. Had he fought me fairly and alone, I should have soon settled the fight."

"Yer fight like an angel, considerin' your size and age," said Rob Rackstraw, with the air of a critic.

"And what have you got to say?" said the girl, turning to Collin.

"Say!" cried the country lad, "that I'm as good as he any day, and each time I meet him I'll give him a tanning, I wull; and, as for you, you ought to be 'shamed of yourself, a big gal like you, to come out among a lot o' lads foighting. But theer, ev'rybody laughs at Wild Winny, but I'll do more than laugh, I wull. If you coom across me again wi' yer mop I'll spank yer as if yer were a boy—theer now."

"In this case, gents afore ladies," said Rackstraw, as he gave Collin a heavy blow on the mouth. "That's a kind o' tap you never drank at afore; all home-brewed. Lots kept on the premises. Served by the proprietor—orders punctooally attended to. Don't hit round—it's agin the rules. Hillo! that's put up the shutter, I think."

This was a playful allusion to both Collin's eyes being damaged by a skilful blow planted fairly between them.

"And that's domino."

The last words recorded the fact that Rackstraw had so thrashed his enemy that the fight was over.

No one had attempted to prevent this fight, partly because they considered Collin deserved what he got, and partly that Rob Rackstraw's movements were so rapid, that it was over in less time than it takes to tell it, and Collin lay stretched upon the ground, his face covered with bruises; and then, as if this scene had not been comic enough, another character appeared.

A top window in the lone house was thrown open, and the face of a woman appeared thereat.

A plaid shawl was pinned across the woman's ample chest, and, as she stretched forth her arms, which, by the way, were naked in consequence of the sleeves of her gown being rolled up above her elbows, she looked like a funny picture framed in the window-frame.

"Meerder, meerder!" she shouted, at the top of her voice, meaning, it is presumed, murder, but her teeth being clenched together and her voice unusually shrill, she pronounced the word that way. "Meerder! Oh, that I should have lived to see the day when people fight like brute beastesses. Oh, my poor, dear Collin—oh, oh, oh, oh!"

Here she sobbed for a few moments; then, catching hold of the window-sill, she began stamping violently, at the same time uttering shrill cries of—

"Meerder, meerder, meerder!"

"Scraggs," cried Wild Winny, impatiently, "how dare you behave like this?"

"Oh, I cannot help it, mum! I've a woman's 'art—a female 'art a-beating in my breast, and I can't stand like a stock and a stone a-looking on while other people go a-knocking other people about. I 'as a 'art as beats for my feller critters. I am a poor, weak female—see I am, and my feelings overcome me, they do. Oh, it's 'orrid!"

Here she screwed up her eyes and mouth, shaking her head as if she had bitten an exceedingly sour lemon.

"Don't be foolish," replied Wild Winny. "Come down immediately. Do you not see people laugh at you?"

"People that 'as no 'arts always laughs at people who 'as 'arts. I will come down. But, oh! my 'art, my 'art, it feels so full."

With this she withdrew her head and closed the window.

"I hope you have not hurt that fellow," said Jack to Rackstraw, pointing to Collin, who was still stretched on the ground, snorting heavily.

"I generally do hurt when I hits," replied Rackstraw, "and I should not wonder if his jaws did ache a little bit; but he ain't as bad as he pretends to be. He's a-shamming. Here, wake up, my carroty friend, and stand on your pins, and have another dose of my mixture."

The last part of the speech was made to Collin, and was accompanied with a push of the foot.

Scarcely had his foot touched the prostrate Collin than Sally Scraggs dashed forward, and, trying to seize him by the hair—she could not because of its extreme shortness—cuffed his ears soundly.

At first Rob Rackstraw seemed quite unable to make this out; but the blows were such as not to leave him long in doubt as to how matters stood.

Slipping his foot behind Miss Scraggs, he placed his arms suddenly across her body.

A sudden jerk and Miss Scraggs fell in a sitting posture on—we were about to say the ground—but she never reached that; she fell with all the weight of her well-rounded form on the prostrate body of her lover.

" Oh ! " yelled Collin, and never was such an enormous " oh ! " heard before.

" Get up. You're a-crushing on me. Oh ! get up."

Obedient to her lover's command Miss Scraggs attempted to rise, but her foot slipped, and she reseated herself.

Again Collin groaned as a pavior does when he drops his rammer.

" This is too ridiculous," said Miss Winifred. " Get up, Scraggs, or I shall discharge you instantly."

" Oh, that I should hear those words from those lips ! " cried Miss Scraggs, swinging herself backwards and forwards, quite regardless of the cries and groans which came from her extraordinary seat.

" Oh, that I should live to hear these words addressed to me from one I have cherished with all my 'art ! Gentlemen, I am a woman of feeling—a female of feeling "—Scraggs always seemed to have some vague idea that a " woman " and a " female " were two different creatures. " I assure you that I feel— yah ! "

With a sudden agility one could scarcely believe so rotund a person could have shown, Scraggs bounded on to her feet, and began rubbing the thick part of her leg.

The truth must be told; the ungrateful Collin, getting tired of his lovely burden, had drawn a large pin, which fastened his smock-frock at the throat, his buttons not being always carefully attended to, and had run it into the leg of the woman with a 'art.

Jack and his schoolfellows laughed with delight as they saw this, but not so Wild Winny.

With an angry glance she turned upon the others, and exclaimed—

" I came here, seeing you attacked by greater odds; I did not think I should be laughed at."

" A thousand pardons," cried Jack; " I would not laugh at you for the world. But really your servant is so comic, that—"

" Go into the house, Scraggs," said Wild Winny, sharply; " and you, Collin, take off these rough fellows."

" Why should I ? " said Collin, beginning to blubber again; " I don't see that I's to be treated like that. I've been wolloped by two chaps. I've been sat upon and nearly smashed by she as I've loved, and 'ad all the wind knocked out of my body, and then I'm told to go away. But I'll be revenged—that's what I'll be—you doan't know some of uz lads 'as as coomed up here to seek higher wages, but you soon shall, so I tell 'ee. So coom, lads, we'll be off now, but time will be when we'll coom back and have our fun out."

" I say," cried Rob Rackstraw, " afore you go just you look here. I am one as wants higher wages, and, what's more, I shall get 'em easy, 'cos for why? I never got my last at all. But if you ever comes to me, I'll give you as much more payment as you wants. I ain't a stingy man in that way. But now just listen to these words. If ever I find you have done this 'ere young lady a 'arm— if you ever rise one finger agin her, I'll so dust your jacket that it wouldn't need another dustin' for forty year, even if you were a miller. So look out. Now put that in your pipe and smoke it as you go home."

The countrymen made no reply, but turned away and marched down the road.

" I guess they ain't Welsh ? " said Rob, quietly.

" No ; they are English country lads, come to seek their fortune here," replied Winny.

" And you boys—"

Jack's cheek flushed at this.

" You boys, you go to Hawkhouse, I suppose ? " said Winny. " You had better wait here for a little while and let those fellows go on."

"I do not see the least occasion for that," replied Jack, quickly; "I am not afraid of them."

"He's a bantam, and that's what he is now, and no mistake," cried Rob Rackstraw, smacking his knee. "I seed him a hitting out right and left, and they were pretty good smacks as he gave. Just a little tooition—a little of this here sort"—here he did a quiet dance all over the place, now guarding and then striking out as swift as lightning—"and he'd be a made man. If I stop here, I'll teach him how to use his 'fives'; you see if I don't."

"And if you do not stop here, may I ask where you intend going?" said Winny, smiling.

"Can't say. Ven I started all the vay from London, if anyone had told me I should have come into the land of mountains, goats, and pretty girls," he added, looking slyly at Winny, "I should have called that there man a liar, and if it was a woman, a mistaken one. I'm a kind of thing like a gossamer spider. I'm blown here and there, east and west, and—ha, ha, ha! I'm blowed if I know where I shall be next at all."

"At all events, you have done me good service," said Winny, "and if you like to receive my hospitality and sleep in yonder barn you are welcome."

"Won't I! you don't know all that I have had to put up with. Lor'! ma'am, a pigstye was a bed of roses to me sometimes. I accepts your offer with thanks, and if I can only do a little in this way"—here he went through a lot of pugilistic attitudes—"well then, I'm on, and no mistake. You've only to say the word and it's 'one, two,' double knocker under the chin, or a slice off the under cut, and one on his tupenny in a moment."

"I trust that I shall not have to call for your assistance," laughed Wild Winny; "I have had enough trouble already. But go into the house, and Miss Scraggs will look after you."

"And I'll look after Miss Scraggs," replied Rob Rackstraw, as he strutted into the house with his hat cocked on one side, his arms akimbo, and his left eye winking violently

"Gentlemen," said Winifred Summerbell, bowing to our hero, "I wish you good-bye."

"Madam—Miss Winny, I beg your pardon," cried Jack Firebrace, "but do allow us to thank you for the kindness—"

He paused, for the door was slammed in his face.

"Well, that is polite at all events," he laughed; "but it don't matter. Come along, lads."

"I say," whispered old Flick, "wasn't she a pretty girl, rather!"

"The young lady was extremely pretty," said Jack, quietly; "but I would rather not speak on the matter just now. Come along; let us race down this lane."

Off they went with all the glee and fun which only schoolboys can show.

They shouted, they ran, they jumped, when suddenly Jack took the lead of the party, crying out—

"Now I'll be hare; let him catch me who can."

Away he bounded, and had just reached a clump of wood, when a stone struck him full on the temple, and he fell senseless to the ground.

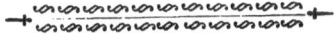

CHAPTER VIII.

JACK FIREBRACE MEETS WITH A COWARDLY ATTACK—HE IS TAKEN TO WILD WINNY'S—THE STRANGE ADVENTURE IN THE DESERTED WING.

"I'd give a hundred pounds, that is, if I had them," said old Flick, "to know who did this coward's act."

"It's a cruel shame. Look how he bleeds," said Tomkins. "Where can we take him?"

"We can't carry him all the way to Hawkhouse," said another boy.

"Of course not," said another; "we must take him back to Miss Summerbell's house."

"But will they take him in?"

"Of course; Miss Winifred is one of the kindest-hearted girls living."

"Ah, and the greatest madcap also," laughed another lad. "You should see her ride Swift, her pony."

"It is a sight," said Tomkins; "over brooks, hedges, gates, and ditches—nothing stops her."

"Never mind that now," exclaimed old Flick, impatiently. "We had better set to work to carry him back to Miss Summerbell's. Come along, lads; just some of you help me to pull up a few stakes from this hedge-row, whilst a few other fellows can cut some of the bushes about here. With these we will make a rough kind of litter, and carry him on our shoulders."

No sooner were the orders given than the lads set about obeying them with a good will.

Pocket-knives were opened, and the soft bushes were cut down most ruthlessly.

The stakes were pulled up and laid down, and bound together with the boys' braces.

On this the soft shrubs were strewn, and then Jack Firebrace was lifted gently on to it.

"Now, lads," said old Flick, "lift him up carefully; take care not to shake him. Here, let me put my jacket as a kind of pillow beneath his head. Poor old Jack! That's the style; now gently does it. Up he goes."

With the greatest tenderness they lifted our hero upon the litter and bore him back towards the lone house where dwelt Madcap Winny, or Wild Winny, for by both names she was well known in the country-side.

Sadly and silently they marched along; but had not gone far before they heard a very melodious whistling of the then popular air of "Tom Tough," and as they turned a sudden bend in the lane they came upon Rob Rackstraw.

"Hillo, my hearties! wot's up now?" cried Rob. "You ain't gone into the undertaking line of business I hope. Who is the gen'leman who has kindly placed his body at your disposal?"

"I am so glad we have met you," said old Flick. "He is the same gentleman who was fighting the country lout just now when the young lady came up."

"And how did he get that crack on the nut?" demanded Rob Rackstraw, as he examined Jack.

"The cowards, whom you and Miss Summerbell saw attack us, must have thrown a stone at him."

"Humph! I tell you what it is, youngsters," said Rob; "this is a very serious affair, and your friend's life is in danger. What are you going to do with him?"

"We are going to get some help for our friend," said Flick.

"I s'pose you are going to the house where Miss Summerbell lives?" questioned Rob.

"That is what we intend doing. We feel sure she will help us," replied Flick.

"In course she will; I take it upon myself to answer for her. She'll be delighted to see you all."

"You take it upon yourself to answer for her!" said Flick, unable to conceal his amused surprise.

"Exactly. I bid you welcome," replied Rob.

"And may I ask you what—or, rather, begging your worship's pardon—who are you? I should much like to know what you mean by calling Miss Summerbell's house 'yours.' I suppose there is no great secret about that matter, is there?"

"No, sir. I'm her butler, her ostler, her coachman, her groom, her bodyguard, her factoakum."

"Factotum, I suppose you mean," laughed Flick. "So the young lady has taken you into her service?"

"You have hit it exactly," said Rob Rackstraw, "and I am to be her adviser and—but here is the house. Welcome to the Lone House, gen'lm. Come in and make yourselves as happy as you possibly can. This way, and I'll inform the lady."

He ushered them into a dim passage, the dark oak panels of which were decorated with Indian war-clubs, New Zealand idols and paddles, besides many other curiosities brought from foreign shores.

From the roof hung ostrich-eggs, in company with swordfishes, sunfishes, and baby crocodiles, so that the place had somewhat the appearance of a small museum.

This strange passage opened into a comfortable sitting-room, massively, if not elegantly, furnished.

Pictures representing ships under full sail when tempest tossed—showing strange seamanship, but artists like always to make nature in a passion when at sea—were hung upon the walls, together with some half models of hulls.

All this told the boys that Mr. Summerbell was a sailor, and one of the true English sea-dog sort, who loved his profession with all his heart and soul; delighting even when ashore to have it near him; but that he also loved his only child, Winifred, and took great care of her education, was shown by a small but select collection of books arranged on top of each of the dwarf cupboards, which were placed in the recesses at each side of the fire-place, a piano, on the top of which was a guitar and several volumes of music.

Altogether there was an air of comfort and luxury about the place the boys did not expect to find.

They had scarcely removed our hero from the litter on to a comfortable sofa, when Winifred entered the room, followed by Rob Rackstraw and Sally Scraggs.

"There's the young gen'lm, my lady, as the coward struck down with a stone. If ever I get hold of Mr. Collin Clout I guess that I'll clout him to-rights."

"Oh! man," cried Sally, holding up her hands, and turning up her eyes, "you surely would not go to stand up for such unchristianity as that? How do you know that Collin did it at all? I hate them nasty schoolboys altogether. They're bundles of imperence tied up ugly; that's what they are. As for Collin, I've always found him as kind and affectionate as a sucking dove, that I have."

"He looks a sucking dove, surely!" said Rob Rackstraw, in a voice that made the boys laugh.

Whilst this pleasant little conversation was going on, Wild Winny had carefully bathed and bound up Jack's wound.

"It is not serious," she said, after a pause; "he will be well to-morrow. To-night he will remain here."

"Lor', miss, what'll your pa say!" screamed Sally Scraggs. "I couldn't stop in the house a hour with a young man. Consider, miss, we are unprotected females. What will the world say? I shudder to think of it."

"My eye!" roared Rob; "hasn't my sister's cat got a long tail! I'll be bound you would like Collin to stay here?"

"Collin is a hinicent, hingered hangel; that's what he is. I'd trust myself and all I possess to Collin, if—"

"He would take you," put in Rob, with a sly wink to old Flick.

"Hugh! you brute!" ejaculated Miss Scraggs, making a clutch with her fingers, as if she were plucking out someone's eyes. "I would not take you if your hair was hung with diamonds. A 'orrid, low creetur, that you are!"

"Silence!" said Miss Summerbell, who, for the first time, seemed to be aware of the quarrel between her two servants. "Sally, prepare a bed for the gentleman at once. Robert, saddle Swift and ride over to Dr. Lamberhurst, and ask him to come at once. Gentlemen, may I offer you some refreshment before you go?"

Flitter saw that this was a pretty good hint that Miss Winifred, however kind she intended to be towards Jack, had no intention of letting the unwounded remain under her roof longer than she could help.

He therefore took upon himself to decline the proffered refreshments; at the same time venturing to ask if he and his companions might be permitted to come and fetch Jack Firebrace on the morrow.

Winifred Summerbell at once gave the lad permission to call for Jack.

So away went the lads, as happy as happy could be.

"Let us have a game of soldiers," cried Tomkins; "and we will march up to Hawkhouse in good order."

"All right—capital!" shouted the others. "Flitter shall be the captain. Come, Flitter, form us into a regiment."

"Very well; I will be your captain for the present—but mind, only for the present. After this Jack Firebrace must be the leader of the school."

"Hurrah for Jack Firebrace, the leader of the school!" shouted all the boys.

"Now, then, my lads, fall into your

ranks, and count so that we may know all are here," said old Flick.

The lads obeyed the order, and at once began counting " one, two, three," and so forth; but when they had finished they discovered that two boys were missing.

One of these, of course, everyone knew was Jack Firebrace—but who was the other?

" Count over again," shouted Felix Flitter; and once more they counted, but only to meet the same result.

" I know who it is," cried Tomkins; " it is that wretched little sneak, Goblin Jim."

" Why, yes, of course it is," replied old Flick.

" It's my opinion that he threw the stone at Jack," said another; " he is demon enough for anything."

" That gives us another view of the case," said old Flick; " perhaps it was not Collin Clout after all."

" I rather fancy it was both of them," replied Tomkins. " I have often seen Goblin Jim and this fellow Collin together, and I believe that they are great friends."

" Here is more and more mystery," said old Flick; " but never mind that now. We have all sworn to stick to the captain, and we will see if we cannot overmatch both Goblin Jim and his companion Collin. But it is now quite dark. Won't there be a row when we return to the school? Never mind, it was not our fault that Mr. Pliant should sit on a wasp's nest and then plunge into a pool of mud. So, come along, lads. Forward! march! double quick time ! "

They toiled on until they were close to a part of Hawkhouse—a ruined and straggling wing, which ran a long way from the chief building.

The decayed and crumbling walls of this building were clad with ivy.

This place had for some reason been the most shunned by the boys of any part of the building.

It had obtained the name of being haunted, although no one could exactly tell why, and that particular wing was known as " the haunted wing."

As far as the boys really knew, owls, bats, and rats were the only inhabitants of this desolate place.

As we said before, the boys had just arrived by this desolate ruin.

They all halted and glanced nervously round at the gloomy pile, but no one spoke.

Suddenly a deep roar of laughter burst from within the desolate ruins.

The boys huddled together like sheep.

They clasped each other's arms, their teeth chattered, and their knees knocked together.

" Wha—wa—what's that ? " gasped one of the boys, with an awful shudder.

" How—how—how should I know ? " replied another. " Do stand still, and don't shake so."

" Hold your tongues," said old Flick; " you need not quarrel about who shakes the most; all are shaking."

" I candidly confess that I am shaking," said Tomkins. " I wish Jack Firebrace was with us now; he would not laugh at ghosts much longer, I think. Oh ! there it is again. Hadn't we better all run away ? "

But it was one thing to say run away, and another thing to do it.

The fact was that every boy, from the largest down to the very smallest, felt that to run just at that moment would not be very convenient, and therefore no one seconded the proposition.

Again and again the bursts of laughter startled the stillness of the night.

Then, to the horror of the boys, who crouched close to a stunted oak, the windows of the deserted wing were illuminated by a red glare, making it look as if the whole place were on fire.

" Ha, ha, ha ! " roared the mysterious creatures in the building; " bravely sung, good Vandervord. And now for a draught of brandy."

A kind of humming silence fell upon the scene, and then a deep voice called out—

" Give us a true song, Jackson ; one that smells of sea-salt and powder. I hate love-songs. What's the good of asking a girl if she loves you? You love her, and that's sufficient. That's my opinion."

" Wisely said," laughed the rest, and then followed a general call for a song, preceded by a short pause.

After a few seconds a rough but not

unmusical voice poured out the following ditty—

"Ye land-lubbers living upon the dry shore,
　Who know not the smell of gunpowder and grog,
Who shiver and shake when the wild tempests roar,
　Come list to a yarn of a jolly sea-dog,
His name it was Jack, and a gunner was he,
　As brave an old tar as you'd meet in a day;
But one winter's night he went out on the spree,
　And Old Nick passing by whisked poor Jack away.
　　　Singing—To di roll lol di, tol di roll lay."

Taking advantage of the noise, and becoming doubtful of the supernatural nature of the revel, Flick crept close up to the building, and, climbing up the thick ivy, peeped in at one of the windows.

The scene he beheld was a strange one in the extreme.

A party of some twenty men were seated round a large fire, drinking and singing together.

They were dressed in the usual style of sailors: thick pea-jackets, large sea-boots, and tarpaulin hats.

The chorus being over, the sailor who was singing began the second verse.

The chorus was taken up fast and furiously by the rest of the company.

Having succeeded so far Flitter thought that he might do more, and therefore endeavoured to crawl close to the window; but unfortunately, as he stretched forth his hand to catch another branch of ivy his foot slipped.

He swung for a few seconds high up in the air, and then, to his horror, he felt the ivy slowly but surely giving way.

Crash! down it came, bringing with it a quantity of loose masonry, and, to Flick's horror, making an awful noise.

In a moment the fire was darkened.

Then there arose such yells and screams that Flick's blood positively curdled in his veins.

He sprang to his feet and beheld his companions flying, as fast as their legs would carry them, towards the school; and, thinking their example good, he lost no time in following them.

He was a swift runner, and easily overtook them, but no one stopped to ask questions.

Onward they sped, until, turning a sharp corner in the old wall, the boys halted instantly.

Before them stood the figure of an old man, with a long, white, flowing beard.

This strange figure was clad in a monk's robe, and a string of beads hung from his side.

To meet an old gentleman clad in that manner, in such a place, and at such a time, would have been astonishing enough, but this peculiar old gentleman seemed to emit a peculiar light of his own, in which he moved, having about six inches of light all round him as a kind of halo.

Overcome with fear the boys dropped upon their knees, and, with open eyes and mouths, and hair standing erect, gazed in horror at the dreadful ghost, who, with outstretched hand, seemed as if warning them back.

"Children of clay," said the spectre, in a hollow voice, "why do you cross the path of the disembodied? Know ye not that this place has been the scene of great crimes? I am called Father Anselm the Martyr. I dwelt with my holy brethren in yonder building, passing our days in acts of devotion, and, when the storm cast ships upon this ironbound coast, my brothers and I tried to rescue the sailors. One night we rescued a band of pirates—we knew not but what they were honest sailors—and took them into our house. In the dead of night they rose and slew us all, departing with the riches of our monastery. But their punishment has been sure. On certain nights they have to hold their revelry over again in yonder hall, and act as they did in the life. Beware how you meet them! Woe unto those who do wrong! Woe, woe!"

The last words were uttered in such heart-rending and piercing tones that the boys closed their eyes in horror, for they expected every moment to see a troop of imps scourging the terribly wicked pirates all round the castle-walls in punishment of their bad crimes.

But after a few moments, when they opened their eyes, they were alone.

They sprang to their feet and dashed off as fast as they could, never pausing until they reached the school, where they found Mr. Gruesome in a great state of nervousness as to what had become of them

They related the circumstances which had detained them, and he appeared perfectly satisfied; but Flitter forbore to mention what they had seen and heard in the desolate wing of Hawkhouse.

CHAPTER IX.

JACK AT THE LONE HOUSE—HE HEARS A STRANGE HISTORY.

WHEN Jack Firebrace awoke the next morning, the sun was shining in at his bedroom window.

He sprang out of bed and took a good look at himself in the looking-glass.

"I certainly am not a beauty," said Jack, as he saw the plasters which Doctor Lamberhurst had used to bind up the cut on our hero's temple. "I can't say that it has improved my personal appearance. I scarcely look in proper condition to pay a visit to a young lady, let alone breakfast with her; and, oh! I am so hungry. I must do the best I can to remove the marks of blood. If ever I find out who did this I will pay him out, and with interest, too."

He bathed his wound carefully, and then, having completed his toilette, drew a few curls over his temple so as to hide the wound from general observation.

He once more went to the window.

The garden was filled with flowers, and was laid out with exquisite taste.

Beyond it was the stable, where Rob Rackstraw was busy grooming the pony, Swift, a vicious little animal.

But he had met his master in Rob Rackstraw, who seemed to know by instinct when the pony was going to kick out, and always managed to escape without appearing to put himself out in the least, all the time whistling away as merrily as possible.

But Jack did not watch this little game long, amusing as it was, for there was "metal" more attractive among the flowers.

There, with a pretty little garden-hat upon her head, a small basket on her arm, stood Winifred, plucking roses and other beautiful flowers, which she arranged in a bouquet.

"How jolly handsome she is!" soliloquised Jack Firebrace. "I wonder if she is always as fiery as she appeared last night. Well, I suppose I must go down and pay my respects. It won't do to be too quiet. She will burst out laughing at me if I do the spoony; ask me to put on the gloves or try the foils. Perhaps she will suggest a little game of cricket. No, I must not be bashful; that game would not do at all. Whatever she does she is sure to look pretty, whilst I fear that whatever I do I shall be certain to appear awkward. Well, I can't help it; I must try my luck.

"I don't know how it is," muttered Jack. "I could face that brute Collin without the slightest tremor, and now I am only going to speak to a girl, who seems as beautiful as she is kind, my nerves seem all in a shake, and I feel much inclined to run away."

Ah, Jack, Jack, Jack! how many a gallant man has felt the same feeling in similar circumstances!

However, Jack put on as firm an air as he could, did not blush more than he could help, bowed politely to the lady, and attempted to make a speech, but found himself stammering awfully.

Winifred Summerbell looked at him in some surprise, her large bright eyes fixed upon his, and then she burst into a musical laugh—such a laugh, so full of fun that it made Jack Firebrace angry and yet compelled him to laugh.

"I really am sorry that I should have given you all this trouble, Miss Summerbell," he stammered. "To be sure the stone did hit me a nasty crack, but I daresay it was not meant for me—for I should not like to think that anyone did such a cowardly trick as to knock a fellow down when he had not the slightest chance of helping himself."

"I am glad to hear you say so, Mr.—Mr.—I pray you pardon me, but I have forgotten your name."

"It's not a very pretty name," said

our hero. "I am called Jack Firebrace."

"Jack Fireplace? Ho, ho, ho! what a strange name! But I should think that it was only a name given to you by your schoolfellows. No human being can be called Fireplace."

"I should hope not indeed!" exclaimed Jack, somewhat indignantly. "I said Firebrace."

"Oh, I beg your pardon, Mr. Firebrace. I am really sorry that I should have misunderstood you."

"Pray don't mention that," cried Jack. "I daresay I pronounced the name carelessly. I am very careless in that way. I must try to correct that fault under Mr. Gruesome's tuition."

"Under Mr. Gruesome's tuition?" said Winifred, with an evident shudder.

"Yes, Mr. Gruesome, of Hawkhouse School. You surely must know him!"

"Pardon me, I do not know him," replied Winifred, sternly. "I live here without knowing my neighbours, save Farmer Jenkins—that is to say, I know them all, but seldom speak, and never visit."

"It is strange that one so young should lead so lonely a life," said Jack Firebrace.

For a moment the girl looked annoyed, then puzzled, and the next a smile broke over her face.

Putting her hand out with a pretty show of confidence, she said to him—

"Mr. Firebrace, I feel certain that I may trust you."

"I can assure you, my dear Miss Summerbell, nothing should make me divulge your secret."

"It is no secret," replied Winifred; "only I know my dear father does not wish it to be generally known. You must know—there, don't bother with your cap, but put it on and let us sit down on this bank, and you hand me the flowers as I re-arrange this bouquet. Well, Mr. Firebrace, you must know that my father is captain of a large ship. He has been a sailor from a boy, and swears that if it were not for me he should like to die at sea. He is so—so clever and brave. I love sailors."

"I should like to be a sailor," replied Jack Firebrace, dreamily.

"Don't be silly; and give me that heartsease. Well, many years ago, my mother's brother had married out in India, and had written home to say that his ship—for he, too, was a captain of a merchant vessel—would soon start for England.

"He was as dear to my father as if he had been his own brother, and I have heard my poor mother describe how pleased he was when he received the lady's likeness, and that of her little boy. Well, the ship sailed, but never reached the land. Only one of the crew ever was seen alive again."

"Merciful Heaven; and were they all shipwrecked?" demanded Jack.

"That was the general belief; but my dear father would never believe it. Some years afterwards an old sailor arrived in London, and declared that the ship had been attacked by pirates, and all the crew murdered, all save himself. Most people thought the old man mad, and refused to listen to his story, whilst others went so far as to hint that if foul play had been used, old Silas must have had a hand in it, or he would never have escaped.

"Unfortunately, my poor mother had died a year before the old sailor returned.

"My father searched far and near for the old man, but he disappeared suddenly and mysteriously. Whether my father had some proof that the sailor's story was true I cannot say. All I know is, that he firmly believed it, and applied to a Mr. Griffiths Grindwell, a rich London merchant and shipowner, to help him in his search.

"What passed at their meeting I do not know, but they quarrelled, and my father took this place down here for me, and soon after started for sea again; but before he went he took an oath that he would leave no stone unturned until he discovered the murderers of his old friend and his wife and child.

"Soon after I came here Hawkhouse was taken as a school. Mr. Gruesome, it appeared, was a kind of poor relation of Mr. Grindwell, who had taken the house to start him. On his return from sea my father learned this, and at once forbade my ever going near Hawkhouse, and also named two rich and powerful gentlemen as my guardians.

"To one of these gentlemen I have to report myself once a week, and to declare that I have had nothing to do with Hawkhouse."

"Miss Summerbell," said Jack, "I must in very honesty confess that this same Mr. Griffiths Grindwell is my guardian. I—I do not know who were my parents—both are dead; and Mr. Grindwell, although not too kind, has brought me up. I must be candid enough to own that I never can like him. Sometimes I fancy he would be cruel, but that he fears me."

As he spoke a look of such utter aversion stole over Jack Firebrace's face that Winifred could not doubt him.

"Well," she laughed, "I will see what can be done. I want a companion, and you will do very well. You have courage, and I like that. I love freedom, fun, and mischief. Oh, if I had been born a man, how I would have sailed the sea with my father! I would have bound myself to discover the murderers of his friends, and then away to a life of adventure. That shall be the life my husband shall follow!"

"That shall be the life I will follow!" cried Jack, carried away by the young girl's enthusiasm. "I swear that I will try to discover the murderers, and will seek adventures, and—"

"Oh, what a charming Don Quixote!" laughed Wild Winny; "he is going to avenge the deaths of people of whom he never heard, and of whose existence, until just now, he was perfectly ignorant. If you take up all adventure as eagerly as that, you will have enough to do to get safely through the world."

"I am, after all, only a schoolboy," said Jack; "but the mouse, if you remember, helped the lion once, and maybe I shall be able to help your father."

"I wish you would show me how," laughed Wild Winny.

"Your father evidently thinks Mr. Grindwell could aid in discovering the fate of his friend. I have to meet Mr. Grindwell, and I may discover something. I cannot tell you the horror in which all the boys hold that dreary old Hawkhouse; they think it is haunted. I myself have seen strange sights there which make my blood run cold in my veins. That dreary house holds deep and dreadful secrets, and, come what may, I will unravel them. Who can say that in so doing I may not be able to discover that which your father so wishes to know? Tell me, will you accept my services?"

For a moment the young girl looked steadily into Jack's eyes, and then placed her hand in his.

"I do accept your services. I don't know whether it is the love of adventure that I have so strongly in me, but I do feel greatly interested in what you say, and hope that you may find some clue to the mystery in that house."

Jack shook hands with Wild Winny and was about to enter the house, when they were startled by hearing a long loud ringing at the bell, followed directly the door opened, by a deep stern voice inquiring for Mr. John Firebrace. What happened we shall relate in our next chapter.

THE BOYS OF HAWKHOUSE SCHOOL.

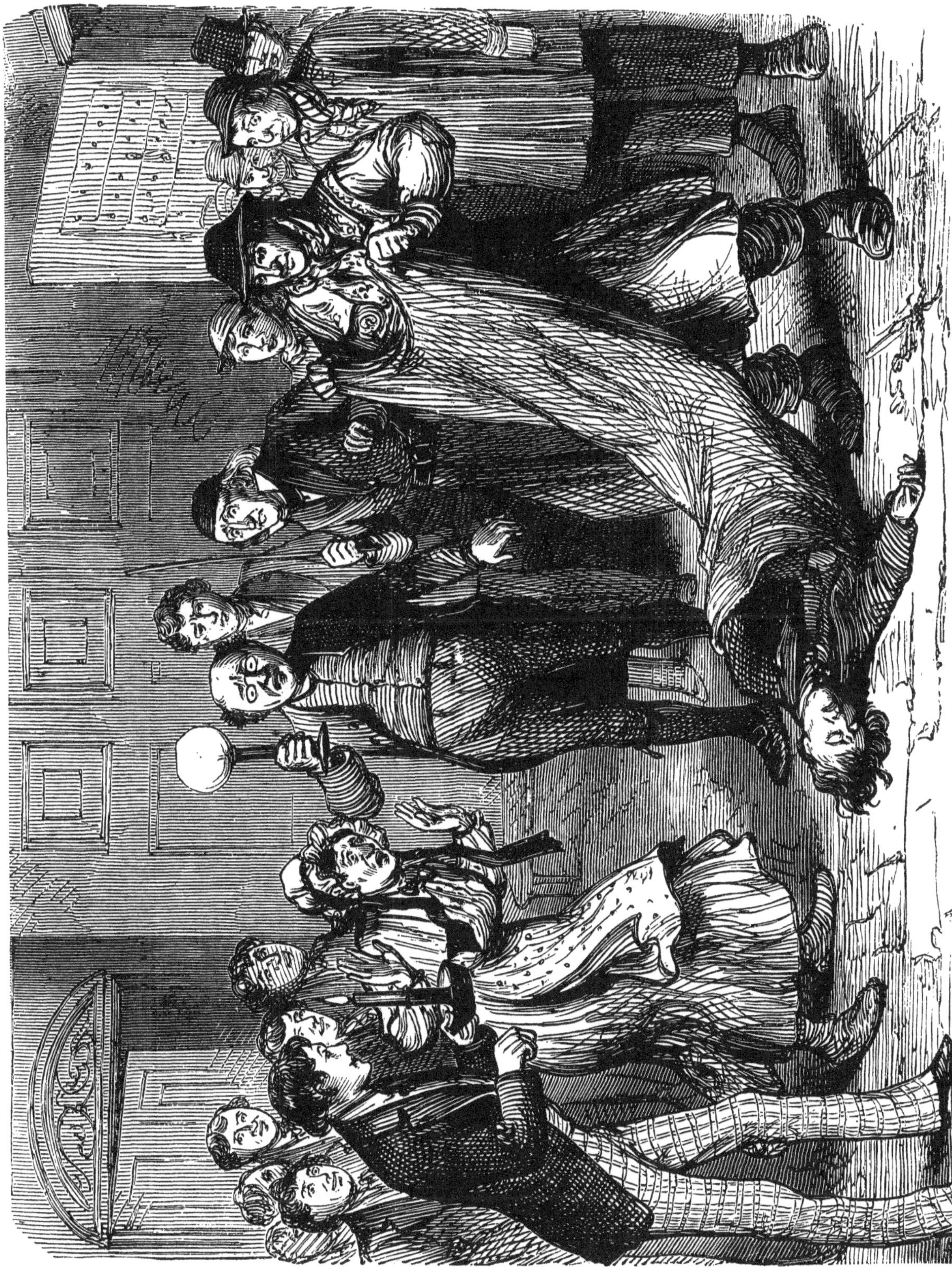

"HE TOOK HOLD OF THE SACK AND SHOT OUT THE IMPRISONED BOY."

No. 4.

PRICE ONE HALFPENNY.

[PUBLISHED EVERY MONDAY.]

CHAPTER X.

JACK FIREBRACE DECLARES WAR AGAINST GRIFFITHS GRINDWELL, WHO ORDERS
HIM TO BE TORTURED.

"I RATHER think Mr. John Firebrace is here," said Rob Rackstraw, who had answered the door.

"Then bid him come here quickly. I have no time to waste on such as he— or you !" said the stern voice.

"You're a nice, civil-spoken gentleman, you are. You look as if you lived on buttered thunder, you do !"

"Robert !" cried Winifred, as she entered the passage, "who is that at the door ?"

"I don't know, my lady ; he hasn't told me his name, and in his case I should not like to judge from appearances ; he might think I was rude and a-using bad language."

"Silence, sir ! how dare you speak so to a visitor of mine ?" cried Winifred, stamping her foot.

"Didn't know that he was a visitor of yours, miss," replied Rob, coolly ; "he never asked for you."

"Enough of this," said the stranger (who was no other than Mr. Grindwell), as he attempted to push past Rob Rackstraw ; "I have come here for my ward, John Firebrace. Stand on one side, boy !"

"No, you don't pass here," exclaimed Rob, sparring up. "No you don't. You may have come for your ward, but, if you don't look out, you will get something else afore you go home to that unhappy lady as calls herself your wife."

Mr. Grindwell stood still for a moment, and then beckoned for Sidney Morrison, who entered, followed by a thick-set, evil-looking fellow.

"I do not wish to use force," said Mr. Grindwell ; "so I warn you I have come here to claim my ward. And once more, I say, stand back !"

"Mr. Grindwell," said Jack, stepping forward, and trembling with passion, "if I am your ward I am not your slave."

"So, so ; the young cock begins crowing early," said Grindwell, with a laugh. "You are not my slave, eh ? By my word, I have a good mind to ship you on board one of my vessels, and see what you would call yourself then. I must tell Gruesome to be more strict with you. Look ! this is the kind of thing I cane impertinent boys with."

As he spoke he raised his whip, and struck our hero heavily across the shoulders.

With a yell of rage Jack sprang forward and clutched Grindwell by the throat, shouting—

"Devil ! I will strike in return."

"Take the brat off, or I will kill him !" roared Grindwell between his teeth ; "take him off, some of you."

But that was not so easily done.

Rob, having pitched Mr. Sidney Morrison out of the door, was now bobbing around the evil-looking man, planting what he called "One, two !" on the man's head and body, and keeping him well employed, so that he was quite unable to come to his master's assistance.

Meanwhile Grindwell had shortened his whip, so that with the butt-end he was able to deal our hero a fearful blow over the forehead, sending him to the earth almost insensible.

He was about to repeat the blow, when there was a sudden cry of—

"Hold !"

And then two pistols, placed close to his face, made him start back and gaze in surprise at the slim form of Wild Winny.

"So you are Miss Winifred Summerbell, are you ?" said Grindwell, after a moment's pause.

"I am ; and you are ·my father's enemy, Griffiths Grindwell. Villain ! leave this house instantly."

"Like father, like daughter," said Grindwell. "Well, lass, I do not wish to stop here ; I have come for that boy. We want no more crazed people."

"He has learned your secret, villain, and he is and shall be my friend," cried Winny.

No sooner had she said the words than she repented it.

Griffiths Grindwell had not a pleasant face at the best of times—it was now perfectly fiendish.

His dark brow lowered, his lips became livid, and his eyes gleamed with a baneful fire.

"So," he hissed between his teeth, "you have followed close upon your father's footsteps! You would step in between me and my ward? Have a care; no one crosses my path with impunity. My mottoe is '*Nemo me impune lacessit!*'* Come," Jack, he continued, suddenly changing his tone to his oily manner, "I am sorry I hurt thee, lad. Get up and follow me. Forget my temper, and I will try to forget yours."

Jack Firebrace at first seemed inclined to resist, but Wild Winny made him a sign to submit.

"I am ready," said Jack; "but I am at a loss to know how I have deserved this treatment. I have received a serious blow from a stone, aimed by the hand of some hidden foe; I am brought here insensible; this lady behaves to me most kindly. Surely, as my guardian, you should thank her and not insult her."

"Boy," said Griffiths Grindwell, in a stern manner, "you know not what you talk of. This girl and her father are my foes, and I have taken an oath that, as far as is in my power, neither I nor mine shall have anything to do with them."

Here young Rackstraw spat on his hands and sparred about, saying—

"Oh, I should like to punch somebody!"

"A nice household!" sneered Mr. Grindwell; "all mad together, I should think—quite mad."

"Anyway, old Sourface, we shouldn't like you to be our keeper," replied Rob Rackstraw.

"Good-bye, Mr. Firebrace," said Wild Winny, suddenly resuming her old careless, dashing way; "you know that we have promised to be friends, and therefore we will be. When my father comes home—which he will do in a month or so—I shall tell him all about

---

*No one provokes me with impunity.

this, and see what he has to say to Mr. Grindwell; and I do ask you not to trust that man."

"I thank you, Miss Summerbell," replied Mr. Grindwell, with a bitter laugh.

"You are welcome, sir," replied Wild Winny.

"Pardon me, Mr. Grindwell," said Jack, "but I should like to know something of my parents; I think there should be no secrets between us."

Grindwell curbed his contemptuous mood, and merely said—

"Between us, John Firebrace? I think you should have no secrets from me. That I should tell a lad like you my secrets—a boy I have taken charge of out of charity—is not likely. It is your duty to have no secrets from me, and if I find you have I shall know how to punish you."

"I never asked your charity," said Jack Firebrace, hotly. "I only wish to know who and what my parents were, and I shall be contented. I can go to sea; I can and will earn my own living without your help. I tell you, Mr. Grindwell, I never have and never can like you!"

"Humph!" sneered Grindwell, although his trembling lip showed how much he felt the boy's announcement; "I believe what you say. You came of a family who always neglected their duty. However, I shall assert my right as your guardian, and will compel you to obey me."

"Then," replied Jack Firebrace, "I here tell you that I will not own you as a guardian. I am this young lady's friend. I know not the mystery that hangs between you and her father, but I will try to clear it up. I tell you plainly that we are from this time forward open enemies, not hidden ones, as we have been."

"Enough; we do understand each other now. Mr. Sidney Morrison, you have heard this nice young gentleman's statement?"

"Certainly, certainly, Mr. Grindwell," said the usher, in a dazed manner.

"Good. You will therefore see that he is placed under strict discipline. If we cannot tame such a spirit we must break it. Now seize the boy, and bear him away."

The usher and the evil-looking man seized Jack Firebrace and held him a prisoner.

"Oh, say the word, ma'am, and I'll precious soon knock out that there gentleman's skylights and—"

Poor Rob Rackstraw said no more, for a blow, delivered with the force of a sledge-hammer by Griffiths·Grindwell, laid him low on the ground.

"That comes from being imperent to one's betters; it serves 'em both right!" cried Sally.

"Go downstairs, girl!" Winifred Summerbell cried, stamping her foot with passion.

Sally Scraggs obeyed, but not before she had exchanged a meaning glance with Griffiths Grindwell.

By that glance Grindwell knew that the lovely Sally was no friend to the Summerbells or their friends, and that her good offices might easily be obtained by a little gold.

"You coward!" cried Wild Winny, "to strike the lad like that!"

"Listen to me!" hissed Grindwell through his clenched teeth, as he caught Winifred by the wrist, grasping the girl so tightly that she could have screamed with pain, but her pride forbade her; "you say you are friendly with this boy; if you be so, avoid him; do not speak to him, for if he meet you I will so punish him that he shall grow to hate you!"

"Do not listen to him, Miss Summerbell," cried Jack Firebrace. "I will be true to you whatever may happen, for I love you. Be true to your word, and we will conquer yet!"

"Silence the idiot!" roared Grindwell, stamping with rage.

Vainly Jack struggled to get free from his captors.

He was borne out of the house, placed, bound, on horseback with the man with the evil look, and in this manner conveyed back to school.

"Now, lad, your punishment begins," said he, when Hawkhouse was reached.

Then, pale with passion, the foam of rage flecking his lips, Griffiths Grindwell turned and left the room, slamming the door behind him.

CHAPTER XI.

JACK FIREBRACE PRISONER—HIS TORMENTOR—THE TABLES TURNED—THE SECRET OF THE WELL—THE RACE TO THE VILLAGE.

In a lonely tower, a jug of water and a small loaf of black bread by his side, his elbows resting on the window-sill, his eyes fixed vacantly on the heaving sea, and whistling plaintively, stood our hero, Jack Firebrace.

Mr. Sidney Morrison had shown rather an unpleasant aptitude in carrying out Mr. Grindwell's instructions.

Jack had been set the hardest tasks possible in his lessons.

For this he did not care, for, being naturally quick, he had learned them, and come off with honours.

But he was forbidden to go beyond the precincts of the school; the other lads were punished if they spoke to him; and Mr. Morrison read him long lectures on ingratitude.

For two days Jack put up with this; of course he was annoyed, but he bore it with patience.

He amused himself by finding out means whereby he could communicate in a measure with his faithful lieutenant, old Flick.

Letters were hastily scribbled and placed beneath inkstands, so that the masters could not see them; but old Flick knew where to find the notes, and took them up in a careless manner, as if they were pieces of waste-paper.

In this manner the two lads had managed to inform each other of what had passed since Jack had been struck with the stone, and to concert plans whereby they intended to be revenged on Mr. Morrison, to whom they naturally had taken a great dislike, and, if possible, to escape from the school.

Poor Mr. Pliant shook his head and groaned at all this.

Unfortunately for Jack, Mr. Sidney Morrison had seen him place one of his notes beneath an inkstand, and had sprung forward to seize it.

Jack snatched up the slip of paper, struck Sidney Morrison back, and, seeing no other way to save his friend old Flick, who would sure to be punished for receiving the note, swallowed the paper.

For this he was doomed to one week's solitary confinement, and his food to be bread and water.

It was his third day of confinement, and Jack had grown weary of seeking for some means of escape.

The walls of the chamber were of stone.

It was about twelve feet square and about fifteen feet high.

The door was composed of thick iron, strongly studded and bolted and barred.

The window was merely a rough hole cut in the wall, admitting the chill damp air. This, as we have already shown, was so low down that Jack was able to rest upon the window-sill; but outside a descent of sixty or seventy feet went sheer down to the sea.

One more opening there was in the room, and that was a small aperture above the door, and close to the ceiling.

"I believe they wish to drive me mad," said Jack, aloud, for the silence had become unbearable. "For three days I have not heard a human voice or seen a creature, save the rats, and there are rather too many of them. Each morning a loaf of bread and a jug of water is lowered from that hole above the door by means of a string, so that I may not even have the pleasure of beholding my gaoler, or exchanging a word with him."

He paced up and down his room for some time, and then paused to examine some rusty chains which were fastened by ring-bolts to the wall.

"If these old walls could speak," he observed, "they would doubtlessly have many strange stories of man's cruelty to his fellow creatures to relate."

"They would, they would," cried a shrill voice. "Ho, ho, ho! They have seen many a dark deed of blood!"

Jack gazed around, but not a creature could he see. Everything was as still as usual.

"This is strange," he muttered.

"Surely I must be dreaming! I must be mad, for I could swear I heard a voice reply to me."

"Mad you may be, dreaming you are not. A voice did reply to you, John Firebrace," cried the invisible one.

Jack placed his hand to his forehead, and stood motionless with horror.

"Hearken to me! I am the evil genius of this place, John Firebrace," continued the voice. "In that room many and many a poor creature has been done to death by my orders. Ho, ho, ho! That chain you just touched: many and many a man has felt the canker of its rust eat into his bones. I am doomed to come to all those who are to die in this room—ha, ha!—die in this room."

"If you are the spirit of the place," said Jack, who had in some measure recovered his courage, "show yourself to me. I am not afraid."

"That is forbidden me. But you will see me soon enough when your time comes. Ha, ha, ha! To the creature in the flesh I may not appear; but when you have quitted the flesh, then, John Firebrace, you can see me."

"When I have quitted the flesh!" repeated Jack. "Will that be soon?"

"You will quit the flesh before you quit that prison. I tell you your fate is settled. Ho, ho, ho, ho! your fate is settled."

There was something in the shrill laugh and demoniacal voice which seemed familiar to Jack.

Dropping on his knees, our hero pretended to shiver with fear, and, clasping his hands, he began imploring mercy.

"Mercy, mercy!" he cried, at the top of his voice. "Oh, have mercy upon me! I am too young to die."

"Ho, ho, ho!" roared the Goblin; "here is brave Jack Firebrace imploring for mercy. Ha, ha, ha, ha! ho ho!"

"Is he?" said Jack, quietly, as he rose to his feet. "You see I can act a part as well as you can, Master Goblin Jim. I do not know where you are, but if I could find you I would break every bone in your goblin skin."

"Ha, ha! I hear you. So you were acting, were you?" said Goblin Jim, appearing at the aperture over the door, and seating himself therein, so that his legs swung inside the prison. "You act very well, Firebrace. I shall come and see you act every moment I have to spare. It's true I am not the evil spirit of this place. Nevertheless, what I told you is true. You will never leave this place alive."

Enraged at the little monster's brutal glee Jack Firebrace seized his loaf of bread, and flung it with all his might at Goblin Jim.

It hit him full in the chest, and his head went back and his heels flew up. But the wall was evidently a thick one, so that Jim quickly recovered himself, and, resuming his seat, held up the loaf.

"Waste not, want not, my boy," chuckled the Goblin. "You won't have any more of this nice black bread until to-morrow at noon, and yet you go flinging these things about in any style. You really should be more careful, my dear boy."

Jack mentally thought so to, but he was far to proud to own it.

"Here, I won't rob you of it," cried Jim.

And he pretended to throw the loaf to Jack, but maliciously threw it out of the window, so that it went plunging down into the sea.

"Dear me! why did you not catch better?" chuckled Goblin Jim. "Now you will have to fast. Well, the clergymen say that fasting is good for the soul, and, when people are in your state, they should look to that."

Jack turned impatiently to the window, determined to appear not to heed the little demon.

"Jack, Jack! Look here, Jack Firebrace," said Goblin Jim, in a wheedling way. "Here is such a nice pie."

Jack Firebrace cast a glance upwards, and saw that Jim really had a nice meat-pie in his hand.

"My mother made it for me," cried the little wretch. "It's beefsteak and kidney—a glorious pie, full of gravy—oh, so nice, my boy! Just look;" here the little brute took a good big bite, so that the gravy from the cake really did run down his chin. "Wouldn't you like a bit, Jack? I'm sure you must be hungry. I ain't, a bit. But the pie is so nice. See me eat it, my boy."

Here the little wretch took another good bite, and smacked his codfish-like lips dreadfully.

"Wouldn't you like to be a good boy and good-looking like me, and get such nice pies?"

"I would not be such a diabolical little whelp for all the world," said Jack, contemptuously.

"Envy, Jack, my dear boy, nothing but envy. The fox and the grapes, you know. I can't eat any more pie just yet."

With that he placed the pie by his side, so that Jack could just see it, and began swinging his legs.

"Oh!"

Suddenly he uttered a yell, and pitched forward.

He grasped at the sides of the aperture, but they were quite smooth, and he pitched headlong into the dungeon.

Jack sprang forward to catch him, but Jim only fell a couple of feet or so, and then hung suspended, a rope having been quickly passed round his waist before he was shoved over.

Who had done this Jack could not tell, but had no doubt that it was some friend.

The person at the other side of the aperture who held the rope-ends could lower or haul up Goblin Jim just as he liked, and it appeared that he wished him only to be a few inches lower than the sill upon which the pie was, for up to that he hauled him; and there swung Jim, the picture of misery, his head and heels almost on a level.

Then a hand grasping a thick cane came through the aperture, and the next moment the air was resounding with the sharp yells of Goblin Jim, as the cane descended with swinging force upon the now uppermost part of his person.

Vainly did the little wretch kick and struggle; his prayers for mercy were useless.

"Oh, oh—murder!" he shouted; "I'm being killed!"

Up and down the cane went as if it were wielded by an arm of iron that could never tire.

Swish! slash! cut! wish! it went, and at each cut Goblin Jim uttered a dismal yell.

At last the cane and hand were withdrawn, taking the "glorious meat-pie" with them.

Then to Jack's delight the bolts and bars of the door were undone.

The door was opened slowly, and a hand was thrust into the room, beckoning our hero to come forth.

He needed no second invitation, but rushed from his prison.

"My dear old Flick!" he exclaimed, but his friend very quickly placed his hand over his mouth.

"Hush! don't make a noise," he whispered; "above all, do not mention names. Help me to bar and lock the door."

This was soon done, and then Jack perceived that Goblin Jim had mounted to the aperture outside by a ladder.

"I followed the little wretch," whispered old Flick, "and whilst he was engaged at his diabolic fun I slipped this rope round his waist, gave him a push, and over he went. After that I gave him a taste of a cane—the first I believe he has ever had, and therefore I believe he is less likely to forget it. Now, Jack, we will undo the rope, lower him down, and then pull only on one end of the rope, so that it will slip out of his belt, and we can haul it in, leaving him a prisoner in your stead."

"No one will come to me before to-morrow at noon," said Jack, "and then they will only lower in the bread and water."

"The brutes!" exclaimed old Flick. "Well, we will make our way into the village; we shall have plenty of time before us. So come along, Jack."

"I am ready," said Jack, "but I am precious hungry."

"Here is that little wretch's meat-pie. Cut off the part that is bitten and eat the rest."

"All right, old Flick."

So Jack ate the pie up, and you may easily believe enjoyed it heartily.

"Now, Jack," said old Flick, "we must cut along as quickly as we can. I have kept my eyes open, and found out one or two things about this old place. Why, it is honeycombed like a rabbit-warren; I do believe there are secret passages and false walls everywhere about it. Just look down here."

As he spoke old Flick pointed down what appeared to be a well.

"It's a nasty-looking place," replied Jack, after he had gazed down.

"Just look at the winch; why, it has not been used for years. But here is a mark round the roller. It looks as if a rope ran over it quite free, and that that had been done lately."

"You are right, Flick, my boy; and, look here, the roller as you call it is fixed."

"Just so. Well, it struck me I would examine the well further."

"Why, the foul air would kill you, Flick."

"So I thought: but just put your head a little way down it and smell, as I did."

Jack did as his friend asked, and drew back with a look of great surprise.

"Well, what do you make out of that?"

"Why, it is quite cold, fresh air, and smells rather of the sea," cried Jack, in amazement.

"Just so; that tempted me to try and explore it. I seized the chain as I do now, and, swinging myself over the low wall, commenced the descent in this style. Come on, Jack, old fellow, only take care not to tread on my hands."

As he spoke Flick commenced descending into the well rapidly, and Jack at once followed him.

They were soon in almost total darkness, and the mouth of the well seemed, to Jack, to be closing in upon them.

"Stop where you are now, Jack, and hold tight to the chain for your life. I am going to swing it."

"All right," said Jack; "fire away."

In an instant Jack felt the chain vibrate, at first slowly, and then quicker, until it assumed the regular motion of a pendulum.

At last the motion ceased with a jerk that nearly threw Jack off the chain, but he held firmly on, and found that the end of the chain had evidently been fastened to one of the walls of the well, for it no longer hung down perpendicularly, but sloped perceptibly.

"Now, Jack," cried Flick, out of the darkness, "come on slowly; I am ready to receive you ; but don't leave go until I tell you. Come along, and be careful."

Jack descended slowly, and was soon touching the point where the chain was fastened.

As his foot touched this place he felt his friend's hand touch his knee.

"Keep firm hold of the chain, Jack," said Flick, "but come lower down."

Jack did this, and, to his astonishment, soon perceived an opening in the side of the well, down which a pale, greyish light shone.

"Now, my dear Jack, we must crawl along this passage."

"What a queer old place!" said Jack. "I expect many dark crimes have been committed about here."

"I am sure I do not know," said old Flick.

They made their way as quickly as they could along the dark passage.

Stooping down they entered the narrow passage which led into a natural cave, and, after creeping and crawling on a little way, they came to the entrance, which was concealed by bushes.

Shoving these bushes on one side they found themselves at the bottom of a well-wooded hollow, out of which they clambered, and at last stood on the side of the hill on which was perched Hawkhouse.

"This is a strange way to escape," laughed old Flick, who seemed to recover his spirits directly he felt the fresh air blowing upon his cheeks; "but, nevertheless, I should think one old Gruesome would never find out."

"I am not so sure of that," replied Jack, who seemed to be deep in thought. "You say there are ghosts seen in Hawkhouse. Is Mr. Gruesome or Mrs. Drysdale afraid of them?"

"No; neither is Goblin Jim."

"Don't you think that they know the true nature of these bogies too well to be afraid of them?"

"You mean that they are not ghosts at all, eh?" inquired old Flick.

"Most decidedly I do. It is my firm belief that some great crime goes on in that old house. The peasantry are so afraid of the bad name this castle bears that they will not approach it after dark. With the exception of ourselves, the boys in the school have only to hear a noise in the middle of the night, and they bury their heads beneath the bedclothes, and would scarcely move if the whole place were on fire."

"That is so. But what are we to do?"

"I am determined to find out the truth of this business. When once I know what it is, if it be as bad as I expect, I will at once escape from Hawkhouse, seek out the nearest magistrate, and confide everything to him."

"No, no, my dear old fellow. We had better make up our minds to bolt, make our way to the nearest seaport, and go to sea."

"No; I have pledged myself to find out this mystery, and I will do it, come what may," cried Jack Firebrace.

"Well, if you will you will, and that is all about it," said old Flick; "and if you stay, I will stay."

"You are a regular brick, old boy," said Jack; "never fear but that we will beat them yet. Now, then, for a race. The first one who reaches the ale-house shall have his ale and a crust of bread and cheese at the other' expense."

"Right. Start fair. One, two, three, and away!"

Off they ran at full speed down the hill, keeping nearly side by side; but as they entered the village they both were stopped by a strange sight.

CHAPTER XII.

WHAT HAPPENED IN THE VILLAGE—THE PURSUIT—THE ESCAPE—JACK TAKES PETER PIGWELLAN INTO HIS CONFIDENCE.

"HA-R-R-R! get out, you old wizard!" "Ger-r-r-r! Pelt him with mud; throw stones at him!" "He is mad! He is possessed of the devil!" "Duck him in the horsepond!" "Tar and feather him!" "Tear him to pieces!"

Such were the cries which Jack and his companion heard, mingled with hootings and groans of the most terrible description, whilst the stamping of feet and confused noise showed a large crowd was approaching.

"What on earth is up now?" said old Flick. "I think we had better get out of the way, Jack."

"And I think that we had better stay here," replied Jack. "These wretches are evidently pursuing some helpless creature."

He had scarcely said the words when Peter Pigwellan came rushing round the corner of the street, his dress torn, blood upon his brow, his whole person covered with dust and dirt, and his hideous face rendered even more repulsive than usual because of the terrible expression of rage, mingled with terror, expressed thereon.

Behind him came a shrieking, yelling crowd of fisher-lads, farm-boys, and—with shame be it said—men and women, all of them hooting, reviling, and pelting the poor unlucky creature, delighting in his agony.

Amongst these Jack beheld his old enemy, Collin Clout, who was urging the folks on to cruelty.

"Go it, lads," cried the ruffian. "Gi' it to un 'ot. He's the fellow as raises the wind and sea to swamp yer boats."

"Ger-r-r-r-r!" groaned the crowd, and a shower of stones fell round the unfortunate deformed boatman.

"Why do you ill-use me thus?" exclaimed the unfortunate creature, as he clutched the stone projection of an old fountain, which was built in the wall. "I have done you no harm. I am old and helpless. I might have made a good and comfortable living if you would let me alone, for I can catch more fish than any other fisherman."

"Ay, that he can," roared out one fisherman; "but he does it by the aid of the devil."

"Ger-r-r-r-r! down with him!" "Stone him!" "Kill him!" shouted the crowd.

Again the crowd poured forth their execrations, accompanied with a violent shower of stones.

With a yell of mingled rage and despair, Peter Pigwellan threw up his arms and fled for safety down a narrow lane.

Whooping with delight, the crowd rushed forward to pursue the unhappy wretch, but Jack sprang forward, and with his friend, old Flick, stood in the narrow entrance to the lane.

"Stand back!" cried Jack. "Why should you torment a fellow-creature in such a manner?"

"He's not a fellow creature," shouted one of the ringleaders of the mob. "He is a vile old wizard."

"Be he what he may, he shall not be tormented in this manner!" replied Jack Firebrace, firmly; "so keep back."

"Here, let me come and speak to that young sprig," called out Collin, forcing his way through the crowd. "I have a little account to settle with yon, my fine fellow. You know what I mean."

"I know that you are a bully and a coward," replied Jack, "and that you flung a stone at me once, which might have killed me. Then you would have added murder to your other vices."

Collin bit his lips and turned deathly pale.

"Oh! that's all very fine," he cried. "You fell whilst running, and struck your head against a stone. You were not hurt a bit, but made it an excuse to skulk from school. But you were found out and lugged back again. Ho, ho, I hope they tanned your hide well. Look at 'im, neighbours; ain't he a fine gentleman? Ho, ho, ho, ho!"

"You may laugh as much as you like," replied Jack, turning very red. "I have carried out my purpose—the old boatman has escaped. Remember, you have had one lesson, and may have another."

Turning on his heel, Jack Firebrace was about to walk away when Collin seized him by the collar.

"Not so fast—not so fast, if you please!" he laughed. "You don't get away in that style, I can tell yer."

"Unhand me, rascal!" cried Jack, shaking off the fellow's grasp, and standing on the defensive.

"Don't let him pass!" shouted Collin, who did not seem inclined to try our hero's strength alone. "He has escaped from the Hawkhouse School. He's the lad as has nearly broken his kind guardian's heart.

"I was up at the school t'other day, and seed Mr. Grindwell, and he told me all about it. 'Here's half a guinea for you, my lad,' he said. 'Let the people down in the village know that Firebrace is a prisoner, and should he escape, and they meet him, I will give a guinea to them if they bring him back.'"

This announcement was received with a loud cheer by the crowd.

Jack saw that it would be useless to argue the case.

He, therefore, sprang forward, and delivered a hearty blow between Collin's eyes, sending him reeling back on the crowd.

"Quick, Flitter!" he cried, "make a run for it! Come along, old fellow, and rob them of their guinea!"

Away scampered the lads as fast as their legs could carry them; but at the end of the lane Jack, not being well acquainted with the place, turned to the right, whilst Flick turned in the proper direction, which was to the left.

Neither perceived the separation until it was too late to attempt to rejoin the other.

Flick climbed up a rock, and, perching himself thereon, watched the chase.

If he went down and joined the crowd he felt certain he should be dragged back to the school, and be severely punished, whilst he could do no good to Jack.

On the other hand, if he returned quietly by the secret passage in the well to the school, the villagers might not be able to recognise him as one of the truants.

Casting one more glance at the crowd, which was now making its way to the coast, he hurried to the hollow in the hill-side, and was soon making the best of his way back through the well into t..e school.

Meanwhile, Jack was gaining ground rapidly on his pursuers, but, not knowing the country, he was hurrying down to the beach, where he knew he couldn't escape them.

"Never mind," he said to himself, "there are plenty of stones there, and I will defend myself as long as I can, and,

when that is no longer possible, I will take to the water, for I will drown sooner than be taken."

With a wild "Halloa!" he sprang on to the beach, and dashed up close to old Pigwellan's curious house.

Hastily gathering up a number of pebbles, he received the foremost of his pursuers with such a rapid and well-directed discharge of stones that they halted, not a few of them having received rather severe blows.

But the pause was only for a moment, and then they rushed forward with re-doubled fury.

Jack Firebrace retreated on to the rocks on which the deformed boatman's house stood, and once more discharged a shower of stones.

As he did so he heard the old boatman call in a low voice to him—

"Run, lad, behind this house; I will save you, as you saved me. Quick! lose not a single moment."

Jack Firebrace sent in another volley to the enemy, and then dashed behind the house, and had scarcely turned the corner when he was seized by the arm, and hastily drawn through a secret door into the boatman's house, and the next moment the door was closed.

"Hush! do not make a noise," whispered Peter Pigwellan; "hark! the wretches are at fault. They cannot make out your disappearance. Here, hide beneath these sails. I don't think they will attempt to enter. If they do, I will give them a good charge of wild-duck shot, and make their faces as hideous as is my own."

As he spoke he took down a long duck-gun from the wall, and, looking to see that it was loaded all right, quietly seated himself on a barrel to await the attack, should it come.

Jack was hidden beneath the sails, with his head so close to the planks that he could hear a good deal of the conversation that went on between his pursuers.

"Why, where on earth has the little varmint gone to?" exclaimed one; "he can't 'a' crawled under a stone like a crab."

"When I saw him come on these rocks I thought we had him all safe, for the sea runs in here, so that he could not escape," said another, and then added in a doubtful voice, "unless he can swim, and has taken to the sea."

"Nonsense!" cried another, "he can't have done that. Besides, there is not the least sign of him. To be sure, he may be drowned."

"I wish he was," growled Collin, "I should get a good reward."

"He must have got into this house," suggested one.

"We will soon see to that," exclaimed a number of men; "we will have the old wizard out."

Some of them began beating loudly on the door of the fisherman's house.

Rising from his seat, Pigwellan sprang upon a table, from which he was able to reach a window that was made close to the roof.

Throwing open the casement he thrust out the muzzle of his gun, and exclaimed—

"How now, you land-sharks? Would you break into my house? Stand back, or I will fire upon you."

The crowd needed no second order, but fell back in a manner which spoke badly for their bravery.

"We don't want to hurt you, Master Pigwellan," said Collin, who acted as spokesman; "you see, I'm almost a stranger here, and I did not know you when I pelted you just now. I worked some time on Mr. Grindwell's estate in Somersetshire.

As he spoke the old boatman made a quick sign with his hand, a sign which Collin at once returned.

"Well, there's a young fellow that has run away from the school up yonder. We want to take him back again, and we think he may have hidden in your house. So if you will let us in—"

"Let you in!" sneered Peter Pigwellan; "let the wolf into the sheep-pen. No, I have seen no lad—I want not to see anyone. Begone!—no man shall enter here while I live. Begone! I say, or some of you will be dead men."

"But, neighbour," Collin expostulated, "I know that Mr. Grindwell will be vexed if this lad escapes, and I know he will reward them as take him."

Jack's heart rose in his mouth, as, from his place of concealment, he saw Peter pause as if undecided.

"Begone! I say once more. I know not the boy you seek. If you missed him on the rocks, seek him there. Now go."

So saying old Peter Pigwellan drew in his gun, and closed and barred the window with great care.

For some time Jack and the old boatman remained silent until they heard the crowd retire; then Peter very cautiously opened the door, and looked out to see if anyone were watching.

"They have all gone—you are safe," he said, as he closed the door; "you have served me and I have served you. Now, tell me, are you really a ward of Griffiths Grindwell?"

"I am," replied Jack; "at least, he tells me so. I have no reason to keep my history secret. So I will tell you all."

Jack, with the frankness of his nature, confided his short history to the old boatman, even telling how Mr. Sidney Morrison had been ordered to torture him, and how he had been imprisoned, the way he had escaped from the school, leaving Goblin Jim in his stead. In fact, he told the old boatman everything, save that Felix Flitter had helped him.

When he had done the old man paced up and down the room, rubbing his hands and chuckling.

"Good, good," he muttered; "the finger of fate is in this. Summerbell, too! I have lived here in this hut so long, and did not know that. Ho, ho, ho! what a fool I have been! I will be equal with him—I will be equal with him. Look here, my young master," he said, turning suddenly on our hero, "you have trusted me with a terrible tale. I am old, ugly, scorned, called mad and a wizard, yet you have trusted me with this strange story!"

"But you have been kind, and have protected me," replied Jack, boldly. "I know that you will not betray me."

"True; you have done well to trust me. What can I do to help you? Will you escape from the school? If so, I will put off in my boat after dark, and land you some distance from here, where you will be safe."

"No; I will return to the school," replied Jack, boldly. "I will discover the mystery of my birth."

"Right, boy, you are right!" cried Peter. "You are a bold lad, and I will help you. You have done well to trust me. Oh, you stare, and think I have no power to aid you. But Providence has caused us to meet. Now, mark me; if your life is threatened—and it may be—come to me at once. If anyone is with you, pretend to jeer me, laugh at my deformity, call me a fool, throw stones at me if you like, do anything; but do not let them think that we are friends."

"Throw stones at you I shall not," replied Jack. "If I were to do that they would suspect something, and so it would get known that we were better acquainted than they could wish."

"True; but I scarce dare trust the tutor Morrison," murmured the old man. "He is held in a hand of iron— a hand which never yet spared its victims. Stay! I might counteract the evil—I can! I will!"

Rushing to a drawer the old man drew it open, and took therefrom a sheet of paper and pen and ink.

With these he quickly wrote a short note, which he folded carefully, and sealed with a gold seal, which he took from behind a loose plank. This done, he addressed the letter to Mr. Sidney Morrison.

"That will do—that must do. He is a coward, and will obey me. Now, my lad, it is nearly dark, and is time you were back in your prison-house. Ha, ha, ha, ha! it shall no longer be a prison-house to you, for you shall be free to come and go as you like. Stay; let me gather up some things which I need, and then we will be off together."

To Jack's surprise he took a large sack, a small sail, a quantity of lanyards, and a coil of half-inch rope, which had a stout hook attached to one end of it.

"Now, my lad, come along," chuckled the old fellow. "We will meet cunning with cunning, mystery with mystery; thus will we conquer them. Come; but remember, you must be as secret as the grave."

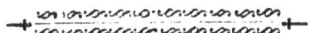

CHAPTER XIII.

THE ALARM AT HAWKHOUSE SCHOOL—MR. GRUESOME IS MYSTIFIED—THE USHER HAS ANOTHER FIT.

THERE was a great and terrible commotion in Hawkhouse School.

Mrs. Drusilla Drysdale was wailing and wringing her hands in the deepest despair.

Mr. Percy Pliant, who still bore some marks of the wasps' stings, sat behind his desk, staring vacantly into space.

Mr. Sidney Morrison, with folded arms, leant against the wall, his hollow eyes fixed upon the ground.

The boys were seated upon the two rows of forms.

Up marched Ebenezer Gruesome, cane in hand.

Behind him came Goblin Jim's mother, uttering loud lamentations.

"Oh, my dear boy—my beautiful pet!" screamed the Ghoul; "I never shall look upon his lovely face again. Where can he be? If I find out that a boy has hurt my Jim, I'll skin him!"

As she spoke she made a clutch at Tomkins, and looked so vicious that the unfortunate youth uttered a dismal howl of terror.

"Don't howl there," yelled Gruesome, belabouring the unlucky boy with all his might. "I'll give you something to cry for. Take that—and that—and that!"

Each word was fully emphasised by a cut of the cane.

"There," said Mr. Gruesome, with an air of satisfaction, "I feel much better now."

"I don't," sighed poor Tomkins.

"Where did you see your boy last?" demanded Gruesome of the old house-keeper.

"He came down into the kitchen, the pretty innocent, and ran away with a new meat pie."

"Oh!" said Mr. Gruesome, after a short pause; "so the infernal little rascal was stealing one of my meat-pies, was he?"

"Well, yes. It was all his fun, you

know. The pretty lamb did it to tease me, that was all."

"Indeed! When he returns," said Mr. Gruesome, cutting the air with his cane, "he had better bring me back the meat-pie."

Again the fearful cane swished through the air, and all the forms whereon the boys sat trembled.

"Mr. Pliant," cried Mr. Gruesome, "don't sit there looking like a fool, sir, if you can help it, which I doubt; but tell me at once what you think of this case. I suppose you do sometimes have an opinion?"

"Oh, yes, to be sure," exclaimed Mr. Pliant, starting back so suddenly that he hit the back of his head against the wall.

"Well, then, if you have an opinion, please to give it."

"Of course, Mr. Gruesome, only —only in this case I haven't the slightest idea—"

"Bah! you are a fool!" growled Mr. Gruesome.

Mr. Pliant smiled a sickly smile.

"Mr. Sidney Morrison," said Mr. Gruesome, "what is your opinion, sir."

"Well, sir," replied the usher, quietly; "I have watched Mrs. Drysdale's 'pretty little lamb,' and never saw a monkey more full of mischief and spite. Most likely the little brute is laughing at us now from some corner or another."

Mr. Gruesome glanced up to the ceiling as if he expected to see Goblin Jim hanging up there like a bat.

"Don't you believe him, master," cried Mrs. Drysdale. "Some of his school-fellows have hidden him away. Perhaps they have murdered him!"

"Murdered him!" exclaimed Sidney, starting back, and brushing the cold perspiration from his forehead. "Murdered him? Who speaks of murder in this terrible house of mystery? Who dare do so?"

"No one wants to mention the word," stammered Mr. Gruesome, who seemed to be in great awe of his assistant. "Hold your tongue, Drusilla," he muttered to his housekeeper; "you will have him in a fit again, and then Heaven only knows what secrets he may blurt out before the boys. I—I tremble to think about it."

The only person in the place who did not notice this scene was Mr. Pliant.

"I think you are mistaken, Drusilla," said the schoolmaster. "Why, the boys are all here, so that they could not have injured your son."

Flick, who was seated with the other lads, having got back to the school without being noticed, could scarcely keep from smiling.

"Yes, all are here excepting that rebellious rascal, John Firebrace, and he would commit any crime," cried Mrs. Drysdale.

"You need not fear that lad," said Morrison. "He is, as you know, a prisoner."

"Of course he is; had he not been a prisoner I should have—bless me, who can be knocking so at the door?"

The knocking was indeed enough to frighten anyone, for it was both loud and continuous.

"Mr. Pliant!" cried Mr. Gruesome, who had become white as a ghost and trembled in each limb. "Mr. Pliant!"

"Sir," replied Mr. Pliant, starting out of his reverie, hitting the back of his head again a fearful blow, and upsetting an ink-bottle, the contents of which ran down his trousers quite unnoticed by him.

"Mr. Pliant, there is somebody knocking at the door. Go and open it."

Mr. Pliant unbarred and unbolted the huge door, which was made of thick oak.

No sooner had he done so than a crowd of people pushed him on one side and burst into the hall.

"Mercy! mercy! mercy!" shrieked Gruesome, dropping on his knees and clasping his hands. "I am innocent!"

"Why, what's up wi' yer, Master Gruesome?" demanded the foremost man, who was no other than Collin. "We be all friends, right good friends too, who come to do you service."

"Oh! is it you?" said Mr. Gruesome, staggering to his feet, and wiping the cold perspiration off his brow. "You see, I am old and nervous; this place, too, is so lonely, and—and—but what is the meaning of all these people here?"

"Why, we have come to tell you that your pupil, John Firebrace, has run away," said Collin

"Run away!" exclaimed Sidney Morrison. "It is impossible. He is confined in one of our strongest rooms."

"Yes, good people, you must be mistaken," said Mr. Gruesome. "I tell you he is under lock and key."

"Then he has escaped," said Collin. "If you find him a prisoner now, why, you may call me a fool."

"Thank Heaven, Jack has escaped them," thought old Flick. "Had they caught him they would have killed him."

"If you saw him," said Sidney Morrison, "why did you not seize him and bring him here? You know you would have been well rewarded."

"That's right enough," replied Collin; "we did try to catch him. He made straight to the sea, and we made up our minds that we had him all safe. But not a bit ot it. After pelting us with stones in a way I never saw the like of before, he coolly rushes on to the Hawk rocks and disappears. All we know is, that we can't find him anywhere. How he got away I don't think old Old Nick himself could tell."

"Your story is utterly absurd," said Mr. Sidney Morrison. "Doubtless, you think to be rewarded? You are mistaken."

"I don't want to be rewarded," growled Collin; "all I know is, I saw him and his guardian. Mr. Grindwell told me to watch."

Bang! bang! bang!

Again the knocker on the door rose and fell.

This time it was with a jerky sound—a mysterious sound.

Mr. Pliant, acting as porter, opened the door at once.

Attached to the knocker was a huge sack, which wriggled about, showing it held a living creature.

"Why, what on earth is this?" exclaimed Mr. Pliant, who, being short-sighted, placed his face close to the sack to examine it. "What on earth is this?"

The creature inside the sack made a violent struggle, and Mr. Pliant received a blow, making him beat a hasty retreat.

Everybody pressed forward to examine the lively sack.

"Dear me!" exclaimed Mr. Gruesome, peering at it, much in the same way as a jackdaw cocks his head on one side to look into a marrow-bone. "Dear me, here is a label on it, and something written in large letters thereon."

Mr. Sidney Morrison raised the label, and, keeping at arm's length from the sack, for the creature inside was making desperate plunges, read as follows—

"I, a friend of the school, captured a runaway pupil of yours, and return him in this sack. Before you take him from the sack flog him as he deserves; do not spare the cane."

"There now!" cried Collin, triumphantly, "is it impossible, Master Schoolmaster? You're a fine fellow to have him safe in prison. Ho, ho, ho! Golly! don't he kick in the sack? So ho, Master Firebrace, you're caught at last, you brute!"

And Collin gave the captive a blow on the head that brought forth a dismal howl.

"Flog him as he deserves! Ah! yes, yes; I will flog him as he deserves," chuckled Gruesome, as he wetted his hand so as to take a firm grip of the cane. "I only wish Mr. Grindwell was here, so that I might show him how much I dislike ingratitude."

Here he turned up the cuffs of his coat.

"I never thrashed a boy in a bag before, but I like the notion. Now, Mr. John Firebrace, you'll have it hot and strong."

With a fiendish grin he raised the cane and began thrashing away at a fearful rate, screaming out at the same time— "Take that—and that. Ho, ho! so you laugh at me?" this was the muffled shrieks of the helpless victim. "I'll give you something to laugh at. Oh! I wish I was stronger, for your sake, that I do. Oh!"

Here the wretch's arm stopped from sheer exhaustion, and the cane rolled on to the floor.

"I'll have a go in now," cried Collin, and, seizing the cane, he showered in a terrific number of blows.

Whack—whack—whack—whack!

"Shame, shame, shame!" cried old Flick and the other boys, disgusted at the cruelty.

"What! dare you rebel?" shrieked Gruesome. "I'll have you all flogged in a sack, that I will. I rather like the idea."

"Oh, won't my Jim enjoy the fun!" chuckled the Ghoul. "Give me the cane; I must have a cut or two at the wretch Firebrace."

She snatched the cane from Collin's hand, for even the countryman was tired, and, with shrill shrieks of delight, gave as many cuts at the defenceless creature as her weak, shrivelled arm would permit.

"There, there, I think John Firebrace has had enough now," laughed old Gruesome. "Let us take him down and turn him out."

The schoolboys clustered together, shuddering and angry, but they dared not speak.

The sack was untied from the knocker, and allowed to fall heavily on to the floor.

It remained perfectly motionless, for the creature inside was now quite still—seemingly devoid of life.

"I—I hope we have not killed him," said Gruesome, in a terrified whisper, to Mr. Sidney Morrison; "you see, there are witnesses, and—and they would call it murder, and then—"

The usher turned pale, pushed him hastily on one side, and strode away to the farther end of the hall.

"Killed him!" exclaimed the Ghoul, who had caught part of the schoolmaster's words. "Not we. Why, he is like a cat; he has got, at least, nine lives. Get out—come, get out! We know that you are shamming, so get up at once."

She bestowed several hearty kicks upon the prostrate boy, but he did not move.

"I'll let the cat out of the bag," cried Collin. "Stand on one side, marm; now out he comes."

As he spoke he took hold of the two bottom corners of the sack, and shot the imprisoned boy out like a hundredweight of coals.

A scream of horror from Drusilla.

A yell of rage from Gruesome.

A cry of astonishment from the ushers and the crowd.

But, above all, arose a shout of delight from the boys.

"Hurrah!" shouted Flick; "it's not Jack Firebrace after all—but that little wretch, Goblin Jim."

"Hurrah, hurrah!" cried the school boys; "serve the Goblin right."

"Oh! my boy—my dear, good, darling boy, my little lamb!" Mrs. Drysdale cried, embracing her son.

No one spoke.

"Why, dash my buttons!" cried Collin, "I have been punishing the wrong boy."

"Oh, oh, oh!" sobbed Goblin Jim, as he returned to consciousness; "this is all through that wretched brute, Jack Firebrace."

"Jack Firebrace!" yelled the rest, in astonishment.

"Yes. I went to have a talk to him through that large opening in the wall, and give him a piece of meat-pie, which mother gave me," said the wretched youth, "when someone threw me into his room, and I was left all alone. I kicked and I screamed, but no one came, and then I lay down to sleep, and I slept. But, oh! I was so hungry, for they took away my pie.

"Well, I was sound asleep, when suddenly a big, rough cloth was thrown over me, and before I could speak I was hurried into a sack—jolt, jolt, jolt—and I was hung up on that knocker, and then—oh, my!"

The little brute curled and wriggled about in such a manner that the boys laughed and shouted in imitation of him.

"Oh, my!"

"Silence! you little whelps," shrieked Mrs. Drysdale.

"Silence! Oh, my!" again shouted some of the boys.

"Mr. Gruesome," remarked Sidney Morrison, hoarsely, "we have had enough of this ridiculous show. Let us not lose one moment, but at once start these fellows off, and then go and see if Firebrace is still in confinement."

"Right; we will do so."

Then, turning to the crowd, he said—

"My good friends, I fancy I have been the victim of a practical joke."

"I know I have," moaned Jim, as he attempted to rub himself all over at one time.

"Therefore, my friends," continued Mr Gruesome, "I beg of you to come and see if we are right who say Firebrace has not escaped, or you are right who say 'We have seen him at liberty.'"

THE BOYS OF HAWKHOUSE SCHOOL.

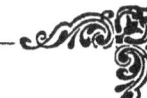

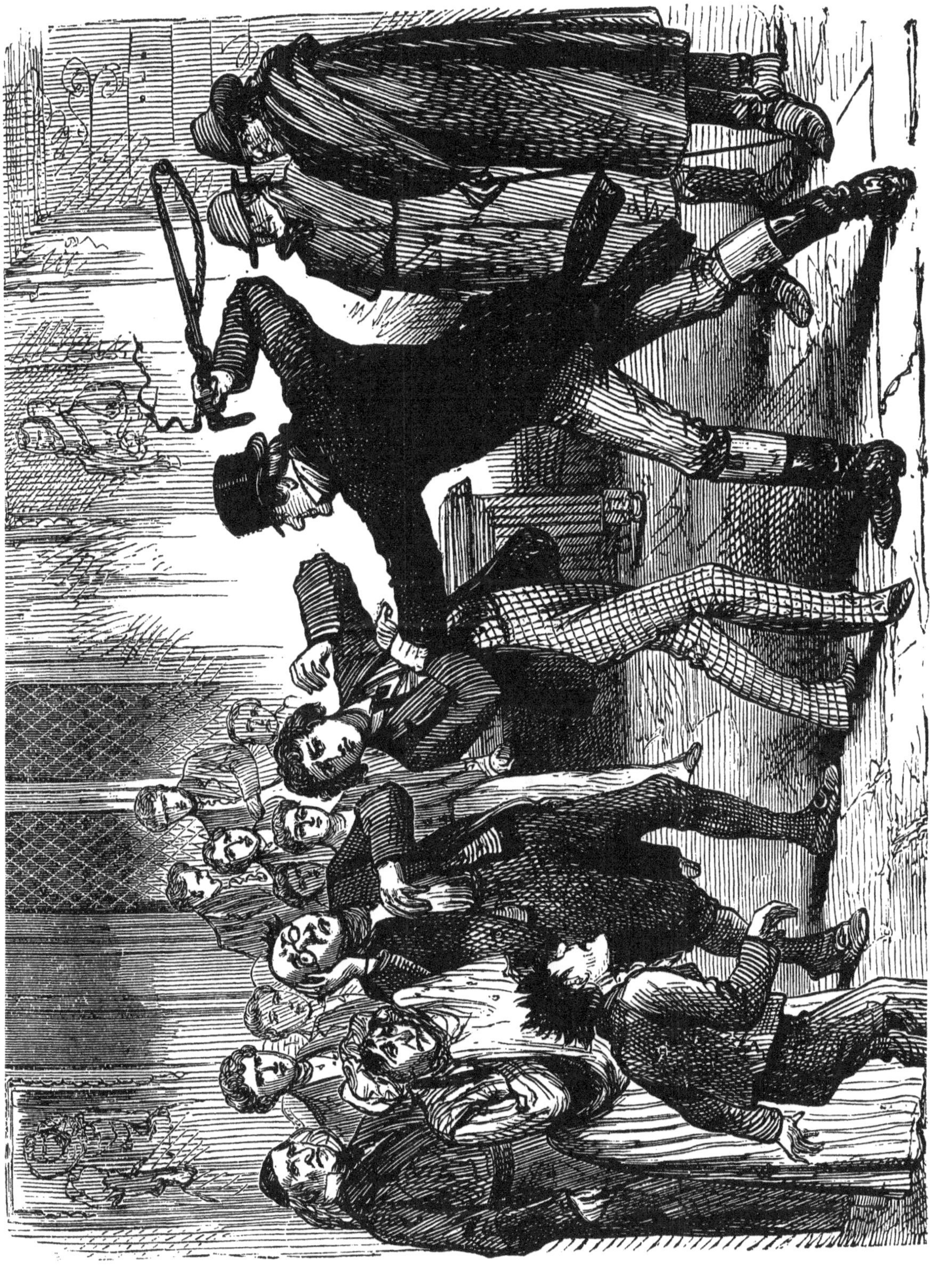

"GRINDWELL SEIZED HIM BY THE ARM, AND STRUCK HIM WITH THE WHIP."

No. 5.

PRICE ONE HALFPENNY.

[Published Every Monday.]

"We will, we will," cried the crowd. "Let us see for ourselves whether it was the lad or not."

"If it aren't the one he said it were," cried one big fellow, pointing to Collin, "I'm danged if I don't thrash him for leading us on a wild-goose chase!"

"Yes, and if you find him there," cried Collin, "call me an idiot."

They mounted the stairs, opened the door, and held the light high up.

"Look!" cried Sidney.

They did look, and there was Jack Firebrace snugly curled up on his mat and sound asleep in the corner.

CHAPTER XIV.

HAUNTED OR NOT HAUNTED?—THE MYSTERY OF THE HALL—THE "HAND OF GLORY."

WITH low exclamations of surprise they gathered round the couch, or rather mat, on which Firebrace slept.

"I am danged if I can understand the thing at all!" cried Collin. "It must have been his ghost I saw."

As for old Flick and the other boys, they were nearly mad with delight to find Firebrace all safe.

Poor Flick was as much mystified as any of them.

"Of a truth this is most strange," said Mr. Pliant.

"Oh!" cried Clout, "these lads can tell you they saw him and another young chap. We were having a bit of fun with old Peter Pigwellan when in comes that young fellow and his friend, and makes so much noise that we were going to pitch into them, but they bolts away. You can swear to the lad, can't you, mates?"

"Ay, that we can, right enough!" shouted the men.

"But let us look at the matter quietly," said Mr. Pliant. "You say that another lad was with him. Is this the other lad?"

And here the good-natured usher gently shoved forward Master Jim, who was still rubbing his aching back.

"That like the other lad!" growled one of the fellows; "not a bit of it. Why, t'other was a good-looking fellow. That's about as ugly a little imp as ever I saw. This chap," he continued, placing his hand on old Flick's shoulder, "is a deuced deal more like the one—"

"Call my darling boy an ugly little imp, you bold-faced scoundrel!" cried

the enraged Drusilla, dragging her own sweet infant towards her. "Oh, you false-tongued villain! I should like to tear your eyes out."

Jack Firebrace, who had been listening to all this whilst he pretended to be asleep, thought that it was time to say something.

He therefore started up on his mat, rubbing his eyes and yawning in the most violent manner.

"Halloa!" he cried, "what is the meaning of this? Am I not to be left in peace even here? Do you think that starvation is too slow a death, and have come to finish me off at once?"

Here he gazed defiantly around.

But as his eyes fell upon Flitter he sprang up, and, shaking his hands, said—

"Dear old Flick, how glad I am to see you! I almost despaired of ever seeing you again."

At this capital piece of acting even Collin Clout opened his eyes and stared.

"Dear me! I think I shall go crazed!" cried Mr. Gruesome. "It equals all one has read of the doings of Dr. Faustus. I begin to think that the devil must have a hand in it."

Scarcely had he said the words when shrill peals of laughter, mingled with a bellowing which would have done honour to the bulls of Assyria, rang through the castle, until the very air seemed to tremble at the sound.

This was followed up by the clanking of chains and the banging of doors, mingled with terrible screams.

Then, as suddenly as the noises had commenced, a dead silence came.

A terrible silence!

The peasants, the boys, and the others gazed in mute horror around.

No one dared to move.

Again the silence was broken by a cry—a terrible, agonised cry—more horrible than all the rest. The cry of—

"Murder!"

One short word; but so fraught with terror that it made the listeners' blood curdle in their veins.

Crash! crash! crash!

Mr. Gruesome clasped his hands together and groaned violently, whilst he gazed anxiously round, as if for assistance.

"Something dreadful is going on here. The house is falling about our ears!" cried old Flick. "Let us hurry from the building at once."

Away rushed the whole of the people to the main hall of the building.

But they paused as they came to the door—paused in horror!

For the hall, which only a short time before had been left by them empty, seemed now filled with a noisy set of men, who were evidently quarrelling and fighting, for the clash of steel could be distinctly heard amongst the smothered muttering of oaths and curses which were heard indistinctly, as if spoken by men whose teeth were clenched, and whose muscles were made rigid as iron from the exertion of fighting.

"What can be the meaning of this?" gasped Mr. Pliant.

"I do not know," replied Mr. Gruesome, who seemed as much afraid of the noises as anyone there. "At least," he continued, "I never heard anything like it in this part of the house, and—"

"Bang!"

A terrific report, as if an old-fashioned blunderbuss had been discharged close to the door.

In an instant there was a general stampede from the door, as if they feared the supernatural quarrellers would soon come pouring forth and charge the mortals.

"What on earth are you running for?" cried Jack Firebrace. "Let us see who is in the room."

"Who will go first?" said old Flick.

"I will," cried Jack, proudly. "If they are men, surely all of us are a match for them? If they are ghosts they cannot hurt us. I never heard of a spirit being able to knock a fellow down, unless it happened to be of the brandy kind. So come along, lads."

Jack seized the nearest light, and at once led the way towards the hall, from whence strange noises still came.

Boldly seizing the handle Jack threw open the door, exclaiming, at the same moment, in a bold voice—

"Men or fiends, we defy you! Come out, and let us see what kind of creatures you are."

Swash!

Then came a deluge of cold sea-water all over them, putting out the lights at once.

All was now dark as night, whilst the air rang with wild, discordant peals of laughter.

"Murder! murder!"

"Help! fire! thieves! ghosts! help! help! help!"

"The devil has come!"

Such were the yells that the frightened people uttered as they fled.

At length they paused, and, clustering together like a lot of frightened sheep, took courage again.

A light was demanded eagerly, and one of the peasants, having produced flint and steel, tinder and matches, after a little trouble one was procured.

From this light others were ignited, and, in a little time, the illumination was grand.

They were now able to gaze into each other's pale faces, but, it must be owned, they saw but little to reassure them therein.

For a few seconds they stood lost in their fear, and then from the boys arose one wild cry—

"Where is Jack Firebrace? He must be in that fearful hall!"

Certain it was that Jack Firebrace had mysteriously disappeared from amongst them.

"I see what it is," cried Collin. "The devil has come to claim his own, and has done it, too."

"We must make our way back to the hall and try to save him," cried old Flick, boldly.

"You may do what you like," growled

Collin, " but I shall not put my carcase in the devil's claws. Maybe he likes schoolboys too well to touch them. They say he is the father of mischief, and I know schoolboys are mischiefs."

" I won't go," " Nor I," " Nor I," growled the other peasants, drawing back in great dread.

" You miserable cowards ! " cried Flick, who, now that he knew Firebrace had been taken away, had recovered his own courage, and determined to face Old Nick himself, if need be, to recover his friend.

" Maybe we are cowards. Ecod ! a man don't know what he is when he cannot believe his own eyes. I don't think that we have more fear than most folk, and will face any man living ; but I don't believe that honest folk have any call to face the devil at all. What do you say, my lads — am I right or wrong ? "

" You are right—quite right," cried the others, who were only too glad to make any excuse to keep from the hall.

" Come along, lads," cried old Flick. " It shall never be said of me that I left a friend in danger ! "

With a hearty cheer the schoolboys dashed forward to the door of the hall.

Flick caught hold of the handle of the door, but could not turn it.

The door was fastened.

Mr. Gruesome, Sidney Morrison, and the others followed at a respectful distance.

The usher, Sidney Morrison, had a dreamy, vacant look.

His face was livid.

Vainly did Flitter and his companions use their utmost endeavours to break open the door.

The strong oak and massive locks resisted their efforts ; indeed, they scarcely made it shake.

" Jack ! Jack Firebrace ! " shouted old Flick. " Do speak to us, old chap. Tell us you are safe."

No answer from the haunted chamber ; only a confused sound as if of mumbling, whispering voices.

Then there arose a wild strain of plaintive music, and the door opened slowly, as if by unseen hands.

All in the room was dark and still ; not a sound of aught but the low murmur of the waves.

Holding the lights before them the boys crept slowly into the hall.

To their surprise all was exactly as they had left it, save that the floor was wet with water.

The furniture was undisturbed, and everything was as peaceful and quiet as could be.

On a couch, apparently fast asleep, was Jack Firebrace, looking as well as he ever did in his life.

They approached the couch and leant over him, to make sure that the sleep was not that of death.

" Gracious powers ! " exclaimed Flick, " what is this on his chest ? It is a dagger and a written paper."

As these words fell upon Sidney Morrison's ears he started violently ; then, pushing the boys aside, approached the couch.

" Let me see what is here," he cried. " Stand back, boys, stand back, and let me see the paper."

It was only a rough piece of paper, on which was written, in red ink, these few words—

" Harm not this lad. The dead *can* work amongst the living. Beware ! I am near to protect the innocent. Be warned, or the ' Hand of Glory ' * will seize the dagger and strike. Beware— beware ! "

Sidney Morrison groaned aloud, and crumpled the mysterious document in his hand.

" Merciful powers ! " he cried, " does the avenging angel persecute me still ? Can I have no rest, no peace, no mercy ? "

" I cannot understand all this," said Gruesome. " Who has written that, and what does it all mean ? "

" Mean ! " shrieked Sidney ; " it means that there is no rest in this world or the next for the creature who has shed his fellow's blood ! "

" Mr. Morrison," cried Pliant, holding up his hands in horror, " you cannot know what you are saying. You must be mad ! "

" Mad—ay, mad ! " continued Sidney, in the same agonised tone ; " would that I were mad. My brain burns like that

* The " Hand of Glory " was a name given to a dead man's hand, prepared by many ghastly and unholy rites, which was believed by superstitious people to permit the holder to pass through bolted doors, or even stone walls.

of the first murderer who slew his brother Abel! Oh, mercy, mercy, mercy!"

As he spoke, he covered his face with his hands, letting the mysterious paper drop upon the floor.

"This is very mysterious indeed," said poor Pliant; "it makes me shiver all over. What can this paper mean?"

As he spoke he took up the paper, and read the contents in a slow, distinct voice.

"'Beware! beware!' Well, of course we will all beware; but if we are to beware, I should like to know of what and of whom we are to beware? The writer has not even put his signature to this peculiar document, but has only appended a curious seal, the device of which is confused, and by this light I can scarcely make it out. It looks like—"

"Fool!" cried Sidney Morrison, hastily snatching the paper from the under-usher's hand. "Would you drive me mad?"

"I beg your pardon, Mr. Morrison," replied Mr. Pliant. "I confess I don't know anything about the paper. I feel certain that it was not meant for me, and, like a firm Protestant as I am, I can safely say I defy the devil and all his works."

Having said this, Mr. Pliant folded his arms, and remained silent.

"Pardon me, Mr. Pliant, I meant no offence," said Sidney. "Of course, I know as little as you do about this ridiculous paper, with its diabolic threats and mysterious seal. I look upon it as some deeply-laid plan of Master Firebrace's, so that he may escape his just punishment."

Scarcely had he said the words than the large windows at the end of the hall were dashed open, and standing on the sill was the figure of a man, dressed in the fashion which smugglers of the seventeenth and early part of the eighteenth century assumed.

His face was perfectly livid, almost a blue, and a flickering light played about it such as the pale phosphorescence on decayed matter.

His eyes were large and glassy, two large tusks protruded from his upper lip, holding it back, giving the face the deadly snarl of the wild boar.

But, terrible as this all was, it did not nearly affect the trembling spectators as much as that which the phantom held in his hand.

It was the shrivelled hand of a corpse, which had been severed from the carcase just below the wrist, so that part of the arm served to hold it.

The fingers were spread out wide apart, and from the top of each finger there sprang up a small, bluish flame, which emitted a ghastly light.

"Liar!" cried the horrible figure, as he pointed with one hand at Sidney. "Behold the Hand of Glory! Beware! Do my commands and you may yet be saved. The seal upon that paper came from this ring. Ha, ha, ha! do you know it, Master Sidney Morrison?"

With clasped hands and straining eyes stood Sidney Morrison, unable to move a muscle.

"Be warned in time; do as I bid ye," continued the strange figure. "That boy must not be harmed, or all here shall perish. Look well at the ring, and obey the Hand of Glory."

As he spoke he pointed to the ring, and then seemed to leap from the window into the air, and disappeared.

With a wild yell Sidney Morrison threw up his arms and cried aloud—

"The ring! the ring!"

He dashed to the window, threw up his arms, and fell senseless on the ground.

The antique ring was that of the murdered man in the cave down by the sea.

CHAPTER XV.

WHAT HAPPENED IN THE HALL OF HAWKHOUSE SCHOOL—SUDDEN APPEARANCE OF MR. GRINDWELL—JACK HAS A STRANGE DREAM.

WHEN Sidney Morrison fell most of the boys and all the grown-up people ran to his assistance; but old Flick and one or two others remained with our hero, and tried to arouse him from the deep sleep which had apparently seized his whole frame, as it were, making him unconscious even of pain; for, in his anxiety to resuscitate his friend, old Flick slapped his hands, and pulled his hair in anything but a pleasing or gentle manner.

Mr. Morrison was the first to recover consciousness.

He drank some water, which they held to his lips, eagerly, and then gazed dreamily around.

"Where—where is he?" he gasped. "Oh, that horrid, horrid sight! Is there no peace for me? None, none!"

"You will excuse me, Mr. Morrison," said Mr. Pliant; "you will excuse me, but I think you had better go to bed. I scarcely think that this is a becoming spectacle for a lot of young gentlemen to witness. I freely confess that the horrid sights and terrible noises we have all seen and heard are enough to make the best of men tremble; but not one of these young lads has fainted, and I do not understand the effect these noises have had upon you, unless"—here Mr. Pliant looked sharply at Mr. Morrison—"unless it is a case of guilty conscience."

"Villain!" cried Sidney Morrison, springing to his feet, and seizing the astounded tutor by the throat and shaking him violently; "dare to breathe one word like that again, and I will throttle you."

"Mer—mer—mercy!" croaked out poor Pliant. "Ler—ler—let me go, will you! Ler—ler—let me go, let me go!"

"Go, fool!"

And as he spoke Morrison threw Pliant off, who, falling against Drusilla, sent that good lady to the ground, the usher falling on top of her, and thus they rolled over and over.

No sooner did Goblin Jim behold his only friend in this distress than he flew at once to her relief, and, twisting his bony little fingers in the unfortunate usher's hair, began plucking at it violently, whilst he kicked and bit with the energy of a demon.

"Take him off, take him off!" roared Mr. Pliant.

Mr. Gruesome seized the cane, which had once before been so well employed that evening, and rained down a shower of blows on the tangled heap of human creatures.

The dry form of Mrs. Drusilla Drysdale received a great many sharp cuts of the cane, whilst Goblin Jim, owing to his agility, managed to escape most of the blows intended for his person.

At last Mr. Pliant could bear it no longer. He was in the middle of the muddle.

Beneath him was Mrs. Drusilla Drysdale, who seemed to be nothing but nails.

Above him was Goblin Jim, pulling out handfuls of his hair.

What mortal man could stand such dreadful torment as this?

He kicked, he plunged, and at last, by a strong effort, twisted himself right over, quite reversing the position of affairs—Goblin Jim being beneath, Mr. Pliant in the middle, and Mrs. Drysdale at the top.

So enraged was Gruesome that he could not see whom he was striking, and consequently Mrs. Drysdale became the recipient of all the blows, and she took very good care to let everyone know that she was.

As for Goblin Jim, he stood a very good chance of becoming nothing but a gigantic smear, for the usher and his mother's entire weight was upon his wretched little form.

He gasped for breath, and was about to give himself up for lost, when, luckily for him, chance sent his teeth through the fleshy part of Mr. Pliant's leg, and, with his natural disposition to cause pain, he kept them tightly fixed there; and now Mr. Pliant mingled his shrieks with those of the housekeeper, until Mr. Gruesome was obliged to leave off out of very fear that the people in the village would be disturbed by the terrible noise.

Collin and his companions separated the combatants.

"Oh, my bones and body!" gasped Mrs. Drusilla Drysdale, after a long pause, during which she had been rubbing herself all over. "Oh! I am crushed to pieces, I know I am."

"Pieces!" yelled Goblin Jim, who never showed any respect for his mother; "pieces! Powder, you mean."

"I—I shall never be able to speak again," said Mr. Pliant. "I feel I shall never speak again. Oh! how my face does smart; I haven't a bit of skin left on it. Oh, oh, oh, oh!"

"The boy is still in his strange sleep," said Sidney, who had been watching Jack Firebrace all the time that the pantomime of Mr. Pliant and Mrs. Drusilla had been going on. "The boy still sleeps."

"I think that he must be in a trance," said old Flick; "it is no ordinary sleep. Perchance it is death."

"Death!" cried the usher, in tones which rang through the room, "death! Oh, that I could die—had courage to die! Better to die, if he be dead, than to meet such a fate as mine."

"Hush, hush, hush, Mr. Morrison!" cried Gruesome; "you must not speak like that. The—the house is haunted, I confess; but it was so long before I came here, and there—there is money for you. Now begone."

Here he threw some money on the table, which the peasants were not long in seizing upon.

"Keep silent in this and you shall have some more. I would not have Mr. Grindwell know this for worlds."

"Mr. Grindwell!" exclaimed Jack Firebrace, starting from the couch.

But, with surprise, everyone saw that, although Jack spoke, he appeared still to be in a deep sleep.

"Hark!" he exclaimed, as he still went through the action of one listening attentively, "hark! I hear the sound of horse's hoofs galloping up the road. They approach nearer and nearer. Hist! what is that?"

At that moment the great clock in the hall chimed nine.

"It is the hour," said Jack; "the very hour. Hark! the horse comes nearer and nearer. Who asked for Mr. Grindwell? Who spoke of Mr. Grindwell? I tell you he is here; close to the gate of the house."

Once more there was a pause, and then followed a loud knocking at the front door, which was no sooner opened than Griffiths Grindwell, booted and spurred, spotted from head to foot with mud, entered the hall.

As he gazed at the astounded crowd, his brow grew darker, and he gathered up the lash of his long hunting-whip, as if he were about to lash a kennel of hounds who had broken loose and been doing some damage.

Behind Mr. Griffiths Grindwell came two men, who might have been friends, or might have been superior servants, for their long riding-cloaks concealed their figures, and their slouched hats almost hid their faces.

As Griffiths Grindwell entered the hall Jack Firebrace sank back on the couch as if still asleep.

"What means this gathering?" cried Grindwell, in imperious tones. "Is this the way that you keep school?"

"Nay, nay, worthy sir. This has been truly a terrible night. We have had such scenes played here that I tremble to think on."

"Go to, Master Gruesome; I thought you had a mind above such folly as these old wives' tales. Does the wind whistling through a keyhole and the slamming of a door frighten thee? Go to, man, I am ashamed of you. If you have no more sense for teaching than you show in this matter, it would indeed be well to get these lads another master."

"Pardon me, sir, pardon, I pray you. I tell you it is not only the ordinary sounds that we have heard lately; far more than that to-night: we have seen some awful things. Not in the part of the building where we generally hear the noises, but in this hall. The door was closed against us, and—oh! I hope I may never see the like of it again."

For a moment even Griffiths Grindwell seemed overcome with surprise, but, after a little time, he recovered himself.

"Tut!" he cried; "I want not to hear of such foolish stories; it suits not my mood to-night. How now, Master Sidney? Has the devil caught hold of you also and scared your wits away? One would think that we were in an asylum for idiots instead of a school, to see such vacant looks. What means all this? Why are these villagers here? Speak, someone, or must I force the words from your throats?"

"If you please, Mr. Grindwell," said Collin, in answer to that gentleman's impetuous interrogation, "if you please, sir, axing your pardon, but, you see, that young fellow as I told you about had escaped from the school, and I and my mates, we coomed all the way up here for to tell the schoolmaster of it."

"What!" cried Griffiths Grindwell. "Dare you tell me that John Firebrace has escaped? By heaven! if this should prove to be true I'll kill you all."

"No, no, no," cried Gruesome; "that cannot be believed—I mean, you must not believe a word that fellow says. See, Firebrace is on that sofa, fast asleep. He has never left Hawkhouse since you gave those strict orders. Oh, my poor brain!"

"Can you explain this, Mr. Pliant?" demanded Griffiths Grindwell, after a short pause.

"Explain! I have been near throttled, after being insulted, by Mr. Sidney Morrison. I have heard sights and seen sounds—no, no, I don't mean that. I have seen sounds and heard sights—no, no, that's not what I mean; indeed, I know not what I mean. If I stay here much longer I shall go mad! I know—I feel I shall!"

"It seems that everyone is mad!" cried Grindwell, stamping with rage. "Mistress Drysdale, can you not explain?"

"Oh, my bones and body!" sobbed the old woman. "Oh, my limbs and legs! I am smashed—quite smashed!"

"If it should please yer honour," said Collin, pulling his forelock, "I think I could explain something and—"

"No, no, good fellow," replied Grindwell, suddenly changing his tone, "I do not wish to hear your version of the tale now. Here is money for you; go to the 'Goat Inn' and enjoy yourselves. But remember this—when you open your mouth to pour your drink down, take care that not a word of what you have seen here slips out of your lips."

"Thank your honour kindly, thank you," said Collin, as he took the handful of silver. "I'll see that all is kept quiet, your honour."

When the door was closed, Mr. Grindwell placed his back against it, and, in tones of fierce anger, cried—

"Who let this rabble rout into this house? Speak, or must I cut the words out of you with my whip?"

And, as he spoke, he cracked his heavy hunting-whip until the others cowered back in alarm.

"Awake—awake—awake, John Firebrace!" shouted a deep voice, which rang through the room.

It was a human voice certainly, but no one in that company had ever spoken so loudly, or could ever do so.

In a moment Jack sprang to his feet, and cried, as if continuing a conversation—

"Villain, give me back my father and mother! You have shed their blood, and I will have revenge, or die for them!"

"What fresh trick is this?" exclaimed Grindwell, starting back, and turning very pale; "this must be seen to!"

Jack paused.

"Come!" cried Grindwell, seizing him by the arm, and at the same time striking him a heavy blow with his whip, "I will have no more of this mountebank business! What is the matter? Dare to refuse to tell me all, and I will punish you as you were never yet punished."

"It is a horrible dream," said Jack, in a low tone, "a fearful dream. I dreamed that I was on board a ship with my dear father and mother. The wind whistled through the rigging, making the snow-white sails bulge out; the blue waves danced past us.

"All was gaiety and life, until in the distance came the merry sounds of music. The mess rushed to windward, and in the distance they perceived a beautiful bark coming towards us.

"Gay colours were flying from the mastheads, and there appeared dancing and music on board, as if the sailors were keeping some gala-day.

"Nearer and nearer she came, until close upon us; then she suddenly altered her course, and bore down right upon us.

"There was a crash, and the next minute more than a hundred men, sabres and pistols in hand, leaped upon our decks, and fell upon our crew, killing and wounding right and left.

"One tall man first shot down my father, and then with his cutlass pierced my mother to the heart. I sprang forward to avenge their deaths, but at that moment I awoke. It was a fearful dream—more than a dream; a revelation."

"How say you, a revelation?" asked Grindwell, who now looked almost as frightened as the others.

"Yes; my father, who was said to have been shipwrecked was murdered by pirates."

Griffiths Grindwell started back as if someone had hit him a heavy blow; but quickly recovering himself, he burst into a rough, discordant laugh.

"This mouldy old house has turned all your brains," he cried. "Did you see the face of your father's murderer, eh?"

"Yes," replied Jack, quietly, and looking steadfastly at Grindwell; "I shall know him when we meet."

"And what was he like?" demanded Grindwell, assuming a careless air.

"He was like you," replied Firebrace, "only his hair was different, and he had a scar—"

"Enough—enough of this folly!" cried Grindwell, quickly. "Mr. Morrison, I must speak to you alone. Mr. Pliant, see that these boys are attended to. If they have any more such dreams as these, you have a cane, and with it must beat better sense into them. As for you, young gentlemen, I fear that Mr. Gruesome is not strict enough with you. I shall give him a lesson. If you see a ghost, put your head beneath the bedclothes, and keep still. Ghosts may creep through keyholes, but they never creep through bedclothes. Mark this; if anyone of you dare leave your bed to-night under any pretence whatever, I will thrash him as long as I can stand over him."

And with this most cheerful farewell he motioned his black-robed attendants to leave the room.

"Jack," whispered old Flick, "what is the meaning of all this? It strikes me you know more than you say."

"Of course I do, replied Jack Firebrace, in the same tone; "take care that we are not observed. It is said that walls have ears, but these ones have eyes too. Take care; when I have a fitting opportunity I will tell you all I dare."

"But just tell me one thing," urged old Flick. "Was not that dream entirely made up—eh?"

"Yes and no. If you mean I did not dream it, you are quite right, for I never was asleep the whole time."

"And the ghosts! Did you see any ghosts?" urged old Flick.

"No—not one; indeed, I don't think there are such things. Now do keep quiet; you have seen the way I have been treated. Even this evening Mr. Grindwell struck me a brutal blow with his whip; he shall pay dearly for that blow."

CHAPTER XVI.

AN EXPLANATION—THE GHOST IN THE DORMITORY—JACK'S DISGUISE—HE STARTS IN SEARCH OF ADVENTURE AND GETS PLENTY.

It would be of no use to ask our readers to believe that the things we have described were really and truly the works of beings of another world.

The truth is that they were cleverly but easily-contrived tricks, mostly performed by Peter Pigwellan, who knew every trap, secret passage, sliding panel, and hidden staircase in Hawkhouse, and there were plenty of them, for the old building had not a solid wall in it, and many of the windows were made with springs, so that when they appeared bolted and barred, anyone acquainted with the mechanism had only to touch the spring and the window opened as if by magic.

All these contrivances old Peter had turned to the very best of purposes.

It will be easily understood that Peter Pigwellan had not the slightest difficulty in taking our hero back to his prison, or in dragging Goblin Jim away.

Moreover, by the aid of speaking-trumpets, he had been able to increase the power of his voice so as to cause the disturbance in the house.

It was Peter who had thrown the water from a large pail over the people; it was Peter who had dragged Jack into the room and closed the door, and it was Peter who had told Jack of Grindwell's approach, and dictated to him how he was to act.

The reader will see now that Jack's dream is easily explained.

As for his prophecy, that was a mere repetition of a secret message which Peter Pigwellan had received, telling him that Mr. Grindwell was on his way to Hawkhouse, and would arrive there at nine o'clock.

The rest of the business was done to throw the house in confusion whilst Peter gave his plans to Jack, and this was all the more easily done as no one had ever heard ghosts in that part of the house before.

Having explained to the reader that which he might have looked on as absolutely impossible, we resume our story.

Jack had turned quietly into bed, and soon was snoring, perhaps louder than anyone.

Suddenly the yelling and screaming of the haunted room commenced with re-doubled force, and the boys, remembering the orders of Mr. Griffiths Grindwell, at once bobbed their heads beneath the clothes.

Tramp, tramp, tramp! down the long dormitory came heavy footsteps, accompanied with the clank of chains.

"Mercy reaches not your ears," cried a plaintive voice. "Will not even my tears move you?"

"I have no mercy; thou must die!" was the reply, in stern tones.

Then there arose an awful scream, the stamping of feet, a strange, rushing noise, and then all was still again.

"Oh, oh, oh!" groaned Tomkins, who trembled so that he shook his bed-stead. "I shall die with fear."

"What do you think of that, Jack?" demanded Flick, in a low whisper.

But Jack Firebrace made no reply, being otherwise engaged.

He slipped out of bed, put on black trousers and a black jacket, which he buttoned up to his chin.

This done, he produced from his trousers pocket a black cotton night-cap, a pair of black socks, and a pair of large black thread gloves.

First of all he drew the black night-cap right down over his face, so that it completely hid his head down to the neck.

He then, with a penknife, cut two slits in the cap just above the eyes, so that the strained web, stretching apart, made two small eye-holes through which he could see.

"Now for my socks and gloves; those on, and I think I might pass for the blackest bogy that ever lived," he thought.

And certainly he might, for not one particle of white could be seen about him.

Indeed, he so matched the blackness of the night that it was difficult to see him at all.

And this was the reason why Jack Firebrace had adopted this dress.

Creeping on his hands and knees he managed to leave the dormitory with-out being noticed; and then once more he stood erect.

From the deserted wing of Hawkhouse, where he had been so lately imprisoned, the mysterious and ghost-like noises still came.

"No wonder the ignorant peasants are afraid," thought our hero. "But it shall go hard if I do not destroy this nest of smugglers—ay! worse than smugglers. But the time has not come yet. I must find out much more about them than I know at present, and wrench from Griffiths Grindwell the true history of my birth and my parent's fate. There is danger in it; but it shall be done."

Keeping close to the wall Firebrace crept towards the deserted wing.

As he came nearer and nearer the noise grew louder, and at last he saw dim-looking beings, which seemed to flit about in the most mysterious manner, each one appearing to have a livid light shining from its bosom.

A more ghostly effect could not be imagined.

Still keeping in the shade, Jack managed to approach so near to one of these groups of men that he could hear what they said.

"Ten thousand devils!" said one fellow, as he stretched his back, which had become stiff from rolling a cask along, "I think that the skipper must have gone mad to make us stack away the cargo in the old mill at once. He has as little regard for a man's backbone as he has for his own conscience."

"And that's saying a good deal, and no mistake, Herr Vandervord," laughed another.

"But there's worse than that to come," said another ; "I just heard the second mate tell Peter Pigwellan so."

"A million devils !" cried the sailor called Vandervord ; "what worse can come than this ? Here have we had a rough passage, where every man was kept night and day at his watch, and yet no sooner get shelter here than we are ordered to unload, and then the skipper orders us to help the land-runners * to get the casks stacked down in the deserted mill. Nothing can be worse than that."

"So you think, Vandervord," replied the other. "Now listen to me. Directly we have run the casks and stowed them away all safely, we shall be ordered on board again, and then up goes the anchor, every stitch of canvas is set, and away we run for the coast of France without staying long enough on shore to take a mouthful of meat or a tankard of ale."

"Then by all the devils !" cried Vandervord, seating himself on the cask he had been rolling, "I will do no more work. I will let him do it himself, that is what I will do, as sure as my name is Vandervord. And you may tell Mynheer Ranulph, or Griudwell, or whatever name he likes to call himself."

Scarcely had he said the words when he was seized from behind and hurled with tremendous force on to the stone flooring.

"Dog !" cried Griffiths Grindwell, for it was the skipper who had dashed the mutinous Dutch sailor to the ground, "dog, dare you mutiny ? Say one word more, and I will blow your brains out."

And, as he spoke, he pointed a pistol at Vandervord.

"But, Mynheer Grindwell," grumbled the now perfectly subdued Dutchman, "I am worn out—my bones ache."

"What ! you dare to answer me ? Off with his jacket, men, and fasten him up to yonder ring-bolts."

Vainly the mutinous Dutchman pleaded for mercy.

In less time than it takes to write it he was stripped to the waist, and his wrists secured by thin ropes to two ring-bolts fixed in the wall, about six feet from the ground, and about five feet apart.

His face being towards the wall, his bare back was exposed ready for the flogging he knew he would receive.

"I shall be merciful this time," said Griffiths Grindwell, with a fiendish look which belied his words, "and shall only give you one dozen ; but for every groan you utter, or cry, be it ever so slight, you shall have an extra dozen. After that you shall play horse. Jackson, step forward and let me see if you have lost your skill with the cat."

The man thus addressed stood considerably over six feet high, and was broad in proportion. He had fiery red hair, and a nose which had been hooked, but from a blow from a cutlass, had been beaten on one side.

He squinted so horribly that the pupils of his eyes could scarcely be seen, giving him a fearfully vicious expression.

He was dressed in a loose sailor's dress, the front of his shirt being thrown open to show his muscular chest, which was as hairy as that of a bear.

With a grin Jackson stepped forward and drew from his belt the instrument of torture.

"Stay one moment," cried Vandervord. "I have one request to make."

"Be quick ! what is it that you desire ?" cried Grindwell.

"I only ask that I may be allowed to have a bullet placed between my teeth,"* said the wretch.

"As you will ; but if I know anything of Jackson, that won't keep your tongue quiet."

One of the sailors stepped up and put a leaden musket-bullet between the man's teeth.

The unhappy Dutchman clenched it tightly, and then, closing his eyes, awaited his fearful punishment.

Jackson drew the lashes through his hand gently, slowly swinging his body at the same time, and then his brawny arm flew upwards, but only to descend with terrific force, bringing the thongs of the fearful whip down upon the white back of Vandervord.

The whole flesh seemed to quiver for

a moment, and then deep blue wheals rose up as if by magic.

Jack Firebrace had to use all his presence of mind to prevent himself from screaming as he saw this fearful scene, but the tortured sailor did not utter a single groan.

Blow after blow fell, and each time the executioner, enraged at not being able to make his victim scream out, redoubled his violence, until even the smugglers, brutalised and cruel as they were, felt sick and shuddered.

The eleventh blow was such a fearful one that many of the sailors involuntarily uttered exclamations of horror.

In a moment Jackson paused, and, turning to Grindwell, said, with a grin—

"I made him cry out then, your honour—

"You are mistaken," said Grindwell; "it was only these chicken-hearted knaves. You have one more chance, so don't despair."

The brutal wretch rested a space to recover his strength, and then delivered the last terrific lash.

No cry or groan escaped the victim, but half of the bullet fell to the floor, and he spat the other half out as his comrade undid his wrists.

"You have failed this time, Jackson," said Grindwell, with a laugh; "but never mind, he is your horse for to-night. And harken, my lads, all of you; news has reached me that a man-of-war is close by, cruising after the 'Flying Fish.' To work at once, for I swear I will kill the first man who utters another rebellious word!"

With that he turned upon his heel and walked away.

And now Jack Firebrace had the pleasure of seeing the game of "horse," once so popular a punishment.

With a long piece of rope Vandervord was harnessed to a kind of sleigh, on which were placed a couple of barrels of spirits, the usual load for a man being only one.

Jackson then seized him by the arm, and using a thin rope as a whip, made him drag the load along as if he were really a horse, and, as he felt his pride wounded at the failure he had just made, it is certain that the driver did not spare the cattle.

In this manner the casks were dragged to a trap door, outside which were some countrymen to receive them.

Jack guessed—and guessed rightly—that there was a secret passage leading from Hawkhouse to the mill, where old Flick and he had first met Peter Pigwellan.

"We must be sharp with the lot," said one of the countrymen, holding up a lantern; "the storm is coming up, and I have heard say the coastguard are on the alert."

Jack gazed at the speaker from his hiding-place in surprise.

It was Collin Clout!

CHAPTER XVII.

OUR HERO HAS A GAME OF JACK-IN-THE-BOX, AND FRIGHTENS THE SMUGGLERS, AND OVERHEARS A CURIOUS DIALOGUE, IN WHICH HIS FUTURE FATE IS DISCOVERED.

YES, Collin Clout, the so-called country lad, was in Grindwell's pay, and captain of the land-runners.

Firebrace could quite understand now Collin's anxiety to prevent him escaping from Hawkhouse, and also why Master Clout had on some occasions spoken with a strong country dialect, when at other times he had rather a Cockney accent.

It was a disguise throughout to blind the eyes of the Custom-house officers.

"If I am found here," thought Firebrace, "they will make short work of me."

This was anything but a cheering prospect, and Jack began to look about him in hopes of discovering some way to beat a retreat, for he had seen quite enough to show him the nature of the ghost that haunted Hawkhouse.

Whilst these thoughts were passing through the mind of Jack Firebrace, a great commotion commenced at the mouth of the well up which the casks of spirit had been brought.

The smugglers clustered together and conversed eagerly, and then, to Jack's dismay, seemed to point in his direction.

"I wonder if they have discovered me," he thought. "I don't think so. Nevertheless, I should be thankful to find some kind of hiding-place. What is this—a chest?"

Yes, sure enough, in a recess Jack discovered what appeared to be an old oak chest.

In an instant he had raised the lid, and, having stepped inside, shut himself in.

It was a large sea-chest, such as sailors use to serve as a wardrobe and chair.

There were no handles to it, but two holes had been cut at each end of the box, and through them had been run a piece of rope, which served all the purposes of handles to lift the chest about.

At first, when Jack noticed this, he little thought how useful the discovery would be to him; but he had not long to think of these things, for he had scarcely hid himself in the chest, when he heard the heavy tramp of the smugglers as they came towards him.

"This is the chest," said one, giving it a heavy kick with his boot. "Just sling it on your shoulder, Bill, and carry it away."

"Is it locked?" demanded another sailor. "If not, the things may fall out."

"There are only papers in it," replied the first man. "However, I may as well lock it to make it all safe."

To our hero's dismay, the fellow thrust a key into the lock, turned it, and so made Jack a prisoner.

It was then that Jack was thankful for the handles, the holes in which they were placed admitting quite enough air to prevent him being suffocated, and also to allow him to hear all that passed.

The chest was dragged up, and, after many bumps and thumps, heaved onto the man's shoulders.

"Did you say that there wasn't anything inside this here chest," growled the man, as he panted along.

"Certainly," replied the other; "there is only a lot of papers belonging to the skipper."

"Then all I can say is, that I think Davy Jones must have got into the chest," growled the fellow.

"Davy Jones!" thought Jack; "that's not a bad idea. If they open the chest I will try to escape as the devil."

"Tut, tut, Bill! you are always grumbling. The box ain't a lady's work-box, but good old oak; but there's not ten pound weight of paper in it."

"There may be only ten pounds of paper," retorted the other, "but, curse me, there must be something else."

"Well, never mind old fellow, here is the well, and we can lower it down into the cave," laughed the first man.

The box was eased down from Bill's broad shoulders.

"It does seem a tremendous weight," said the man who had locked the chest. "If I had not put the things in it myself, I should swear it was full of stones. When we have it stowed on board we will examine it."

"On board!" groaned Jack Firebrace. "They will take me to the smuggler's ship, and there, it matters not what part I play, they will find me out and kill me."

"Wake up there—wake up there!" cried Griffiths Grindwell, as he hurried up to them; "we have no time to lose."

"There is something strange about this here box, your honour," said Bill; "it ain't 'is nat'ral weight, not a bit of it."

"Fool!" cried Grindwell, impatiently. "How can the box have grown heavier? Here, haul the box up and lower it down the well at once! Make haste, or we shall be found out."

The box was soon slung up to the pulley and then lowered as rapidly as possible down the well.

The sensation was not a pleasant one, but Jack stuck his knees and elbows as tightly to the sides of the chest as he could, and by these means he managed to keep himself from being one mass of bruises and contusions.

It was with no small sense of relief that he felt the chest touch the ground, and the men unhook the rope with which it had been lowered.

The chest was pulled roughly on one side and there left to await its turn to be shipped away.

Jack Firebrace could hear the scuffling of feet and the confused sound of men's voices speaking in whispers.

"I wonder what those villains are up to now!" he thought. "They are evidently not easy in their minds. Well, I can't say that I am either."

And it must be confessed that, bold as our hero was by nature, the position he found himself in was not cheering.

Taking out his penknife, Jack cut off one of the knots of one of the rope handles, then by pulling the other knot, he was able to drag the rope inside, and thus leave the two holes free, so that he could breathe easier, and also get a slight glimpse of what was going on outside his narrow house.

He could make out that he was in a cave—a cave by the seaside—for he could hear the beating of the waves on the shore; but beyond a glimpse now and then of some legs, he could not see anything; but this enabled him to know that the smugglers were busily engaged at some work which they were executing with as little light as they could.

Presently the confusion grew louder, and Jack heard the rough voice of the man who had locked the chest—who, by the way, was no other than Jackson, who had so cruelly flogged the luckless Vandervord.

"Quick! most of you to the boats!" he cried; "shove off at once and get on board the 'Fying Fish.' Get everything ready to start at a moment's notice. Luke Bradley, Mat Murdoch, and Bill Blast stay with me here; the captain will want you. And look you, lads; have everything ready to shake out the sails to the wind directly a blue-light is seen to flicker on the rock just above Peter Pigwellan's hut. Then up with your helm and away to France."

"But the captain and the others, will they not join us?" demanded one of the men.

"No; he has other work to do. Away with you, lads!"

The men made the best haste they could down to the boats.

"Heaven be praised!" thought Jack.

"At all events, I shall not be carried out to sea and made to walk the plank."

"Here's that cussed box!" said Bill Blast, giving the chest a violent kick. "My back aches from it yet."

"Most like it does; and had we known what the skipper meant, we need never have moved the thing," said Jackson.

"I only wish that you had known what the skipper meant and not removed it," thought Jack.

"But what are we going to do with it?" asked another.

"Well, you see, the 'Wasp' is sailing up here on the look-out for our vessel, and the captain don't wish to have his papers overhauled should she happen to catch the 'Flying Fish.'"

"There be some queer deeds amongst them papers," said one of the men.

"Ay!" growled Jackson. "The skipper keeps his log as if he were the captain of a man-of-war instead of what he is."

"And those log-books are in that chest," grumbled Bill Blast. "I know'd as how there was something wrong with them; it was all his sins as did it. They are heavy enough to break his friend Old Nick's back, let alone mine."

"You had better not let him hear you say so," said Jackson. "He will most likely break your back in something after the style he treated Vandervord."

"I think it would be as well for me to take one of these log-books," thought our hero, "as it might be very useful on some other occasion."

So putting his hand upon the first book which came in his way, Jack Firecrace slipped it under his jacket.

"But what are we to do with the confounded chest?" asked Bill Blast. "I should like to break it up."

"No, no; that would not do at all, the pieces would be found. We must bury it, my lads—bury it deep down in the earth."

All Jack's hope of liberty was gone.

Had he been taken on board he might have been thrown into the sea; that would have been bad enough. But buried alive was something terrible, awful, fearful!

Should he scream and at once tell them a human creature was there?

If he did, would not that be to sign his

own death-warrant? for they would kill him at once.

But what of that?

Better to die in an instant than to suffer the slow pangs of death by being buried alive!

A cold sweat broke out over Jack Firebrace's brow. Do not think he was a coward.

Who—who in this world could look forward to such a horrible fate as being buried alive, with calmness?

He remembered having heard or read somewhere, about a beautiful French lady who had, to all appearances, died and been buried.

He remembered that her lover, who had been away at the time of her death and burial, returned to the village, and, determined to gaze upon her face once more, had re-opened the tomb, there to find the lady with clenched jaws, eyes still staring, although the sight had long since left them; her nails dug into her flesh; her knees bruised in trying to burst open the coffin; her shroud bedabbled in blood.

All showed the terrible agony the lady must have suffered.

These thoughts flashed through Jack's mind with the speed of lightning.

However, he did not move. He made no cry.

All his idea was to fight his way out of the difficulty if it were possible.

"I have the skipper's orders to take out the books and then bury the chest," said Jackson.

Jack Firebrace breathed again.

At all events he should not die that horrible, terrible death—being buried alive.

It is true that Jack had only the faintest chance of escape.

But hope grew strong in his heart, and he waited anxiously for the time to come when the chest should be opened.

"Bring the chest more out here, Bill," said Jackson; "more in the light so that we can see better."

"Phew! it is a weight!" grumbled Bill Blast. "I never seed such a box. If it was chockfull of gold it could not be heavier. As sure as I'm a living breathing man, I believe that the devil has got into that there chest."

"I believe that the devil has got into that old muddled head of yours," laughed Jackson, as he turned the key in the lock. "Don't I tell you that I only put the books into the chest, and that I know there is not a single thing besides in it. As for the devil—why, I've heard a great deal about him, and—ho, ho, ho!—I should like to see him."

Scarcely had he uttered the words, than Jack Firebrace sprang up in the box, dashing the lid up, at the same time uttering the most unearthly yells, and waving his arms about in a frantic manner.

For a moment the men looked at the horrid figure (for, what with his black dress and the flickering, uncertain light of the torches, it must be confessed that our hero made a very hideous appearance); then crying loudly—"The devil! Mercy!" they fled out of the cave, falling over each other in their terror.

Jack uttered another unearthly yell; then, finding that he was alone, he glanced hastily round for some place to hide in.

This was soon found, for the cave was one of that irregular kind, filled with dark recesses and smaller caves, half-way up the cliff, caused by the waves in stormy weather.

Having selected one of these hollows, Jack dashed out the torch, and then crawled into his place of concealment.

He could still hear the men's cries for help and shouting—"Old Nick has come for some of us!" then Griffiths Grindwell's stern voice, commanding them to silence.

"What means this hubbub?" he cried. "You cowardly hounds; do you wish to bring the officers upon us?"

"It's the devil himself—he is in the box—he is in the cave!" shouted the men.

"Silence!" cried Griffiths Grindwell, "you bawling idiots! Jackson, you used to be brave. Explain this noise."

In tones which yet trembled, Jackson related what had happened in the cave.

"You must all be mad or drunk," growled Grindwell, when he had heard the story.

"Neither, an it please your honour," replied Bill Blast. "When I lifted that there box I says, says I, 'The devil is in it,' for it was that heavy, I nearly broke my back, and it grew heavier every step I took."

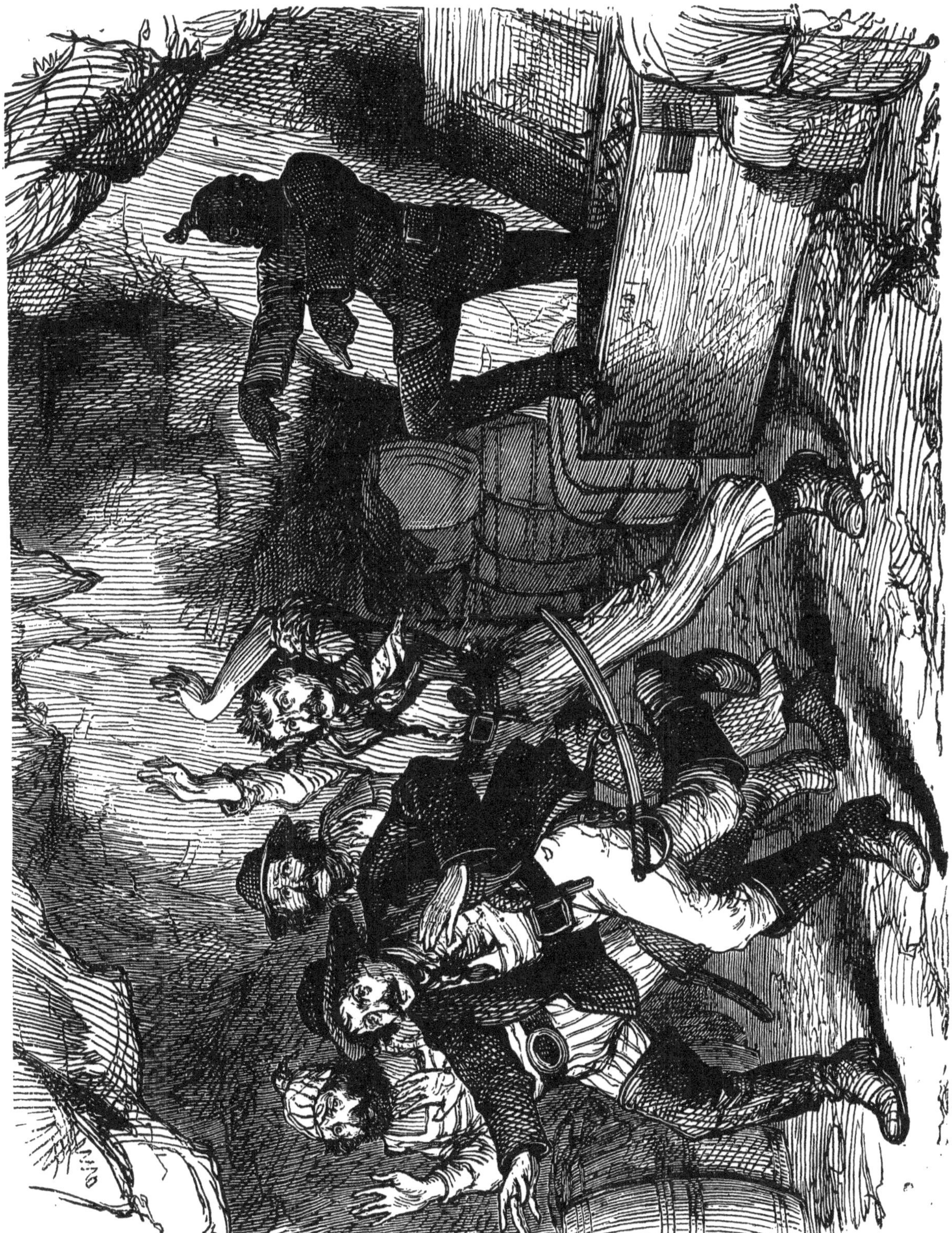

"JACK SPRANG UP, YELLING AND WAVING HIS ARMS ABOUT."

No. 6.

PRICE ONE HALFPENNY.

[PUBLISHED EVERY MONDAY.]

Grindwell looked sharply at the men's pale faces, and saw that they evidently believed the story.

Seizing a fresh-lighted torch from one of the men, he hastily entered the cave, and examined the chest.

All appeared to be safe, for in his hurry, he did not stay to count the books, and therefore did not miss the one which Jack had taken.

"And what was this creature like?" demanded Grindwell, turning to Bill Blast.

"Well, sir, he was a big, tall man, at least seven feet high."

"More than that, Bill," put in Mat Murdoch; "he was nine feet at the least, and as black as a coal."

"Well, maybe he was," replied Bill, who, for once in his life, allowed himself to be corrected; "maybe he was."

"But it wasn't his height as I cared for," said Luke Bradley, "it was his eyes. Oh! them fearful eyes."

"Oh, they were fearful eyes indeed," cried Jackson, "as large and deep as soup-plates."

"And as hot and glaring as red-hot iron."

"And his horns!" cried Bill.

"And his tail! it twisted and twirled about like a fiery serpent!" exclaimed Mat Murdoch.

"Peace fools!" cried Grindwell. "Out with the books at once, and then bury the chest. And mark me, lads, if I hear anything more of this, I will flog you all round."

Having given this order, Grindwell turned towards a tall man who was clad in a long black cloak reaching down to his heels, and a slouched hat drawn so low over his face as to conceal his features.

With this mysterious figure Griffiths Grindwell conversed some time in whispers, whilst the men removed the books from the chest. Having done this they drew from a hole in the cliff a couple of spades, and were about to dig a hole in the back of the cave, when the cloaked man stepped forward and stopped them.

"Not there—not there!" he cried; "as you value your lives, do not touch that spot. You—you know not what is there."

In his anxiety to stop the men he knocked his hat off his head, and to Jack's surprise, discovered the features of the new usher, Mr. Sidney Morrison.

"Ha, ha, ha!" laughed Griffiths Grindwell, in reply to Morrison's excited speech; "you need not fear to disturb *him*. He sleeps sound enough you may be sure. But perhaps it were better to let his bones rest in peace. They say 'Dead men tell no tales,' but I have known some very nasty revelations come out of the appearance of a skeleton."

"For mercy's sake be silent," implored Sidney; "remember we are not alone, and—"

"And what?" demanded Grindwell, suddenly seizing Sidney's wrist with a grip of iron. "Do you think that I fear these men betraying me? No; there is not one amongst them who is not deeply dyed in blood. I hold their lives in my grasp, as I do yours. Fear not, I will not betray you—that is if you obey me. Remember, you are my creature!"

With a moan of agony Sidney reeled back to the side of the cliff, as Griffiths Grindwell flung away his hand.

"The chest is buried, yer honour," said Mat, touching his forehead; "what are we to do with the books?"

"Place them in a heap here," said Grindwell, pointing to the spot which the usher had begged them not to disturb.

The men took the books, which were merely quires of paper stitched clumsily together with covers of brown paper, and threw them all of a heap at the back of the cave.

Grindwell drew from the place where the men had concealed their spades, a tin can containing some kind of spirit.

With this inflammable liquid he saturated the books, and then taking a torch from one of his men, lit the pile.

In an instant a bright flame shot up illuminating the whole of the cave, and making Jack tremble lest he should be discovered.

"That is the way I destroy all the evidence against me," laughed Grindwell. "Now, my men, to your posts. You know the signal—one port-fire shown so that it only can be seen on the south-west. Now go!"

The men left the cave, and Grindwell and Sidney stood face to face, and as they thought, alone.

"This is a strange story, indeed," said Grindwell, after a pause; "one could almost believe that the old house is really haunted."

"You cannot doubt my word," replied Sidney. "There is the paper that I found on the lad's chest."

As he spoke, he held out the slip of paper which had been discovered on Jack Firebrace, when he pretended to be in a trance.

Grindwell snatched it from him, and read it aloud—

"'Harm not the lad. The dead can work amongst the living. Beware! I am near to protect the innocent. Be warned in time, or the Hand of Glory will seize the dagger and strike. Beware, beware!'"

"Oh, it is terrible!" cried Sidney Morrison; "surely this is the finger of fate, pointing out the guilty."

"Pshaw! Sidney Morrison, you are a coward. I know you well, and have studied you from a lad."

"Coward!" cried Sidney; "who would not be, with such a terrible fate hanging over their heads?"

"You talk like an idiot! Look at me! I have stood upon my vessel's deck when the shot has whirled past me, tearing away the rigging, and splintering the masts. I have had a dozen cutlasses slashing at me right and left, and but one ever wounded me, and for that cut, many lives have paid, and many more shall. You, Sidney Morrison, are cowardly, as well as avaricious! Do you think *when I paid that bill* I did not know that you had committed forgery?"

With a low groan Sidney Morrison hung down his head.

"Tut, man! I will not hurt you. You shall have wealth, and live right merrily with me. Listen! All you have to do is this. When I sailed the West Indian seas every ship I took I destroyed. My plan was to bind the crew and passengers hand and foot and batten them down in the hold. Then, having removed all the merchandise I could, I sent a cannon-ball through the vessel's side, below water-mark. Ten minutes afterwards all signs of the ship had gone. No witness could be found, save at the bottom of the sea."

"Merciful Heaven! this is most terrible!" muttered the unfortunate usher.

"Well, amongst the papers of one ship I found many deeds relating to vast estates, both here and in the West Indies. Some of these I have been able to secure, others I have not yet dared to touch. But none of them are firmly mine. Now, you shall make the deeds good. In the old house yonder, I have had parchments placed where they may get stained and mildewed, so that they may appear old. That is your work to look after them. Your reward shall be wealth, and probably I may adopt you as my son. Do you agree?"

"I must. I cannot help myself. But this paper found on Firebrace! The terrible seal upon it! Look! it is the seal of the dead man's ring!"

"Yes, you are right. Let me see if the murdered man's grave has been touched," replied Grindwell, taking a torch and examining the ground.

He pushed the ashes of the burned log-books on one side with his foot, and, in doing so, struck against something which, on closer examination, turned out to be the bone of a man's arm, from which the hand had been severed.

Grindwell turned deathly pale on seeing this.

"Sure enough, the grave has been opened again, and the hand cut off. Who could have done this?" said Grindwell, fiercely.

"It has not been done by mortal means," replied Sidney Morrison, with a shudder.

"Tut! Whoever has done it bears us no good will, whilst he is friends with Master John Firebrace. That boy must be removed. He has crossed me several times already. I cannot strike the blow myself. Could you not do it, Sidney?"

"No, no. I could not—I dare not do it. No more blood—no more blood. I cannot bear it."

"At all events, it must be done," replied Griffiths Grindwell, shrugging his shoulders, and glancing contemptuously at the usher. "Our safety depends on it, and I am not one to let such things stand in my way long."

Sidney Morrison shuddered at the cold tone of this bad man, but Jack looked in vain for a sign of pity.

For a moment Griffiths Grindwell

remained thinking the matter over, and then said—

"I must put this into the hands of Mistress Drysdale. She has a clever head for mixing potions which cures all ills."

"Do you mean to poison the lad?" asked Sidney Morrison in a hoarse whisper.

"Not I," replied Grindwell, with his sardonic laugh. "But perhaps something he may take will not agree with him."

"I understand," said the usher. "And then we shall be free. I breathe again. Oh, how I fear death!"

"So do all, coward!" muttered Griffiths Grindwell. "But there; you know what you have to do. Do it well, and I'll protect you. Hark, someone comes!"

"Master! master!" exclaimed Peter Pigwellan, hurrying into the cave. "The 'Wasp' has just rounded the point!"

"So soon!" exclaimed Griffiths, stamping with rage. "At once tell the men to show the signal. Away with you! The 'Flying Fish' can show her a good pair of heels, and must lead her a good chase from here. Away, away with you!"

CHAPTER XVIII.

THE "WASP" AND THE "FLYING FISH"—A FEARFUL PLOT—THE ALARM-BELL— JACK SPOILS MR. GRINDWELL'S TREACHEROUS GAME.

BOOM!

"Hark to the cannon! the pursuit has begun," cried Grindwell. "Quick, Morrison, follow me. We must once more become peaceful citizens, you the quiet scholar, and I the steady-going merchant, who wields the pen and knows nothing of the sword."

Laughing at his own conceit, Grindwell extinguished the torches, and our hero could hear their retreating footsteps die away in the distance.

"Well, I think I have had a jolly lucky escape," said Jack.

He listened attentively to try if he could hear anyone near him, but, so far as he could make out, he was quite alone.

He drew forth the log, and, having thrust it to the very end of the hole in which he was concealed, crawled out himself.

"I've fallen into a jolly good thing, certainly," thought Jack. "I can't make Pigwellan out altogether. As far as I can see, I am in a regular nest of murderers by sea and land. There is someone buried over there, that's certain, and I am to be doctored by that wretched old creature, Mrs. Drusilla Drysdale the Ghoul. I have heard some people look back on their schooldays

with delight. I can't say that I shall do so with mine.

"Hark!"

Boom! boom!

"There go the cannons again. The whole place will be alarmed, and they will discover that I am not in my bed. What is to be done? Peter Pigwellan might be able to show me some way back, as he did before, and—Bang! There, they are firing again. I must try to find Pigwellan, come what may."

With this determination he made his way to the mouth of the cave, and was soon standing on the sea-shore.

The sea was running very high, and a heavy gale came tearing round the point, and roaring about the crags.

Dark masses of cloud were scudding along at a furious rate over the moon, so that at some moments the scene was completely shrouded in darkness, whilst at other times it was completely illuminated by the white light of the moon.

Jack Firebrace clung closely to the cliff, so as to avoid the boisterous gusts of wind.

As he pulled on his black nightcap and gloves, he gazed out to sea, where a beautiful sight presented itself.

The smuggling ship, the "Flying Fish," was dashing along at full speed, every stitch of canvas spread, looking as saucy a little craft as ever sat on the top of the heaving waves.

Behind her was a beautiful preventive cutter, crowding all sail in chase.

The cutter steered right for the schooner, and every now and then sent a shot from her bow-chaser after the " Flying Fish "; but the latter vessel kept well ahead, now and then firing a shot from her long swivel-gun which was placed well aft, and rather aided than impeded the schooner.

However, as far as Jack could make out, neither ship received any damage from the interchange of fire, so, after watching them for a few moments, he once more pressed on towards Peter Pigwellan's hut; but paused, and crouched down behind a rock when he perceived Grindwell now dressed as a peaceable merchant, standing with the two men who had arrived with him from London, and Peter Pigwellan, close to the door of the cabin.

" Mr. Grindwell," cried one of the strangers, " that little schooner of yours is a beauty—how she cuts the water ! "

" I trust that your craft being pursued will not injure us."

" No; the ' Wasp ' has been cruising about here for the last month past in hopes of catching the ' Flying Fish '; but I have my private signals all along the coast, so that when she is here, the ' Wasp ' is away, and when the ' Wasp ' comes up to this bay, my little barque is always warned off the shore. I let her be pursued to-night in order that she would draw off the ' Wasp.' "

" It was rather a dangerous game," said the other gentleman.

" And therefore the kind of game I like. Besides," he muttered, in a lower voice, " I have a debt to pay, and will pay it to-night. There goes the ' Flying Fish ' spanking away. In half a minute she will have rounded the point and be out in the open sea."

The clouds had now massed over the moon, so that the night was perfectly dark.

The wind increased in violence until it blew a perfect hurricane.

Taking advantage of the darkness and the noise made by the wind and waves, Jack managed to creep close up to Grindwell without being perceived, and

to hide himself behind Peter's boat, which was pulled high up in the rock by the side of the cabin.

From this hiding-place he was able to see and hear all that went on, and he noticed that Peter seemed frightened and nervous.

At last, in desperation, Peter caught the smuggler's arm, and forced him away from the others.

" What means all this, Griffiths Grindwell ? " demanded Peter, sternly. " Have you more of the fiend's work in hand ? "

" And if I had," replied Grindwell, haughtily, " what is that to you? Do you forget that you are in my power ? "

" No," replied the old man, quietly; " but I have warned you that I will have no more blood."

" Go to, old man," Grindwell laughed, " you are only half-witted, or I should be angry."

" Half-witted ? Yes; and who drove me so ? who made me work chained like a galley-slave ? who tortured me until I became mad ? You did, Griffiths Grindwell."

" Silence your blabbing tongue ! " cried Grindwell, as he clutched the old boatman fiercely; " I allow no one to speak like that ! "

" Tell me that there is no evil meant here," urged the old man; " you have the mark of blood between the eyes."

Jack Firebrace peeped up into Grindwell's face, and noticed that he had a deep red mark between the eyes !

" No more of this. What evil should I mean ? Come, Peter, we will go into your cabin, and you must give us a cup of brandy. Come, my boatman, old Peter is a man who knows what brandy should be, and will give us some of the very best, I can tell you."

Old Pigwellan, who seemed greatly relieved by Grindwell's change of manner, hurried into the hut, and hastily produced a flask of brandy and some good-sized drinking-glasses, which he filled with the strong liquor, not forgetting one for himself.

" This is the right sort," Grindwell cried, as he tossed off the brandy; " this never paid duty. Come Peter, get us some pipes and tobacco; my friends and I will enjoy ourselves at your expense."

The old boatman hastened to a

cupboard to get the tobacco, and, taking advantage of his back being turned, Grindwell hastily drew from his pocket a small packet containing a dark powder, which he emptied into Peter's glass; then, with a wink to his companions, he refilled all, crying out as each took his glass—

"Now, gentlemen, let us drink, 'Long life and success to all here.' Drink, Peter; that is a toast you cannot refuse."

"Nay, that will I not," chuckled the old man. "'Long life and success to all here!'"

He tossed off the brandy at one gulp, put the glass down, gazed feebly around him, passed his hand slowly over his forehead, then staggered forward, made several clutches in the air, and fell senseless to the ground.

"Confound the old fool!" Grindwell said, as he bestowed a kick upon the prostrate body of the old boatman; "I shall have to make short work of him one day. But come, gentlemen, or we shall miss our chance."

They all came out of the cabin, the door of which Mr. Grindwell locked and pocketed the key, and passed so close to Jack Firebrace, that he could have touched them, and commenced climbing up the cliff.

"I wonder what work they are up to now?" thought Jack; "no good, I'll be bound. Stay! perhaps this wretched man Grindwell is going to take them back by some secret way to the Hawkhouse? I'll follow; so here goes."

Keeping as much as possible behind projections in the rock, Jack followed up Mr. Grindwell and his friends.

They paused near the foot of the cliff, and appeared to be busily engaged lighting a lantern.

By its light Jack Firebrace saw that a rope, having a cradle at the end, had been lowered from one of the windows in Hawkhouse on to the beach.

In this cradle one of the men was placed, having the lantern in his hands.

The man in the cradle jerked the rope as a signal, and in an instant he was quickly hauled half-way up the cliff.

Here he swung backwards and forwards the lantern.

Meanwhile Grindwell and his companion stood with their faces looking out to sea, watching for something.

Jack was puzzled.

What could they be taking all this trouble for?

As he watched the lantern, he could not help remarking how much the light looked like that on the mast-head of a ship when a vessel is rolling about on a stormy sea.

"A vessel on a stormy sea!" He saw it all now; they were wreckers!

He looked out to sea, and there, only a short distance from the shore, was a light, which in size and movement exactly resembled the one on the cliff.

It was the light at the masthead of the vessel which was being lured to destruction.

What could he do to save the doomed vessel?

If he shouted he would not be heard by those on board the ship, whilst the wreckers would instantly throw him into the sea to perish.

One hope, and but one hope remained, and that was to awaken Peter Pigwellan, for he saw now that the sleeping draught had been administered to the old man so that he should not be able to prevent this diabolical act.

Cautiously Jack Firebrace crept back to the cabin, and tried to force the door open, but without success.

"By Jove! that is a lucky thought," muttered Jack; "the sliding panel at the back of the cabin by which he saved me from that fellow Collin, may be undone. I can but try, and may Heaven aid me!"

He hurried to the back of the cabin, and, to his great delight, found that the panel could be slipped back with ease.

The next moment he was kneeling by the old man's side, trying to awaken him.

He dashed cold water in his face, chafed his hands, and called him by name.

At last he succeeded so far that Peter Pigwellan opened his eyes, and dreamily listened to Jack's hurried words.

"Hawkhouse! escape—trap yonder —beneath table!" murmured Pigwellan, and then fell back fast asleep.

"It is useless," said Jack; "yet stay! His words may have some meaning in them. At all events, I can but try."

He hurried to the table, and, snatching

up the little lamp, began to examine the floor.

Just beneath the table at the end of the cabin he perceived a small trap-door.

He opened it, and discovered a ladder which led to a narrow passage.

Jack had no time to consider.

He at once descended, carefully closing the trap after him.

The passage continued straight on for some thirty yards, and then turned abruptly round to the foot of a winding staircase cut in the rock.

Holding his lamp above his head so as to see plainly, Jack hurried up the staircase.

At last he came to an abrupt halt, for the stairs seemed only to lead to a blank wall. But our hero knew too much now of secret passages for this to puzzle him, and at once, with the aid of his lamp, commenced searching for some secret spring, feeling convinced that what looked to him like a wall was in reality a secret door.

He found a knob, pressed upon it as hard as he could, and the door slid noiselessly back.

He closed the door, and having ascertained that it was quite fast, paused for a moment, to consider what to do next.

He found himself in the long corridor that ran right across Hawkhouse to the old tower, and the windows of which faced the sea.

Hastening to a window, he gazed out to sea, and saw that the misguided ship was rapidly approaching the beach.

What could he do to warn her off the reef of rocks.

"The alarm-bell!" he cried, as the idea flashed across his mind; "it may tell them that they are sailing towards the coast; and at least it will arouse the villagers, and they will find out that there is a wreck on the coast."

He ran to the tower, but to his dismay found that the rope of the alarm-bell had been cut.

Seizing the rotting timbers, Jack managed to creep up until he had climbed to the beam on which swung the alarm-bell.

He took one hurried glance at the sea, roaring and tearing far down beneath him, as if the ghosts of the drowned sailors were swinging about on the raging waves, ready to welcome their friends on the doomed ship; then, with a shudder, he fixed his eyes on the bell, and crawled out towards it.

At last he reached it, and found to his delight that the rope still ran round the wheel.

In an instant he had seized it, and the bell commenced tolling out deep tones of warning and alarm.

"Confusion!" shrieked Griffiths Grindwell, when he heard the bell. "Who has done that? It has ruined our plot."

"Nay, not so, not so," said the others. "They are too near the beach now to escape. They must be wrecked."

"Look yonder," cried Grindwell; "do you see those lights flashing out there?"

"Confound it! What can be going on? The whole place seems alive with people," replied one of the men.

"The alarm-bell has aroused all the honest fishermen, and they are despatching messengers to the preventive stations. The game is up, gentlemen. Give the signal, and let our friend be lowered to the ground again."

The signal was given, and the man who held the decoy-lantern at once extinguished it, and was lowered to the sands.

"They cannot rob me of all the reward for my night's work," laughed Grindwell, "for not one of the crew of that vessel will reach land—that is, alive."

"Are you sure of that?" asked the other. "Were I convinced that such was the case, I would have less fear."

"Fear!" exclaimed Grindwell, with scorn. "I had hoped, Clement Bulstrode, that you knew not fear. I tell you that never did a ship strike upon yonder reef that one man was saved alive. I ought to know, who have wrecked so many ships here."

"Leave that to me; but if one of those men in yonder ship escapes, our lives will be in danger. We must pretend to save them, but, should one come ashore alive, he must quickly die. You know what I mean."

Whilst this conversation had been held in hurried whispers, Jack Firebrace still tolled the bell.

On came the ship, until, with a fearful crash, she rushed upon the rocks.

Screams of horror, which rose high above the storm, told the sad story of the despairing crew.

The masts went by the board, the rugged rocks tore the vessel's sides, the cruel waves foamed about the ship as if rejoicing in her fate, now and then making a clean breach over her, and carrying many of the sailors to a watery grave.

Swinging himself backwards and forwards on the rope, Jack managed to get at last close to one of the walls.

He clutched the oak, let go the rope, and in a few moments was once more standing in the corridor.

He heard a confused murmur of voices and the sound of hurrying feet.

The inhabitants of Hawkhouse were aroused.

"They must not catch me here," thought Jack, so he quickly touched the spring of the secret door, entered the passage, and closed the door again.

This done, he hurried cautiously down the steps, and at last reached Pigwellan's cottage.

All was as he had left it.

There slept the drugged boatman, snoring heavily.

"I must not stay here," muttered Firebrace. "Those wretches might find me. I'll slip out onto the beach, and trust in fate."

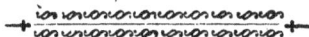

CHAPTER XIX.

JACK'S ADVENTURES AT THE WRECK—A STRANGE MEETING—HUMAN OR SUPERHUMAN?

THE beach was now covered with countrymen, sailors and fishermen, amongst whom Jack recognised Collin Clout.

"How the deuce could the fellow have got himself into that scrape?" said a burly man dressed in the uniform of a naval lieutenant. "There must have been precious careless men on board, or"—and here he glanced sharply at Mr. Grindwell, and then up to Hawkhouse—"or some light must have been shown from a window in that wretched old building. If I had my way I would have it pulled down. It only serves as a haunt for ghosts, or worse."

"Nay, Lieutenant Purvis," replied Griffiths Grindwell. "What harm does or can old Mr. Gruesome the schoolmaster and his scholars do to vessels out at sea?"

"I don't know," replied the lieutenant, gruffly. "All I can say is, that since he has been here wrecks have been too frequent."

"To-night, at all events, the Hawkhouse has done some good. I was the first to see the ship, and at once tolled the alarm-bell."

Jack Firebrace, who, concealed behind a group of sailors, heard this startling statement, felt inclined to spring forward and declare it false; but he thought it would be far more prudent to remain still and see how matters turned out.

Lieutenant Purvis looked at Mr. Grindwell as if still doubting the fact.

"What can we do to help you?" said Griffiths Grindwell, softly.

"That I cannot say; no boat can reach them where they are now; the Black Rocks are as sharp as a shark's teeth—ay, and they who once get near either of them have not much chance of escaping. Besides, we have no boat that can venture out."

"No boat?" exclaimed Griffiths Grindwell; "but there are the preventive boats, and then, in the bay over yonder below the village there are plenty of fishing-boats. Surely they can put out to sea?"

"They would not get ten yards from the shore before they would be capsized," replied Lieutenant Purvis.

"You know best, lieutenant," said Mr. Grindwell, in a sad voice; "but it seems a terrible thing to be standing here witnessing so many of our fellow-creatures dragged down to a terrible and untimely death; their shrieks for help ringing in our ears, and yet not to be able to help them."

"Halloa! why, what is that out on the rocks?" cried the lieutenant.

It was Peter Pigwellan.

Peter had recovered from his drug sooner than Grindwell had calculated.

He had recovered his senses, and, hearing the shouts of the men, he hastened at once to the secret panel, and in a few seconds was out on the rocks steadily watching the wreck as it broke up.

He understood all that had happened, and, rushing to his fishing-boat, began to use all his strength to launch her.

"Oh, that I had someone here to help me!" he shouted, "I might still save some of the unfortunate creatures."

"I am here, Peter," cried Jack, coming up and seizing hold of the gunwale of the boat; "come along, old man; we will save them."

"Good lad—brave lad," replied Peter; "Heaven will help and protect us. Come; now, both together. Ho, ho!"

The boat moved and slid quickly down.

It touched the water, and as our hero and Peter sprang in a receding wave carried her clear of the rocks.

They seized an oar each and pulled with all their might towards the distressed vessel, shouting a word of encouragement to her crew and passengers.

"They are mad—they are going to their death!" cried Lieutenant Purvis, as he saw the boat put out to sea.

"May they be drowned!" muttered Grindwell; then added aloud—"Did you see who were in the boat, lieutenant? They must, as you say, be mad."

"How the deuce can I tell who went into the boat on such a dark night as this?" growled the lieutenant; "all I could make out was that it appeared to be an old man and a lad. Why the deuce could they not have shouted for help? I would have gone with such brave fellows in a cockle-shell."

At this moment a vivid flash of lightning illumined the whole scene, and by it the spectators on shore were able to make out the fisher-boat working its way boldly against the billows, in a vain endeavour to reach the wreck.

All was darkness again, and the air was filled with the tremendous roll of the thunder.

"Who can the fools be?" muttered Grindwell, as he put his hands before his half-blinded eyes. "May—" but the words died away on his lips, for the excited spectators uttered a cry of horror.

He had seen the bright light of the second flash of lightning through his fingers, but before he could remove his hands all was darkness.

Again the deafening roll of the thunder pealed along.

"There! hark to the crash!" cried a sailor.

The ship had divided and gone to pieces.

Griffiths Grindwell could scarcely repress a cry of triumph when he heard the news; but he checked it and asked—

"And the boat—the boat with the gallant fellows who went to the rescue? Did you see what had become of them?"

"They were close to the ship when she broke up," replied one man; "wait until the next flash, then we shall know."

"Light a torch; has anyone a portfire?" shouted Lieutenant Purvis. "Why don't another flash of lightning come?"

It came, bright and vivid as ever, rending the black clouds and lighting up the dark sea.

Wreck and boat had both disappeared.

"May Heaven have mercy on their souls!" sobbed the lieutenant, who, like all truly brave men, was tenderhearted.

At that moment the sharp ring of horses' hoofs was heard on the rocky road leading to the beach, and a lady accompanied by two gentlemen, and followed by a groom and a maid-servant, all on horseback, dashed up to the spot.

"Where are the poor people?—where is the wreck?—are they saved?" cried the young girl, as she sprang off her horse.

"Alas! no, Miss Winny," said Lieutenant Purvis, as he took the young girl's hand. "God have mercy on them! All have perished."

"Merciful Heaven! this is terrible! When did the wreck break up?" exclaimed Wild Winny.

"Only just as you came up," said the lieutenant, kindly; "two brave fellows who went to the rescue perished also."

"Here, we have brought down a port-fire or two," said one of the gentlemen who had come down with Winny. "We will light one and send the light over the water."

"Ah, Captain Firbank," cried the lieutenant; "you are here. You must excuse me because of the darkness. I did not know you, and you also, Dr. Lamberhurst."

At this moment the port-fire flared up in the tin shade, and threw a bright blue light over the water.

"It is hopeless. There is not a living thing to be seen," said Lieutenant Purvis, sadly.

"We are saved!" whispered Griffiths Grindwell to his companion, as he turned to walk up the beach.

"No, no! they are not all lost!" cried Wild Winny, in tones that made Grindwell's blood run cold. "See yonder! There is something struggling with the waves. It is a man—two men —quick, lads! Twenty guineas to the first brave fellow who helps them ashore!"

"Another twenty if they are alive!" shouted Captain Firbank, wildly pulling off his coat.

"Rackstraw, get the blankets ready," cried Dr. Lamberhurst: "here, Peggy—Jenny—what's your name—"

"If you means me, sir, I begs to say my name is Miss Sariah Scraggs," replied the indignant maiden.

"Confound the girl!" cried the doctor. "Get out the brandy and the hot-water bottles."

"That's for you, Sally," laughed Rackstraw. "Take my advice and don't interfere with doctors. They are as sharp as their own lancets, as hot as their own blisters, and to some people worse than physic."

Meanwhile the commotion down by the sea was growing stronger and stronger.

All strove to get a place close to where a few daring men were striving to save the men from a watery grave.

The waves came pouring in with tremendous force.

Now that the sailors saw that life might be saved there was no shrinking back; each one was ready to face grim death in the endeavour to save his fellow-creature.

They formed a kind of chain, linking themselves firmly hand in hand, the foremost man being clutched by the man behind him only by his leather belt, so that he might be able to clutch with both his hands at the drowning men, whilst those behind kept him from being washed away, and also to help him drag the luckless victims ashore should he be able to seize them. But the waves broke with such violence on the shore that the men were knocked down and forced to retire, thinking themselves lucky in being able to get off with a good drenching and some heavy bruises.

But the men from the wreck were still battling their way towards the shore.

One of the sailors threw out a rope, with a faint hope that one of the two might clutch it.

They hauled the rope a little way back.

There was a weight upon it.

With a lusty cheer they hauled it in.

A crash, and a fearful wave broke upon the beach, making the fishermen run back a dozen yards.

But they held on to the rope, and, as the wave receded, had the joy of discovering the two men stretched on the beach.

The hearty cheer raised by the honest fellows was taken up by those on the outside of the crowd, who could not see what had happened; but they knew from the sound that it meant some good had been done, and they shouted for joy.

What sweeter incense than that could have been raised from heaven?

Grindwell had been thrust back in the most unceremonious manner by the preventive officer and his men, so that he was one of those who knew not what had happened—but not one of those who shouted.

He moved anxiously about trying to learn the news from those who stood nearer, but all were so excited that they could not give him any intelligible answer, merely repeating the words— "Saved, saved, saved!"

But now the crowd separated, and a youthful figure, wrapped in a large blanket, is hurried towards the place where Sally Scraggs has the hot-water bottles, the flask of brandy, and other comforts for the shipwrecked.

Grindwell glanced carelessly at this figure—it was not the one he cared for—most likely only the cabin-boy.

Then came some strong men bearing what appeared to be the lifeless body of a man.

Grindwell, alias Randulph the smuggler, bent anxiously forward to see if he could catch a glimpse of the face of the man they so carefully carried.

The question with him was: had death seized the right victim?

Grindwell was able to see that the younger man—a lad—was seated now near the cliff, with Rackstraw attending on him.

He also saw the elder man stretched on the ground, whilst Dr. Lamberhurst did his best to restore animation in the apparently lifeless form.

"Here!" cried Dr. Lamberhurst, as he put his ear to the man's chest to listen if he could detect the beating of the heart; "here, one of you hold the lantern a little more this way. How do you think that I can see to go on with my work when you sway the light about in that style?"

"Give me the lantern," said Winifred, snatching it from the man's hand; "I will hold it for you, doctor."

"That is a brave lass!" cried the doctor. "Why, what on earth is the matter now? Winny, Winny, my lass! What is it, my child?"

Miss Winifred Summerbell uttered a loud scream, and, bursting into a flood of tears, dropped on her knees.

"Matter!" she cried. "Oh, Dr. Lamberhurst, do you not know him?"

And here she pointed at the sailor.

The doctor again leaned over and gazed earnestly into the mariners's face.

Taking advantage of a movement in the crowd Grindwell did the same.

"Gracious powers!" cried Dr. Lamberhurst. "It is Edwin Summerbell, your father!"

Grindwell stayed to hear no more, but hastily turned and fled.

When he found himself alone he gnashed his teeth, and, raising his clenched hands towards the sky, exclaimed—

"What fiends are these that now spring up to baulk my will? But I will not give in—neither man nor devil shall turn me from my path. Till now I have always conquered, and will do so still."

As if in reply to this impious speech a flash of lightning shot from the heavens, and striking a tree a few paces from where the smuggler stood, withered it up at once.

But it was not this grand but terrible sight that made Grindwell start—it was the face of Jack Firebrace, pale as a corpse, which seemed to come suddenly out of the darkness and glare upon him.

"Am I mad or dreaming?" cried Grindwell. "Was it really a ghost? Is this lad in league with creatures of another world? Tut! what care I? He is in my power, and I will destroy him if he be human or superhuman!"

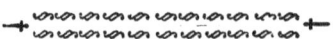

CHAPTER XX.

GRINDWELL DECIDES UPON OUR HERO'S DESTRUCTION—MRS. DRUSILLA UNDERTAKES THE MATTER—JACK'S DANGER.

GRIFFITHS GRINDWELL hastened as fast as he could to the gate of Hawkhouse School.

Having reached it he knocked loudly for admittance.

Pushing Drusilla Drysdale on one side as she opened the door, Grindwell snatched the candlestick out of her hand.

"Gracious goodness! Mr. Grindwell,

what is up now?" cried the old woman, angrily.

"Close the door and your mouth at the same time, you old beldame," cried Grindwell, as he walked away.

On he strode up the stairs and along the dark corridors of the dismal, ghostly mansion, and behind him, panting for want of breath, came Drusilla Drysdale.

Grindwell paused when he reached the door of the dormitory, and beckoned her towards him.

"If you please, sir," she said, in a meek voice, "you took away my light; and you looked so ill, that I thought I had better follow."

"Enough, enough, good dame," said Griffiths Grindwell; "I shall need your help. To-night one of these boys has left the school."

"Lor', sir, you don't say so!" exclaimed Drusilla. "If it be true, then it must be that young demon, Firebrace."

Grindwell made no reply, but, looking steadily at the old hag, nodded his head.

"I knew it," she hissed, shaking her bony fist in the air; "I knew it was that little brute."

"So," said Grindwell, with a low, sardonic laugh, "the lad is no favourite of yours, eh?"

"Favourite!" grinned the hag, "I hate him! I detest him! He is not a boy—he is not human—he is a little wizard."

"Then you ought to like him," sneered Grindwell; "for, if report speaks truly, you are a witch, and Jim your familiar imp."

The old woman wrinkled back her lips and flattened the skin of her forehead, until with her green eyes she looked like some hideous creature of the cat species about to spring on its prey.

"Fools and such folk will talk," she hissed. "But tell me this: how could that lad get out of his prison when bolted in? How did he manage to get my beautiful boy put into that prison? Can you tell me that? Do you think that Clout made a mistake? Do you think that the others made a mistake?"

Grindwell made no answer, and seemed lost in deep thought; but listened as Dame Drusilla Drysdale continued—

"Not they. Besides, does not my dear boy James swear that he saw him leave the prison? Then how does it come that my pretty pet Jimmy is spirited out of this house into a sack, where he gets nearly beaten to death? Can you tell me that?"

Grindwell shook his head.

"No; then I will tell you," cried the old lady, triumphantly—"it is witchcraft; or that the boy was born for some special purpose, and possesses powers which are more than human.

"Start not, Griffiths Grindwell; such things have been, and if that is the case he must succeed. If it be only witchcraft," and here the old lady chuckled fiendishly, "why I know the way to counteract that business. I know spells as powerful as most spells, which close the eyes in death."

"What do you mean by 'born for a special purpose'?" demanded Grindwell, as he plucked nervously at his cravat.

"Why, I mean," said the hag, in a low voice, speaking each word slowly and distinctly, "I mean, to detect murder, to baffle and defeat crime—most likely to bring some great criminal to the justice he has for so many years escaped."

As the old woman hissed this into her master's ears her eyes glittered with delight as she watched his startled look.

"Tut! you are an old fool, and I but little better for listening to you," he said, shaking her bony grasp from his arm; "but hark you, Drusilla; whatever this lad may be I am determined on one thing. If I find him in that room," here he pointed to the dormitory, "I will believe that he is a spirit, and will leave him to your tender mercies. Do with him what you like; only remember, he must be dead in twenty-four hours."

"Ha, ha! I understand," grinned the old woman; "but you will find him there, I warrant you. Had you seen him a hundred miles from here he could have been back before you, had he so chosen. He is an elf child—a demon. Go in and see."

Grindwell opened the door and entered the room.

The beds seemed all undisturbed, and every boy's head was beneath the bedclothes.

"Which is his bed?" demanded Grindwell, in a whisper.

"I don't know," replied the hag, "but

we must find out. Call them up; we shall soon see if he is here."

"Boys, get up! Get up, I command you," cried Grindwell, in a voice of thunder.

"Oh, oh, oh! here's another ghost!" cried the boys, burying their heads farther beneath the bedclothes.

"You wretched little idiots, if you do not do as I tell you at once I will have you flogged all round," shouted Grindwell.

In an instant all the boys were sitting up in bed, for the word "flog" drove away all ideas of ghosts.

Griffiths Grindwell looked at the boys, and, strong man as he was, could not help starting as his eyes rested on Firebrace.

Yes, there was Jack Firebrace, rubbing his eyes and yawning as if he had just awakened from a very heavy sleep.

"He is here," hissed Drusilla Drysdale into the smuggler's ear; "you see I am right; and he dies within twenty-four hours."

"Hush!" whispered Grindwell, and then turning to the boys he continued— "Which of you boys left the dormitory to-night?"

"No one, sir," cried the boys, in so loud a chorus that Grindwell could not hear if Jack Firebrace answered.

"If you did not leave the dormitory you have been out of bed. Just now I heard you running about and screaming."

The boys looked at each other in such evident wonder that Grindwell saw at once that they had done nothing of the kind.

He therefore determined to turn it off as best he could, and said—

"I do not think I could have been mistaken; still, there are strange noises in this old house. The wind blows down the chimneys and along the corridors, making rumbling noises, so that I may have been mistaken."

"If you please, sir," said Tomkins, "when we first came to bed, somebody came in here clanking chains, and said—"

"Nonsense, nonsense, boy, I do not wish to hear such trash as that. Firebrace, you used to be a truthful boy—"

"And trust I am so now, sir," replied Jack, who, by the way, though hating to tell a lie, had no foolish scruples about

doing so to such a wretch as he had proved Grindwell to be; "do you think I have altered at all?"

"No, no; I have no reason to think so," said Grindwell, hastily; "but tell me, have you seen or heard anything to-night? You know what I mean?"

"I heard what Tomkins did, sir; and at once placed my head beneath the clothes as you ordered."

"I did not want a repetition of Tomkins's story," said Grindwell, sharply; "have you heard anything else?"

"I have heard a great deal of shouting, which seemed to come from the sea-shore. I have heard the thunder and the wind."

"Of course you have. I should like to know who has not?" exclaimed Grindwell.

"Please, sir, I haven't heard any of it!" cried one of the boys, who, hearing Grindwell say he should "like to hear who had not," and being anxious to please that gentleman, hoped to do so by this piece of information.

"Then you must have been deaf!" replied Grindwell, impatiently. "A ship has been lost, with all her crew, in the bay."

"Dear me, how horrible!" exclaimed all the lads, in a breath.

"And are you sure, Mr. Grindwell," said our hero, fixing his eyes upon that gentleman—"are you sure no one is saved?"

"I—I—I believe not," said Grindwell. "Good-night, all of you."

He hurried from the room, followed by Mrs. Drysdale.

"Well," cried Drusilla, "and what do you say now? Am I right that he has supernatural powers, eh?"

"I do not understand it," muttered Grindwell; "but whilst he lives I shall have no security. He must die. It is strange, but if I ever feel sensations of fear and remorse it is when that boy's eyes are fixed upon me."

"Then we must close them," chuckled Drusilla Drysdale. "Won't Goblin be pleased when it is done!"

"You surely will not tell him?" cried Grindwell, in amazement.

"Sha'n't I! but I shall, though. Goblin, as the boys call him, knows as much as you do. He will help me in the matter."

"And have you no fear that he will let this secret out amongst his companions?" asked the smuggler.

"None! You may leave Hawkhouse to-morrow as safely as if the deed had been done before your eyes, my boy."

The two plotters then walked quietly down the corridor.

"Can he leave?" thought Jack Firebrace, as he crept into bed, for he had been listening to the conversation through a crack in the wainscot; "it will not be my fault if he do. So Goblin Jim is in it, eh? I will pay him out."

With that he turned over and went fast asleep.

CHAPTER XXI.

A CHEERFUL TEA-PARTY—THE AWFUL CONCLUSION.

"I say, Jack Firebrace!" cried Goblin Jim, at four o'clock in the afternoon of the day after the wreck.

"Well, what do you want with me?" said Jack, carelessly.

"I've got such a lot of news for you, Jack. You know I always did like you, Jack. You are a favourite of mine, Jack."

Firebrace could scarcely keep from kicking the little wretch, but he forbore the luxury, and said—

"Well, I must say that I have not noticed it; but still as you say so, I am bound to believe your word."

"That's what I like about you, always so straightforward. No humbug, you know. Mother—you know mother—nice woman, ain't she?—well, she's fond of you, too."

At this last announcement Jack Firebrace could not help laughing outright.

"Oh, it's a fact, though, and I can prove it to you, that I can. What do you say to that, eh?"

"Well, I have always thought that it was my misfortune to have incurred her displeasure."

"Not a bit of it. She is awfully fond of you."

Jack was not quite so sure about that, but at the same time he did not think it worth while to contradict Jim.

"Yes, you know, and what is stranger than all, she's roughest to those she likes best. But that is neither here nor there. Mr. Gruesome is very ill, and something has gone wrong with Sidney Morrison—he's a lively fellow, and would do well as an undertaker—and Mr. Pliant has tea with the boys. So mamma is going to let me ask one of the boys to tea with me in her room, and she told me she should like you, and I said I loved you; so come along, tea's all on the table.

"I'll soon be with you," said Jack.

And away danced Goblin Jim, looking the picture of evil.

"Now is the moment for action," thought Jack.

And he slipped into the dormitory, opened his box, and took out some lumps of stuff which looked like soda.

These he thrust into his pocket, and then scribbled a hasty letter, which he carefully sealed and addressed to Winifred.

Having completed these arrangements, he went out into the playground to old Flick, to whom he told the startling news.

"Going to tea with the Goblin! you don't mean it?" said Flick. "Why, what is up now? I hope they don't mean to poison you."

"I really do not know," replied Jack.

"Don't go, Jack—don't go. You may depend upon it that they mean you some mischief. You have not told me all that has happened, I know. You have been up to some of your games, and they have found you out, and now mean to kill you."

"Perhaps you are right," said Jack. "But I mean to have good evidence to lay before a magistrate before I have done. I must also find out what Grindwell knows of my parents. In the meantime I mean to have some fun. Where is the gunpowder you said you had?"

"Hidden under a loose stone in that old outhouse," replied Flick.

"All right; come along with me, and I will show you a little invention of my own, which I have called Nerve Startlers."

They entered the outhouse, and whilst Flick got the gunpowder from beneath the stone Jack produced a bundle of uncut goose-quills. He cut off the barrel or hollow part of the quills and filled them full of gunpowder, and then plugged up the open end with damp clay.

"This is all right," he said, as he put the "Nerve Startlers" into his pocket. "Now I have got my ammunition on board I am ready for the fight. Take this note, Flick; you see it is addressed to Miss Summerbell, and if anything should happen to me see that it is delivered into her hands; but if I return unhurt you must give it back to me unopened. Good-bye, old Flick!" he cried, as he wrung his friend's hand warmly—"Good-bye; we shall meet again."

"But, Jack, old man," cried Flick, "stay one moment; I wish to speak to you—don't leave a fellow like that."

All his cries were in vain. Jack hurried off and soon presented himself in Mrs. Drusilla Drysdale's room, where he found Goblin Jim.

"Welcome, Master Firebrace!" cried Mrs. Drysdale, who was making the tea, whilst Goblin Jim was toasting some muffins and crumpets—"or, rather, I should say Mr. Firebrace, for you look quite like a man, I do declare."

"You are very kind, I am sure, ma'am," said Jack, pretending to be rather nervous.

"There, there, sit down and make yourself happy. That is, if anyone can be happy in this house. Don't burn those muffins, Jim," said the old woman. "What a boy that is! If he ain't drawing his fingers over the top of the buttered toast and licking them afterwards. I never did see such a child!"

Drusilla Drysdale then hurried into a back room to fetch some article for the tea-table which she had forgotten.

Taking advantage of her absence, and Jim being engaged toasting the muffins, Jack carefully examined the teacups.

One cup was quite clean, another the same, but that which was nearest Mrs. Drysdale's chair had a little white powder in it.

Cautiously lifting the cup which held the white powder Jack emptied part of the poison into another cup, and then with the tip of his finger removed a few more grains, so that now two cups held a small quantity of poison, but not enough to kill anyone.

Then Jack took the liberty of putting the clean cup close by Mrs. Drusilla Drysdale's seat, and the poisoned ones where the others had stood, and it must be confessed he felt much more comfortable when he had completed this little arrangement.

Thrusting his hands into his pockets he commenced whistling softly, and lounged up to the fire as if to watch the toasting.

"I say, Jack, don't these things smell nice? Oh, crikey! ain't I hungry, just. Do make a good tea; eat as much as you can, for I don't think you will have many chances of having another like it—that I don't."

Jack could not help shuddering when he heard this, for it was said with such an air of fiendish delight.

"I have no doubt we shall all enjoy it," he replied; "I intend to make myself agreeable."

"Do, do; try to come out strong in the forgiving way," chuckled Jim.

This last observation seemed to please the Goblin so much that he had to turn away and cover his face with his hand so as to hide his laughter.

Jack seized this opportunity to drop his "Nerve Startlers" amongst the coals in the coal-scuttle.

"Look out, Jim! why, what the deuce are you after? you'll burn that muffin to pieces. Muffins were not meant to clean the bars of a kitchen grate with. What a fellow you are; you have made it as black as soot!" cried Jack.

"I can't help it—I can't help it. It is so jolly funny. Oh, my; I know I shall kill myself with laughing."

And dropping the toasting-fork Jim cast himself on the hearth-rug, and holding his sides rolled about screaming with laughter.

THE BOYS OF HAWKHOUSE SCHOOL.

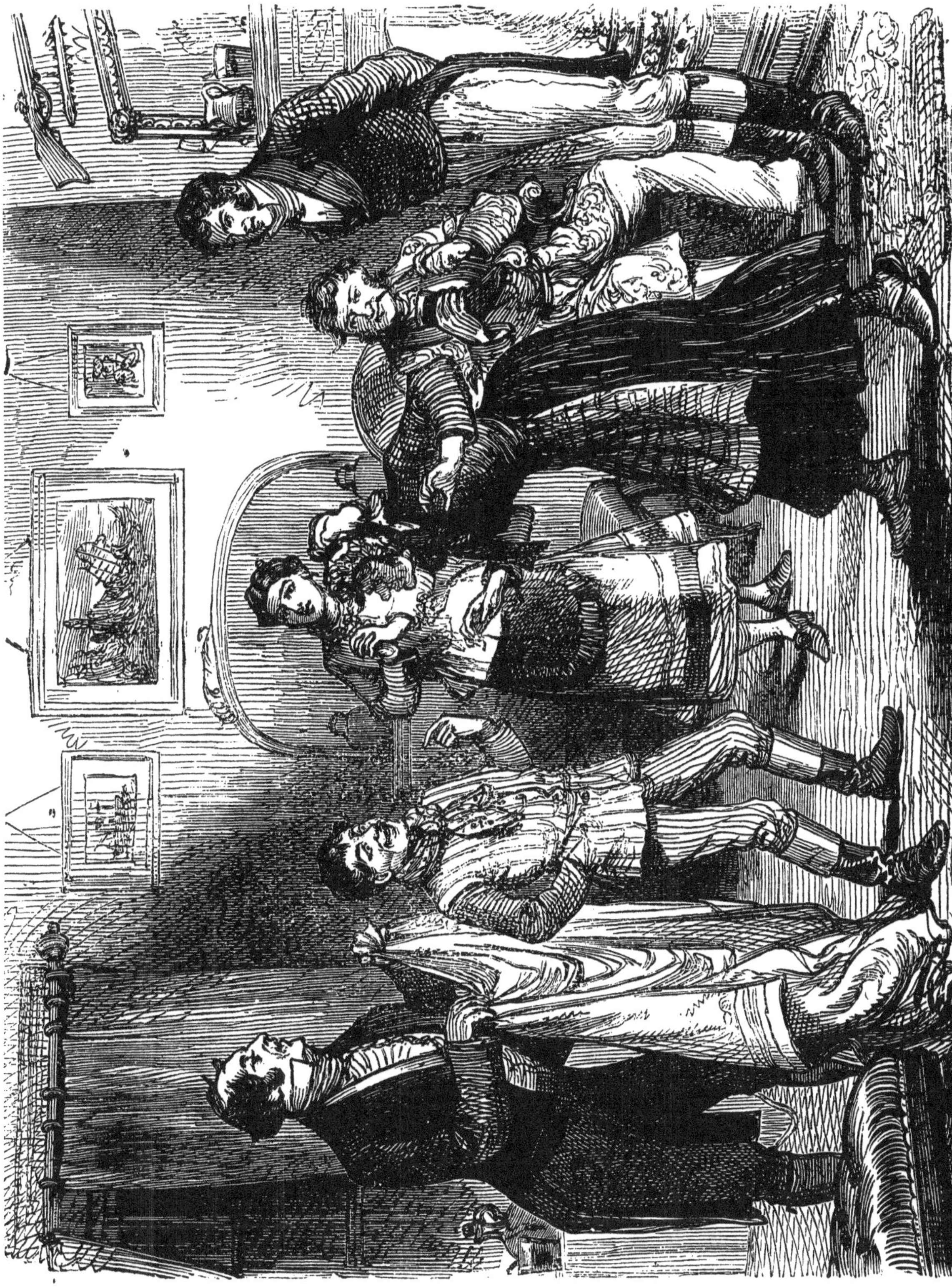

"THE DOCTOR TORE OFF THE BLANKET, AND BOB RACKSTRAW STOOD BEFORE THEM."

No. 7. **PRICE ONE HALFPENNY.**

[PUBLISHED EVERY MONDAY.]

Jack seized the toasting-fork and most likely would have dug it into the little wretch, so maddened was he to think that any human creature could rejoice at another being put to an untimely and painful death; but at that moment Mrs. Drusilla Drysdale hurried into the room, and, seizing the Goblin by the hair of his head, hauled him on to his feet.

"Leave off, can't you," shrieked Goblin Jim, striking and kicking at his parent; "what's up now? Can't yer leave a fellow alone?"

"Oh, you ungrateful little wretch! oh, you unmannerly little brute; to think of your behaving in this manner before a gentleman."

This seemed to make Jim more wild than ever, for he twisted about like an eel in his endeavours to escape.

"You must pardon him, Mr. Firebrace, you really must. It's the last time he shall have the honour of having tea with you—that I vow. And I always keep my word."

The last remark gave Goblin Jim another cause for mirth.

He held his stomach, and, doubling himself up, danced about the room laughing and screaming.

"Oh, don't!—oh, don't!—oh, don't! I can't stand it; you will be the death of me. I know you will—I know you will!"

The mother watched the fiend-like antics of her son with evident pride.

Then turning to Jack, said—

"He's such spirits, that boy 'as. I can't tell where he gets them from in this dreary house. Come, sit down, and let us have tea."

Jack bowed as he took his seat, accepted some muffin which the Goblin handed him, and then carefully watched the way in which Mrs. Drusilla Drysdale poured out the tea, for he naturally felt anxious as to which cup she would give him.

"Throw some coals on the fire, Jim," said Drusilla, as she poured a little tea into each cup.

"Thank goodness, she has not noticed that I have changed the cups," thought Jack.

The cups were soon filled, and, to our hero's delight, Mrs. Drysdale handed him the one without the powder.

"The murdering old cat," he thought "she would have given me the whole of the poison if she could."

"As I was saying," said Mrs. Drysdale, pouring her tea into the saucer, "as I was saying, this is a dreary house. You must excuse me taking tea in the kitchen, Mr. Firebrace" (this was a playful allusion to her drinking out of the saucer instead of the cup), "but my poor old lips can't stand the heat as they used to do, and I am that thirsty I could drink the sea dry."

"Oh, what a whopper you do tell, old woman!" roared Jim; "you know you always do drink out of the saucer."

Mrs. Drysdale glared spitefully at her son; then she renewed her conversation—

"As I was a-saying, this house is a dreary one. I know it makes my old bones shake with fear. Oh, them ghosts, they do so worrit me. Do you fear ghosts, Mr. Firebrace?"

"No, madam," replied Jack, quietly; "I have done no wrong, and therefore have no reason to fear them."

"Perhaps you do not believe in them?" said the old lady, glancing sharply at Jack.

"Pardon me, but I am rather superstitious. I believe in omens," replied our hero, gravely.

"Omens—omens!" exclaimed the old lady, "I don't know what they are. What are they?" demanded Drusilla.

"Warnings of impending death or misfortune, such as strange things flying out of the fireplace," answered Jack, who for some seconds had been watching the flames playing round one of the loaded quills.

"Don't believe in them," said Mrs. Drysdale, gulping down her tea and setting down the saucer.

Bang—whizz—whizz—flash—bang—bang!

Away went two of the quills right across the room, making a terrible smell.

"Lud a mussy! What is that?" cried Mrs. Drysdale, starting back so violently that she nearly upset the tea-things.

"I should think that was a warning—or an omen of someone's death," said Jack, solemnly.

Goblin Jim looked pale and frightened; however, he ran to where the quill had fallen and picked it up.

The question arose what was it, for it was so burned that no one could tell it was a quill.

"It's not a coal or cinder," said Goblin Jim, "and it smells just like burnt bones."

"Nonsense!" cried Jack, pretending to be awfully alarmed; "you don't mean to say that it is a dead man's bone? if so it means danger to you."

"What!" shrieked the Goblin, dropping the quill upon the floor in a great fright.

"A dead man's bone!" repeated our hero. "Let me look at it. I have read of them, but never seen one."

He picked up the burnt quill, examined it, and then, with a most tremendous sigh, laid it on the table.

"What is it?" demanded Mrs. Drusilla Drysdale. "What is it, I say?"

"It is a dead man's bone," replied Jack. "They say that when one of these fly out of the fire a murder or several murders have been done in the house, and for everyone which flies out after the first a death from unnatural causes, such as poison, is sure to follow. But I can't believe that it is true. Do you?"

"Certainly not," said Drusilla Drysdale; "certainly not. It is all a cartload of rubbish. Sit down to your teas."

Bang—whizz—whizz—whizz—flash! and another flew out right under Mrs. Drysdale's nose.

"Drat the thing; I wish they would not come so near to me," cried Mrs. Drysdale, evidently uneasy.

"It is another," said Jack, in a sepulchral voice. "That means a death to come. I—I don't feel comfortable."

"Do you feel sick, giddy, tongue hot, and a burning in the chest!" demanded the old crone, eagerly.

"The old beldame thinks the poison is at work," thought Jack, and then answered that he felt better.

"Oh!" said the hag, "I suppose these stupid things frightened you. Another death. Ah! I wonder who it will be?"

This speech proved so very comic to the Goblin that he nearly rolled off his chair with laughter; but his laughter was checked by a perfect shower of the "Nerve Startlers." A bundle of them having slipped over a falling coal and rolled into a red-hot hole, of course were discharged instantly.

"Murder!" shouted the Goblin, as some of the quills struck him on the head.

Mother and son gazed in horror at each other.

One death they could understand was likely to happen, but who were the others?

Of course Jack pretended to be as much frightened and astonished as anyone, and so well did he act his part that Drusilla Drysdale and Goblin Jim never suspected him of the trick for a single moment.

"What can this mean?" gasped the old hag, nervously; "more deaths them are! I do not understand it."

"I should think that a murder will be done," replied Jack, solemnly; "and that the officers of justice will discover the foul crime and bring the perpetrators thereof to the scaffold."

"Yah!" screamed Jim. "Mother, I—I don't feel well. I think I'll go and play—I—I don't care about stopping here. Oh, my, I've got such a pain!"

"Don't be a fool, Jim," cried Mrs. Drysdale, "stay where you are."

They resumed their seats, but neither Drusilla nor the Goblin seemed as cheerful as they had been.

However, Jack kept the conversation going by telling them the most dismal ghost stories he could remember, and his memory was a good one, whilst his knowledge of ghostly lore was of the greatest.

At last, he declared his ability to tell the future by the grounds in his tea-cup.

Mrs. Drysdale, who did not seem quite well, nervously invited him to make a trial, and our hero accepted the task.

In the first place he took Drusilla's cup and saucer, and having wiped the latter perfectly dry, commenced swinging the cup, which was not quite empty, round and round.

As he did this he managed to slip into the dry saucer a lump of the crystal (which we have before mentioned he had taken from his box), and which was a lump of the chemical * now used to make the toy known as Satan's tears, and which ignite directly they touch fluid.

He did this without either of the spectators seeing him.

Suddenly he turned the cup over into the saucer, when the tea touching the chemical, it at once ignited, and, of course, up went a perfect cloud of smoke from beneath the edge of the teacup.

"Oh, mother, something's wrong!" shouted the Goblin.

"Mercy on us! what is that?" screamed Drusilla Drysdale.

"I don't know!" exclaimed Jack, springing from the table as if in the greatest fright, and managing to upset table and tea-things with one shove.

Crash! crash!

"Oh, my! Help! Mother, mother! Help! I shall be crushed to pieces beneath the table!"

The voice was Goblin Jim's.

No sooner had he perceived the smoke from the tea-cup than he shrank away, and when Jack lifted the cup and he saw a blue flame burning in the midst of the tea, his courage left him entirely, and he sank down on the hearthrug, making sure that the Evil One was close at hand. So when Jack upset the table it went crashing on Goblin Jim's stomach.

Great was the confusion as they hauled the Goblin forth, and at the same time Mr. Pliant, followed by all the boys, rushed in to ascertain the cause of all the disturbance, having heard the outcries in the schoolroom.

There stood Goblin Jim, looking a very sick goblin indeed, for all the spirit was completely washed out of him.

"Help, help!" he cried. "I'm so sick. Oh, oh, oh! my stomach. My throat burns. Oh, mother! Help! something's wrong inside me."

But Mrs. Drusilla Drysdale was too ill even to attend to her own dear son.

"What on earth is the matter?" demanded Mr. Pliant. "Are you all tipsy, or what is it?"

"Oh, I shall die!" yelled Goblin Jim. "Oh, those dreadful dead-men's bones; we have taken the poison instead of—"

"Hold your tongue, you little fool!" screamed Mrs. Drysdale, who, poisoned as she was, still had her wits about her.

"What's the good of holding one's tongue when one is likely to die. Oh, oh, oh! I wish someone would fetch a doctor! it's all here, here!" and the Goblin placed his hand over his stomach.

"You—you—little fool!" cried Mrs. Drysdale, trying to keep down her anguish. "I think you must be—yah! Oh—dear—yah! I'm—oh—I—don't —know—I'm poisoned!" she screamed, at last. "We are poisoned by that— oh, my—imp of a boy."

And here she pointed straight at Jack Firebrace.

"Poisoned by Firebrace!" exclaimed the school, in alarm.

"It is false!" cried Jack.

But before he could utter another word he was clutched from behind, and, looking up, he beheld Grindwell and Sidney Morrison, who were both holding him a prisoner.

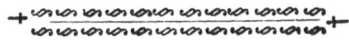

CHAPTER XXI.

WHAT HAPPENED ON THE SEABEACH AFTER GRIFFITHS GRINDWELL LEFT.

WE must now go back to the seashore and describe what happened there after Mr. Summerbell, Winny's father, had been so gallantly rescued, and how our hero escaped back to the Hawkhouse.

Of course everyone's attention was turned to Summerbell.

At last their endeavours were crowned with success.

"Father, do you not know me?" demanded Winifred, in tones of anguish.

* Sodium.

"My—my dear," said Dr. Lamberhurst, "you must not excite your father now. We must keep him quiet."

But Captain Summerbell had a different opinion, for as the doctor was pouring a little warm brandy and water into his mouth he caught the tumbler from him, drained off the contents, opened his eyes, smacked his lips, and sat up.

"Heaven be praised, then, it ain't a dream!" he exclaimed. "Then I'm not down in Davy Jones's locker?"

"Not a bit of it, my old friend; but tell us how this all happened."

"Heave to a moment; how many of my poor fellows are saved?" demanded Summerbell.

"Alas! my dear friend," said Dr. Lamberhurst, "I fear not one has escaped. You were saved by a miracle."

"Avast there; those sort of things don't turn nowadays. Winny, my lass, give me another kiss, my girl; and Firbank, old messmate, just mix me another glass of grog—the doctor's too liberal with the water."

"But, dearest father, will you not come home?" said Winifred, anxiously.

"All in good time, my lass, all in good time. But, truth to tell, my old hulk was so knocked about that I'm blest if I think I can move just at present. God help the poor creatures that have gone to the bottom, and may He bring the cruel wretches who misled us to justice."

"Misled you!" exclaimed those who were standing round; "misled you; why, what do you mean?"

"Why, I tell you that I saw false signals."

"Better not speak now," said Lieutenant Purvis, of the coastguard; "those things had better be thought well over before spoken. I don't believe a soul in this village would draw a ship on to the rocks, but when once she is on they might not be particular in helping themselves to any little article which happened to come ashore."

"You may believe what you like, sir," said old Summerbell, as, with the doctor and Captain Firbank, he rose to his feet; "you may believe just what you like, but I have another kind of story to tell, and as soon as you come up to the house you shall hear all about it.

My poor comrades are now sleeping beneath the deep. I had one man to avenge, now I have fifty; and I'll avenge them all, or die for it."

The old man held up his hand towards heaven, and shook it, as if invoking aid from above.

"Suddenly he paused, and passing his hand over his brow as if gathering his senses, he exclaimed—

"What a fool I am—an ungrateful fool! Where is the lad as saved me? Fancy my not thinking of him!"

"Never mind him," said Firbank; "thank goodness, he is all right. Yonder he is, seated in his blankets, with your daughter's servant attending on him. They shall follow us; come along."

"Come, papa, dear," said Winny, "I do not wish you to be ungrateful, but you see Sally is attending to the noble fellow."

Captain Firbank and the doctor assisted Mr. Summerbell and his daughter into the carriage, then sprang in themselves, and drove off rapidly in the direction of the Lone House.

Lieutenant Purvis, having told off some men to look after any wreckage that might come to shore, crossed to where the rescuer of Captain Summerbell was lying, still wrapped up in blankets, his head placed on the knees of Miss Sarah Scraggs, who was consoling him like she would a baby, even going so far as to lift up one end of the blanket to insert the neck of a bottle into his mouth—but the bottle contained something very much stronger than milk.

"Well, my lad, how are you now?" asked the lieutenant, as he knelt by the side of the youth.

"I'm a wee bit better than I was," gasped the youth; "but, oh! I'm so co-wo-old—so co-wo-old!"

"Poor fellow," said the lieutenant, kindly; "he is evidently a landsman, and has not been used to the sea; and yet how bravely he fought his way! It was a mercy either escaped—a miracle that they both did. Give him some brandy. He shivers as if he had got the ague."

The gentle Sarah raised the corner of the blanket and inserted the neck of the brandy bottle.

It was seized with avidity, and released with the most evident regret.

"Well, landsman or seaman," laughed Lieutenant Purvis, "he can take his grog pretty readily."

"Oh, wo-wo! I am so co-wo-old. I shiv-iv-iver and sha-a-a-ake like a aspen."

"A Cockney for a pound," muttered the lieutenant. "It is very strange that these Cockney lads always seem to have plenty of pluck and endurance. Let me have a look at you, my lad."

He endeavoured to lift up the blanket, but it was at once pulled down, and the face concealed.

"Why, what's the matter with you?" inquired Lieutenant Purvis. "You are not ashamed to show your face, are you?"

"N-n-n-o; but, oh! that awful sea. Booh! I can feel it now a-heaving all around. Oh! I feel so sick."

"Take some brandy, my boy," cried Sarah Scraggs, in a tone which she tried to render persuasive, at the same time administering a dose, which was at once accepted.

"Humph!" muttered the lieutenant to himself; "I doubt whether it was a case of pluck, after all. I rather fancy that he is only the cabin-boy, and I believe that he clung to Summerbell as much for help as he did for anything."

"Which I am ashamed on yer," cried Miss Sarah, who happened to overhear this speech. "Haven't you a heart in your breast, Mr. Purvis? Here is a feller-creature, more, a humane cretur" (Miss Sarah evidently thought these were two different and well-defined things), "as 'as been a-risking his own precious life to save a seafaring man, and you've the heart to say that he aint't done it on purpose. Oh! I hate such meanness! Take some brandy, my dear. Do now."

The distressed creature in the blanket took the medicine prescribed without a murmur; he rather seemed to like it.

"I don't want to say a word against him," laughed the lieutenant; "only I never saw a fellow alter his character so quickly in my life."

"And well he might change!" cried Sarah. "I know it made me creep all over; my back opened and shut, my heart leaped right into my mouth, and

my stomach turned completely over. Oh! I felt horrible, that I did."

"I should rather think you did," the lieutenant laughed. "You should go to the College of Surgeons; you would be one of the most wonderful specimens of the freaks of Nature ever shown. You should take my advice and go."

"I am much obleeged to you, sir," said Sarah, tossing her head; "but I ain't a-going to make a object of myself."

As she said this the youth in the blanket shook so tremendously that she had to administer another dose of brandy.

"Here, lads," cried the lieutenant to some of his men; "just hoist this poor fellow into yonder cart. Do not hurt him; he has done a noble action to-night, and he is ill, so treat him gently. This lady—I beg your pardon, this anatomical wonder—will accompany the gentleman, and I have not the slightest doubt will take care of him on the road.

"Now then, Polly," said one of the fellows, good-humouredly, as he gently shoved Sarah on one side, as that lady did not seem quite inclined to give up her charge; "now then, Polly, give us a wider berth."

"You impudent brute!" cried Sarah, giving the man a swinging box on the ear, "my name's not Polly."

"Polly or Molly—Sally or Sue," cried the man, rubbing his check, "you've got a jolly hard hand, and a large one."

It was remarkable how the blanket shook.

The ague was apparently getting worse and worse.

Again brandy seemed necessary, and again was it, like the proverbial smallest offerings, thankfully received.

"Come, my lass," said a grey-headed sailor, "we've the captain's orders to put this young fellow in the cart, and we must do it. So, fair actions if you please. I likes a woman when she behaves as sich, but when she's a wixen, why, I likes to have her teeth drawn, and I generally has my way. I beg your pardon. By your leave."

The old tar managed to give Sarah a sudden shove with his elbow, and over she rolled down the beach.

"Now then, lads," he said, "hoist the feller into the cart. She'll follow quick enough. To my thinking, the young chap is in more danger now than he ever was in his life. I'd as soon be drowned as marry that girl."

The youth in the blanket was as tenderly lifted off the ground and placed in the cart as if he had been attended on by gentle, tender-bred ladies instead of rough old sailors.

But all who have been to sea know the wondrous gentleness shown by all gallant seamen to the sick and wounded, be they friend or foe.

"Where is he! where is he!" exclaimed Sally Scraggs, picking herself up out of a heap of shingle. "They are a-killing of him; I know they are! Oh! where is he? His wounds will bust out a-fresh, and he hasn't any brandy when the ague fits come on again. Oh! you cruel wretches! If he dies of ague and cold you'll burn, and that's a comfort."

"He's all safe and sound. Come! jump in, will you," said the man who sat on the front of the cart, ready to drive off.

Miss Sarah Scraggs started and looked at the driver.

But the night was dark, and the man had a thick comforter round his throat and a slouched hat pulled down over his face, which he turned away from the sweet Sarah.

"Will anyone help me to get into this 'orrid vehicle?" exclaimed Sarah, looking at the cart, which was one of the kind generally used for carrying bricks.

"In course we will," said one of the sailors; "make haste. Now put one leg over the side of the cart; up you go, and—"

"What!" cried Sarah, in tones of offended modesty; "do you think me a hopera dancer or a hofficer of the horse marines? No, sir, never! There is the valliant rescuer of the father of my missus. He may die for want of a feminine woman's care. But I cannot help it. He may perish; all may perish; but I can't demean myself by behaving like a hofficer of the horse guards blue at the sound to mount. No! I will look at him, and leave him to die."

She leaned over the the side of the cart to draw aside the blanket, and gaze upon the man she felt she loved—nay, felt she adored.

Seeing her in this position one of the sailors removed his straw hat, and, putting his head down as a bull does when about to charge, ran at her, and, with a sudden jerk, much resembling that of the brute just mentioned, sent Miss Sarah Scraggs right into the cart.

"Drive on, mate!" shrieked the sailors, amidst a roar of laughter. "Drive on."

The man lashed his horse, and away they went, jerking and bumping over the heavy roads.

At every jolt poor Sarah set up a yell.

"Oh! wo—wo—wo-oh!" groaned the sick man. "I—yi—yi—yi—yi—yam so cold. Der—der—der—do give me some brandy."

"Oh! that I should have forgotten my own brave, galliant, devoted young man," cried Sarah, dropping the brandy-bottle from her fair lips and placing it to those of the youth. "Drink, dear, drink, and shake off the ague."

This last bit of advice seemed rather to bring on the ague fits, for the bottle rattled against the patient's teeth, and he drank so much brandy that he nearly choked himself, and had to be patted on the back by the gentle Sarah.

"My dear," whispered the sick man, directly he could recover his breath; "how can I repay you for this?"

"Don't ask me," giggled Sarah, pretending to hide her blushes, a most useless thing, for two reasons.

In the first place, there were no blushes to hide; and in the second, they were now in a road over which the trees hung so that they could not see each other's features, the night was so dark.

"I am not wealthy," continued the youth. "I have reasons to think my parents are noble. Until now I had but one object in life. Now I have two. One is to gain your 'and and 'art."

"Oh, sir, I feel I can't refuse so galliant a man, but you do take me by surprise. I've 'ad many a proposal afore — I might say hundreds, and not go beyond the truth."

Here the ague seized the unlucky fellow, and Sarah had to administer more brandy.

It composed him, and then she continued—

"But, before I pledge my word, I think it is but right that I should know what is your other object in life."

"You shall have it, my duck. I have wandered far and near to find a rascal called Collin Clout, whom I mean to kill."

Crash!

Down came the butt-end of the driver's whip, aimed at the head of the sick man, but, luckily for him, missing its mark, and, unluckily for Sarah, falling with a heavy blow upon her left shoulder.

She fell, howling with pain.

The horse started off at a furious rate, and up sprang the sick man.

At the same moment the driver clambered over into the cart, and grappled with the youth in the blankets.

Backwards and forwards they swayed, the cart rattling on, their teeth clenched, their eyes fixed on each other's face.

Even above the rattle of the cart could be heard the heavy breathing of these men struggling for life.

For a few seconds Sarah thought she would remain where she fell, at the bottom of the cart.

But she soon discovered that two people jumping about on her was not pleasant, and therefore determined to get up, which she did, and, as luck would have it, as she rose she seized upon the whip, which had fallen.

Clambering over the front of the cart she managed to get hold of the reins.

Then, flogging the horse as hard as she could, she drove him on towards the Lone House.

The next moment there was heard a deep, dull thud as the man who had once driven the cart rolled out into the road.

"Missed him!" muttered the strange sick man, "but it is not safe to jump out after him."

And the next moment after that reflection he dropped down to the bottom of the cart and curled himself up in his blankets, seemingly as ill as ever.

On flew the lovely Sarah, whipping her horse and screaming as she went.

At last she arrived at the Lone House.

Her screams brought a number of people to the door, and then—Miss Sarah Scraggs fainted.

"Lift them into the house," said Dr. Lamberhurst; "they are both ill. How that fellow loves to roll his blankets!"

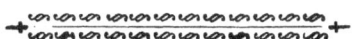

CHAPTER XXIII.

WHAT HAPPENED AT THE LONE HOUSE BEFORE THE ARRIVAL OF SALLY SCRAGGS— —THE CAPTAIN'S YARN.

On the carriage arriving at the Lone House, which happened some little time before Sally drove up in the cart, Mr. Summerbell was helped out, and after a pipe of tobacco and a good stiff glass of grog declared he was all right, and then he commenced to relate his adventures.

"D'ye see, my dear old friends, I fitted out my ship as part trader and part privateer—for I took out a letter of marque—and carried six eighteen-pound carronades and two long bow-chasers, besides a heavy swivel-gun amidships, and had a pretty good complement of men, now all gone to their

last account, and may the Lord have mercy upon them and take into account that they died doing there duty and try-to sweep from the seas a set of rascals who are at war with mankind."

The old man paused for a moment, and passing his hand over his eyes, dashed away a tear.

"Well, we put into Candia to repair some damages which we had received in a white squall, when I happened to hear the news that a ship called the 'Flying Fish' had had to put in there, and I learned that she was commanded by Matito of the Evil Eye—a one-eyed vagabond who had once served under the man whom I have sworn to hunt down—I mean Red Randulph.

"I found she had only started twenty-four hours before I arrived—that it was supposed she had run a cargo of black slaves to Turkey, and was now off on her way to Tunis for another.

"In twenty-four hours we were all ready—the decks kept as ready for action as we could, and every stitch of canvas was spread in hopes that we should overhaul the 'Flying Fish,' for we had not the slightest doubt she was a slaver.

"Well, away we went, with a fair wind and a flowing sea.

"At last, having met with dirty weather in the Bay of Biscay, we put into the little port of Beauvoir, behind the Island of Noirmoutiers.

"Here, to our joy, we heard that the 'Flying Fish' had been there.

"Off we set in pursuit, and got a glimpse of her just off the Scilly Islands. She evidently was signalling someone on shore, but on seeing us she spread her white wings and sped away as fast as she could, and we after her.

"Darkness prevented us continuing the chase, so we kept under easy sail, beating about in hopes that we might come across her by accident.

"I had just turned in for a few hours' nap when I was awakened by my mate reporting to me that there was a ship some few miles south making signals to the shore by rockets, and that someone on the shore was replying to them in the same way.

"Out I turned, and now I knew that the vessel must be the 'Flying Fish,' for this reason. The spot on the shore from which the replies came was a bleak promontory, with no human habitation within some miles of it.

"'Now, my lads,' I cried, 'I have them as sure as a gun.'

"To cut a long story short, we made all the sail we could; but she had gone, and, what was much the worst of it, she did not get the bad storm until some time after we did. Down came the blinding rain, whilst the wind shrieked through the shrouds as if it would blow the very hair off our heads.

"Of course we did not know how to steer to find her, for the night was as black as pitch, and they don't have the lights on the west coast of England like they do on the east coast.* So I beat out to sea, but still keeping a southerly course.

"Well, the wind grew so strong that one would have thought that the devil was out, bent upon mischief.

"I gave up the chase, and got all my sails close furled. For some hours all went well, when suddenly we heard the sound of guns.

"'That's some ship in distress,' said my mate to me. 'Where the deuce can she have got to?'

"'That's no ship in distress,' said I; 'you may be sure. That's our friend the "Flying Fish" fallen in with one of the king's cruisers,' and I put it to the men, and they one and all said they would run any risk sooner than remain idle, and so, perhaps, let the 'Flying Fish,' which they had been pursuing so long, escape.

"We heard the firing nearer and nearer, until it ceased suddenly.

"I guessed we were near about this point, but the night was dark and the sea running high, and the wind as we doubled, you know, put the shore on our lee-bow, so I was about standing out to sea again when I saw the light on a ship's masthead a good deal nearer the shore—ay, fully a couple of miles it seemed to us.

"There she rode steadily enough, pitching about to the waves, now reeling and dipping as the sea heeled her over; but she was evidently riding at anchor, for she did not go forward at all. So the mate and I argued that we had better make all the sail we could and get close to her, and there anchor for the night.

"On we came, steering right to the light. The night was too dark to let us see more than that, but the nearer we got the more we were certain that the light was that of a ship riding at anchor.

"Suddenly we heard the tolling of a bell—a deep-mouthed, clamorous bell.

"Our hearts grew sick, and the face of the bravest man on board turned white, for that moment the light went out.

"We knew we had been lured upon

---

* This observation still holds good, although the lighting of the coasts all round has greatly improved since the time of which we write.

the rocks by wreckers; each one felt that he had not an hour to live."

"Oh! dear, dear, father!" cried Winifred, throwing her arms round her father's neck and kissing him, "how terrible!"

"Ay, lass, it is terrible. The mate and I grasped each other's hand—one hard grip—not a word spoken; but we knew we wished each other all that one dying man can wish his fellow-victim.

"Sailors have no time to speak on such occasions, and that makes them so long telling about a storm on land.

"Of course, I gave orders that all should go well to work, shorten sail, and try to 'bout ship; but she missed her stays, and we went with a tremendous crash upon the rocks.

"Our men were washed down into the sea.

"Suddenly our ship split up, and I found myself buffeting with the waves. The rush of the waters revived me for a moment, and, as I rose to the surface, I felt myself clutched by the collar.

"I looked up.

"A flash of lightning made the whole scene as clear as day, and, by its light, I could see the face of the man who had hold of me. Who do you think it seemed to me?"

They all shook their heads, and leaned forward to hear what he might say.

Dropping his voice to a low whisper, he said, in earnest tones—

"It was my old friend Jack Falkland, who was murdered by Red Randulph!"

"Impossible!" cried the others. "The person who saved you was a mere lad."

"That may be. I only tell you that Jack Falkland had hold of me, and I know no more, for I became insensible again; but I am sure, if it were not my old friend Falkland, that it was his spirit who upheld me until help came. I take it as a warning that I am still to meet with Red Randulph and have my revenge!"

"That," said Captain Firbank, "you must know is absurd."

"I beg your pardon, sir, but I do not think that it is at all absurd," replied Summerbell. "I believe there are spirits, sir, who warn us of danger near at hand."

It was just at that moment Sally's screams were heard, and they at once rushed out and carried her and the blanketed figure into the parlour.

What happened after we reserve for another chapter.

CHAPTER XXIV.

SALLY TELLS HER STORY—ROB RACKSTRAW IN A NEW CHARACTER—THE PLOT—
MR. SUMMERBELL'S VOW OF VENGEANCE.

WHEN they had carried Miss Sarah Scraggs and her new sweetheart—her young hero, as she delighted to call him —into the parlour, they eagerly demanded to know what was the cause of all the outcry, and what had become of the driver of the cart.

"I don't know; I can't say!" cried Sally, bursting into a fit of tears. "It do seem hard, that it do, that a poor girl can't do an act of kindness but she must be hit about in this way. Ho, ho, ho! my poor head!"

"Ho, ho, ho!" groaned the man in the blanket.

"My good girl." said Captain Firbank, "do let us know what has happened? No one will injure you now."

"I know that, sir, and thank you kindly," said Sally; "but you must let me get my breath."

"Take a little drop of brandy, my dear, and see if that will do you good," said Dr. Lamberhurst.

"I don't mind if I do," replied the gentle Sarah.

And she evidently did not mind. Indeed, she liked it.

"Well, go on, my good girl; go on

with your tale," said the doctor, impatiently.

"Well, we were driving along, and I was nursing that young man's head, for he was very ill, and he asked me if I would marry him."

Here a most awful groan came from the blankets, making all start with surprise.

"Are you ill?" demanded Captain Firbank, anxiously, as he tried to uncover the man's face.

"I shall be better soon," murmured the man, keeping the blankets firmly down.

"Well, I was about to say that I would consider and consult my friends, for you know a young woman should be careful before she answers questions like that, for, though I must confess his beauty had touched my 'art, yet he was a stranger to me and I could not say 'Yes' at once."

"Decidedly not; but do go on, there is a good girl."

"Well, sir, then up sprang that vile wretch as was a-driving of us, and he hit a terrible blow with the handle of the whip at our heads, which was close together, and the blow falling on me, I fell to the bottom of the cart a-screaming like mad. Then up got the gentleman as was ill, and knocked the driver out of the cart. Then I seized the reins, and knew no more until we came up to the door.

"There is another mystery here," said Captain Firbank. "This sick man is strong enough to knock a fellow down, and yet we find him wrapped up in his blankets, unable to move and evidently wishful to hide his face."

"If he requires my aid I must see his face," said Dr. Lamberhurst.

"I—I—don't want your aid, doctor," stammered the poor fellow. "I am quite well, I thank you, doctor; and I hope you're the same."

"Nonsense, nonsense," said the doctor, kindly; "there can be no harm in my feeling your pulse. Put out your hand."

"I—I am quite well, I thank you. I don't like doctors, and I won't take physic. I'll go and sleep."

He jumped up, and was hurrying towards the door as well as he could for the long blanket, when the doctor caught hold of him.

"Not so fast, my good lad," he said; "we have had quite enough of mysteries to-night; and, if I am not much mistaken, you can clear up a good many of them. So off with that blanket, and let us have a good look at you."

As he spoke he tore off the blanket, and Rob Rackstraw, in all his native impudence, stood before them.

"Robert Rackstraw!" cried Wild Winny, clasping her hands, and then bursting out in a loud laugh.

"Robert Rackstraw!" cried Sally. "Oh, the deceitful monster! oh, the false little wretch! Let me get at him, that I may tear his eyes out. To think that I should have been silly enough to nurse him and to give him brandy—and such brandy, too. It is a disgrace, that's what it is. Don't wink at me, you impudent brute, don't."

"Don't be hot-tempered, Sally. Didn't you say that you loved me? and didn't you drink some of the brandy?"

"I wish it had been poison for your sake, that's what I do," cried Sally.

"Thank you for all your kind wishes," said Rob Rackstraw, coolly; "the same to you, and many on 'em."

"You—you—you atom—you thing—you low thing—I—I don't know what to call you."

And bursting into a tremendous fit of tears, the disappointed maiden buried her face in her hands.

Rackstraw looked hard at the doctor, then winked at the people assembled, and pointed with his thumb over his shoulder.

"She's a rum one, she is. Can turn on the water like one o'clock; and can't she spoon—oh, no! not at all."

"Come, Sarah," said Captain Firbank, sternly, "what is the meaning of this?"

"Well, sir, the truth to tell, I don't know myself. I am as much at sea as that gentleman was a little time ago."

Here she pointed to Captain Summerbell.

"Who is this fellow? What is he, and what does he want here?" demanded Mr. Summerbell, angrily, looking towards Rob.

"That young lady can tell you, sir, how I came here," replied Rob, quietly.

"I'm like the rest o' th' things in this here precious place. I'm a mystery, that's what I am. Anyways, I have done some good here."

"Come, come, my man," said Captain Firbank, sternly; "it's no good you trying to make out that you saved Captain Summerbell. The gallant fellow who did save the captain was given into your charge. Now, where is he?"

"Look here, sir," replied Rob, coolly; "I never *did* say that I saved Mr. Summerbell—who, I hope, is none the worse for his ducking."

"Not at all; but just tell me at once what has become of the young gentleman whom we left in your charge?"

"Well, now, that's the question I have been asking myself all the way along, and can't answer,'" said Rob, looking puzzled.

"Can't answer!" exclaimed Dr. Lamberhurst; "you surely don't mean to say you let him go?"

"No; oh, no! I didn't let him go; he vanished, went into air, or vapour, or melted away, or something."

"Good heavens!" cried Captain Summerbell, who, like all sailors, had a good deal of superstition; "it was the spirit of my dear old friend."

"Well, sir," said Rob, doubtfully, "I don't say that he was not a spirit. All I know is, he drank a lot of spirits; but just as I heard them shouting about you, when they recognised you, you know, sir, I only turned my head to see what the noise was, and when I turned round again the blanket was empty—he had gone!"

"Gone!" they all exclaimed, in the greatest surprise.

"That's just it," said Rob.

"There is some dark and evil game going on here," said Dr. Lamberhurst. "A mystery we must clear up."

"That's just what I said, sir," cried Rob, hitting the palm of his left hand with his right fist. "I'll find it out one way or another, cost whatever it may.'

Rackstraw's cool, calm, somewhat impudent way changed so suddenly to one of fierce determination that all were surprised.

"Wait one moment and I'll tell you in a few words, and what really did happen down yonder in the cart."

He walked quietly to the parlour door, opened it suddenly, and looked out.

Being perfectly satisfied that no one was in the passage listening, he closed the door gently and locked it.

Whilst this was going on the rest of the company remained silent, watching his movements in amazement.

All but Wild Winifred thought that the fellow had drunk too much.

She thought that he had suddenly gone mad.

Rob Rackstraw now walked close up to the table and put his fingers to his lips to warn them to be silent.

Then he put his hand into his coat-tail pocket and drew therefrom a pair of highly-polished steel handcuffs.

"Perhaps, gentlemen," said Rob, in a different, but still Cockney tone, "these will tell you what I am."

"You are a constable?" exclaimed Captain Firbank, in surprise, as he examined the handcuffs.

"Right you are, sir. All the way from Bow Street, London. I'm down here on some special business. Private business."

"That we can easily imagine," said Dr. Lamberhurst. "But it is not quite so easy to see why you have come to us."

"Well, I have my reasons. I know there are some queer characters about this part. So as a groom's disguise is as good as any, and as I saw that I could watch as well from this house as any other, I determined to take service with this young lady, and I flatter myself that I have made a regular good servant; but you know best about that, miss."

"I am quite satisfied," laughed Wild Winny. "There could not be a better groom."

"Thank you, miss. Well, when I saw that the lad who had saved Mr. Summerbell had hooked it, I says to myself— 'There is a game up here.' So what do I do but slip into the vanished fellow's place, and act his part just to see if anything would turn up. I had not been long there before one or two queer-looking men came up and tried to get a peep at my mug; but I would not let them."

"I suppose not," laughed Captain Firbank. "But pray make haste with your story."

"Well, to cut a long story short, Miss Sally Scraggs came up and began hugging me about so—beg pardon, miss, for mentioning it before you—but she did, calling me her hero, though why hers I can't tell. Well, when I was put into the cart all went well; but I kept an eye on the driver, whom I believed to be a fellow who goes by the name of Collin Clout down here, but whom I believe to be no other than Slimy Samuel, a party I've been looking for. Well, as we went jogging along, spoonying and drinking the brandy, I caught sight of our friend the driver listening, and so I says to Sally—

"'Sally, I have wandered far and near to find out a rascal called Collin Clout, whom I mean to kill.'

"I had scarcely said the words when down came the butt-end of the driver's whip on Sally. My beautiful Sally had shielded me without knowing it. Of course I knew at once that I had my man to deal with, and up I sprang. He was too quick, though, and before I could get hold of him he rolled out of the cart; but I know I disfigured his mug for him."

"And this man Clout, what do you think he is guilty of?" demanded Dr. Lamberhurst.

"All kinds of things. He is in league with forgers. He is a receiver of stolen goods. I don't know what he is; but I can tell you what he is not—and that's virtuous. Now, gentlemen, as I said before, I am down here on business, and I think I can help you and you can help me. The forgeries have something to do with that old brute, Griffiths Grindwell; of that we are sure. For my own part, I put it down that this Hawkhouse School is only a blind, and that we shall find a very different game is being carried on to what we think."

"And in which way can we assist you?" demanded Mr. Summerbell.

"Oh, in many," said Rob.

"Well, explain."

"At present, keep quite quiet; let me remain here as your servant and muzzle the gentle Sally. She's very lovely, but she's like a great sea-serpent—a little of her goes a long way," replied Rob.

"Well, we will do what we can," laughed Dr. Lamberhurst; "but you know it is not so easy to muzzle a woman."

"Oh, I don't mean to muzzle her so that she sha'n't make love to me. I rather like that. What I mean is, arrange that she shall not be able to meet this Slimy Samuel, or Collin Clout. If she does that I know the fellow will soon make her his spy, and we shall be watched inside the house and out."

"And what are we to do in the meantime?" demanded Captain Firbank. "We can't be idle!"

"If you don't mind putting yourself under my charge I think I can make you all useful. Don't quarrel, but appear more friendly to Grindwell. If you really want to deceive an enemy become his friend, or if your enemy happens to be a woman make love to her, only don't marry her, or you'll get the worst of it."

"You are a perfect philosopher," the doctor laughed.

"I ought to be, sir. I have had a great deal of misfortune in my life, and that's a good schoolmaster."

"Well, we are all agreed to do as you wish," cried Captain Firbank. "We will call on Griffiths Grindwell tomorrow."

"You may, I will not!" Summerbell said, springing to his feet. "Never will I cross that man's threshold as a friend. When I enter his door it shall be to drag him to justice. He shall have no loophole for escape—no chance of his life. I will have no secret enmity with Grindwell. I hate him. Mine shall be a fair and open fight. I declare solemnly that I believe Griffiths Grindwell lured me on to this shore for the purpose of wrecking me! I believe that it was the spirit of my friend—my murdered friend Falkland—that saved me, and never will I cease from my task of vengeance until I have brought these murderers to justice.

"Griffiths Grindwell refused to help me, and yet he knew that Falkland, his wife, and baby were murdered. My mission is from Heaven, and by its hand alone will I be guided."

CHAPTER XXV.

JACK FIREBRACE IS MADE A PRISONER AND CONDUCTED TO THE WIZARD'S TOWER—
HE RECEIVES A TIMELY WARNING—MR. GRINDWELL OFFERS TO RELEASE JACK—
JACK PREFERS STAYING IN THE WIZARD'S TOWER.

WE left our hero, as the reader will doubtless remember, under the accusation of having poisoned Goblin Jim and Mrs. Drusilla Drysdale, who were suffering great pain from the effects of the drug they intended administering to our hero.

"I can't make this out," said Mr. Pliant. "Certainly these two people seem as if they had taken poison."

"I fear they have," replied Jack, quietly. "I think you had better send for the doctor."

"Dear me; you take the matter very coolly," said Pliant. "But perhaps that had better be done."

"In the meantime," said Sidney Morrison, "Mr. Firebrace must go back to his prison."

"Don't put him—oh! my stomach—in the same place—oh—as he was in before!" groaned Goblin Jim. "He can escape—oh!—out of that, you know—oh! It's my belief that he is in league with the devil! Oh! my stomach—oh!"

"That is true; he did escape," said Sidney Morrison. "Where, then, can we put him?"

"Oh, I know!" groaned Goblin Jim, who, in the midst of his pain, still could bring his evil little wits to work cruelly. "I know where to put him—the Wizard's Tower! There he cannot escape. Oh, oh, oh! How I burn! How I burn! Oh! my stomach."

"Let Firebrace be taken to the Wizard's Tower at once!" cried Sidney Morrison.

And in an instant our hero was taken away to the Wizard's Tower, the very name of which made the other lads' blood run cold.

It was a small tower, built just over the spot where the old chapel stood (which we mentioned in our first chapter).

The story of murder connected with this old tower was certainly one not calculated to make a prisoner there feel comfortable.

Jack knew the dreadful repute of the tower, and it must be said that he did not like his prison.

However, as he could not banish the fact altogether from his memory, he tried to laugh at the story.

"Hulloa, what is this?" he muttered, suddenly, as he tapped with his knuckles upon the wainscot. "I'm hanged if this ain't hollow!"

As he tapped, a strange, grating noise was heard behind the panel, and the next instant it flew back, disclosing the features of Peter Pigwellan.

"Why, Peter!" cried Jack, delighted at seeing his old friend again, "I feared you were drowned."

"There's no fear of that," Pigwellan said, with a bitter laugh. "When my boat turned over in the surf I clung to it, and was carried round into the next bay. I called to you to do the same, but you did not hear me. Still, I knew that you would be saved. I knew it, for heaven has work for you to do. By your hand alone must justice fall upon Red Randulph. Ah! what am I doing?" he exclaimed, stamping with impatience. "Here am I wasting my time, when every moment is precious. Mr. Firebrace, your death is determined upon. I am here to warn you."

"What is their scheme?" asked our hero. "It shall go hard if I do not frustrate it."

"This evening, the 'Flying Fish' will come up to the bay. The 'Wasp' has missed her, so she is not in danger."

"I am sorry to hear it," said Jack; "but I should have thought that, after the other night's adventure, the coast-guardsmen would have kept a better watch."

"They will keep out to sea," replied Peter. "A boat with some armed men will be sent into the cave behind the rock on which my hut stands. You will presently be released from this prison. You will find Mr. Grindwell will profess to be sorry that you should have been so wrongfully treated. All those who have annoyed you will be reprimanded by him. He will give you a note to bring down to me. As soon as you are on the beach the men from the schooner will bind you, throw you into their boat, and take you on board the 'Flying Fish.' I dare not think what fate will meet you there."

"Hush! I hear someone coming," said Jack.

"Yes; your foes come. Be bold; be firm. Remember yours is the cause of right, and you must succeed."

With a wave of the hand, Peter Pigwellan drew back, and the panel closed.

A few seconds afterwards the key turned in the lock of Jack's prison; the door opened, and Griffiths Grindwell entered.

"Jack," he exclaimed, "I am sorry to find you here still. I have made inquiries into the case, and I have discovered that it was all the fault of that stupid old housekeeper. She put some mixture into the tea with the idea of drawing out the strength, and took an extra dose. Hence the fearful pains she and her son have suffered."

"I am glad to hear that the truth has been found out," replied Jack; "but it it is strange that it did not affect me."

"As you say, it is strange—very strange," replied Grindwell, in some confusion. "But you are evidently of a strong constitution."

Griffiths Grindwell then advanced to the window and looked out to sea.

"The ship does not come in sight," he muttered to himself, "and I have sworn that it shall be done to-night."

Jack watched him carefully.

"Come," said Grindwell, suddenly, "you must not stay here. They say that this old house is haunted, and I will freely confess that I would not pass a night in that room for a hundred pounds."

"There is some game up here," our hero thought. "The ship has not arrived, I see. Now he wants to get me to some other room. I must stay here.

"The truth is, sir," said Jack, "I have heard the history of this old place, and I agree with you, if a ghost is to be found anywhere, it must be here. I, therefore, should like to spend a night here."

"Have you no fear of ghosts?" demanded Griffiths Grindwell, in a low voice.

"No. I have seen things which other people have called supernatural, but if they were I was not at all frightened. So I should like to stay here."

"So be it," said Grindwell, with a grim smile; "but remember this—if you remain here it will have to be as a prisoner. For many years that door has never been unlocked of a night, and I will not permit it to be so now. You will have some provisions sent you, but the doors will be locked. Be warned in time. It would be useless to call for help from here, and it is said that the evil spirit of this tower has torn to pieces many people who have ventured to sleep in this chamber. Now, what will you do?"

"I will remain here," said Jack, boldly.

"Be it as you will," said Griffiths Grindwell, with a sharp glance of hatred at our hero, "but, mark me—whatever happens to you no blame can attach to me."

He left the room and locked the door, but soon returned with a basket containing cold meat, bread, and a large bottle of brandy.

These he put before our hero on a table, and then walked quickly to the window and gazed impatiently out to sea.

"Confusion!" he muttered; "where can Martin Malochi be? He was not wont to play me such tricks as these."

Then turning to the table, he said—

"There; eat and drink well. I have done all I can for you. Perhaps I ought to insist upon your not staying here; but I like courage, and therefore shall let you have your own way. Good-night."

"Good-night," replied Jack.

And the door closed.

Our hero could not help shuddering as it did so, for a sort of chill seemed to blow in from the sea on him, whilst the night wind whispered—

"Alone, alone, alone in the haunted tower!"

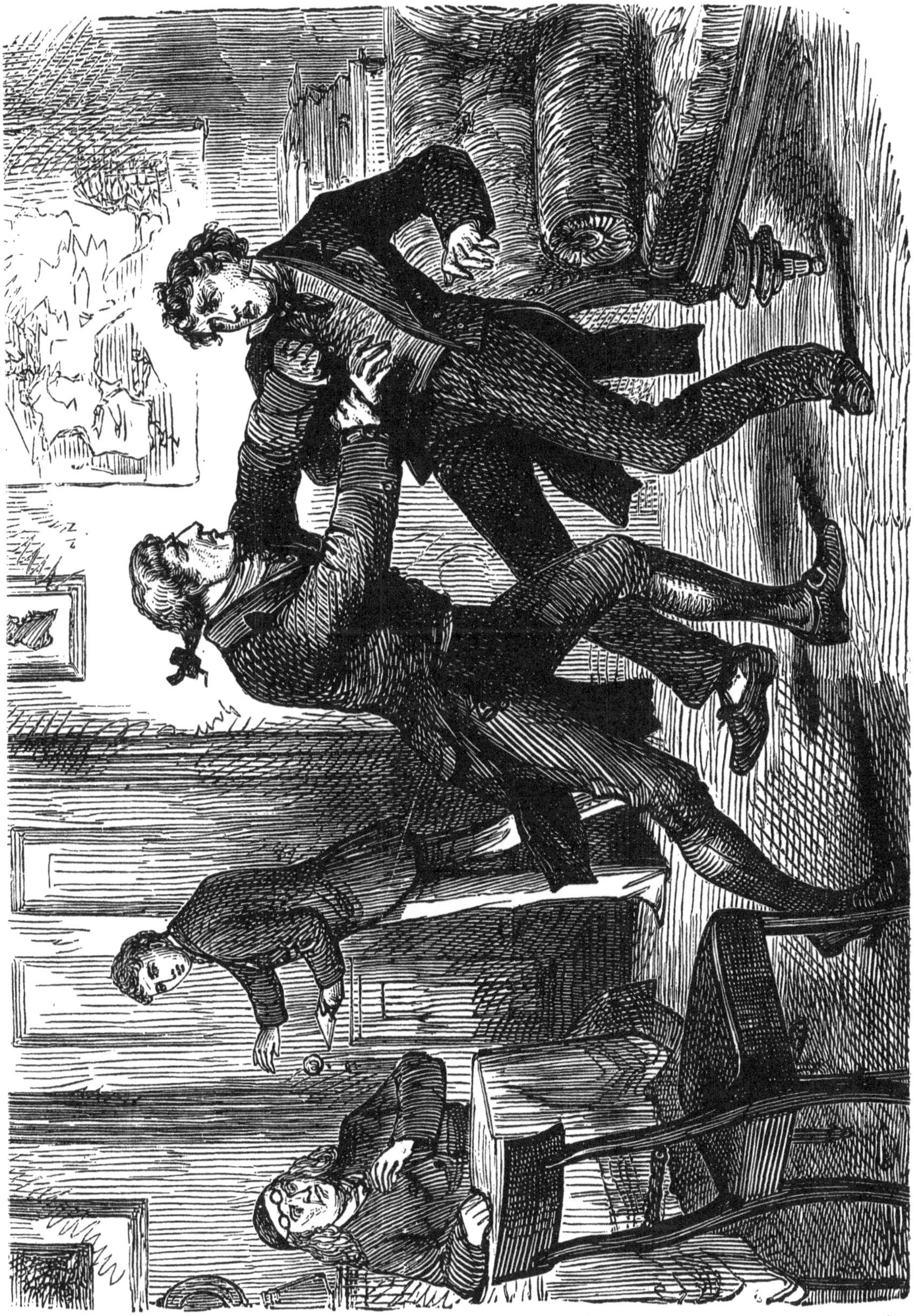

“‘SILENCE!’ EXCLAIMED GRINDWELL AS HE FORCED THE YOUNG MAN BACK.”

No. 8.

PRICE ONE HALFPENNY.

[PUBLISHED EVERY MONDAY.]

CHAPTER XXVI.

WHAT HAPPENED IN THE WIZARD'S TOWER—THE SPECTRE—THE DEADLY BLOW—
SPIRITS VERSUS GHOSTS—BLOW FOR BLOW—A TERRIBLE LEAP.

"THEY cannot have doctored the meat and the bread," thought Jack, when he was alone, "so I will have a good feed to start with."

Jack was a true boy of England, and preferred to fight upon a full stomach to an empty one.

He turned his attention to the bottle, out of which he took a very modest sip; but even that nearly choked him.

"I don't like that," he muttered; "besides, if I did, I dare not drink it. I want all my wits about me to-night. Now to have a look round again. I wish Pigwellan had showed me the secret of the panel. Stay! he said it would lead me to death. I understand now. Whoever these fellows are who are against me, they guard that passage. If they attack me it is by that way they will come."

He walked to the window and gazed out at the sea, and marked the position of the tower.

It was perched up on the top of the old grey cliff, and seemed, as the wind shook it, about to topple into the sea below every minute.

The sea-bird's plaintive cry sounded in the night air, proclaiming the coming tempest, and the bats came dropping down from the oak beams of the roof, where they had clung all the day, dozing the sunny hours away, so as to be ready to flit about at night.

"I don't half like this now I am here," said Jack, as the bats flashed past his face. "The more I think of old Grindwell's look at me, the more I am convinced that he has hit upon some different plan to that which Peter told me about. I must keep on my guard. I wish I could find some weapon."

He looked about, and noticed an old rickety oak table standing in a dark corner.

"He soon wrenched a leg off it, and, to his joy, found it made a capital club.

"So that is meant for my bed," he said, as he looked at an old worm-eaten couch. "It was very kind of them to think of me in that way, but I most decidedly shall not use it. I know what I will do, though," he cried, suddenly.

As he spoke he stripped off his coat boots, and cap.

"Now for it!" he cried.

Then he collected all the old ragged cushions out of the chairs and couches so as to stuff the coat in order that it might appear as if it had a body inside it. This he laid down on the couch, and covered it over carefully with the blankets, and being away from the window, in one of the most gloomy corners of the room, it would have deceived the most sharp-sighted person.

Having done this, Jack coiled himself up under the large table in the centre of the room, and soon was asleep.

The great clock of Hawkhouse had tolled out the midnight hour when our hero awoke.

He could not have told what had awakened him, but he awoke with a feeling that something of evil was near.

A strange unearthly light shone over the floor, and seemed to come from the secret panel.

Jack peeped up and beheld a tall man with a long black beard, dressed in a long black flowing robe, round the borders of which were worked strange hieroglyphics.

Presently he glided towards the table and peeped over towards the couch whereon was the counterfeit Jack.

The stranger evidently required something to give him fresh courage, for he stretched forth his hand, seized the brandy bottle, and smelt it.

The scent seemed to agree with the ghost, for after another good smell he took a deep draught.

"Ha!" he whispered, softly; "that is the real good sort—just the thing I like. But business first, pleasure afterwards."

He was about to put the bottle back on the table, but could not withstand the temptation of another pull.

And it was a pull; Jack began to think that he would never leave off, he was such a time at it.

But at last the ghost put down the bottle, and hiccoughed most violently.

"Very—hic—good brandy. I'll first finish the young gentleman, and then I'll finish the drink."

The fellow advanced on tip-toe to the bed—no easy matter for him to do in his state—then drawing a long knife, plunged it several times into the stuffed coat, which luckily Jack Firebrace had put in his sleeping-place.

Jack gave two dismal groans and then a deep sigh.

"Ah," said the fellow, "I think I have done for him now, so I will drink his very good health."

Once more the bottle was glued to the would-be murderer's lips, and he drank a deep draught.

Jack crawled towards the secret panel, determined to venture trying to make his escape that way, for he dreaded that the fellow might go back to the couch, and, discovering his mistake, rectify it in a manner anything but pleasant to our hero.

He was close to the door when he heard the man put down the bottle, at the same time exclaiming, with a drunken sigh—

"Empty, quite empty. Like—hic—the other pleasures of this life, it didn't last long—hic. Now I think I'll go."

Jack laid himself flat on the ground as the fellow reeled towards him, but he soon perceived that the man rolled so from side to side from the effects of the drink that he would be safe to kick against him.

It would have been useless for Jack to have sprung up and tried a fair fight, for the fellow was a brawny, muscular man, and, although overtaken with drink, was probably accustomed to brawls, and most likely at the first blow he would be able to pull himself together, as the saying is, and wresting the stick from our hero, perhaps kill him with it.

These thoughts flashed through our hero's mind as quick as lightning, and he at once determined how to act.

Still keeping stretched on the ground, Jack just raised his head so that he might place his right hand, which held the oaken stick, in such a manner that he could make a sweeping blow with it.

The man advanced, steadying himself as well as he could by the furniture.

He was now within a couple of feet of Jack, who, collecting all his strength, swept his club round, delivering a most awful cut across the ghost's shins.

A frightful yell arose, and the pretended ghost rolled over on to the floor, kicking and screaming with agony.

Jack sprang up, and made a dash towards the secret panel.

But to his horror he found it closed!

"I'm in for it now," thought Jack. "There can be no way for me to escape from this wretch; so I'll fight to the last."

But at this moment the man looked up and happened to see Jack by the ghastly light of the brazier, which was fast sinking.

"Help! help!" he yelled, in abject terror. "It is the boy's ghost. Mercy, mercy!"

Jack at once saw that the man had taken him for a spirit, and determined, if possible, to keep him to that idea.

"Cruel murderer!" cried Jack; "henceforth you shall never be alone. My spirit shall haunt you for this foul crime."

Stretching out his arm Jack advanced towards the man, who, in abject fear, retreated from him.

"Come!" cried Jack, stretching out his arms as if to embrace the fellow. "Come! I will bear thee away to the grave!"

For a moment the man stood petrified with horror, and then, with one bound, sprang on to the ledge of the window.

"Come back! come back!" screamed Jack, now thoroughly alarmed, "I am not dead! I am no ghost!"

It was too late!

The man was not only drunk from the brandy, but the liquid had been drugged.

This, added to the fright which he had received, drove him raving mad.

He turned round and faced our hero, who, in his turn, started back in horror as he beheld the man's terrible, demoniacal look.

The fellow threw his arms up into the air, burst out into a wild scream of laughter, and sprang out into the night.

Jack rushed forward.

But nothing was to be heard save the roar of the sea as it dashed against the foot of the cliff, and the shrill scream of the tempest as it rushed round the tower.

Jack reeled away from the window and fell senseless upon the floor.

CHAPTER XXVII.

JACK ASTONISHES GRIFFITHS GRINDWELL—AN OFFER OF FRIENDSHIP—THE LETTER —GOBLIN JIM IS TOO CLEVER BY HALF.

It was just the break of dawn as Jack awoke from his stupor and gazed slowly around him.

At first he thought that all that had happened must be a hideous dream, but he found that the dummy figure had been stabbed over and over again.

So there could be no doubt that it was intended he should be murdered.

"Well, it was not my fault," he said. "I only pray that Heaven may have mercy upon his soul."

He hastily put the cushions back in their places, slipped on his coat, cap, and boots, and removed all marks of any person having been in the room save himself.

This done, he went to the window and tried to see if the body were on the sands.

The tide was out.

The golden sands, ribbed by the ripple of the receding waves, lay stretched beneath him.

He gazed at the rough stones at the foot of the cliff, but could see no trace of the man.

Could he have escaped?

No.

The sea must have swept him away.

Jack sighed as he thought of the man's terrible death, and then gazed out to sea.

There in the bay, with her sails all snugly furled, was the "Flying Fish," and a boatful of men was pulling from her towards the shore.

"So," thought Jack, "I am only out of one danger to get into another. Well, come what will, I will never give way."

He threw himself carelessly on the couch, taking care to have his oak stick, or rather leg of a table, near him.

Presently he heard footsteps coming along the passage.

The key turned in the lock.

The door opened, and Grindwell peeped in.

At first he thought that Jack had been killed, and that it was his dead body stretched on the couch.

"Confound that fool, Bill!" he muttered. "I told him to remove it so that I could give out that the boy had made his escape; and now—great heaven! what is this?"

The last exclamation was caused by Jack springing up, yawning violently, and looking fixedly at Grindwell.

"Oh, how early you have awakened me!" cried Jack, stretching himself; "I feel much like the young gentleman in Dr. Watts's beautiful poem, 'You've awaked me too soon, I must slumber again!' It was a nasty night, very!"

Griffiths Grindwell looked confused, and did not know how to answer the lad.

Jack saw this, and determined that he would puzzle the wretch as much as he could.

"You don't look well, Mr. Grindwell," he said. "I trust that you slept well last night?"

"Yes—yes—I slept well—very well last night—but you—you in this terrible chamber; how did you sleep?"

"Pretty well, I thank you; but the rats and the mice they made a terrible noise. Some actually bit my clothes."

Griffiths Grindwell took up the brandy bottle, and examined it by the light of the window.

It was empty.

By the expression of his face as he put it back on the table, Jack knew it had been poisoned.

"And did you drink all that brandy?" demanded Griffiths, looking very red.

"Who else is there to drink it?" laughed Jack. "The rats may have had some for all I know. But I certainly won't stop another night here!"

"No, that you shall not!" replied Griffiths Grindwell; "to that I pledge my word."

As he spoke he took up some of the things on the table to examine them, and Jack noticed that his hand trembled.

"Did—did you not see anything at all? I mean, did you not see the spirit of the Wizard?"

"I saw something, but who or what it was I don't know. It made several stabs at this couch. Why, I do declare, my coat has been stabbed through and through. This is most strange. Do you understand it?"

Griffiths Grindwell stepped forward, and, with trembling hands and eager eye, examined the coat.

There could be no mistake in those cuts. He knew the style too well to doubt that; they were stabs!

"Did—did you not feel these stabs?" he demanded. "Are you not wounded?"

"No, I did not feel them in the least. I have not a scratch upon me. Those ghosts don't hit hard, they say."

"But what became of the man—I mean the ghost—after he had stabbed at you?"

"I don't know where he went to!" replied Jack; "I only know that he disappeared suddenly."

Jack said this so innocently that Griffiths Grindwell was overcome with astonishment.

"The boy must be more than mortal!" he muttered. "No man could have drunk that brandy and lived!"

"I think I have rather astonished him!" thought Jack. "Fortune favours me, so I shall fight on to the last."

"Well, Mr. Firebrace," said Griffiths Grindwell, "you must certainly be praised for your courage. I have met many bold men in my time, but I don't think many of them would have cared to pass such a night in such a place. You are growing too big for school, Firebrace," he continued, as he clapped the lad upon the shoulder; "you should go to sea, and have a crew of brave fellows under you who obey your slightest order. 'Tis grand to stand on the quarter-deck of your vessel, and feel that you are master of the ship and all on board of her.

"To see, as the orders fall from your lips, the white sails flutter down from the yards, then swell out to catch the breeze—the vessel heels slightly over, and away she bounds trembling from stem to stern, riding the waves like a thing of life. Or, in the hour of battle, when the ship belches forth her deadly fire, the cannon-balls crash into our bulwarks, sending the splinters in shivers both far and near, down goes the mizen-mast; but what care we? We are yard-arm to yard-arm with our foe! The order is given, 'All hands on deck to board,' and with a ringing cheer we spring up the shrouds, and like a swarm of locusts pour on to the enemy's decks. Then comes the soul-stirring word, 'Victory!' You are the conqueror! as you stand upon the quarter-deck, which, but a few minutes before, was your enemy's."

In speaking Griffiths Grindwell had quite forgotten the oily London merchant, and had become once more Richard Randulph, the privateer.

"Tell me, Jack," he said, suddenly remembering that he was not on board his own ship, "tell me, is that not a glorious picture?"

"Yes and no," replied Jack, in stern tones; "yes, if the ship you command is an honest merchantman, or better still a man-of-war, and the enemy you conquer is an outlaw, for such sea-devils deserve no mercy. If it be the pirate who gains the victory I would sooner be the conquered, and would prefer death to suing for mercy from such a base wretch. To such a demon, the more he triumphs the deeper is his disgrace. What creates admiration and love in another man causes hatred and contempt in him."

"How!" cried Griffiths Grindwell, pale with passion, and stepping forward, as if to strike the boy; "dare you tell me this?"

"And why not?" replied our hero. "What can a respectable London merchant have to do with such villains as I spoke of? Nothing; besides, so good and kind a man as you are can surely never excuse these fierce murders."

"No, no, of course not," exclaimed

Grindwell, hastily. "Still, I fancied that you loved the sea."

"Of course I do; only," here Jack sighed, "I am always in a scrape. Ah, and what is more, I am charged with many things I do not do. For instance, why should I try to poison Mrs. Drusilla Drysdale and her beastly little imp of a son?"

"Yes, yes; there have been a great many mistakes happen of late," said Grindwell, with a sneer; "but trust me, they shall not happen again. For the future I will be certain—quite certain."

"Thank you for nothing," thought Jack.

"Come, come; we will now breakfast," said Grindwell. "When the meal is over you shall take a letter from me to old Pigwellan, the deformed boatman. You shall go to sea one day, and in the meantime Pigwellan shall take you out in his boat and teach you how to sail and steer. Come, I will make something of you before I have done."

Jack followed Mr. Grindwell at once, but he felt that a plot far deeper than all the rest was laid against his life.

The breakfast passed off very slowly indeed. Grindwell asked just a few questions about the adventures of the night; Mr. Gruesome nibbled his crisp toast as if he were munching the dried bones of dead men, while Mrs. Drusilla Drysdale glared horridly at Jack.

Mr. Sidney Morrison, pale and haggard, sat silent at the table, neither eating nor drinking, but with hollow eyes glaring at our hero, not unkindly, but with a look of wonder and horror.

"One could almost fancy one was having breakfast with a lot of departed spirits," thought Jack; "this is deadly-lively."

Breakfast done, Mr. Griffiths Grindwell wrote a letter, which he intrusted to Jack, at the same time saying—

"There, take that to old Peter, and tell him to come here at once. You shall have some fine sails on the sea."

He was about to leave the room when Mr. Sidney Morrison sprang up and cried, in an agitated voice—

"Stop!"

"What do you mean?" exclaimed Mr Grindwell, as he grasped the usher by the arm.

"Have you no mercy? Think before you commit this."

"Silence, I say!" cried Grindwell, as he forced the unlucky young man back into his seat; "your madness will carry you too far one day. Will nothing but a lunatic asylum suit you, or," he muttered, "must I hand you to the gallows?"

With a deep groan Mr. Morrison fell back on the sofa, gasping forth in weak tones—

"Mercy! oh, mercy!"

Taking advantage of the confusion, Jack slipped out of the room with the letter.

"Here I am," he thought, "in another trap, and how I am to get out of it I do not know."

He had just put on his cap, and was making his way to the door, when he heard the shrill voice of Goblin Jim calling to him.

"Halloa, Firebrace! where are you off to? I thought you were to be kept a prisoner in the Wizard's Tower?" he cried.

"You see you are wrong, Master Jim," laughed Jack; "I am at liberty to go where I like. What do you think of that?"

Jim looked puzzled, and evidently felt inclined to run out and give the alarm that Jack was escaping.

Jack saw this, and, for reasons which the reader will soon learn, wished to keep Goblin Jim with him.

"Do you see this letter? Do you know this writing?" said Jack.

"I should rather think I do," replied Jim, after he had examined the letter. "It's old Grindwell's fist. I know it."

"He has written to Pigwellan to tell him to take the bearer out in his boat and give him a sail whenever he likes."

"No; you don't mean to say that," said Jim. "Well, I'm blest if you ain't in luck, that's all; I never get a sail."

"I should not think that a great loss," replied Jack, carelessly. "The sea is so rough; and then it is so tiresome to be cramped up in a boat."

"Oh! it's all very well for you to pretend that you do not care about going, now you know that you can go."

"I can assure you that I would rather

not deliver this letter," replied Jack Firebrace, carelessly.

"Oh, yes; I dare say. A very likely thing. If you don't like to take the letter, you let me take it."

Jack Firebrace paused as if he were thinking deeply, and then said—

"I really do not know whether I ought to give you the letter; but I tell you candidly, I would sooner you deliver it than that I should. But I am afraid that Mr. Grindwell may be displeased if I don't go for a sail."

"Oh; he won't mind. But look here. Are you sure that the letter says 'bearer' and not Mr. Firebrace?"

"Mr. Grindwell told me it was bearer," replied Jack; "but after all, perhaps I had better take it myself."

"Ugh! you sneak!" sneered Jim. "I knew you wouldn't let me take it. Catch me ever asking you to tea again, that's all."

At this threat Jack could scarcely refrain from laughing, but he kept his countenance, and holding out the letter, said—

"I can assure you that I don't want the letter. You may take it if you like; but if Mr. Grindwell is displeased, you must bear the blame, remember that."

"All right!" cried Jim, as he seized the letter. "I will settle all that. Won't I have a jolly day at sea!"

He turned, and dashed off in such blind haste, that he ran headlong against old Flick, and down he went.

"Halloa!" cried Flick; "where the deuce are you coming to? If you do that kind of thing again, I'll punch you."

"It's your fault," whined Jim; "you're always doing something as you shouldn't. Just you wait until I come back, and I'll tell my mother about you; and won't you get it hot, that's all! I'll let her know how you've bullied me."

"If you dare to talk to me like that," cried Flick, "I'll give you such a licking that you will repent it."

Flick stepped forward as if to carry out his intention, but Jack held him back, and motioned for him to keep still.

Goblin Jim sped right down the hall and opened the front door, so as to make sure of a good retreat, and then danced and screamed—

"Yah! yer big bully! Why don't you come and hit me? Yer can't; yer daren't—you know yer daren't! Only wait until I come back, and I'll make it warm for you both. I'll tell all about you, Jack Firebrace. I saw you trying to open the letter, and I heard you say that you would not carry any of old Grindwell's letters. You're a nice, grateful boy, you are. I'm ashamed of you! I'll let him know that I snatched the letter from you, and, seeing where it was addressed, took it, and delivered it. You see if I don't get you shut up again in the Wizard's Tower, and you, too, old Flick. You'll be put on bread and water, that's what you will get."

Flick made a dash forward, and Goblin Jim sped away down the hill.

"Come back, Flick, come back," laughed Jack; "the little brute has fallen into his own trap."

CHAPTER XXVIII.

GOBLIN JIM RECEIVES THE REWARD MEANT FOR JACK FIREBRACE—THE "FLYING FISH" HAS A NARROW ESCAPE—JIM TRIES AN EXCUSE AND REAPS THE BENEFIT OF IT—SEA LOGIC—THE GUNNER'S DAUGHTER—KEEL-HAULING—A STING FROM THE WASP.

GOBLIN JIM bounded along grinning with delight, enjoying in fancy the punishment he hoped to get for Jack and old Flick.

"He, he, he, he!" chuckled the little imp of mischief; "I know old Grindwell's plan very well. He's soft-soaping Jack Firebrace so that the other lads may think that he loves the brute. What a spree! I shall get all the pleasure and Jack all the pain, for I have seen what old Grindwell means when he is extra fond of a fellow. He was particularly fond of our late usher, Mr. Willis, and he disappeared. If I am not mistaken Jack Firebrace will disappear likewise.

"Hillo!" he cried with delight, as he stepped on to the sands; "here's a spree; two crabs fighting. One's nipped the other's claws off. He's trying to get away! No you don't! Let the other bite you. There; he's got hold of the other claw now. Oh, how the little one kicks! Ha, ha, ha, ha! He holds him as in a vice!"

Here the little demon danced about in delight, as he beheld the crab's struggles to release itself from its enemy.

"There goes the other claw!" he yelled; "and now one of his legs has gone. Where's a stone? I'll smash 'em both! They both deserve being killed; the little one for being a coward and trying to get away, and the big one for beating the little one! He's a coward!

"Oh, here's a jolly stone! Now, then, for a good shot! Whoop! that's a good one! It's killed the little crab, and half smashed the other! Now, then, to settle the business. Now—"

His tone was suddenly changed, for, at that moment, two sturdy men who had crept up behind him drew a sack over his head.

"Boo — woo — woo — wha — wha— what's the matter?" cried Goblin Jim, struggling violently to release himself.

There was no reply; the sack was pulled down to his feet; then he was drawn down to the sands, and the mouth of the sack fastened tightly with the wretched little brute inside of it.

"Let me out, Jack. I'll tell my mother of you, that's what I will do! I won't be treated in this style, I can tell you!"

"Hold your confounded little tongue, you whelp!" growled one of the men, at the same time bestowing a hearty kick upon Jim's ribs; "if you ain't silent I'll be the death of you, I will."

Goblin Jim took the hint, and was silent. Indeed, if he had tried to speak he would not have succeeded, for fear had taken away all power to cry out.

One of the men seized the neck of the sack, and swung it carelessly over his shoulder.

Head downwards, his knees touching his mouth, bumping about at every step the man took, Goblin Jim was carried down to a boat, into which he was thrown, with about as much consideration as if he had been a bag of biscuits.

"Where can I be?" thought Jim. "Oh! that I had not taken that letter —that letter!" he exclaimed, suddenly. "I see now all about this. Oh! what a stupid donkey I've been; what an idiot I must be! This letter was Jack Firebrace's death-warrant. He knew what it contained—he always finds out everything—and that is why he got me to take it. I shall be killed for him. Ho, ho, ho, ho!" he blubbered; "let me out. I'm not the right boy. Do let me out. Oh, do! oh, do! You have got the wrong boy in the sack."

The only reply to this affecting appeal was a very hearty kick in the ribs, and a command to "stow that noise!"

Jim did not quite understand the language, but he had a strong idea as to what it meant.

"What shall I do?" he murmured to himself; "whatever shall I do? I'll tear the letter up, and then they may not know the order."

He was about to tear the letter, but suddenly stopped and thought better of it.

"No," he said, as he put the note back in his pocket—"no; I will not do that. My only chance is to give them the letter, and prove that I am not the boy that they expect. I wonder where they can be taking me to?" he continued, as he listened to the heavy splashing of oars, and felt the motion of the boat.

He shuddered as he thought he was about to be drowned. He felt for his knife to cut his way out of the sack, but discovered that he had left it at home.

At that moment the boat struck against something hard, and he heard the noise of the men shipping their oars.

"Have you got the young brute?" demanded a rough voice; "or has he managed to give you the slip?"

"Not he. I've got him all safe enough—he kicks and scratches like a cat. I never saw such a spiteful little wretch."

"He'll have plenty of the cat here;

more than he will like," said the first speaker. "Just put a bit of this rope round him, and we'll precious soon have him aboard. Now, then, are you all ready? Run him up there by the yard-arm."

"Yeo—heave oh!"

Up flew Goblin Jim in the sack, his head still downwards, and there he twisted and twirled about like a joint of meat hanging before the fire roasting. Then he was pulled sideways, and lowered on to the deck of the vessel.

Scarcely was this done, when a loud voice rang out clear and sharp the command to get the boat on board.

Then followed some confused sounds of men hurrying about, and from what Goblin Jim could make out it appeared that a strange sail had hove in sight, and that the crew did not like the looks of her.

Then came the loud voice of the captain, which sounded through his speaking-trumpet like the roaring of the sea.

"All hands make sail! Mr. Bulstrode, set some of the men to throw water on the sails. Keep her before the wind. We shall beat her now, hurrah!" laughed the captain. "Confound it! What is she doing now?"

"She's exchanging signals with the land, sir. I can't make them out; they are private signals," replied the mate.

"We are in a mess, I fear," said the captain; "this comes from Richard Randulph's infernal fool-hardiness. I told him that we should be watched all along the shore. See yonder! thunder and lightning, there is a cutter coming out there from under the shelter of the cliff. She's a revenue cutter, and has six brass guns."

"I suppose we had better clear for action?" said Bradly, the mate; "the men will fight, for they know very well that they cannot escape death if they are taken."

"True; get all ready. Send the men aft; I would speak to them."

"An action!" thought Goblin Jim. "Oh, lor'! oh, lor'! here am I imprisoned in this wretched sack, and the bullets will be flying about, and I sha'n't be able to see them coming, or dodge them. It isn't fair—that's what it isn't; I shall be killed, I know I shall. Oh, how I wish Jack was in the sack!"

"My men," cried the captain, when the fellows had assembled aft, "you see these king's men have set a sort of trap for us, and there is only one thing left us to do, and that is to make a running fight of it, for if we yield we shall be hanged without mercy, and for my part, I would sooner die fighting than dancing about in the air with a hempen collar round my neck, like a black doll outside a rag-and-bone shop. One word more, my lads, and then to your posts. The first one that shows the white feather I'll cut down with my cutlass. Now be off, and see that you fight like men."

With three cheers for their captain the men hurried off to their posts, determined to fight to the death.

Leaving Jim in his sack, half dead with fear, and kicked and trampled on by the sailors as they hurried about, we will just watch the manœuvres of the "Flying Fish" to escape from her enemies.

"Keep her away two points," cried the captain, "so as to run her right under the cutter's nose. Bradly, stand by the larboard guns. Now, here she comes! Look out! She is only throwing herself up in the wind to get aim. There it comes."

Bomb—crash! and a heavy shot came tearing its way between the masts of the "Flying Fish," but doing little or no harm.

After the first shot the cutter made all sail straight down upon the smuggler, but so well managed was the latter that she glided in front of the cutter twenty yards from the tip of her bowsprit, and, as she went, fired her cannon right into the cutter, tearing up her rigging and killing numbers of her crew.

"Luff—luff!" yelled the captain; "we are safe, my boys, safe. We know the 'Wasp' can't catch us, and as for the cutter, she will have enough to do to look after herself. Hurrah! my lads."

Goblin Jim hardly knew whether he ought to be glad or sorry when he heard that they would not be overtaken. If he had felt certain that he could not be killed in the action, he would have been thankful for the "Flying Fish" to have been taken, for as it was he now saw no prospect of escaping from these desperate men, whose natures were so like his own, that they really loved cruelty for the very sake of cruelty.

He heard one or two dropping shots, but the reports of the cannon became fainter, and at last ceased altogether.

"Keep a sharp lookout, Bradly," said the skipper, "and send two of the men below with that young monkey."

Again the Goblin was hoisted up, and carried down the hatchway on a man's back. He groaned aloud, but no one paid the slightest heed to him.

"There he is, cappen," said the fellow who had carried Goblin Jim, dropping him heavily on the floor: "he ain't dead yet, I think."

"Throw him out of the sack," growled the captain. "I don't know what's come over Randulph. He used to be no end of a fine fellow, but now he's as squeamish as a girl. At one time he would have killed the lad himself, but now I've got to do his dirty work. Turn him out, and let's have a good look at the whelp. We'll have some fun out of him."

The string wherewith the mouth of the sack had been tied was cut, and Jim was shot out on to the cabin floor.

"Hillo, my young shaver," cried the captain, "what's the matter with you? Just get on your pins, and let us have a look at your ugly mug. I can't say that I am particularly struck with the cut of your jib."

"Oh, if you please, sir, it is all a mistake," whined Jim; "I ought not to be here, but another boy."

"If you ought not to be here," laughed the captain, casting a fiery glance out of an unusually large eye, which squinted horribly, "why the deuce did you come? If you have made a mistake, that's your lookout, not ours."

"Well, if you please, sir, Mr. Griffiths Grindwell—"

"Who?" demanded the captain, screwing his awful eye round to look at Goblin Jim.

"Mr. Griffiths Grindwell, if you please, sir," faltered Goblin Jim.

"Oh, you mean Richard Randulph, or Red Randulph, as we used to call him in the West Indies. It is the same man."

"Perhaps you are right, sir—I have heard Mr. Gruesome mention that name. Yes, I remember; he said, 'Richard Randulph, shed no more blood. Beware!'"

"Oh, you know he said that, do you?" said Matito of the Evil Eye, for he was the captain; "you know he said that?"

"Oh, yes, I can swear to it, for I listened at the keyhole."

The captain winked at the men, and a more than usually malicious look gleamed from his terrible eye.

"You are a nice boy—a very nice boy. No wonder that you were liked in such a place as Hawkhouse. Pray go on with your story."

"Well, sir, Mr. Grindwell gave a letter for another boy to carry to old Pigwellan, the deformed boatman, and I, thinking it was given him so that he might get something good, took the letter from him, and took it down to the beach to deliver it, when—"

"Yes, yes, we know all about that," interrupted Matito. "Where is that letter?"

With trembling hands Goblin Jim drew the note from his pocket, and handed it over to the one-eyed captain.

Matito opened the letter, and read the contents over once or twice.

He then placed the letter down upon the table, and putting his huge red hand on it, said, in tones of thunder—

"This letter does not mention anybody's name; it only gives me orders to treat the bearer with severity, or even to take his life if I like."

"But, sir, this is only a mistake—a most unpleasant mistake."

"For you I should think it was an unpleasant mistake," replied the captain, with a brutal laugh.

"It can't be meant for me," said Goblin Jim, "because I am like one of the family at Hawkhouse, and I know a lot of the secrets of the place. I've seen some of these gentlemen here play ghosts when there has been a cargo to run. I was the one who saw the way the brig was wrecked on the sands the other night."

"Oh, you did, did you?" said Matito, drawing in a long breath. "What a remarkably sharp boy you are!"

"That I am. You should hear how my mother speaks about me. She says she will back me to find out a secret against anyone. Ah! and I can, too.

I know more about the secrets of Hawkhouse than any other boy in the school."

"Just as I thought, just as I thought," said Matito. "One of you fellows go on deck and tell Mr. Bradly I want him, the rest take this lad into yonder cabin and see that he don't escape. The young fellow is too clever to be left at liberty."

Jim was dragged away, and thrown into a dark cell.

In about a quarter of an hour he was called back into the room, where he found the captain and his officers seated at a table, drinking hot grog and smoking black pipes.

The captain had evidently been making the most of his time in drinking, for he was evidently partly intoxicated already.

His features were puffed and red, and his eye rolled about in an awful manner.

"We have been considering your story, young gentleman," he thundered out, "and we have come to the conclusion that you are so very clever that we can quite understand why our good friend Randulph, or, as you call him, Grindwell, should be anxious to get rid of you. Confess, now, that you were told to bring that letter to Pigwellan."

"Me confess that?" screamed Goblin Jim. "Me confess that I am Jack Firebrace? Impossible! I can't do that!"

"I know nothing about your Jack Firebraces or anything else," replied Matito. "All I know is you were sent here for a certain purpose, and, by Jove! you shall confess yourself to be whosoever I please. Hark'ee here, my lad. If my employer sent you to me for a certain purpose, and I do not carry out that purpose, and his plans fail, I should deserve punishment, eh?"

"Ye-es, sir; I suppose you would; but, oh! mercy, mercy! oh, do have mercy upon me!" shrieked Goblin Jim, clasping his hands and dropping on his knees.

"You keep quiet and listen to my arguments," said the captain. "I've got a bit of sea logic, as we call it, which I think will put matters all right, and, therefore, ought to be pleasing to all parties concerned. Now, what do you say to that?"

"I—I am delighted to hear it, sir," said Jim, rising up, for he felt convinced that the captain had hit upon some plan to kidnap Jack Firebrace.

"That's better. Well, then, in order that I may punish the person according to the captain's orders, and to prevent the wrong person being punished, I intend to flog you until you confess that you are the right person; then there can be no mistake in the matter. I think that's clear enough—ain't it, gentlemen?" he demanded, turning to the officers and men.

"Clear as a fog at sea," laughed the fellows, who seemed in a high state of jollity as they beat their hands in applause.

Goblin Jim looked round at the men in horror, scarcely being able to answer the argument.

"Ha, ha, ha!" he laughed. "You are pleased to be funny, gentlemen. The captain's wit tickles you."

"Something else will precious soon tickle you," cried Matito, rolling his evil eye about in an awful manner.

This last remark had the desired effect of bringing the look of abject terror back into Goblin Jim's face.

"Surely, surely you don't mean to do anything so dreadful as that?" he cried. "I tell you that I am not the boy meant."

"And I tell you most positively that I know you are," said Matito. "Bo's-wain, marry this young gentleman to the gunner's daughter; she's a good wife, and will bring him to reason soon."

"Marry the gunner's daughter!" screamed Goblin Jim. "But I never have seen the young lady—I don't know her; and then, I am not of age. Mother won't let me marry, I know. Besides, I'm not in my proper parish, and you have not put up the banns."

"We will put the bands about you in rather less than a couple of minutes, my fine lad," said the bo'swain.

Vainly did Goblin Jim protest that he did not wish to enter the marriage state.

He only made the men laugh more.

And now his prayers and supplications were turned by desperation into a useless endeavour to resist the men.

He kicked, he scratched, he bit, and he yelled; but in spite of all he was soon slapped down over the breech of a cannon.

His arms were lashed down, so that he appeared to be embracing the cannon, and his feet were fastened in ring-bolts in the deck.

"Now, my lad," laughed Matito, "that is the gunner's daughter. How do you like the young lady, eh, my fine fellow?"

"Take me off! oh, take me off!" cried Goblin Jim. "These strings cut my wrists and my ankles. Take me off! oh, take me off!"

"No, no; just tell me if you are the right boy now."

"No, I am not the right boy," shouted Goblin Jim! "you know I am not. Oh, won't Mr. Grindwell give it— Yah! Oh, oh! Yah!"

At a sign from Matito, the boatswain, who had been standing by Jim's side, raised a knotted rope's-end, and let fall two or three heavy cuts upon poor Jim's tight trousers, thereby causing that young gentleman to finish his speech abruptly.

"Mercy! oh, yah! mercy, mercy! oh, yah!" cried Jim, struggling to release himself.

"Give me a few more!" roared Matito, whose evil eye lit up with redoubled spite as he heard the boy's shrieks.

The boatswain was nothing loth, and not only did he redouble the force of the blows, but also poured them in so fast, that Jim at last began to think that he should never be able to sit down again; indeed, he felt as if he should have nothing left to sit upon.

"Now, my gentleman, I have no doubt the gunner's daughter has taught you wisdom. Are you the boy mentioned in this letter? Mind, your friend, the boatswain, is all ready behind you to remind you if your memory is bad."

"Yes, sir, I am the lad," whimpered Jim, who had no inclination to have any reminder from the boatswain.

"Ah, I thought so. Cast off the lashings, but don't let him get up yet," said Matito; "there is nothing like a rope's-end in all the world to bring a young lad's memory straight; just impress that on his mind, boatswain."

Down came the rope's-end, and up flew Jim, who, a few moments before, would have declared it impossible to rise.

"By Jove! how active he is," laughed the fellows round. "It is evident that he is not in love with the gunner's daughter."

"Oh, oh! I should rather think I was not," bellowed Jim. "It's my belief that I am cut to ribbons."

"Sit down and hold your tongue!" shouted the captain.

"I have no objection to holding my tongue," said Jim; "but sit down! I thank you, I can't. I don't think I shall ever be able to sit down again."

"Bo'swain, I think our young friend here wants the gunner's daughter again. Ask him if he does."

"No, no! I don't, indeed I don't. Where do you want me to sit down? I'll sit down; only give me a cushion, a soft one."

"Sit on that gun-slide!" shouted Matito.

And down dropped the unhappy Jim as if he were shot.

"My orders are, now that this young gentleman confesses that he is the boy mentioned in here," said Matito, holding up the letter as he spoke, "that I keelhaul him from stem to stern of the 'Flying Fish.' So one glass more, gentlemen, and then we will be off."

Jim looked round inquiringly at the speaker, unable to make out what on earth he meant by "keelhaul."

He had not much longer to wait in doubt, for two of the sailors seized him, and dragged him up.

It was a beautiful moonlit night, and the sea was rather smooth; but the weather was decidedly cold.

Goblin Jim watched two of the men passing a thin rope beneath the ship in such a manner that it quite encircled it from bow to stern, half being beneath and along the keel and half being along the deck from stem to stern.

They then took two other ropes, which they fastened to the long one at right angles, so that they would pass under the ship across the keel, and be brought up on each side.

Jim was wondering what all these preparations could mean when he was suddenly seized and stripped naked.

"I say, look here!" he cried; "don't

do that! It's cold, you know. I can't stand this terrible cold."

"You will find it colder presently," said the captain, with a grin.

And in two minutes he had fastened Jim to the long rope, and his arms and legs to the two cross-ropes, so that as he lay on the deck he made the figure of an X.

"Now then, lads, when I call 'Three' pull slowly on the rope, you at the bows coming aft at a quiet walk. You fellows who have the larboard and starboard guy-ropes keep them even, so that he makes an even run along the keel. Bo'swain, stand clear to heave him over when you hear the word. Now, my lads, are you all ready?"

"All ready, sir," cried the boatswain and men, who seemed to be enjoying the sport with a great relish.

Poor Jim knew not what they were going to do, but he was too well aware that they meant to torture him.

"One! two! three!"

Scarcely had the captain uttered the last word, when the boatswain caught up Jim, and hurled him into the sea.

Down, down, down, he went, and naturally his first impulse was to strike out and swim, so as to rise to the surface.

But, do all that he could, he was carried down by a lead fastened to the long line, and his arms and legs were kept spread out by the two guy-ropes.

In this manner he was slowly dragged under the keel of the ship.

His arms and legs were nearly wrenched from their sockets, as the men, who held the guy-ropes, moved uneasily, and so pulled more one way than the other.

The water rushed into his mouth and ears, and, in a moment, all Goblin Jim's wicked deeds flashed across his mind.

Bitterly he repented them now, for he firmly believed that the cruel wretches meant to keep him at the bottom of the keel until he was drowned.

But suddenly the keel seemed to vanish, and he was hauled up into the ship's bows, having gone right along under the keel.*

When they hauled him on deck, Jim fell down on his face, for he was more than three-parts drowned.

* Keelhauling was invented by the Dutch, and was used sometimes as punishment in our navy. Of course now it is abolished.

"Come, get up," yelled Matito, giving him a frightful kick, "or I'll make you. You have got to do that little journey three times."

But Jim was too far gone to care what more they did to him.

He lay there quite regardless of the captain's oaths or blows.

"Here, bo'swain," shouted the captain, "just give him a touch with your rope's-end. That will bring him up sharp."

Down it came, and a faint "Oh, yah!" came from the Goblin's pale, quivering lips, but he did not stir.

"Try again," cried the captain.

The boatswain sprang forward, and once more raised his brawny arm aloft, flourishing the rope's-end so as to get all the force he could.

It was about to descend when a loud report was heard, and the next instant a round-shot came screaming through the air, dashing off the boatswain's head, and then plunging over the ship into the water beyond.

For a few seconds the outlaws stood horrified, and then a hearty cry arose from all.

"It is the 'Wasp!' the 'Wasp!' She is bearing down upon us."

Whilst the captain and the crew of the "Flying Fish" had been drinking in the cabin, and enjoying the horrible torture they had inflicted upon Goblin Jim, the "Wasp" had pressed on all sail, and had cruised about in hopes that she might fall in with the "Flying Fish."

As the moon came out they had seen her hove-to, preparing for the keelhauling, and at once the captain had made straight to her, not firing until he was within range, and then sending the round-shot across her bows, which had the effect of saving Jim from a further taste of the rope's-end.

Uttering the fiercest oaths, Matito rushed aft, and, seizing his speaking-trumpet, gave the words of command—

"Loose the royals—sheet home the fore-royal — weather-sheets home—lee-sheets home."

"Ay, ay, sir!" shouted the men aloft, as they obeyed the orders with wonderful speed, for they knew it was a case of life or death.

"Overhaul your clew-lines—steady, steady!"

"Ay, ay, sir; all clear."

"Taut-leech—belay—well the lee-brace—haul taut to windward. Mr. Bradly, take the helm. Steer back to Hawkhouse. We may escape them yet. If not, we will have a tough fight for it, and, as Red Randulph put us into this scrape, he shall take his share of the danger. Down there, flat on the deck!" he shouted, as another round-shot came tearing through the air, and down all the sailors fell on their faces.

"She fires too high," laughed Matito. "Let her blaze away as long as she don't hit us. See, we have increased our distance from her."

The men gave a hearty cheer as they saw this, and the "Flying Fish," as if encouraged by their applause, sprang swiftly through the waters.

CHAPTER XXIX.

GRINDWELL HAS AN UNEXPECTED VISIT AND A TREMENDOUS SURPRISE.

GRIFFITHS GRINDWELL was walking near the beach when he was informed that visitors were awaiting him in the dining-room of Hawkhouse.

Grindwell was surprised at this announcement.

However, he composed his face into the blandest expression he could possibly form, and entered the room where his visitors had assembled.

As his eyes fell upon them his brow grew darker, and he pressed his lips firmly together.

The visitors were Captain Firbank, Dr. Lamberhurst, and Lieutenant Purvis, of the coastguard.

"Pardon me, gentlemen," said Grindwell, bowing stiffly, "but this is a most unexpected pleasure. Pray be seated."

"We have not come here, Mr. Grindwell, to pay a friendly visit," said Dr. Lamberhurst, "but rather to make a few inquiries about the wreck which last occurred on these sands. By a most miraculous chance the captain of the vessel escaped. He is, it is believed, the only man who has ever escaped from a ship which has struck the Shark's Back rocks."

Grindwell made no reply.

He merely shrugged his shoulders, smiled, and bowed.

"That man, Mr. Griffiths Grindwell, was once your friend—indeed, for many years he sailed one of your ships. His name is Edwin Summerbell."

"So I heard someone say the other night," replied Grindwell. "He was once, as you say, in my service, but he did not suit me."

"No; for he is honest," said Captain Firbank, bluntly.

Griffiths Grindwell made no reply; but his right hand crossed as if by instinct to his left side, as if feeling for a sword.

"You are pleased to be polite," he said, suddenly recovering himself; "but I am not the man to seek quarrels."

"A good doctrine," said Dr. Lamberhurst; "but I think we can settle this case without quarrelling. We only want to ask you one or two questions, which we feel certain no honest man would refuse to answer."

The others nodded their assent and looked hard at Griffiths Grindwell.

"An honest man!" exclaimed Grindwell, raising his eyebrows; "you are scarcely complimentary, my friends. Still, I will answer you as far as is in my power and assist you to the fullest extent—if the cause be honest."

"Then, Mr. Grindwell, we will go to the point at once. Mr. Summerbell declares that he was lured on these rocks by false lights. In fact, that the ship was decoyed by wreckers. The light, as well as he can calculate from the bearings, must have been shown on the Hawk's Rock about half-way down the cliff. You understand me?"

"Yes, I understand you," said Grindwell. "You speak plainly."

"Good. We wish to know if you can in any way explain those lights?"

"And this is your first question. Bah! do you come here to insult me?"

"You deny all knowledge of these lights?" demanded Captain Firbank, sharply.

"I refuse to answer any such questions," replied Grindwell. "I believe that this is a conspiracy got up by that fellow Summerbell, and in which conspiracy, gentlemen, you have but too readily joined; but, mark me! I am as a rule an easy-going man. Still, if you dare to place yourself in my path I will crush you."

"We have no fear of you," replied Captain Firbank; "and as—"

"My dear Firbank, do be patient," said Dr. Lamberhurst. "Why do you lose your temper?"

"There is one thing more I must ask you, Mr. Grindwell," said Lieutenant Purvis. "Large cargoes of contraband goods have been run somewhere on this part of the coast."

"In that case I should advise you to stop them. It is not only your duty, but your interest to do so. It is not mine," said Grindwell.

"To stop them is most certainly not your business," said Captain Firbank. "It may be to run them."

Grindwell's eyes flashed fire, and he clinched his hands as if about to strike the captain to the earth.

"I have borne enough of this," he cried, passionately. "Do you think I will be insulted in my own house? Begone, I say, and tell the idiot who sent you that I despise him."

"Now, really, Mr. Grindwell," said the good doctor, "you are too hasty. We do not for one moment mean to say that we believe you are answerable for these things; but there are servants in this house. They may be in league with the smugglers, and we feel certain that you, as an honest merchant, would feel as glad to stop their traffic—"

"Hearken to me, sir!" cried Grindwell, who, although trembling with passion, managed to speak in a cold, firm voice, "hearken to me! Had you come here and asked me to help you in the name of the law, I would have tried to have done so. It has pleased you, however, to come with threats. They never have and never shall move me. I know nothing of this matter. If I were a

lieutenant of the coastguard"—here he looked at Lieutenant Purvis—"or a half-pay officer"—here he looked still harder at Captain Firbank—"I should feel it my duty to find out these men. As it is, it can't be any business of mine. Gentlemen, our interview is at an end."

"One moment—just one moment," said Dr. Lamberhurst.

Grindwell, who was moving to the door, paused.

"You have placed, I believe, a pupil in this school of the name of John Firebrace."

"Ha!" said Grindwell, with a short laugh, as he swung round so as to face them; "and what of him?"

"We wish to speak to him," said Dr. Lamberhurst.

"By what right? You are no relations of his. He is my ward."

"We are friendly towards the lad, and would help him. You cannot object to that?"

"By heaven, I do object to it!" cried Grindwell, roughly. "I know the cause of your visit. A conspiracy—yes, there is a conspiracy. Where is the boy? Tell me that. You have induced him to run away. Where is he?"

"We induced the boy to run away from school!" cried all the men together. "We do not understand you."

"No," he sneered, "perhaps not. I suppose you don't know that he has run away? Oh, no! Now, mark me!" he continued, his eyes flashing fire, and his lips trembling with rage, "mark me! He has been enticed from home—by you—by you, gentlemen, and that false hound Summerbell. Nay, do not frown at me; I dread not your looks. I can wield a sword as well as any of you."

Here Grindwell paused suddenly, looking as if he had made a slight mistake in mentioning the sword.

However, he very quickly recovered his self-possession, and continued—

"Yes, gentlemen, the sword. Why do you stare so? I am a peaceful merchant, one more used to the quill than to the sword; but I still say that I fear you not. Now go; I will have no further converse with you. Bring back the boy, and all shall be forgiven; if you do not do so, I shall hold you answerable, and will move the law to do its worst for you."

THE BOYS OF HAWKHOUSE SCHOOL.

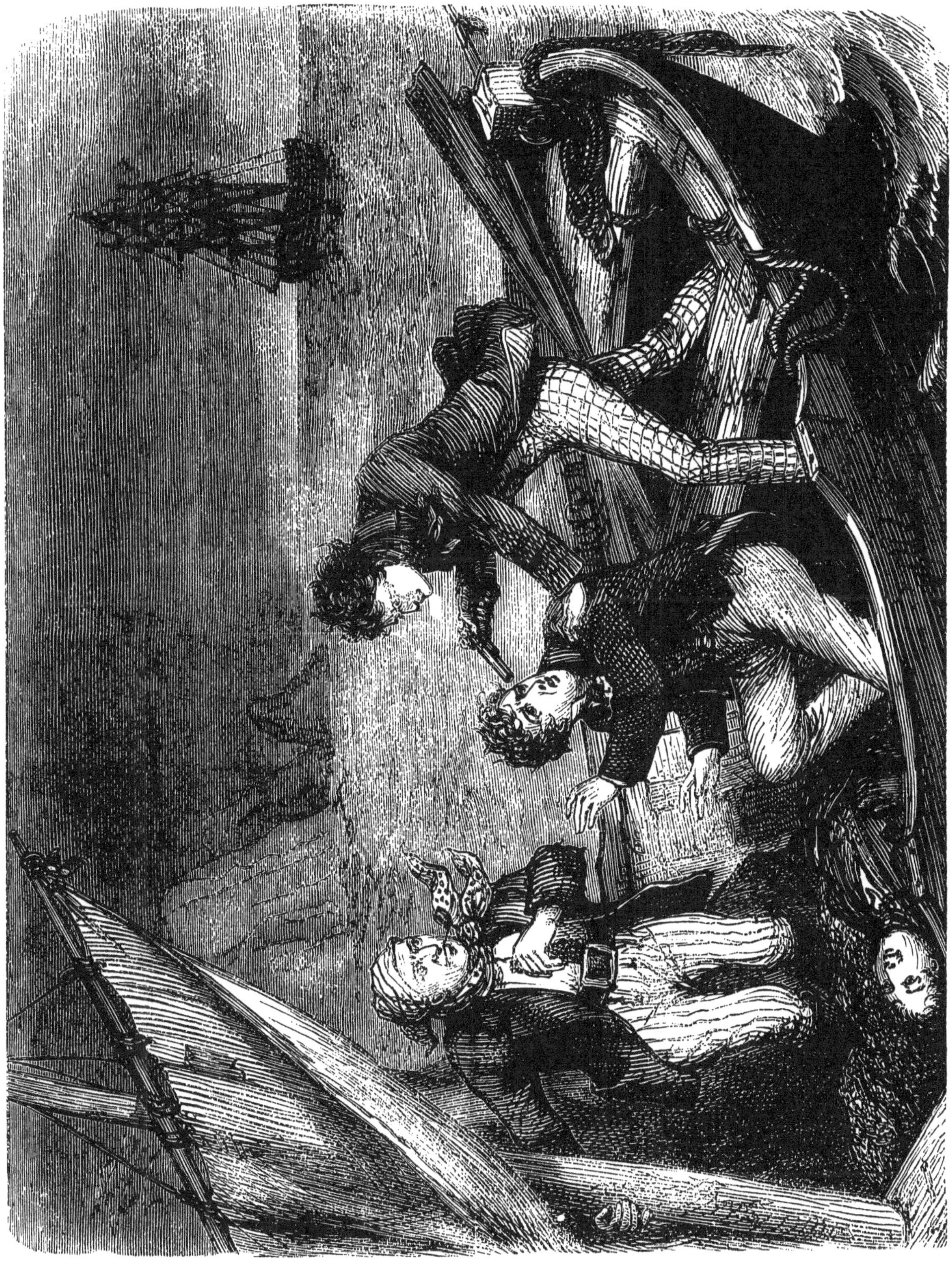

"OLD FLICK, STANDING UP, HELD A PISTOL TO MORRISON'S HEAD."

No. 9.

PRICE ONE HALFPENNY.

[Published Every Monday.]

"Can this, be true?" exclaimed Dr. Lamberhurst, turning round to his friends.

"True!" thundered Griffiths Grindwell. "Dare you doubt my word in my own house? Begone with you ere worse come of it."

The men saw that it was useless to argue further, and therefore in sullen silence left the room and house.

"Ha, ha, ha!" grinned Grindwell, as the door closed, "you want Jack Firebrace, do you? No, no, my friends; he is settled at last, and by what I have done I will cast a slur upon the characters of these honest gentlemen that they shall find it difficult to remove. They who cross my path once never do so again; that boy Firebrace is one who has done so; but he has gone to his death."

"Hurrah! it is a finer day for a sail than I thought it would be," said a merry voice behind him.

Griffiths Grindwell started back in horror, and turned round.

There, seated quietly on a window-seat, reading a book, was our hero, Jack Firebrace.

"You—you here, Firebrace?" cried Grindwell, looking steadfastly at Jack, "or are you a spirit?"

"A spirit? No! I am flesh and blood right enough. Whatever should make you think me a ghost, Mr. Grindwell?"

Grindwell paused, and wiped the heavy dews off his brow, and then said, in a soft, half-laughing manner—

"What wonder you startled me! Did I not give you a letter to take to old Peter Pigwellan, containing an order that he should take you out in his boat whenever you like? At first I thought you were drowned, and that your ghost had appeared to me."

"No; oh, no," said Jack, calmly. "The fact is I did not feel inclined for a sail this morning, so I stopped at home."

"You might have told me so at first," exclaimed Grindwell, angrily. "What have you done with the letter? Give it me, boy."

"I did not know that it would matter. I met Jim, the housekeeper's son, and as he seemed anxious to go for a sail I gave him the letter, and he took it down to the bay—"

He said no more, for, with a yell of rage, Grindwell had sprung upon him and had grasped him by the collar.

"Wretched brute! you have caused the murder of that boy—of my boy! Do you think that you shall escape me thus? Never! Your doom is now certain. Nay; your struggles are in vain. I know not what holds back my hand from striking you myself. But be assured your hours are numbered."

Placing his hand over Jack's mouth to suppress his cries he dragged him down a flight of stone stairs, opened a large iron door leading to a dismal dungeon, flung our hero inside, and closed the door.

CHAPTER XXX.

JACK AGAIN IN PERIL.

THE dungeon wherein our hero found himself confined was so dark that he could not see his hand before him.

He felt about the walls and found that they were of stone—cold, damp, and slimy to the touch.

"What a fool I have been," he muttered, "even to go about without the necessary things to strike a light! To remain here means certain death. But how to escape? It is useless to cry out, for no one would hear me, and if they did they would not help me."

He paced up and down his dreary abode, now and then taking a step too far, and hitting the wall, until by accident he came across a stone bench, on which he threw himself to await his fate.

How long he remained in this miserable place he could not tell.

It seemed to him days; but it might only have been hours, for night and day were the same there.

At last he heard the bolts of the door shoot back.

Then Grindwell entered, holding a torch in his hand.

Behind him came Sidney Morrison, pale and haggard, his hands working nervously, and his eyes cast downwards.

To Jack's great delight, behind the usher came old Peter Pigwellan, looking as hideous as ever; but our hero believed that he detected in the old man's eye a twinkle of merriment and triumph.

"So, my young fighting cock," laughed Grindwell, as he placed his torch in a sconce, "you have not killed yourself, as I hoped you would, in order to save us trouble? Well, you never would oblige anyone—never! So we must do it."

"I am no coward," said Jack, boldly, "and would never commit the crime of self-murder. If I am to die, I am prepared to die."

"It is as well that you should be," said Grindwell. "You shall never see to-morrow's sunrise. I have sworn it, and Red Randulph always kept his oath of vengeance."

"Red Randulph!" exclaimed Jack. "Are you, then, that cruel wretch, whose name was once the terror of the Indian seas?"

"Curses on my tongue for making that foolish slip!" growled Grindwell. "But it matters little now. Your ears will soon be deaf, and your tongue silenced in death. You fool, to have crossed my path! Had you been tractable, I would have made much of you, for you have courage and daring, a quick wit, and a ready hand to the blow; but you have chosen to turn against me, and must perish! Seize him, Pigwellan! tie him hand and foot, and wrap him in this old boat-cloak."

"You shall not bind me," cried Jack, springing up, and, placing his back against the wall, he put himself in an attitude of defence. "You may have the power to murder me, but I will not submit quietly! Come what will, I will fight to the last!"

"You had better give in quietly, sir," said Pigwellan, as he advanced towards Jack; "I don't want to hurt you more nor I can help."

Jack looked fixedly at the old man, and could have sworn that he saw him wink one of his eyes.

"I don't care, cried Jack; "I will not submit. I will call for help, and fight to the last!"

"Mr. Sidney Morrison," cried Grindwell, and a fiendish delight flashed into his eyes, "seize that boy!"

Sidney Morrison advanced to carry out his master's orders, but our hero's fist advanced also, and the usher fell back, caused by a well-directed blow delivered with all his weight from the left by Jack.

But at the same moment Griffiths Grindwell sprang forward and dealt the lad a fearful blow on the head, stunning him.

"Quick, Peter!" he cried; "stuff a gag into his mouth, bind him fast, and tie a shot or a bar of pig-iron to his feet, and then fling him into the sea. Mr. Sidney Morrison, you will go with this man, and see that he does as he is ordered. Do you hear?"

"I—I cannot go—I cannot go!" moaned the tutor. "I cannot shed more blood."

"You will do exactly what I ask you," said Grindwell, quietly; "if you do not there is the gallows."

The usher covered his face and bowed down his head.

"You see you are in my power. Refuse to obey me, and you die. Obey me, and you shall be well off. Now go!"

By this time Pigwellan had bound our hero's arms and legs fast together, and had wrapped him up in an old boat-cloak, so that he looked like a roll of cloth.

This he threw carelessly upon his shoulder, as if it were not the slightest weight, and stood ready to depart.

"Come, Sidney," said Grindwell; "my game is a desperate one, and those who are with me must be as guilty as myself, or they die."

"I am in the toils," said Sidney Morrison, "and must submit. What would you have me do?"

"Assist that man to carry the lad down to his boat. You will then put out as if going to sea. A bag of ballast or a bar of pig-iron must be bound to his feet, you throw him overboard, one splash, and he is gone. The business is soon done, and two are enough to do it."

"I want no help to do a little job like that," said Peter Pigwellan; "I'd much sooner do it alone."

"And I would sooner that he went with you," said Grindwell, sharply. "And, hark ye, Master Pigwellan," he continued, giving the deformed boatman a rather heavy blow over the head with the butt-end of his pistol, "I have had reason of late to doubt your honesty and truthfulness to me. Take care, take care! I am not the man to be played fast and loose with. If I find you playing me any trick I will nail you to the mast of my vessel, even as they nail stoats and weasels to the doors of barns."

"Nail away, Richard Randulph!" cried the old man, with a snarl. "Do you think that no one has a right to speak but yourself? Look at my face! Look at my twisted limbs! Who did this cruel work? You, you, you—and you alone! This was your return for the patient love I bore you. This was done, not because I was false, but because I was true—Heaven forgive me! —too true to one so cruel and vile!"

"Cease your preaching!" cried Red Randulph, stamping with rage. "I can look upon you and laugh—yes, laugh. I chose to make you even more ugly than nature had already done. I did it. Think you that the agony of such a creature as thou art weighed with me? No; my will is my law, and the law of those around me. Whilst I live I will have my way. I will die boldly, fighting, drinking the blood of my enemies to the last."

"Take care, Richard Randulph, lest your good fortune desert you and leave you to perish as miserably as you have caused others to do. You are but mortal. The lightning flash, the blast of the tempest—nay, the bite of the creeping snake may lay you low in death!"

"Begone!" cried Randulph, stamping with rage; "and mark this! If you return not soon with sufficient tokens that the deed has been done I will hang you to the yardarm of the first ship of mine which puts in here."

Pigwellan made no reply, but moved slowly to the door, muttering and grumbling as he went.

"See that the fellow does what I have ordered," said Grindwell, in a whisper, to Sidney Morrison. "If thou art so particular, thou needst not raise a hand in the matter, only give thy orders and see that he obeys them. Remember this. Obey me well, and in a few months thou shalt be free. In the meantime be a man; strike and spare not!"

"I will do your bidding," replied Sidney, passing his hand wearily over his forehead. "Sometimes I wish for death, but the darkness of the tomb, the cold, deep grave frightens me. I dare not die!"

"One word more, Sidney Morrison," cried Randulph, as he clutched the usher's arm, and glared into his eyes in fiendish triumph, "one word more. Look at that long pack there," and he pointed to the senseless form of our hero, enshrouded in the long boat-cloak; "that boy would have become rich, even as I am, had he been obedient. He chose to rebel; he dies! Be wise, Sidney Morrison, be wise; obey orders, or you shall as surely go to the dismal tomb as I now send yonder lad to his."

With that Griffiths Grindwell motioned them to the door, and, taking the torch from the sconce, prepared to follow them.

They passed down the secret passage, which we have before described, and from thence down to the cave.

"Do you know this spot?" demanded Grindwell of the usher, as he held up the torch over the place where old Silas Sidecraft had been murdered.

Sidney Morrison started back and shuddered, but said nothing.

Grindwell, or Randulph, extinguished the torch by beating it on the sands, and then led the way out to the rocks.

It was one of those terribly dark nights when not a star is to be seen, the wind blows in heavy gusts, and the sea moans and moans as if in labour with the coming storm.

The usher stumbled along the rocks, but Grindwell and Peter Pigwellan walked on as if they were on level ground, for they were used to that path.

They reached the boat, and old Pigwellan laid our hero down at the bottom of it.

He then motioned the usher to step in, and take his place in the middle of the boat, which he did, and then the old deformed boatman followed, and fitted on the tiller.

"You keep quiet there," he growled to Sidney Morrison, as he pointed to a seat. "I'll manage the boat. Shove off, sir."

Grindwell seized the boat, and shoved her off; but before he did so, he cried, in low, deep tones, to the usher—

"Remember, Sidney Morrison, I trust in you. If either of you deceive me, I will be avenged, if I travel round the world to find you."

He gave the boat a tremendous push, and she glided from the beach, rising and falling on the treacherous waves.

"Sit where you are," growled Peter Pigwellan. "I'll look after the boat. What does a landlubber like you know about sailing?"

With wonderful swiftness Peter set the sails, letting the boat "go wild" for a few seconds; then he seized upon the helm, and brought her up into the wind.

Out, out into the deep, dark night, dashed the little vessel, and away to sea, flying before the wind.

Old Peter, having her well trimmed, kept his arm round the tiller, and filled and lit his pipe, stuck it into his mouth, and puffed and puffed away, whilst Sidney Morrison sat trembling and shaking with fear.

Not a word passed between them.

The usher sat shivering in the middle of the boat; Pigwellan smoked listlessly at the helm; Jack lay insensible at the bottom of the tiny craft.

"What is that?" asked Sidney Morrison, as he pointed to something that looked like a huge shadow to windward.

Pigwellan glanced in the direction indicated, lashed the helm down, and then, springing forward, lowered the sails.

"What are you doing?" asked Sidney Morrison, in a hoarse whisper. "What is that yonder?"

"Silence!" replied Pigwellan, in low but commanding tones. "What you see yonder is a ship. She's lying off the coast until there's light enough for her to make her way in safety to some port. If she sees our sail, we shall probably be hailed, and then our business will be found out. You keep still, and I will manage all this; you need not fear."

The deep shadow—for in the darkness of the night the ship appeared but little more—grew more and more indistinct, until, at last, it faded away altogether.

"I think it is about the time," he said. "We can do it here all right."

"Good!" remarked Sidney Morrison, with a shudder. "Let us get it over, and return to shore."

"Wait until I make this bag of ballast secure to his feet," said Pigwellan; "and then into the water, and into eternity he goes with one splash!"

He knelt down by the side of our hero, and was busily employed with the ropes on his feet and wrists.

Sidney Morrison saw this, but he did not watch the old boatman closely to note the preparations for the murder.

"Now, are you ready?" demanded Peter Pigwellan, as he rose to his feet.

"Quite," rejoined Sidney Morrison, as he rose from his seat and stooped down to take hold of our hero's shoulder.

"Villain!" cried Pigwellan, angrily, as he seized the usher by the throat and hurled him backwards; "villain and coward."

"What mean you?" demanded Sidney Morrison, gasping in surprise as he gazed on old Peter.

"You, who have known the horror of having blood upon your hands, would you still increase that terrible dread by another murder in order that your own worthless life might be saved? Far better would it be to perish at once than drag on so miserable an existence. Do you think that I came here to murder that boy? No! I came here to save and not destroy! I am bound to Griffiths Grindwell; but, although I cannot leave him, I have saved many and many a one from his clutches. He may kill me, but he shall never drag me down to crime."

"Are you mad?" demanded Sidney. "This lad's escape will destroy us all—all! We have no way to escape. You know Mr. Grindwell's power; but you know not the hold he has over me. It is my life or that lad's."

"Ho, ho, ho, ho!" laughed Peter. "So I do not know the hold he has over you, eh? Look you here, Master Sidney Morrison; what think you of this? Do you know the ring—the silver ring; two twisted snakes, with heads upraised as if about to strike? 'Sblood, if that be not enough, do you know this, eh? This is the Hand of Death!"

As he spoke he held up the skeleton hand, on one of the fingers of which glittered a silver ring formed like two snakes in the action we have already described.

"Mercy, mercy!" cried Sidney Morrison, clasping his hands and falling on his knees as he beheld the ghastly object.

"I will have mercy on you, Sidney Morrison, but only on one condition; and that is that you swear to help me in all my schemes to overthrow those of Richard Randulph. I dare not betray him to the law; I dare not take his life. A mysterious power forbids that; but I can and will frustrate all his evil intentions. Resist me, and this token of your guilt finds its way to the hands of justice."

Sidney Morrison seemed quite overpowered; he rocked himself backwards and forwards and moaned aloud.

"Nay," continued Peter Pigwellan, "promise to obey me, and I will do more. I will clear up the mystery of the murder in the cave, and relieve your soul from the terrible weight of guilt which hangs upon it. Now do you consent to obey me and to keep my secrets?"

"He had better," said a voice behind him, "he had better, or I'll blow his brains out!"

Sidney Morrison glanced over his shoulder and perceived, to his dismay, old Flick standing up in the boat, and holding a pistol in unpleasant proximity to his head.

"You here?" he exclaimed, in surprise.

"Yes; I am here; and a good job for you it is that I am here, for I can add my persuasions to those of old Peter here. I can't say that the argument is a kindly one, but it is a strong one."

"Heaven be my witness," moaned the usher, "I had no wish to become the wretch he has made me."

"I can swear to that," said old Pigwellan; "but it is useless to waste time in vain regrets."

"That's true, Peter," said old Flick. "Come, Jack, old man, get up."

To Sidney Morrison's great surprise, Jack sprang to his feet.

His bonds fell from him, for, as Peter Pigwellan had leaned down as if to tie the bag of ballast to our hero's feet, he had, in truth, unfastened or cut the ropes which bound him, at the same time whispering into his ear that no harm should befall him.

"Now, what is to be done?" demanded Jack, shaking his limbs, which were stiff from being bound.

"Peter had better pull ashore and let us escape," said old Flick; "that is what I think would be the best."

"That won't do," growled Peter; "and, mark this—until the time comes —and come it will, and must—I forbid any of you to betray Mr. Grindwell to the law. I have saved your lives; you must promise me that."

"We do—we do!" answered the lads. "You have stuck by us, Peter; we will stick by you. But why not put us ashore?"

"His people are everywhere. He has spies all along the coast. No; you would be re-taken and murdered."

"He would also discover that we had betrayed his trust," said Sidney Morrison, nervously.

"Fear not," said Peter, with a sneer; "I will protect your miserable life. I have promised to do so, and I will."

"Well, we must make up our minds to something," said Jack. "We can't stop out here for ever."

"I have it," said Peter, "I have it. You saw that ship which came beating up into the bay?"

"Yes, yes!" cried Jack, clapping his hands; "I understand now. You will put us on board of her—"

"No, no, young master; you are too impatient. I dare not put you on board of her. But you can swim?"

"Like a duck!" laughed Jack, for the fresh breeze and the thoughts of liberty filled his heart with delight.

"And you, my young master?" inquired Peter, turning to old Flick.

"Me?—oh, I swim like a stone," sighed old Flick. "I don't think I was born to be hanged, but if I drop into the water the chances are that I certainly shall be drowned."

The old man stamped his foot impatiently and muttered—

"It must be done—but how? If I go near the ship I shall be seen, and no one would forget my face."

"That's true," thought Jack.

"Let me see—let me see!" muttered Peter.

"Then, suddenly clapping his hands, he exclaimed—

"Yes, I know how to do it."

"That's right, Peter," laughed Jack. "What a wonderfully clever fellow you are! We are all attention."

"There's a net in the bows of the boat," said Peter Pigwellan. "Just you overhaul it, young master, and cut off a dozen or so of corks, and pass them over to me to run on to this piece of rope. I'll soon show you how to swim."

This was soon done, and old Peter made a set of corks such as are frequently used by boys learning to swim.

These he bound round old Flick's body so that the corks floated just behind his shoulder-blades.

He then quietly pulled the boat out into the bay until she caught the tide drifting inwards.

"Now," he observed, "in a few minutes we shall be within a couple of hundred yards of the ship we saw. Then you two lads must slide into the water and make your way to her. The tide will carry you. You can swim, Mr. Firebrace, and I need not tell you not to leave your friend, but to guide him as well as you can to the ship. Get hold of the cable, creep up it, and hide yourselves on board. At daylight she will most likely sail out to sea again and go to some port. You come out then and say that you were out in a boat and were upset—say anything; they can do you no harm, and you will be free. But,

mind; not one word about Red Randulph."

"We understand."

"Good. Now, are you ready?" demanded Peter Pigwellan.

"Yes. Good-bye, old fellow; we shall meet again."

They shook hands, and the two lads slipped into the water and were soon out of sight.

"Heaven help them!" said Peter. "Poor lads—poor lads. So young and so cruelly used. It is terrible."

Silently they bent to their oars and pulled towards the shore.

But as they neared it a boat passed them filled with armed men.

"Boat ahoy!" cried a voice from the strange boat; "boat ahoy! Is that you, Peter?"

It was Griffiths Grindwell's voice.

"Ay, ay, sir!" replied Pigwellan.

"You have been a confounded long time about the job. You threw it in, I suppose?"

"It's in the water now. You can ask this gentleman," replied Peter.

"Yes, yes," said Sidney Morrison; "I saw him go in."

"Then the boy is drowned and out of my way? Good! Keep a bright lookout on shore; I am now going on board the ship."

"On board the ship?" gasped Peter Pigwellan. "Which ship?"

"My ship, the 'Sea Hawk'! You must have passed close to her; but you are going blind."

The boat dashed quickly away towards the ship.

Dropping his oar the old man exclaimed—

"Poor lads, poor lads, their fate is sealed. They are on board the pirate-ship."

"What do you mean?" demanded Sidney Morrison.

"The 'Sea Hawk' is Grindwell's old ship—the one he sailed in as Red Randulph. The boys are lost, lost, lost!"

CHAPTER XXXI.

WHAT JACK AND OLD FLICK DID ON BOARD THE "SEA HAWK"—JACK PLAYS A TRICK UPON DUMB PETER, AND TAKES A NEW CHARACTER—THE ATTACK ON THE LONE HOUSE—WHO FIRED THE GUNS?

"Keep well up, old Flick," said Jack; "we shall soon be by the ship. Hist! keep quiet, or we shall disturb the watch."

"I am all right now, Jack," replied Flick, between his shivering teeth; "but precious cold."

They clambered up the cable, and crept into a porthole in the bow of the ship.

"How do you feel now, old fellow?" whispered Jack to his companion, whose teeth were chattering horribly.

"I feel that a good large fire and a glass of something hot would be very acceptable to this child, old man."

"I daresay you do," laughed Jack; "but I scarcely think we are likely to get it here. We have to wait until the ship is well out to sea, and then we must throw ourselves on the mercy of the captain, who may be a brute."

"I don't much fear that," said old Flick, laughing; "he can't be much worse than Grindwell."

"If he be only half as bad it will be quite enough for us," replied Jack; "however, we will make the best of it."

"The best of it," grumbled old Flick, as he crawled with Jack down the fore-hatch. "If we happen to come across anyone just now, it strikes me that we shall most likely have another cold bath."

"Don't be too cheerful, old man. Phew! how this place stinks!" whispered Jack.

"Who is there?" demanded a gruff voice out of the darkness. "What are you whispering for over there?"

"Nothing, mate, nothing; go to sleep," replied Jack, in a rough voice, trying to imitate a sailor; "go to sleep."

"Ah! it's precious fine to say go to sleep," growled the fellow; "but this cursed wound won't let me. Is the captain on board yet?"

"No; but I can't stop—good-night."

And Jack, catching old Flick by the arm, hurried him out of the cabin, but, missing the ladder, they stumbled along into a dark place, and then plunged suddenly forward down the hold of the ship, for one of the hatches had been left up.

Luckily for the lads they fell upon a number of old sails, so that, although much shaken, they were not really hurt.

"That was a narrow escape, old fellow," said Jack.

"I don't know so much about that," replied Flick. "Look here, Jack; judging from the distance we fell, I should think we were now in the hold of the ship. All is complete darkness, and here we are likely to remain, and become food for the rats, for I cannot guess how we are to get out."

"Nonsense, Flick, nonsense!" said Jack. "Keep up your pecker, and all will go well. Let us feel round this wretched place."

"Keep hold of each other," replied old Flick, "for if we are separated, I know that we shall not meet again in this dark hole."

"Why, what on earth makes you so dull, old fellow?" said Jack.

"I don't know, I am sure," said Flick, "beyond that I feel we shall soon have to part, Jack."

"Part!—nonsense! You have a fit of the blues on you, old man. You will soon be better."

"Perhaps I shall—I do not know. Who can be sure of anything in this world?" sighed poor Flick.

Jack made no answer, but, taking his companion's hand, commenced examining the hold as well as he could.

The place seemed nearly empty, with the exception of a lot of casks piled up at one end of it, and a few ropes and sails littered upon the lower deck.

"She don't seem much like a merchant vessel," Jack whispered to his companion. "What can she be?"

"Jack," said old Flick, suddenly,

"we have been betrayed. We are on board the vessel that the coastguard were after."

"By Jove! old fellow, I think you are right," said Jack, after a moment's thought. "Stop, there is a light shining through the planks yonder. Let us climb up on these barrels as well as we can, and see what is going on there."

With the greatest caution they climbed up the barrels, and at last were by the crack through which they had perceived the light flaring.

It looked into a small cabin, in which were seated two sailors—ill-looking fellows enough—smoking their pipes and drinking brandy and water.

"I should like to know what the captain is after," said one of the men; "I can't make him out lately. We ought never to have come back here after the row about the 'Flying Fish.' But there, Randulph would always have his way, let it be for right or wrong."

"It would be a precious look-out for anyone who disobeyed him," growled the other. "Are all the men ready?"

"Ay, ay; they are at their posts; pistols and guns loaded; cutlasses all sharpened; everything is prepared."

"That is right. Hush! there goes the signal; the captain has come at last."

A shrill whistle and the challenge of the watch on deck were heard, then the men hurried out to meet their commander.

"What is the matter, Jack?" asked old Flick. "Why, your hand is trembling, old fellow."

"Keep up your pecker, old Flick, and don't mind me," said Jack. "As you said just now, we are in a great scrape. But keep quiet, and we will do our best to upset all their plots. Hush! here comes the captain."

The two boys again applied their eyes to the crack in the partition, and beheld Griffiths Grindwell enter the cabin, followed by some of his officers.

Grindwell was dressed as a sailor now; by his side hung a huge cutlass, and the butt-ends of a brace of pistols could be perceived protruding from the belt of his trousers. His wig was removed, showing the deep scar that ran across his brow, and a huge false moustache, whiskers, and beard hid the entire lower part of his face.

He walked swiftly into the cabin, and having drunk a deep draught of wine, turned to his lieutenants.

"You have everything prepared?" he asked, in quick tones.

"Everything. The men are told off, as you ordered. But, if I may speak my mind, I don't think it right to leave the 'Sea Hawk' with so few hands aboard."

"That is my affair, not yours," replied Randulph, sharply. "The Government cutter is miles away from here, and will not hear the report of our pistols. But in case they should, have you the guns loaded and shotted?"

"Everything is ready, captain," replied the man.

"Good," laughed Grindwell, with a fiendish look; "I shall to-night have my revenge. Where is Dumb Peter?"

One of the men went to the door and called aloud for Peter, whereupon a wretched lad, clothed in rags, with a face as black as a chimney-sweep's, and hands browned with tar, entered the cabin.

He stood with bent-down head and sullen face awaiting the captain's orders.

"Peter," cried Grindwell, "Peter, you lazy dog, go to the hold and bring a keg of brandy; the men shall have a deep draught before they start. Hurry, you lazy hound, or you shall taste the rope's-end pretty sharply."

The dumb fellow made a kind of murmuring sound and then departed on his errand.

"Old Flick," whispered Jack, "as you value your life, make the best of your way down from the casks; I will follow."

Cautiously they crept down, and by Jack's directions they hid themselves in one of the bulkheads behind the hatch, and then awaited the coming of Dumb Peter, for they knew they were in the hold where the brandy was kept.

Presently a dim light shone from above, a ladder was lowered into the hold, and Dumb Peter, swinging a lantern, came slowly down into the hold.

Scarcely had his foot touched the deck when Jack seized him from behind and threw him on the floor.

"If you attempt to move, I will kill

you," whispered our hero in the lad's ear.

The boy, who, though dumb, was evidently not deaf, made no attempt at resistance.

"Quick, Flick, old fellow, lend a hand here. Put the lantern in a place of safety. That will do. Now help me to strip this fellow. How dirty he is! There, you go on and strip him whilst I strip myself."

"Strip yourself?" demanded old Flick. "Why, what do you mean to do?"

"Never mind, old man; only make haste. Make haste, or we shall all be lost."

Old Flick at once set to work, and in a few moments Dumb Peter was stripped to the skin, and comfortably rolled up in an old sail, to keep him warm, which was bound round with thin rope, so that the lad could not move.

Then Jack, who had removed his own clothes, put on the lad's rags, roughed up his hair, blackened his face with the dust from the casks, and daubed his hands with tar and pitch.

"Do I look like Dumb Peter now, Flick?" he laughed, as his companion, by the aid of the lantern, examined him.

"By Jove, you do! But what are you going to be up to now, Jack?" demanded old Flick, anxiously.

"I don't know exactly. I will do the best I can to find out what those fellows are up to. You stay here, and I will be back to you soon. Anyway, I think at present we had better separate," answered Jack.

"Why? Oh, Jack! let us go together," pleaded old Flick.

"There are not two Dumb Peters, Flick, so only one must go. In this disguise I may discover means for our escape."

"Yes, but they may kill you, Jack; will kill you, if they find out who you are," said Flick.

"Your being with me would not prevent their doing that," said Jack. "You know our agreement, old fellow; don't try to break through it now, when it is most important it should be kept. I am captain, and you must obey me."

"Very well; but I wish you would give me something to do besides watching this fellow."

"All right, and so I will, if you will only be quiet. You heard him say that the cannon are loaded. Well, if you hear anything of a very terrible disturbance on land, creep up on deck, and fire one of the cannons. If it does nothing else, it will alarm these wretches, and may stop them committing greater cruelties."

"All right, Jack; "you may rely upon me. And I'll tell you what I'll do. I'll see if I can't make this fellow tell me more about this ship and its crew. He don't look a bad fellow, and—"

"Peter!" roared a voice down the hatchway. "What are you doing down there, you lazy lubber?"

Jack squeezed old Flick's hand, seized a keg of spirits, flung it upon his shoulders, and, assuming the walk and style of Dumb Peter, crawled upon deck, where he found one of the mates waiting for him.

"Do you think that we can stop here all night, you lazy brute?" cried the man, bestowing a hearty kick upon our hero. "Come, tumble up, or I'll give you such a taste of the rope's-end, that you won't quite relish it, my man."

Jack, who was an excellent mimic, imitated the noises he had heard Dumb Peter make, and shuffled forward to the cabin, where he found Grindwell—or Richard Randulph—and his officers mad with impatience.

Curses and blows were showered upon Jack, all of which he received in stolid silence.

"I think we have pretty well knocked his senses out of him," laughed one. "I never saw such a fool."

"So I am likely to have a nice time of it," thought Jack.

"I fancy we had better take him with us," said Grindwell; "he could serve out the grog."

"Yes, I think he does that with the greatest quickness and pleasure. It's the only thing he can do."

"Well, then, we will take him. If he is shot it won't much matter. If he is taken prisoner, he cannot say much. Here, Peter, serve out the brandy to the men, and then come with us."

This was just what Jack wished, but

he was greatly afraid that the men might know he was not Peter.

However, as it was dark, he went boldly to work, merely taking great care not to let anyone see his face more than he could possibly help.

But the men were far too much engaged with their grog to notice him, and, as he made it very strong, there were no complaints about it, the men drinking it in as quickly as possible.

Then the word was given to man the boats, and Jack, in the character of Dumb Peter, was ordered in the stern-sheets of the long-boat.

Down into the boat tumbled the men, and the word was passed to give way, then, with muffled oars, they pulled in shore towards the Hawk's Crag.

"I wonder if they are going back into the school," thought Jack; "if they are it will be very awkward for me. There, in the strong light, I am sure to be known, and, if discovered, death is certain."

The boat touched the sands, and Jack's first idea was to spring out and run away; but that he soon found would not be easy to do; for he, having charge of a large keg of brandy, two of the sailors, on their own account, took charge of him.

"Now, my men," said Grindwell, in an undertone; "look well to the locks and loadings of your pistols. Keep your cutlasses ready to your hands, and your eyes open to prevent surprises. Now, keep well together. What are you two fellows doing there?"

The last question was put to the two men who kept close by our hero.

"Please, your honour, we're only helping Dumb Peter to carry the spirits along."

"If I find you taking too much of the spirit until we are aboard ship again I'll let daylight into you. But perhaps you had better keep by the lad; he has no reason to wish us well. Now, march."

The two fellows were only too delighted at this permission, and at once caught hold of Jack's arms and bore him away in triumph, the keg of brandy bumping against him at every step he took.

Up from the beach, skirting the hill whereon Hawkhouse stood, rounding the road leading to the village, and then on through a thick wood which led to the mill where Jack and old Flick had first met Pigwellan.

The tumble-down old place was soon reached, and, leaving the little band drawn up in the shade of the mill, Grindwell and one of his officers entered the dilapidated building, from which they soon emerged, followed by several other men, who in silence delivered crape masks to the others.

"Fall in," said Grindwell, and once more the band commenced its march.

They had not proceeded far when Jack heard the crowing of a cock, shrill and clear.

The band halted at once, and replied to this signal—for such it was—by two soft whistles.

The next moment two men leaped over the hedge, and advanced to Grindwell.

It was with difficulty Jack repressed a cry of surprise, for the foremost man was Collin Clout.

"Well," said Grindwell, sharply, "have you been able to make all right?"

"All safe. All you have to do is to advance quietly, surround the house, and, at a signal I will give, which is three taps at the shutters of the lower window, Sally Scraggs will open the door, and let in half-a-dozen. One must go to the upper story and kill that Rackstraw—he is the one most to fear; the next must go to the large room on the second-floor, the one looking over the garden, you know; that's where Mr. Summerbell sleeps."

"Good; I will look after him," said Grindwell. "But two people have ever crossed my path with impunity. One, a boy, now sleeps beneath the sea; the other shall die to-night."

"In the rooms below are the doctor and the half-pay lieutenant," continued Collin.

"Ah!" said Grindwell, turning to his two lieutenants; "I intrust these gentlemen to your keeping."

"They won't bother us much," growled one fellow; "mine sha'n't even groan."

"Then there's the girl; she sleeps next to her father," continued the spy.

"I will look to her," said Grindwell, with a fiendish smile; "are there any more?"

"None; we cannot fail if all keep quiet. If anyone escapes from the house, you must shoot him down."

"The men have their orders," growled Grindwell. "Now, boys, you must advance with your guns ready to fire; but do not put your fingers on the triggers, in case of an accidental stumble, which would be disastrous. You have heard what our spy says. Now, forward!"

Every word of this discourse poor Jack had drunk in eagerly.

No sooner had Jack become aware of the nature of Grindwell's expedition, than he set to work to thwart, as far as possible, the schemes thus cleverly, but diabolically planned.

Taking care to avoid notice, Jack broke a small branch out of the hedge. This he denuded of all its twigs, save a small one about an inch long, which stuck out nearest the thickest part of the stick.

They were now within twenty paces of the house, when again a halt was called and the instructions once more given to the men.

Now Jack, whilst the conversation had been going on, had cleverly managed to place the hooked part of his stick round the trigger of the mate's musket, whilst he attached the other end to a bramble close by.

"Now for the attack!" cried Grindwell, and he stepped forward towards his post.

The mate made one step forward, the stick pulled the trigger, and the next moment a loud report rang through the air, and one of Grindwell's men fell dead, his skull blown to atoms.

In a moment all was confusion.

Many of the men did not know who had fired, and imagined that the people of the house, having discovered the plot, had set an ambuscade ready to shoot them down.

Some turned to fly and threw down their muskets, which, in the dark, our hero took good care to discharge, so as to make the confusion greater, and, if possible, call assistance to the people of the Lone House.

The people in the Lone House were evidently now wide awake and aware of their danger.

Lights appeared in the upper windows, and men's voices were heard calling to one another.

"Forward, forward!" cried Grindwell. "Attack the house at once!"

At this moment a door was flung open, and a figure clad in white rushed forth screaming.

It was the beautiful but somewhat energetic Sally Scraggs.

Bounding forward she threw her lovely form upon Collin, and, casting her arms about his neck, implored him to save her.

"Confound you, you fool, have you left the door open?" demanded Collin, shaking her off.

"No, Collin, no. That wretched old brute, Dr. Lamberhurst, he caught me peeping out and calling you, and, oh—"

"Well, what do you mean?" demanded Collin Clout, quickly.

"Why, the brute, he—he—he kicked me! Oh, I can't tell you where, but he kicked me out of the house and shut the door behind me. Oh, Collin!"

Again she flung herself upon the young man's neck, but, with a heavy blow, he felled her to the earth.

"Forward, my lads, forward!" cried Grindwell, who now seemed in his perfect element.

He waved his sword on high, and with a ringing cheer, called upon the others to follow.

Whatever these wretches were, they had the courage and ferocity of the tiger.

Answering their leader's call with a cheer they presented their guns, and poured in a sharp volley of bullets.

Then, swinging their muskets by the straps over their shoulders, they drew their cutlasses, and rushed forward.

Suddenly from the windows—which directly the attack had been commenced had been darkened—flashes of flame, followed by sharp reports, were belched forth, and some half-dozen of the pirates bit the earth.

"Close under the walls—close under the walls," cried Grindwell. "They cannot fire there."

This advice was far too good to be neglected, and now all the band were clustered close under the wall, which protected them from the deadly fire of the besieged.

Then Grindwell ordered one of the

mates to produce the Greek fire, and use it quickly.

The fellow coolly took out what appeared to be only a couple of ordinary wine-bottles, filled with liquid.

Stepping softly back, he flung one over the wall straight at a window, through which it crashed, and the next moment the whole place was one blaze of light, and with horror our hero perceived the room was in flames.

"Bravo!" cried Grindwell; "that was a good shot. Give them the other to make certain. Let us get this over."

The advice was, in one way, good, but in another, it was unfortunate—that is, looking at things from the outlaws' point of view; for, had the bottle been aimed with the same skill as the first one, the flames would have at once burst forth at two different parts of the house; but it was not so well directed.

It caught the top of the wall, under which the outlaws and Sally were hiding.

There was a dreadful crash; the liquid no sooner came in contact with the air than it became liquid fire, which poured down upon the devoted Sally Scraggs and one of Grindwell's men.

In an instant both were enveloped in flames.

Uttering yells of agony the two miserable creatures threw up their arms and rushed away into the woods, rolling amongst the underwood, vainly attempting to put out the flames; but only setting fire to the dry sticks and dead leaves on which they fell.

Even the pirates, cruel, merciless brutes as they were, shuddered at this terrible fate.

"Leave them to their fate," roared Grindwell; "we cannot save them—they must perish. But we can avenge them, like good men and true. Quick, my lads; shoot at the windows. Do not let one man escape!"

And now all became the greatest confusion and uproar.

Bullets rattled against the walls as the besieged vainly tried to shoot the pirates, who, now and then dashing from their cover, discharged their guns through the windows, in hopes of killing someone, for they dared not stop to take aim, and then rushed back to the shelter of the wall.

And now the house was in flames, the lurid light shooting up into the dark sky.

"They must have perished in the flames," said Grindwell; "they have not fired for five minutes."

At that moment one of the scouts rushed up, and, in hurried tones, cried out—

"Fly, fly; the people of the village are in arms! The coastguard are out, and will be down on us in a few minutes."

"Quick, lads," cried Grindwell, hurrying his men together, "to the beach! We can reach it before the people come. Now run for it. We have done our work."

They were going to rush off when the outer gate of the Lone House was opened, and Wild Winny ran out.

"Ha, I have you at last!" cried Grindwell, as he seized her in his arms; "we must not leave anyone to tell the tale of this fight. Come, my lads, the girl has fainted; she is my prisoner."

He threw the girl as lightly over his shoulder as if she had been of no weight, and then led the way through the woods.

Jack made an attempt to bolt, so that he might be able to bring down the people to the beach, and so rescue Winny; but one of the men, thinking that he only turned the wrong way in his confusion, seized him by the arm and dragged him quickly away.

"It can't be helped," thought Jack. "If I call out I shall only be killed at once, and most likely do no good; whereas, if I go back to the ship, I may be able to save both Winny and old Flick. Save them I will, or die!"

The man who had thus, as he thought, taken possession of Jack, was one of the fellows who had paid the greatest attention to the brandy cask, and so his steps were not the swiftest or steadiest: Jack was, therefore, in hopes he would relax his grasp of his arm; but that was not to be. The man grasped our hero's arm tighter and tighter, as if for support.

Jack now imagined that he and his companion must be much behind the others, and in his heart he devoutly hoped that they might be overtaken by the pursuers.

Suddenly the fellow's foot caught in a

broken branch; he was thrown violently forward, and his head fell with a terrible crack against a tree.

Jack's natural good heart made him stoop down and examine the fallen man.

The fellow was dead as dead could be; so our hero relieved him of his pistol and knife, and then, leaping to his feet, exclaimed—

"I am safe—safe! Thank heaven, I can now give the people warning where they must fly to rescue dear Winny, and to send the coastguard after the pirate vessel. Hurrah! I will save her yet."

He was about to dash off when strong hands caught him from behind, and dashed him to the ground.

"Not so fast, my young master, if you please," said a voice Jack knew too well to be Collin Clout's. "I don't think you will get off quite so easily. I have a little account to settle with you yet. Now's the time for it."

"Unhand me, wretch!" gasped Jack, for Collin was kneeling on his chest, nearly crushing him.

"Don't be in such a hurry," said Collin. "I shall get off presently. But I don't know if you will be any better off when I do. Confound the thing! what the deuce have I done with it?"

Jack could tell that Collin was feeling for something in his pocket, but knew not what.

Suddenly the fellow drew whatever it was forth, and opened it with his teeth.

Our hero knew that it was a large clasp-knife from the noise the spring made.

"Listen to me, Collin Clout," Jack said, calmly. "Death is nearer to you than to me. I can let you go—"

"Can you?" said Collin, with a short, bitter laugh. "You are very kind, certainly. Anything more?"

"Yes; if you attempt to kill me, you will be dead in two seconds," replied Jack, coolly.

"That we will see. I am not to be taken in by such nonsense. So here goes."

"Beware!" cried Jack. "If you attempt to take my life, you are a dead man!"

Collin raised his weapon to strike the fatal blow.

Jack saw the gleam, and, quickly pre- senting his pistol, discharged it full in the coward's face.

One horrid yell, and Collin Clout threw up his arms, staggered to his feet, and fell back dead.

Jack flung away his pistol—for it was now useless to him—and once more dashed off, hoping to make his way through the wood, and get to the village in time to tell the people how they might intercept the pirates; but, in his confusion, he turned the wrong way, and, as he sprang out into a field, was seized.

"Hullo!" cried one; "why, I'm blest if it ain't Dumb Peter! Only to think of his escaping! It makes one almost inclined to kill him."

"No, no, that won't do; let us get on," said the other man.

Jack, seeing that the men were impatient to get down to the boats in order that they might make good their escape, pointed to the forest, and began showing the greatest signs of terror, at the same time uttering sounds meant to convey the idea that the pursuers were close upon their heels.

"I see what he means," whispered one of the men; "the people are in hot pursuit."

Jack nodded his head violently, and continued his gesticulations with increased ardour.

"Come along, then, old Dummy," said one of the men; "for once you have been some use."

But here Jack had another scheme by which he hoped to escape.

He pointed to his foot, hopped along a few paces, then stopping, shook his head.

"He's sprained his ankle," said one. "We must not leave him alive. Let us kill him, and then run."

Jack began to be very sorry that he had done this trick.

However, it was too late to draw back, so he made signs imploring mercy.

"We won't kill the poor little devil," said one of the men; "you take one arm and I'll take the other, and we will run him down to the beach in no time. Now then, my lad, off you go!"

Jack dared not complain at this, and so, held firmly between the men, he was made to go bounding away at a tremendous pace, until, nearly faint with fatigue, they arrived at the beach.

"Into the boats, into the boats!" said Grindwell, in a whisper. "No one has been down to the beach yet. The coastguard have evidently been led off the scent by our spy, and have not seen the brig."

Scarcely had he said the words than there was a quick, bright flash out at sea, followed by a loud report.

It was a cannon from the "Sea Hawk."

"Confusion!" roared Grindwell; "they cannot have attacked the brig. Can they be mad on board?"

Again and again came the boom of the vessel's guns, sending their deep sounds to echo amongst the cliffs.

The men were all in the boats now; the order was given to shove off, and the next minute they were cleaving their way through the water towards the brig.

As Grindwell steered he bent forward, and with his hawk-like eyes peered into the darkness.

There was the ship just as he had left it, save that there appeared some confusion on board.

No other ship was near it—not even a boat was to be seen on the water save their own.

"They cannot have boarded the 'Sea Hawk' and taken her," said Grindwell to one of the men.

"Better hail her, sir, first, afore we pull in close," said the fellow thus appealed to.

"Ship ahoy!" cried Grindwell, "ship ahoy! Why did you fire those guns?"

"We did not fire them," replied a voice from the ship. "They went off by themselves."

"What do you mean by that?" shouted Grindwell, passionately. "Have you not been attacked?"

"No, sir; everything has been as quiet as possible. We saw the light of the house burning on the shore and stood ready to make all sail, when first one gun went off and then another. I think the devil is on board, that's what I do."

"Give way, my men," observed Grindwell; "if he be on board I shall be wanted to kick him out."

With this grim bit of humour Grindwell was soon on board, and then Wild Winny, now wild no longer, was lifted out of the boat on to the deck.

"Count the hands as they come up," he said to his mate, "and let me know how many are missing."

The men crawled up on deck very slowly, for not a few of them had been severely hurt.

Jack was awfully afraid that he would be discovered, but luckily, Dumb Peter was of so little consequence, that the officer in charge did not seem to care much whether he was alive or dead.

"The men are all aboard, sir, except eight missing. The boats are all hauled up," reported the officer.

"Very good; make all sail at once. These guns will bring down the cruisers upon us. When we are out to sea, I will inquire into this matter. Tell Dumb Peter to get me some brandy and supper."

CHAPTER XXXII.

ON BOARD THE "SEA HAWK"—THE INQUIRY INTO THE GUNS—JACK STARTS ON ANOTHER ADVENTURE.

JACK, who, of course, in his character of Dumb Peter, received the order to get the captain's supper, was not a little puzzled how to set about it, for he had not the slightest idea where the larder was.

However, he at last hit upon the right place, and at once set to work, making a most peculiar selection of provisions.

"I wish to goodness that I knew the way the real Dumb Peter does his work," thought Jack. "However, I will give Grindwell a taste for his supper, and I only hope that he will poison himself with it, that's all."

THE BOYS OF HAWKHOUSE SCHOOL.

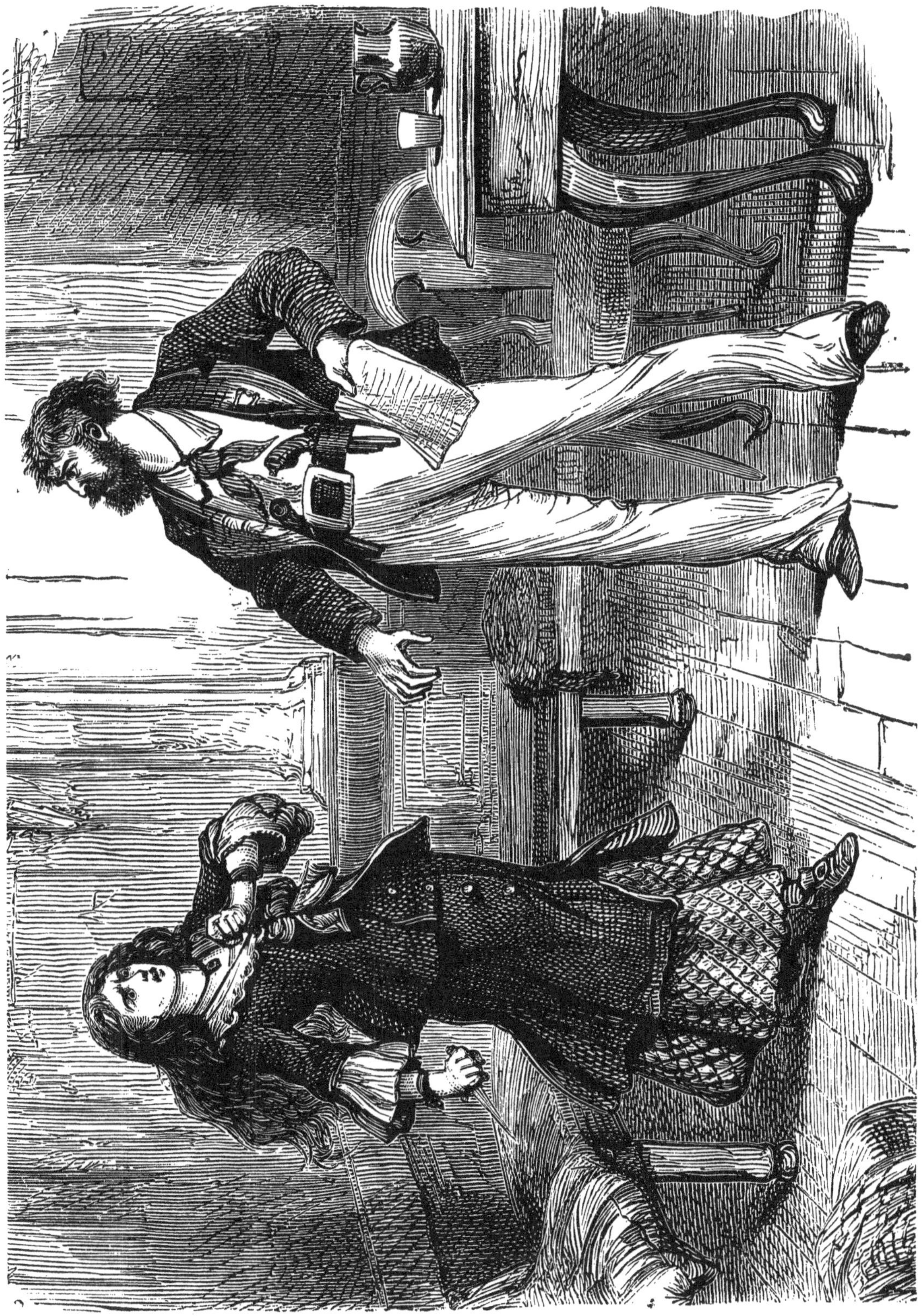

STAND BACK!' SHE EXCLAIMED, AS SHE DREW THE DAGGER."

o. 10.

PRICE ONE HALFPENNY.

[Published Every Monday.]

Seizing a tray, Jack spread a cloth upon it, and heaped all the victuals he could find in a confused mass in the middle, putting a knife and fork and plate by the side.

This done, he hurried away to the cabin; but as he rushed into the room, the mate was about leaving it, and the consequence was they came into collision, Jack flying one way, the mate the other, and the provisions anywhere and everywhere.

"Confound that fellow!" cried Grindwell, seizing a pistol, and firing it at our hero. "I'll kill him!"

But either the excessive passion he was in, or the late events going so much against him, had unsteadied his hand, for the bullet so kindly intended for our hero, was lodged in the thick part of the mate's shoulder.

The man sprang to his feet with a yell of agony, and turned with a fierce look at Grindwell.

"By heaven! you shall pay for this!" he roared, as he stamped his feet with mingled pain and rage.

"Dare you speak thus to me, dog!" thundered Grindwell.

And, with a fierce oath, he flung the pistol he had so lately fired right into the man's face, and this with such violence, that the fellow fell rolling on the deck.

"Get up, you yelping hound!" cried Grindwell. "Up this instant, and hand me back my pistol!"

The fellow staggered to his feet, and, picking up the weapon, handed it to Grindwell in sullen silence.

"You have had a heavy lesson, my friend," laughed Grindwell. "Now go, and don't forget it."

The mate, whose face was bathed in blood, cast a quick look of hatred at Randulph, and then slunk away.

"Come here, you lazy, careless whelp!" said Grindwell to Jack, who was busy putting the things, as well as he could, back upon the tray; "put your tray here. Now hasten away, and get another keg of brandy. I must hold a court-martial upon these men, and find out who fired those guns. There is treachery on board. But I will find the traitors, and then they shall have but a short shrift, and a run to the yardarm!"

Jack was only too glad to get out of the cabin. He made a dash to the larder, and, having filled his pockets with food, and hid a bottle of water under his jacket, he hurried away to the hold, where he found old Flick still watching by the real Dumb Peter.

"Oh, Jack, I am so glad to see you!" said old Flick. "What a terrible night it has been!"

"It has indeed. These wretches have burned down the Lone House, murdered all in it save Winny, and she is now a prisoner on board. Old Flick, come what may, I am determined that, if I must die, I will devise some plan of sinking this vile ship and her crew. Not one on board deserves mercy!"

"Don't say that, Jack; this poor lad does, I am sure. He has been trying to speak to me, but I don't understand him."

"We will see about that presently. Have you found out where he sleeps?" demanded Jack.

"Yes; here, in this miserable hole, in that dark corner, and—"

"Peter!" roared a gruff voice down the hatch.

Jack put his finger on his friend's mouth, placed the provisions, water, and some candles, he had taken from the larder, by the side of Flick, and then hurried quickly away with a keg of brandy.

"Look sharp, you lazy lubber," cried the sailor, giving Jack a kick, to help him along the road, as he said; "look sharp, or it's my idea you will be hung up to the yardarm as a warning to skulkers, my hearty. The captain wants you down in the chief cabin."

Jack hurried along, and found Grindwell seated at the head of a long table, his drawn cutlass and a brace of pistols placed before him.

"Put the brandy here," said Grindwell, pointing to the table.

This was at once done, and with the steel hilt of his sword, he broke in the head of the keg.

Grindwell then took from his pocket a silver whistle, and blew upon it shrilly.

This was answered by the boatswain's whistle, and the merry cry of "Tumble up, tumble up!" sounded through the ship.

The mates came silently into the

cabin, and seated themselves at the table, whilst the men gathered in groups at the farther end of the cabin.

The ship was now plunging through the sea at a fine rate, so that two men for the watch, and one at the wheel, were all that were needed to be on duty. All the rest were in the cabin.

Jack hid himself in a corner, determined to watch.

First, a tumblerful of neat brandy was served round to everyone, officers and men, and then the court was at once opened.

"Now, Mat Weatherstay," cried Grindwell, striking his fist violently on the table, "tell me how those guns went off."

"Well, I'm blest if I know, yer honour. D'ye see, the tide had been running out strong, and so I goes forward, as the ship had swung upon her cable, to look how yer honour was a-getting on with the work on shore. Well, yer honour, I says to my mate, says I—'That's the sound of a musket, that is.' Says he, in his friendly way—'Mat, I'm blest if you ain't the ugliest and thick-headedest old fool out! That there was the sound of a fowling-piece, and not of a musket.' Well, as we was a-talking, more shots come, and I says—"

"To the point, man, to the point!" cried Grindwell, impatiently. "Who fired the guns?"

"That's just it, yer honour," replied Mat Weatherstay. "I don't know; only, as I said—"

"Silence!" cried Grindwell. "If you open your mouth again, I will have your tongue plucked out, as I had Dumb Peter's yonder! Where is Seth Johnson?"

"Here I am, your honour," replied a fellow, whose deep voice rolled out from the midst of his black beard, "here I am, yer honour. But I don't think I can tell you much more nor my mate could about the guns."

"Tell me what you do know, or dread the result."

"Well, we had watched the fire, and we thought we saw you on the shore. We were all straining our eyes to make sure it was our people, when 'Bang' goes one of the guns close by us. We turned round, but there was nobody near the gun. Then off went another and another. We stumbled back in alarm."

"Cowards!" cried Grindwell, contemptuously.

And he tossed off a cup of brandy.

"Asking your honour's pardon, I don't think many of us here be afraid of a fight. I've been side by side with yer honour when we've leaped on board a ship much better manned than we were, and I never drew back; but when I see a light no bigger nor a snuff of a candle go bobbing from one cannon to another, and letting 'em off, and not a being near, that is, as was visible to mortal eye, well, I don't mind owning that I did feel queer."

"That's true enough, yer honour," said an old man, whose broad, hairy chest was that of a giant. "Them sort of things is what makes a fellow think more of his latter end than anything else. I'm willing to have a grapple with Davy Jones if he will only come in a visible and substantial way like; but it's the invisible ones I can't stand. You can't get at 'em, and they do get at you, right into the marrow of your bones."

"So you have turned coward, have you, Jacob?" sneered Grindwell. "I should have thought that we had played too many tricks like those of our own up yonder at Hawkhouse for you to be frightened."

"Tricks we have played, and that's certain; but you see, yer honour, whatever we did there was always someone to be seen. Now, in this case, no one was to be seen, only a thing like a little firefly as flitted from one touch-hole to another, and let the cannons off quickly. That's different."

Grindwell looked fiercely round; but he saw that all his men were of the same opinion; he could see no trace of treachery in their faces.

"Bah! the thing is done," he laughed, as he tossed off another cup of brandy; "let it go. If Davy Jones be really on board, I challenge him to mortal combat. I fear him not, let him come in any shape he likes."

At this wild defiance the strongest sailors shuddered and glanced nervously over their shoulders.

"There!" cried Grindwell; "fill up your cups, my lads, and drink success to the 'Sea Hawk.'"

The fellows shouted with delight, and, having filled their glasses, drank the toast with loud cheers.

"The girl—my prisoner, whom I have just brought on board—will occupy my little cabin. I have locked her in there. Now mark me—the first one who tries to hold any communication with her, dies! Now go."

The men bowed, and in silence left the cabin, and tumbled up on deck.

Jack was about to follow them when Grindwell called him back, and, pointing to the poop of the cabin, where there was what appeared to be an alcove covered with curtains, bade him make his bed.

Jack drew back the curtains, and found that there was a fixed bedstead behind them.

He at once set to work to smooth down the sheets and shake up the pillows, and as he did so noticed that at the back of the bed was a port-hole about a foot and a half square, which evidently was fixed in the stern of the ship.

With the greatest care not to make any noise, Jack undid the catch, so that the window could be easily opened.

He then completed his work, and crept out of the cabin to old Flick and Dumb Peter.

"Dear Jack," cried old Flick, "I am so delighted to see you safe and sound again. What has been up?"

"I have told you the greater part of my news," said Jack; "besides, I have to be off directly."

"Off again?" said old Flick, in astonishment, as he watched Jack making his supper.

"Yes; you forget that I am the captain's servant," said Jack. "Now, whilst I eat, tell me how you fired those guns."

"Did I do it well?" demanded old Flick, as a broad smile played over his face.

"Capitally. For my own part, I can't tell how you can have done it. Cut on, there's a good fellow."

"Well, then, Dumb Peter helped me," laughed old Flick; "he's no fool, only—" here he dropped his voice—"only I think, Jack, that the poor creature is dying—I do indeed."

Jack took up the candle and looked at the sleeping boy.

There was no doubting that cold, pinched look—Death, with kindly hand, would soon release him.

"I have made him understand we are friends to him," whispered old Flick, "and he is so pleased. I told him that I wanted to fire off the cannon without the men knowing, and then he pointed to that locker, which I opened, and found a kind of tarred string of a very loose twist. Following his signs, I found a keg of brandy with the head knocked in. This, I suppose, was our young friend's private cellar. Acting under his advice, I soaked the string in some brandy—But what are you taking off those things for, Jack? Are you not going to play Dumb Peter any more?"

"Of course I am; but now you must take the part for a little time. You are as good a mimic as I am, and can do it as well."

"And what are you going to do?" demanded old Flick, as he stripped off his clothes.

"Never mind what I am about to do," said Jack; "just you go on with your story."

"Well, that is soon done. I then rubbed the soaked string well with gunpowder until the cord was nearly dry, and my hands as sore as possible, I can tell you. This done, still acting under my dumb friend's advice, I crept on deck, and whilst the sailors were all forward twisted the string round the breech of every cannon on one side of the ship, taking great care that it crossed the touch-hole of each cannon, on which I dropped a little loose gunpowder to make sure. Then I dropped the end down on the deck, lit it, and crept away."

"Well, and the effect was—"

"Very peculiar," said Flick. "The spark seemed to burn of a dark red, so dull that one could scarcely see it. It appeared to burn inside the string, but I found that it burned it quite to a light ash, which the softest wind would blow away. At first it burned slowly, but at last burned quicker. Each time it came to one of the touch-holes, 'Fizz' went the loose powder, and 'Bang' went the cannon. I scarcely could keep from laughing as I saw the fellows start back in horror. They watched the cannons so closely, that I had plenty of time to escape."

"Capital! Now, then," Jack cried, as he put on his own clothes, and once more appeared in his old character; "you must, if you are called—or, rather, if Peter is called—go up for him. You will find it dark, but keep your head well down. I shall be back soon," continued Jack. "Take care of him while I am away."

"One moment, Jack," cried old Flick. "You are going on some dangerous exploit."

"Dangerous or otherwise, I must go," said Jack. "You shall know all when I come back."

"Look here, Jack," said old Flick; "here is an old flint pistol I found in yonder locker; you may want it. It is not loaded, but you can load it. Take it with you."

"Hold hard for a moment, Flick," said Jack. "Let me look at the pistol."

He took it in his hands, and examined it closely, and then, thrusting the barrel into a knot-hole in the flooring of the deck, snapped it close off to the pan.

"Better not load such a pistol as that, Flick. However, this other pistol which I have may be very useful. Where is the powder, old boy? I have no time to lose."

"Here is the powder," said old Flick.

Jack took some, and, having seen that the flint was sharp, and gave out sparks as it fell, he wrapped some powder up in a piece of tarpaulin, which he bound on the top of his head with a bit of yarn.

He then wished old Flick an affectionate good-bye, and started on his adventure.

CHAPTER XXXIII.

RED RANDULPH DEFIES ALL GHOSTS—THE APPARITION IN THE ALCOVE—A STRANGE BEDFELLOW.

As Jack left the spirit-room he took a coil of line on his arm, and, having crept cautiously up to the first deck, fastened one end of the line to a cleat by a port-hole.

He then thrust open the port-hole, and lowered the rest of the line into the sea, being careful not to make a splash.

He then noticed how the ship was going, and the way the line went.

The vessel was spanking along at a fine rate, sailing sharp on the wind, and with delight, Jack noticed that the line he had paid out floated close to the vessel's side, and trailed astern.

Slipping through the port-hole, Jack lowered himself into the water, and, swimming as he went enough to keep his head well up, he managed to reach the stern of the ship, and, as she was built low down in the water, without much difficulty climbed up to the port-hole or window, which looked in on to the captain's bed.

He could just look through and see the lights shining from the curtains, and knew that Grindwell had not entered.

He fastened the end of the line firmly round his waist, and then pushed open the cabin-window, and crept in.

Cautiously he peeped out of the alcove from between the curtains, and saw Grindwell sitting at the table.

Before him was the keg of brandy, and Jack noticed, with delight, that he had evidently been drinking freely.

Untying his parcel of gunpowder, Jack emptied it in a little heap on the bed just before him.

He then carefully put the piece of tarpaulin away, and, taking his pistol, which was cocked, in his left hand, he held it down so as to be able to ignite the powder whenever he liked.

"Bah!" exclaimed Grindwell, or Red Randulph, as he drank some more of the fiery spirit; "I used not to have my nerves shaken like this—and now, too, when all my wishes are so well accomplished. The boy sleeps beneath the sea, in the same grave where I sent his father and mother. Summerbell is killed; I saw him fall. The game is now entirely in my own hands, and yet I tremble."

Again he had recourse to the brandy to revive his courage, and then continued—

"It is strange, very strange! Who could have fired those guns! Tut! have I become a child that I should think of such rubbish? It must have been some of the men. No; they dared not do it, there is not one on board dare turn against me. All are so bad, they know that if one swings all must share the same fate."

He rose from his seat and paced rapidly up and down, only pausing now and then to take a drink.

"If I touch on the coast of France the girl must be placed under the care of some fisherman's wife. No, that will not do. She might—nay, she would—break loose and let the world know all. A convent! That would be better—or a madhouse better than all! Yes, I must attempt it. Then back to London, remain for a time quiet and calm in my merchant's office, and I can travel down to Hawkhouse again without fear."

At that moment a tap came on the cabin door, and Grindwell bidding the person "Come in," one of the officers entered.

"It's a dark night, sir," said the man, "but, as near as we can make out, there is a sail on the lee bow."

"How is that? Has she no light visible?" demanded Grindwell, huskily.

"No, sir; but there was a vivid flash of lightning, and the watch swear they saw a sail."

"Tut, tut! the men are half drunk and wholly frightened by that affair of the cannons. Tell them that I have no fear. We are not in the quarter of the globe to meet the 'Flying Dutchman,' and," he added, with a fearful oath, "if I were I'd give the mynheer chase and blow him to the place where they say he will have to go one day."

The sailor shuddered, and turned pale, but did not move.

"Have you anything more to tell me? No more ghost stories, I hope. By my faith, we are children again."

"Johnson, the mate, you shot, is dead, sir," said the man, in a low voice; "he died a few minutes since."

"What care we for that? You take his place. You have a higher place, and I a better officer," cried Grindwell.

"Ay, but his death was horrible. He called all curses down upon this ship, and on the crew."

"Do you think his calling can make them come? Ha, ha, ha! think you that he can command curses, and call up spirits? Ha, ha, ha!"

"But the men say they have seen him since he died, sir," said the sailor.

"If you see him, set him to work. A crew of ghosts, who could work well, would be to my taste. No wages to pay; no fear of their eating or drinking too much; and, if we come to a good hand-to-hand fight, none of them can be killed. What has this fresh ghost been doing?"

"Running about the rigging in the shape of a ball of fire," said the mate.

"And have you fellows been at sea so long, and yet do not know St. Elmo's light? It shows we shall have nasty weather. Bah! Pass the word for Dumb Peter to bring up another keg of brandy. That will put life into the men. Ha, ha, ha! once get plenty of spirits on board, and the corpse will be forgotten."

The sailor went to the door, whistled, and passed the word forward for Dumb Peter and the brandy.

He then returned to the table, and, at Grindwell's command, drank some of the spirits.

Presently the door opened, and in came old Flick, admirably disguised as Dumb Peter, with the keg on his shoulders.

He was about to put it down on the table, when Grindwell ordered him to take it to the men.

Peter—or rather Flick—was about to do this, when Grindwell called out—

"No; stop here, you idiot! I spoiled your talking anything to the men. Call one of the men," he continued, turning to the sailor, "and I will give my own orders."

The officer blew his whistle, and, in a moment, a number of the men came tumbling down the hatch.

"So, so," laughed Grindwell; "are you all so afraid that one dare not move without the other?"

The men took off their caps, and scratched their heads, but made no reply.

"Here, one of you fellows, take this keg of brandy forward and knock in the head; all have a glass round, but mind, no man must be seas over except Johnson, the dead man. Don't wait to sew him up in a sail or hammock. Heave him overboard at once. Now go, all of you but Dumb Peter. He shall help me to undress."

The men were delighted at getting the brandy, and rushed away.

Muttering to himself Grindwell paced about, whilst Flick stood in a corner trembling lest his disguise should be found out.

"Ghosts!" muttered Grindwell. "Why do the fools keep on talking of ghosts? I hate the word."

There was a tap at the door, and the next moment the first mate entered the cabin.

"The men swear, sir, that they have heard all sorts of strange noises in the spirit-room," said the mate.

"Fools! idiots! cowards!" cried Grindwell, foaming with rage; "if there be ghosts in the ship they should haunt me. I have committed more crimes than anyone here, yet no ghosts come to me. I defy them!"

"Beware!" said a deep, stern voice, from behind the curtains of the alcove.

"What is that?" cried Grindwell; "the wind moaning, or the creaking of the vessel?"

"Beware, beware, beware!" cried the voice, and the next moment the curtains of the alcove flew back, discovering Jack Firebrace, pale and wet, his hair hanging down by the side of his face, lank with the cold water of the sea.

Stretching out his hand towards Grindwell, he exclaimed, in a tone of menace—

"You have summoned me from the depths of the ocean, where you sent me. Soon you shall be with me in your watery grave. I warn you in time. Beware, beware! this ship is haunted; no one shall find rest herein. Death is on your head!"

Grindwell dashed forward, but Jack snapped the pistol, the powder flared up, filling the place with smoke, and, taking advantage of the cover, Jack slipped out of the window and dropped into the sea.

Flick, who at once knew who it was that represented the ghost, flew from the cabin and alarmed the crew, whilst the mate fell down in a fit, yelling and screaming as one who had gone mad.

A few of the boldest of the crew crept down to the cabin, where they found Grindwell seated on a locker, pale and trembling, and the place filled with smoke, which certainly did smell strong of sulphur.

"It—it is a dream," cried Grindwell; "a boy who ran away—was drowned. He cannot hurt us. Brandy, lads, brandy; that is the best thing in the world to cure a man's nerves."

As he spoke, he drank off a deep draught of the liquid, and his eyes began to flash fire.

"Look ye, lads," he cried; "it was but a shadow: we'll say it was a ghost, still but a shadow. My bed will be as easy and nice to sleep in as ever, dry and comfortable as any on land. See now, look here."

He pulled the curtains back, but his eyes, as they fell upon the bed, suddenly became fixed and staring.

"What is this?" he cried, as he started back; "the bed is wet, and there is blood, and the quilt is scorched!"

In horror the sailors leaned forward, and they found what their captain said was true.

Of course the reader knows that the wet came from Jack, having been in the sea; the scorching from the gunpowder. As for the blood, that came from the lock of the pistol, catching Jack's hand, and making it bleed.

But the sailors did not know this, and were consequently now thoroughly convinced that it was the ghost.

"Tut, my boys!" exclaimed Grindwell, mad with horror; "if ghosts are aboard, we will take them with us, and so frighten our foes."

"The body of the mate went over from le'ward," said one of the men, who was now quite tipsy; "he went such a splash into the water; and do you know, captain, where he fell in the waters hissed, and the steam flew up."

"Ha, ha, ha!" roared the men

"let's drink his safe journey to Davy Jones's."

"Come, lads!" he cried at last, "one more cup, for I grow tired, and must go to bed."

"To bed, captain?" cried Mat Weatherstay. "Why, you surely would not sleep in that bed?"

"And why should I not?" asked Grindwell, sternly. "I would sleep there if even the dead mate were to jump into bed beside me."

"Ho, ho, ho, ho!" came a hollow voice from behind the curtains.

Each man put down his glass on hearing the mysterious sounds, and gazed with horror at his neighbour.

"Ho, ho, ho, ho!" came the sepulchral laughter again.

The men started to their feet, and, whilst standing ready to fly, gave a terrified glance at the curtains of the alcove.

"Fools!" roared Grindwell; "fools! Does a mere sound make you shrink back? There was a time, Mat Weatherstay, when you would have laughed to scorn the loudest thunder, and loved the roar of the cannon; now, an echo, a simple echo, makes you tremble."

"Ho, ho, ho! Come, Griffiths Grindwell," said the voice. "Come to bed. I'm damp and cold—damp and cold—cold as death!"

A murmur arose amongst the men, and they drew back from their captain.

Grindwell saw this, and at once knew that if he did not do something to procure their respect for his courage, all hope of ever ruling them again was gone for ever.

"Ha, ha, ha!" he cried, as he drew a pistol from his pocket; "thou art cold, eh? Then here is something that shall warm thee."

He fired the pistol, and the ball tore through the curtains, and reached into the alcove.

"That cannot harm me now," said the voice. "Come, come, Richard Randulph, I am awaiting you. There is room enough for two thousand in my bed—the cold bed of the ocean. You and your crew must follow me. Ho, ho, ho, ho!"

Grindwell, with a strong effort, composed his voice and features, and, turning to his men, he gazed sternly at them.

His face was deathly pale; foamflakes stood upon his lips, and his eyes were unusually bright.

"Cowards!" he cried, contemptuously; "think you that I fear this spectre, if it be one? No. When did you ever see me shrink from danger? I gave my word that I would go to that bed, even if Johnson, the old mate, were in it: I will keep my word."

With a step slow, but steady, showing his immense determination, he advanced to the alcove.

"I am coming, Johnson," he cried, as he drew the curtains apart.

He was about to spring into the bed, when he appeared suddenly changed to stone.

With eyes protruding from their sockets, one hand holding back the curtains, the other pointing into the alcove, he turned to his men, and, in a voice of agony, mingled with rage, exclaimed—

"Who has done this horrid thing?"

The men stepped forward, and then, having gazed into the alcove, turned and fled, with loud cries of alarm.

Stretched on the bed was the corpse of the murdered mate, which had been consigned an hour before to the sea!

CHAPTER XXXIV.

JACK CONTINUES HIS PERSECUTIONS OF GRIFFITHS GRINDWELL—THE DEATH OF DUMB PETER—HOW JACK SAVED WINNY.

WHEN the men beheld the terrible ghastly body of the mate stretched upon the bed, they turned and fled, leaving Grindwell, unable to move, by the side of the corpse.

At length he summoned courage, and,

stretching forth his hand, touched the clammy thing.

It was cold and wet.

He could no longer doubt that the body was real. "Then how could it have come there?" he asked himself.

He had never believed much in ghosts, if at all. Still, he had thought such things might be; but could the sea give up its dead? Could the cold clay, which once held the flame of life, animated by the avenging angel, and leaving its watery grave, step forth to call the murderer to his fate?

"If it be so," he cried, in tones which did not tremble, "then is my doom settled. I have faced death a hundred times in the course of my mad career, and will not shrink from it now. Come, my friend, once more will I consign you to the deep. This time you shall not escape me; or if you do, I will indeed praise you."

Seizing the body in his arms, he raised it from the bed, and bore it out of the cabin up to the deck, where he threw it down with a dreadful thud.

It was a dismal night, not a star to be seen; the wind was coming up fast, the sea ran heavily, and a nasty drizzling rain had made the decks so slippery that it was difficult to stand.

"Avast there, you cowardly lubbers!" cried Grindwell, as he advanced to the crew, who were gathered forward, whispering and trembling. "You are a nice set of sailors to be frightened by a dead man! Look, I have brought him upon deck."

The terrified seamen scarcely dared move forward, but such control had Grindwell over them, that they feared him even more than they did the dead sailor, who had so mysteriously appeared again amongst them.

They advanced tremblingly up to the body, and at Grindwell's command one of them held a lantern over it.

"It's the mate, sure enough," laughed Grindwell. "I see it all; the poor fellow was not dead, and having caught in the rudder-chains the cold water revived him, and he crept into the cabin window to die in my bunk."

This was a remarkably clever explanation of the affair, but the men did not believe it.

The way that the body of the mate really did get into the alcove was as follows—

When Jack was swimming back to the port by which he crept into the spirit-room, he felt something cling to the rope, and on examining what it was discovered that it was the dead body of the unfortunate mate.

At first he was horrified at the sight, and tried to shake it off, but the body clinging to the rope made him think that he would put it to some use, and try to awaken some remorse in the cruel breast of the pirate.

For this purpose he made the body fast to the rope, and let it drift to the stern of the vessel.

He then climbed up to the cabin window, and hauled the body in after him—no very difficult matter, for the seaboard of the ship was very low—and having placed it carefully in the alcove performed the speaking part himself, only keeping his head in at the window, so as to be able to drop out before he could be seen.

How well this plan succeeded the reader already knows, and will now see that what appeared to have been done by supernatural agency was accomplished by the most easy means in the world.

"By the powers of darkness!" laughed Grindwell, who, having recovered from the shock the unexpected sight of the body of the man he had so lately murdered had given him, now seemed to enjoy the joke; "by the powers of darkness, I will give him such a weight to carry him down that I don't think he will be in too great a hurry to get up again. Here, one or two of you fellows sling half-a-dozen of your largest shot onto him."

The men dared not disobey, and in a few minutes heavy cannon-balls were slung or tied to the feet of the corpse, which was then, by Grindwell's orders, heaved over into the sea.

One terrible splash, and the dead man sank for ever beneath the waves.

"Now," cried Grindwell, as he turned round and faced his crew, "you have heard my explanation of how that fellow got into my cabin. If any man dares to doubt it, let him at once step forward and say so."

As he spoke he clapped his hand

upon the butt-end of his pistol in a very significant manner.

Not one of the sailors believed in the explanation, but they all protested most eagerly that they did.

"Ah!" laughed Grindwell, "I thought you would. Now, mark me, my lads; you having all agreed that this is the right explanation, had better not alter your opinion, for the first one who dares to breathe a word of doubt I will send after the murdered mate, so that he may ask him how he did do it."

With that he turned upon his heel and descended to his cabin, leaving the trembling seamen to their thoughts.

Jack, disguised as Dumb Peter again, had crept upon deck to listen and see what happened, and no sooner had the body of the unfortunate mate been consigned to the deep than he returned to the spirit-room, where a terrible scene was passing as well as upon deck.

Stretched upon a few old sails, which had been made as comfortable as could be by Jack and old Flick, was poor Dumb Peter, evidently sinking fast.

Flick supported his head, and every now and then bathed the dying boy's lips with water, for they were parched with fever.

Jack had brought from the store-room an old tin pot, and in it had placed some pieces of meat with an onion and a little water, and was hopelessly endeavouring to make a kind of broth.

The dying boy watched, with large and thankful eyes, all these proceedings.

Now and then a smile, so sweet, so gentle, played upon his lips, but died away almost instantly.

"It's very sorry sort of broth," said Jack, as he looked into the pot to see how it had got on, "very. But I cannot get better. Heaven help the poor boy! When I think of all the cruelties to which he has been a victim, it nearly drives me mad."

Jack tried to give the lad some of the broth, and Dumb Peter tried to drink a little to oblige his new-found friends.

But the cold hand of death was too near for the poor lad to obtain warmth, even had the soup been perfection.

He motioned it away with his hand, and smiling faintly shook his head.

"Try him with a little warm spirits and water," said Flick; "it may d good, and cannot do harm."

This was done, but was also refuse by the dying lad.

"I wonder if there's a doctor c board?" said Jack; "if I though there was, I would go on deck and as for him."

"If you could get one, I don't thin he would be able to do much good this case," whispered Flick.

"Nevertheless, I will ask him," r plied Jack, and leaning over the boy, l whispered—"Peter, Peter, can you he me?"

Dumb Peter raised his heavy eyelid and, gazing in our hero's face, nodde that he did.

"Tell me, then, is there a doctor c board that I can fetch?" asked Jack.

Peter shook his head, but presse Jack's hand by way of thanks.

"Is there no one we can tell that yc are so ill?" demanded Jack.

"No," signalled the boy, and then l drew from his neck a small gold ge ring, suspendid by a string.

This he motioned Jack to take, an then clasped his hands in prayer.

The two lads knelt down by his sid and prayed fervently.

It was evident that the poor dum boy was joining in their devotions, fc his lips moved, but no sound escape them.

Suddenly a peculiar rattle was hea in his throat; he grasped the two boy with his hands, sighed heavily, and fe back dead!

At the same moment the candle flare up for a moment, and then sank dow and went out.

"Jack," whispered Flick, "what sha we do? The poor boy is dead."

But our hero could not answer, fc sobs choked his utterance.

It was a terrible position for then very terrible—alone in the dark wit the corpse!

At last Jack roused himself to actio and taking his friend's hand, said—

"Flick, dear old fellow, in a fe hours we may be with poor Dumb Pete I do not think it at all probable th we shall be able to hide ourselves muc longer, and to speak the truth, if I we alone, I would now go on deck, and, possible, kill Grindwell, who is a monster in human shape."

"I am ready to go with you Jack," said Flick; "death would be far more preferable than this life."

"No, no, Flick; we have someone else to think about; there is pretty Winny to save."

"True; but how are we to do it?"

"Look here!" cried Jack; "it has been fated that we should bring to justice the wretch who rules this ship. The cabin in which Winny is a prisoner is only partitioned off by planks from this wretched hole, and in some way we must make our way to her. Death can but be our worst punishment, and for myself, I would willingly meet it if I dragged this fiend down with me. Now, Flick, are you willing to risk your life for this good deed?"

"I am, Jack. If these troubles and dangers have done us harm, they have also done us good. They have taught us to hate evil, and to love good; that life is but like the spark in a fire: one second it burns brightly, and the next it is gone, gone, and for ever. Those who would be happy, must be good, and not fear death."

"Then, Flick, dear fellow, let us at once set to work, for I am sure we shall succeed in upsetting all this bad man's plans. Now, let us lay this poor fellow out, placing his hands as if in the action of prayer; so—that is well. Now we will roll him up in the canvas, into which we will place some of the pig-iron that we saw by the ladder. That is it. Heaven have pity on him!"

This sad office having been performed for the poor dead boy, the two lads remained for a few moments in silent prayer.

"Come, Jack," said Flick, "we must now set to work to place the body in its watery grave."

"Not yet; the first thing we must do is to look after Winny. I have my reasons for this. Now to work; I must creep on deck and see if I can get a lamp or candle."

Jack crept upon the deck, and with difficulty walked to the store-room, for the ship was labouring heavily.

However, he reached it at last, and having found a lantern with an oil-lamp,

he bore it off in triumph to the spirit-room, where he and Flick lighted it.

"I say, Jack," said Flick, "don't you think that we might as well examine some of these chests that are standing about? We might find some weapons. I tell you that I am ready to die, but I don't mean to part with my life at all readily."

"You are right, Flick," said our hero; "but we must take care how we do this. It is evident that any great noise we make here will be heard, and then someone will be sent to see what Dumb Peter is up to."

They crept carefully to the boxes, and having opened one or two found that they were filled with pistols and swords.

"We are in luck," said Jack; "at all events, we shall not want for weapons. Just take a couple of daggers, Flick; the pistols are of no use to us, for we cannot get any powder or bullets."

As he spoke Jack carefully hid two daggers in his rags (for it must be remembered that he was still disguised as Dumb Peter).

"Now to try and save Winny," said Jack.

Once more they crept up the barrels until they were on a level with the cabin wherein Winifred was a captive.

They looked through a crevice, and by the aid of the swing-lamp which hung in the cabin could see Winifred on her knees by the couch, weeping and praying.

"Winifred, Miss Winifred," whispered Jack; "pray don't be frightened; we are here to help you."

Wild Winny started and clasped her hands, gazing round the room in bewilderment and alarm.

"Don't be frightened," whispered Jack, "and, above all, do not make a noise, or you will betray us."

"Who are you?" asked Winny. "Speak—who and what are you?"

"I am your friend, dear Winny," whispered Jack, quite forgetting that he had no right to be so familiar, even under such urgent circumstances—"your friend, Jack Firebrace; and here is old Flick—that is, Felix Flitter. You must remember him. We want to get one of these panels out so that you can pass through it to us, and so we shall be all together. Whatever fate may come we will share it."

Wild Winny could scarcely believe her senses when she heard these words.

"If it be really as you say," she replied, "give me some proof that you are Mr. Firebrace."

Jack thought for a moment, and then said—

"I am the person who saved your father."

"Now I know you are Jack Firebrace," cried Winny, clasping her hands, "and I implore you to save me."

"We will," said Jack.

"Can I not help you in some way?" inquired Winny.

"Yes; listen at the door of the cabin so that you can warn us if anyone is coming near."

"Work as quickly as you can," said Wild Winny; "I will take care to give you warning if anyone should approach."

Jack now took the lantern and carefully examined the partition.

He found that it was strongly made of oak, the framework being at least two inches thick, and the panels an inch.

Quickly the lads set to work to get the beading ripped off, when Winny told them that she heard someone approaching.

Jack was able to pull the panel back far enough to thrust a dagger through.

"Take this, Winny," he whispered; "if they should attempt to harm you use it fearlessly. We will remain here, and if it be necessary we will break through this partition and fight for you as long as we have life."

Winny clutched the dagger and concealed it in the folds of her dress.

Hardly had she done so when the key turned in the lock, the door opened, and Grindwell, who had evidently been drinking, entered.

Having closed and locked the door he placed a paper on the table, and commenced thus—

"Miss Summerbell, for some reason, it matters not what, your father has chosen to take a great hatred to me, and has sworn to be my ruin. Now I have removed all my enemies but one, and that one is your father."

"So," cried Winny, "it was you who lured his ship on to the rocks, and caused the deaths of so many brave fellows?"

"You are right. I did lure the ship on to the rocks with the full intention of killing your father. He escaped me. With the same wish to destroy him I attacked your house. He may be dead; I hope he is; but, if still alive, I intend to make him my friend."

"Your friend!" cried Winny, scornfully.

"Yes. Now listen. I intend touching on the south coast of France and there making you my wife. Here is a paper which you must sign, in which you state that you left your father's home of your own free will, and that you have selected me as your husband."

"Selected you!" cried Winny, as she recoiled from Grindwell's outstretched hand. "Stand back!" she exclaimed, as she drew the dagger Jack had brought her; "stand back, or I, girl as I am, will try my strength against yours, and, if heaven will lend strength to my arm, will kill you."

"Foolish girl," said Grindwell, coolly, "I do not wish to hurt you. Put up that dagger. If I wished to have you disarmed, I have only to blow this whistle, and call some of my men, and you would be instantly overpowered. Now, mark me! You must, and shall sign this paper! I give you but one hour to decide. Refuse me if you dare," he continued, as he struck his clenched fist upon the paper, "and I will then compel you. Choose between this and death; and, mark this: Red Randulph never yet failed to keep his word."

"Think not to terrify me by your threats," replied Wild Winny, boldly; "I am not friendless, even here."

"Not friendless even here?" cried Red Randulph, glancing nervously around. "I do not understand."

"The good are never friendless," replied Winny. "Heaven will raise them up friends."

"Tush!" laughed Grindwell; "besides your father I have, or rather had, only one other I feared."

"And that one was?" demanded Wild Winny.

"John Firebrace; but he will trouble me no more: his body rests beneath the waves."

"But not his spirit, which walks on

board this doomed ship!" said Jack, in a deep and sepulchral voice.

Griffiths Grindwell staggered back, and turned pale as death.

"Whose voice was that?" he gasped.

"What voice?" demanded Winny, who, taking up the idea, determined to make Grindwell believe that there was a ghost in the place. "Tell me; what voice do you mean?"

"Did you not hear a voice speak just now?" asked Grindwell, looking dreadfully pale.

"Why, we are quite alone," repeated Winny.

"It must have been my fancy," said Grindwell, as he passed his hands over his eyes.

"The fancy of an evil conscience," replied Wild Winny; "if, as you say, you have committed these crimes, repent while there is yet time, for something tells me that your course is nearly run."

"Bah! do not think to frighten me with such wild stories," laughed Grindwell. "Ghosts or no ghosts, I care not. I have but one guide, and that is my will. Sign that paper before an hour is over, or I will compel you. Mark me, I never break my word."

"Beware! She shall never sign that paper!" said Jack, placing his lips close to a crack in a panel a little distance from the other.

"What is this dreadful mystery?" cried Grindwell, starting back; "is the ship haunted?"

"It is haunted," cried Jack; "the spirits of your victims are near you, urging you on to destruction."

"Are you—are you the spirit of John Firebrace?" gasped Griffiths Grindwell, as he leaned on the table.

"I am," replied the voice. "I am here with the spirit of the murdered mate to protect the innocent, and punish the guilty. You are surrounded; your days are numbered; thy doom is set, and you cannot escape."

"I do defy ye!" yelled Grindwell; "if ye be spirits, I bear within me a spirit also; and I fear you not. I will fight you to the last."

"Thy doom is settled," moaned Jack, in tones which even made Winifred shudder, so unearthly did they sound. "Thy doom is settled; thou canst not escape. It is written in the book of Fate."

"Be it so; but it is also written that this lady becomes my wife. Hark ye, madam; that paper must be signed within an hour, or I will have you flung into the sea."

With a threatening gesture of the hand, Grindwell turned upon his heel, and left the cabin with a deathly white face.

"Quick, old Flick," said Jack, as he once more set to work ripping off the beading; "we must save her at once."

At last the beading was off, and the panel fell backwards, leaving space for Winny to pass through.

"Now, Winny dear," whispered Jack, "make haste into here. Take care how you tread, for these are all casks, and, if we knock one down, these wretches may suspect something, and come down to search."

"Fear not for me," said Wild Winny; "I have all the courage of a man, and would willingly sacrifice my life to bring that wretch to justice."

"I have no doubt but that one day we shall be able to do so," said Jack. "Now, Flick, we must throw poor old Dumb Peter overboard. They will think the splash made by his body is Winny jumping overboard. Now, then, let us to work at once."

Cautiously they lifted the body, thrust it through the port-hole, and let it fall with a splash into the sea.

"Man overboard!" shouted the watch, and directly there was a great confusion on the deck as the sailors ran to the side in hopes of seeing who was the unfortunate wretch; but the body had been so heavily weighted that it sank at once.

"Call up the men," shrieked Grindwell, as he stamped about the deck with rage; "I think the fellows are all mad."

The men mustered aft according to their captain's orders, and the names of the crew were called out.

Each name was readily answered to, and no one was missing.

"Where is Dumb Peter?" demanded Grindwell.

"Pass the word for Dumb Peter," shouted one of the officers, and one or two men hastened to call the lad.

In a minute Jack, mimicking the slouching gait of the deceased lad, had crawled upon deck in response to the summons.

"Who, then, could have fallen overboard?" demanded Griffiths Grindwell, sternly.

No one answered, for no one dared to answer the question, but, in their own hearts, they believed that the ship was a doomed ship—that the vessel was haunted.

"Will none of you speak?" cried Grindwell. "What man could have fallen overboard?"

"Axing your honour's pardon," said one of the men, "it may not have been a man fallen overboard."

"It could not have been," cried Grindwell; "all the men are here."

"Just so, sir," replied the man; "but there is, or there was, a woman on board."

"She could not escape," said Grindwell. "It is something that has been thrown overboard. Now, mark this! my fine fellows. It strikes me that many of you here are cowards, believing in ghosts and those kind of things. If ever I hear of one of you daring to mention such absurdities I will run him up to the yardarm directly. Now to your posts, and remember I am not the man to be played with."

The men slunk away; and Grindwell, turning to the mate, bade him make for the coast as quickly as he could.

He then retired to his own cabin, where he paced up and down in deep meditation.

"Can such things be?" he muttered. "I cannot believe it. Do the dead really move in spirit amongst us? No; it cannot be. And yet, if at last my plans are all upset? If by these invisible agencies all my hopes are made to crumble into dust, and to leave me at the mercy of my foes! I had longed with all my heart to leave her child all my wealth. He must not know the stain that rests upon his name. Well, I hold Summerbell's daughter as a hostage. She is in my power, and—"

"You lie," said a stern voice; "you lie! she is not in your power!"

Grindwell started, and looked up.

There, showing just between the curtains of his bed, was the face of Jack Firebrace, the face marked with blood, and his hair dripping with water.

"Can this be possible?" muttered Grindwell; then rushing to one side of the cabin, he snatched up a pistol, and fired it at the alcove, but the face was gone.

"It is but imagination," said Grindwell, trembling. "I will not believe it. Bah! if they be ghosts, it is certain that they cannot injure me, for with all the will possible, not one has yet hurt me."

Laughing at his own security, Griffiths Grindwell—or Red Randulph—directed his steps to the cabin wherein Wild Winny had been a prisoner.

"I have come for your answer," he said, as he opened the door, but he had scarcely taken one step into the cabin, when he paused in amazement.

It was empty; not a sign of anyone was to be seen.

Hastily he looked round, but did not notice the panel having been removed. He then looked under the table, and everywhere else where a person might be concealed, but Wild Winny was not to be found. Indeed, that young lady was watching his movements through the chink in the timbers.

The escape of his prisoner seemed to have more effect upon Grindwell than anything else.

He threw himself upon one of the settees which ran round the room, and remained some moments in silent thought.

"So," he exclaimed, at last, "she has preferred death to me. Well, I am rid of her, and she might have borne witness against me. It is better as it is. If I am brought to bay, I can fight to the last. I shall but be more desperate. They will have a hard tussle to overpower me. We make now for the Ile de Bas. There I take in a cargo, and make for the coast of Kent. I land with the cargo, and post to London. If inquiries have been made for me, my good friend, Luke Lansner, will have made that all right. No, I cannot fail. My plots are too well laid for that. So, mortal or immortal, I defy you all."

CHAPTER XXXV.

THE LAST OF THE " FLYING FISH "—GOBLIN JIM MEETS THE REWARD OF ALL HIS TREACHERY AND CRUELTY.

WE left Goblin Jim in a very unpleasant position on board the "Flying Fish," which vessel was being pursued by a Government ship.

Goblin Jim was by nature a coward, and extremely cruel, delighting in witnessing another's pain.

It would have given him the greatest pleasure in the world to have witnessed a sea-fight could he possibly have done so without being placed in danger. The arms and legs of the combatants being crushed to pieces, their groans and their cries would have been delightful to his cruel heart; but when there became a great probability that one of his own limbs might be carried off by a cannon-ball, he wished that people would not go to war.

"Now, then, younker," said one of the men, as he came across Jim hiding behind a carronade, "what are you doing there?"

"Please, sir," gasped Jim, "I'm keeping out of the way of the shots that nasty ship is firing at us."

"Keeping out of the way of the shots, are you?" sneered the man. "Now, look here, my fine young fellow; we had not direct orders to kill you, but we were told that your kind friends would not be sorry to hear of your death. So you will please to come out of that and walk aft with me. I have a nice place to put you upon where you will see the whole of the action—that is, if it comes to that; and if it don't, why, you will be all the better sailor for the experience of riding on the boom of the main-sail."

Vainly did Jim protest that he did not wish to see the action, and that he was very comfortable where he was. They laughed loudly at his complaints, and dragged him aft, where they strapped him stride legs on the boom of the sail, so that he faced the ship which was in pursuit.

As the vessel rode over the waves Goblin Jim rose up and down, now drenched to the skin by the spray, and now high and dry in the air, whilst ever and anon a shot from the chasing vessel dropped unpleasantly near the stern of the "Flying Fish."

All day long Jim rode see-saw on the boom, and when night closed in, it was evident that the "Flying Fish" had distanced her pursuer. Still the captain of the pirate vessel determined to make all safe.

For this purpose he had the light in the stern cabin lit, so that the chase might see them.

He then had a large tub brought upon deck, in which were rigged three sticks, in much the same manner as the sticks or props are to which gipsies fasten their caldron, and between them was hung a lighted lantern.

The lights in the cabin were then extinguished, and the tub set afloat astern. The helm was then put hard aport, and the "Flying Fish" went off on another tack, leaving the tub to mislead the Government vessel, which it did, for when they were about a couple of miles to leeward, they heard the sound of firing, and had no doubt but that the Government ship would fire until they struck the tub and swamped it, and would finally imagine that they had sunk the "Flying Fish."

Goblin Jim was cast loose, and had to wait upon the men, receiving in payment what the men called monkey's allowance—more kicks than halfpence.

"It's precious hard," grumbled Goblin Jim, "that I should be treated so only out of a mistake. I wish Jack had taken his own letter. Oh! won't I have it out of him if I get back to Hawkhouse! I do wish that stupid old wretch, my mother, had poisoned him."

"Now, then, what are you doing there?" growled a man. "You are spilling some of that tar upon the deck."

"Why, you young wretch, how dare you do that!" yelled the captain; "here, Harrison, just dust that young fellow's jacket for him."

THE BOYS OF HAWKHOUSE SCHOOL.

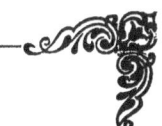

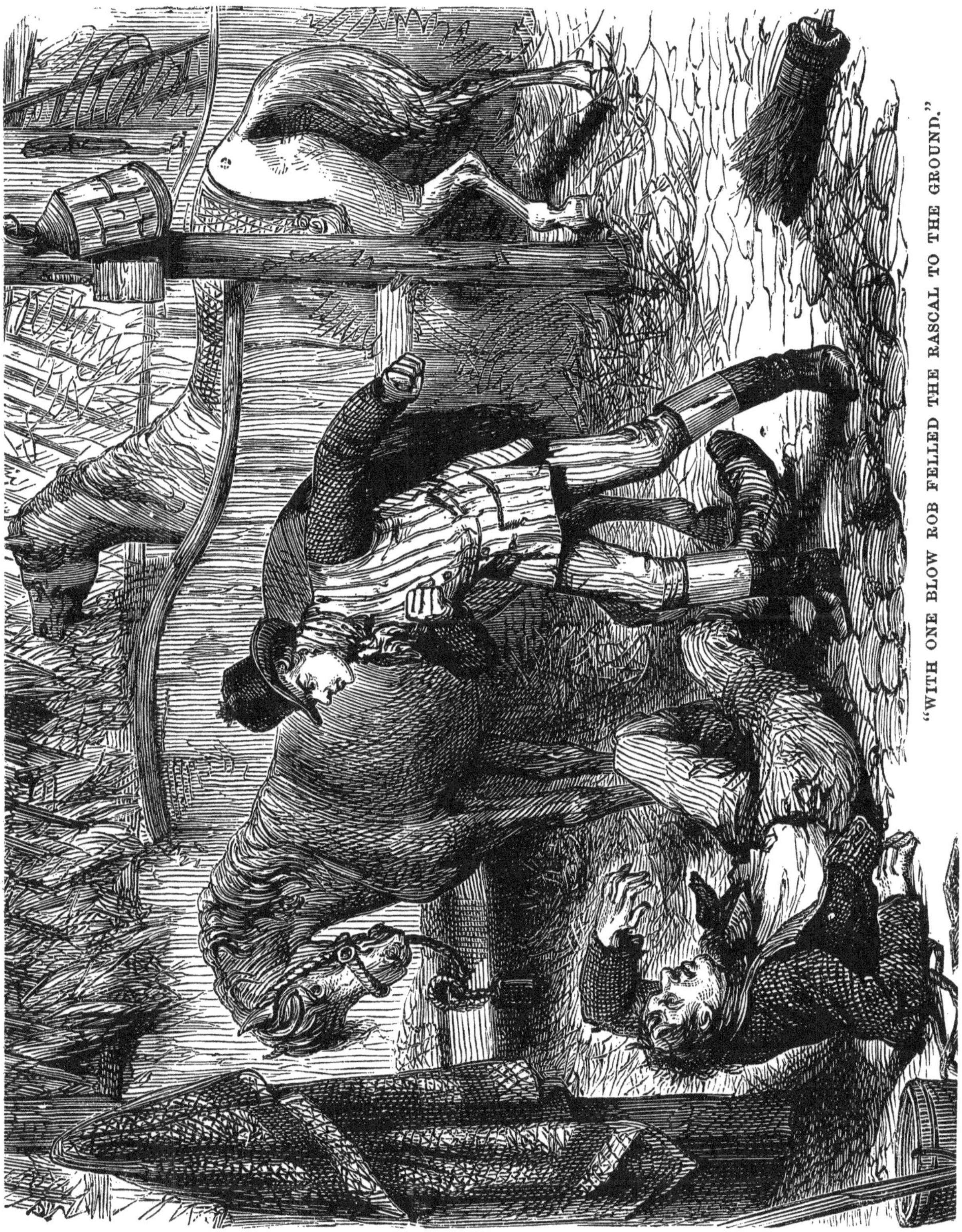

"WITH ONE BLOW ROB FELLED THE RASCAL TO THE GROUND."

No. 11.

PRICE ONE HALFPENNY.

[Published Every Monday.]

The man, who took a savage delight in flogging boys, seized Jim by the collar, and with a nice ratan which he had in his hand dusted Master Jim's jacket so thoroughly that that young gentleman believed that not only his jacket and other clothes were cut into ribbons, but all the flesh on his body.

Most boys can and will roar when chastised, but Goblin Jim roared enough for fifty.

"Hold your tongue, you little wretch!" cried the captain, stamping with rage. "Pitch him into a tub of tar to stop his mouth."

In an instant the lad was seized, and he was dragged forward as the captain walked aft.

Two men seized him by the legs and arms, and lifted him over the cask of tar.

One scream, a long, piercing shriek, then a splash, and Jim sank beneath the tar.

Three times did they souse the unfortunate Jim in this peculiar bath, and then they drew him forth, black from the sole of his foot to the crown of his head.

"Ho, ho, ho!" roared the men, as they gazed at the poor little wretch. "He is as black as pitch."

Goblin Jim was mad with rage, and nearly suffocated with the thick fluid.

All thoughts of fear had now left him, and he rushed frantically at the men, who dodged about to avoid him.

Never was there such a terrible game of touch. The men screamed with laughter, and Jim with rage.

Here and there he darted—now after this one, now after that; now falling over a pile of ropes, and now plunging head foremost into the caboose.

"Get out of here," cried the cook, seizing a red-hot poker; "don't come dirtying my nice clean kitchen."

As he spoke he placed the poker on Goblin Jim's tarry jacket, and in a moment it was in a blaze.

With a yell of agony Jim dashed away, and the fiend-like men screamed with laughter; but their tone soon changed, for as Jim rushed along, blinded by the flames, he struck against the tar-barrel, which was upset, and the whole of it caught fire.

Jim rushed on, and the next moment had plunged headlong into the sea.

And now the terrified sailors perceived that they were doomed to meet the same fate as the lad whom they had so cruelly tormented.

The blazing tar spread upon the deck and flowed in liquid fire down the fore hatch.

Many of the men had become plentifully daubed with tar through the struggles of Jim, and now they, too, were on fire.

These rushed about making frantic endeavours to extinguish the flames, but only succeeded in spreading the conflagration.

Vainly did the captain try to obtain some order, so that the boats might be lowered.

One boat, indeed, was lowered, but so many sailors jumped into it that it was swamped.

As the loaded cannon of the ship became heated they went off, so that she appeared firing her own farewell salute.

And now even the captain had abandoned all hope, for the spirit-room was on fire.

Boom! Crash!

A large column of blue fire shot up into the heavens.

There was a deep, dull report.

And when the smoke cleared away the "Flying Fish" had disappeared.

Thus Goblin Jim had fallen into his own trap, and, through his wickedness, had met with a terrible death.

* * * * *

A heavy sea was rolling in shore and breaking over the terrible rocks which surround the Ile de Bas on the coast of Finisterre—a heavy sea and a rapid tide.

A drizzling rain fell through the thick air, making all things cold and clammy to the touch.

A terrible night, and one fraught with the greatest danger to a ship which happened to be on that rock-bound coast, unless the captain had consummate skill, and knew the coast well.

It was on such a night that the "Sea Hawk" slowly but surely crept nearer and nearer to the shore.

Red Randulph paced slowly up and down the quarter-deck with his lieutenant, now and then pausing to look towards the coast, and then, resuming his walk, he conversed in low tones with his subordinate.

"It is a brutal night," he muttered, as he dashed the clammy rain-drops from his face.

"If I might advise you, captain," said the lieutenant, "I would work out to sea again. This is a dangerous coast. The sunken rocks about here are sharp as needles, and—"

"Tut, tut! I have no fear but what I can sail my ship all safely into the bay. But I fear we may not see the signal, or that our signal may not be seen."

"We must be very close to the shore now," said the mate, who was evidently very anxious.

"Yes. The signal ought to be made. Just burn a blue-light at the foot of the foremast, but be careful not to let it burn long."

The lieutenant sprang forward, and with his own hands lit the fire, which shone brightly for a few moments, and then was quenched by a pail of water being thrown over it.

"There goes the return signal," said Griffiths Grindwell; "so we can steer in here. We ought to find the 'Flying Fish' waiting for us. Let some of the men go out in a boat and tow us in. All hands take in sail; we shall be much safer that way."

"Yes," replied the lieutenant, in a doubtful voice. "But I must confess I do not like the night."

"Tut, tut! The peculiar accidents which have occurred aboard this ship have made you nervous. Trust me, I am too old a hand to risk my ship. See! there is the Bec de Lac all right. Starboard your helm there! Good! and now we are in the current and all safe again."

"That is true," replied the lieutenant, gleefully. "Upon my word, sir, you are a most wonderful pilot."

"I know the place well. Go and get the cables out, and see that the men are all ready to take in the cargo. We must be off to the south coast of England before day breaks. Here we have a double difficulty. If the French take us our ships will be seized and our goods confiscated, whilst we shall be made prisoners of war; whilst, if the English take us, a long rope and short shrift will be our fate. So we had better be careful."

The vessel was now in a deep channel, where she was able to sail close under the cliffs, which rose up abruptly from the sea.

Ropes were carried out from her to the rocks, where some people had assembled to help the smugglers.

At last the ship was hauled in alongside of what appeared to be a natural quay.

Grindwell stepped on shore, and conversed apart with the leader of the shore party, whilst the contraband goods were carried on board the vessel by French fisher-girls.

And now Jack became greatly alarmed about Winny and old Flick.

For himself he felt pretty safe in his disguise as Dumb Peter, but he trembled for his companions.

"Tiens!" cried one of the French girls, throwing off the heavy cloak which she was wrapped up in; "this is hard work. One might as well be a horse to be driven about in this way."

Mumbling and grumbling, the girl passed on to her work.

Quick as lightning Jack had seized the cloak and hurried with it down into the spirit-room.

"Winny, dear Winny!" he whispered; "I must ask you to do something which will demand all your courage."

"You have only to tell me what to do," replied Winny, quietly.

"Winny dear, you must slip on this cloak and join the gang of girls who are bringing the goods on board. Pretend to be one of them. Go with them, and when you are on the high lands take the first opportunity you can to slip away, and hurry to the nearest village or town that you can, and give them notice of this night's work. I would go myself, but you would be discovered for certain during my absence. With these people —I mean the French people—even if they find you, you will be tolerably safe; but if Grindwell discovers you, your fate will be sealed. Can you do this?"

"I will. I speak French pretty well, and will do all that I possibly can to get assistance to stop this ship."

Hastily throwing the cloak over her shoulders Wild Winny followed Jack on deck, and, taking up her place amidst the girls, passed on to the shore.

Jack then stole back to old Flick.

"Flick, old fellow," he whispered, "you must hide yourself under these sails; make haste, for I heard the girls say that this would be their last load, and then we shall have them coming down here to stow them away."

"But what will they do to you, Jack? Some of them are sure to spot you."

"Of that I must take my chance," replied Jack.

"Well, if it must be, it must be," sighed old Flick; "but I do not like leaving you. But promise me that if there is any danger threatening you that you will call me. If you don't, Jack, I'll never forgive you."

"Well, then, I promise. Now, jump beneath that sail, and whatever you do remain still. Make haste; here they come!"

Old Flick had scarcely time to wrap himself up in the sail when the mate of the vessel came tumbling down into the store-room, followed by some score of girls, all carrying rolls of silk and other such goods to be smuggled into England.

"Now, then, Dumb Peter," he cried, "look alive, and hold the light here. Come along, my dears," he continued, turning to the girls, "pack up the goods as quickly as you can, for we must be away before the first streak of dawn."

Quickly the girls packed up the goods, being directed by an old fisherwoman, who was as broad as she was long.

"Ahi, ma petite!" the fisherwoman cried, as she pointed to a vacant space, "why do you not put your bale of silk down here? Ma foi! I really think you must be blind not to see that. Tiens, and you too, Lizette! Allez, allez! plus vite. Make haste; make haste!"

And so this stout but energetic lady kept up a continual run of directions, until, feeling herself exhausted, she plumped herself down upon the canvas wherein old Flick was concealed.

Jack did not know what to do.

At any other time he would have been unable to keep from laughing at his school-fellow's unpleasant predicament; but he knew that to laugh now meant certain destruction for both of them.

"Tiens! but I am tired," cried the old lady, as she bumped down on the top of old Flick. "Parbleu! it is quite a treat to be seated here, and—Yah! Sacre tonnerre! what is that?" yelled the old Frenchwoman, as she sprang from the canvas and placed her hands behind her. "It has pierced me through and through."

"It's all up with us now," thought Jack. "I wish Flick had kept quiet for a few moments longer, though I don't think I should have been able to have stood it myself."

"What can it be?" cried the old woman, giving the canvas another terrible kick. "Ha, ha! I see what it is. It is those careless sail-makers who have left a needle in the sail. We will soon have it out. Oh, I am hurt!"

The Frenchwoman was about to unroll the canvas, and Jack was preparing to defend himself as best he could, when suddenly the idea struck him to extinguish the light.

Turning suddenly round he let the lantern drop, and in an instant all was dark.

Oh! what a confusion of voices arose!

The girls all rushed up on deck, and the old Frenchwoman, gesticulating violently, followed them.

But in her hurry she quite forgot that she was not so thin as the maidens, and consequently she stuck hard and fast in the hatchway, her head and arms above the deck, and the rest of her body, from the waist downwards, below the hatches.

"Oh, oh, oh!" yelled the old woman; "help me out of this! help me out of this!"

"What in the name of all that is evil is the matter with you?" muttered Grindwell, as he clapped his hand over the old woman's mouth. "I think all the world must have gone mad lately. What, I say, is the matter with you?"

Poor Jack, who was standing behind the Frenchwoman, could hear all this.

But, of course, he could not see a thing.

"I don't know! I don't know!" gasped the woman. "Something did stab me and did make me jump. Then the light went out all of a sudden; and then a tremendous big hand, cold and clammy as that of a corpse, did seize me by the ankle. Then I did turn and did fly up here!"

"Ma foi, Jacques!" growled Griffiths Grindwell, "you had better take care of your spirits. Why did you let this old hag come on board?"

"Hag yourself!" screamed the old woman. "I have not touched a drop of brandy except to keep the cold out. I tell you I felt the cold hand quite plainly, and—"

But here all made a motion for her to be silent, for a sound, full of direful meaning to them, smote upon their ears.

It was the sound of a musket being fired off.

"Hist!" cried Jacques; "the soldiers have discovered our plans and are down upon us. Hark! there goes another shot. Quick, quick, all of you, to the shore! You must get the ship out the best way you can, Monsieur Randulph. We must now work each for himself. Tiens! who could have given the alarm? To shore with you all, girls! Keep the road round by the cliffs. Treason is abroad, and we have been betrayed!"

"One moment, Jacques," said Grindwell. "If the 'Flying Fish' puts in here—"

"Sapristi! have I not told you that she will never put in here again? Do I not tell you that a ship put in to St. Pol De Leon this morning, and reported having seen a vessel on fire? They made towards it, but it blew up when they were some miles off. However, they picked up a boat, and that boat had once belonged to the 'Flying Fish.' Sacre! the soldiers are too near to speak now. Adieu! Get the ship off as soon as you can, or you are lost."

Without pausing for a reply Jacques hurried off, dragging the stout Frenchwoman behind him.

The fisher girls who had carried the packages on board had already escaped.

Soon the cliff was quiet and still.

Not a single object could be seen moving on it.

But now and then a dropping shot told that the scouts of the smugglers were anxious to warn their companions to fly.

The ropes were cast off from the cliffs and boats were sent out to tow the "Sea Hawk" out to sea.

Quietly and swiftly was each order carried out directly Grindwell delivered it.

The ship had already entered the deep channel when lights were seen to glimmer on the face of the rocks, and a party of soldiers and douaniers (custom-house officers) came tearing down the road.

"Halte-là!" shouted the officer.

"Heave to or we fire!" cried out the officer of the douaniers.

"Pull away, my men!" shouted Grindwell. "If they fire and hurt us, we can and we will hurt them in return."

"Ready!" came the stern voice of the commanding officer, followed by the rattle of the muskets as they were brought up to the soldiers' shoulders.

"Fire!"

And the red tongues of flame shot from the muskets, pouring a deadly volley into the "Sea Hawk," strewing her decks with the killed and wounded.

"Run out your guns and fire," shouted Griffiths Grindwell, as he stamped with rage.

It was evident from the steady aim and quickness of the fire that the soldiers knew the character of the ship, and determined, if they could not capture her, to destroy as many of the crew as they possibly could.

The guns were quickly run out, and soon their deep mouths belched forth their charge of fire and shot against the rocks, but the soldiers stooped down behind the huge boulders of stone, so that none were hurt, except a few bruises caused by the splinters of the rock which flew off as the cannon-balls struck them.

"Load!" cried the French officer, and the musical sound of the ramrods as they were drawn forth rang amongst the echoes of the rocks.

"Fire!"

Another volley was poured in, but with not such good effect, for the vessel had swung itself out of the channel, and in a minute Grindwell had seized the helm and made her swing round.

"Cheerily, men!" he shouted. "All hands lay aloft and loose the sails! All ready, there?"

"Ay, ay, sir!" cried the men.

"Give them one more shot," continued Grindwell, as he turned to the mate, "and then we are away. Look out, my lads," he shouted to the men aloft. "The gun will be your signal to make all sail."

Boom!

Crash! went the guns, and in less time than it takes to write it the "Sea Hawk" had spread her wings and was speeding swiftly out to sea.

"How many are wounded, Mr. Thomson?" growled Richard Randulph to one of his officers.

"Five are dead, sir, and seven wounded," replied Mr. Thomson; "it has been an unlucky cruise."

"The chances of war, sir, nothing else," said Grindwell, putting on an appearance of carelessness he did not feel.

"It is not only the men we have lost," said the mate, "but the effect on those that are left!"

"What do you mean?" demanded Grindwell, sharply. "They dare not dream of mutiny?"

"No; but they do say things have not gone right with the ship of late—that, in fact, the ship is doomed."

"They are idiots! Serve them out a good glass of spirits each, and have the dead thrown overboard at once."

"But the wounded, sir? What are we to do with them?" demanded the mate. "We have no doctor."

"Give them two or three glasses of spirits and bind up their wounds; they will be better soon."

The mate shook his head and walked silently away.

"What is there against me?" muttered Grindwell, as he entered the cabin wherein, until lately, Wild Winny had been a prisoner. "I, who knew not what it was to have my will crossed, to be now overthrown at all points. Can the dead really come back to thwart the schemes of those who injured them in this life?"

"They can," said Jack, in a deep voice, for he had been listening to all this concealed behind the panel.

But this joke nearly proved fatal to him, for, drawing a pistol, Grindwell fired at the panel.

The bullet passed through the wood within half an inch of our hero's head.

"That was a lucky miss," thought Jack, as he crouched down farther out of the way.

"I defy you all, then," cried Grindwell, in a passion of madness. "Come one, come all, and do your worst. Red Randulph will never submit to anyone of this or the other world. What ho there!" he yelled aloud, and the mate Thomson rushed into the room.

"What is it, sir?" asked the mate who looked eagerly at Grindwell's pale face.

"Put on every stitch of canvas the ship can bear; we must make the coast of Kent as soon as possible.

"I shall leave you then to discharge the cargo, and to make your way back to Hawkhouse. I must to London plots are out to ruin us; traitors are amongst us; but let the men know that if they yield it is only to be hanged," said Grindwell.

"Fear not, sir. The crew of the 'Sea Hawk' must conquer or die."

"Right, my good fellow, right Quick, then; make all sail. We will defy everything. If the next few ventures pay well I will make you all rich men."

With these remarks he dismissed the mate.

* * * *

Leaving Grindwell and his ship for a few moments we will retrace our footsteps for a little, and see how Wild Winny had managed to get to the nearest village to give the alarm.

Climbing up the cliff with the rest of the girls Winny managed so well to imitate their movements that, in the darkness of the night, they took her for one of themselves.

Wild Winny pretended to follow them, but at the first opportunity that offered she slipped away, and ran off as fast as she could down a road which led from the sea-shore.

She had not gone far when she perceived a man, who appeared to be a sentinel of the smugglers, for he was watching eagerly down the road, and held a musket so as to be ready to raise it directly.

To avoid this man Wild Winny crept into a field, and made her way across it slowly, and with caution.

She had just reached the other side of the field when a loud, harsh sound smote on her ear.

It was the neigh of a horse.

The next moment the noble animal, which was evidently some farmer's pet, trotted up to Wild Winny.

Winny clapped her hands with delight,

and hailed the coming of the horse as a good sign that she would be in good time to stop the smuggling vessel, and rescue the two lads who had done so much for her.

She seized it by the mane and sprang upon its back.

The horse seemed pleased to bear her, and, answering to her call, sped quickly on its way.

She passed one or two men, who had evidently been posted to guard the smugglers, and to give them notice of the approach of the custom-house soldiers, should the latter catch sound of the "Sea Hawk" being near.

One of these men saw her, and called upon her to stop, or he would fire.

To this she made no reply, but, grasping her horse's mane with both her hands, she leaned as far as she could over the neck of the horse, bending down low, so as to offer as small a mark to the sailor as possible.

She heard the man utter a fearful oath, and the rattle of his old musket as he presented it.

Then came a loud report, and the bullet sped over her head, doing no damage.

Raising her head she touched the animal lightly with her foot, at the same time giving the "View halloo!" in true old English style, awaking the dull echoes of the plain, making the wild plovers and gulls fly up and scream,

whilst the sentinels of the pirates fired off their guns in all directions in such a manner that they not only alarmed Jacques, as we have already seen, but the soldiers stationed at the neighbouring village.

With a clattering sound Wild Winny dashed through the village until she arrived at the little stone house, which served as a sort of barracks, where the soldiers had rushed out and had just fallen into their ranks.

In as few words as she possibly could Winny informed the officer of the detachment that an English smuggler vessel was at Ile de Bas Cape, that she had escaped therefrom, and at the same time implored him to send his men to overhaul the ship, as their were two young gentlemen on board who had been carried off against their wills, and were now held prisoners on board the "Sea Hawk."

"Morte de ma vie!" cried the French officer; "is it that terrible 'Sea Hawk' again? We will soon be after them, mademoiselle; you will pardon me when I say that I must hold you as a prisoner. I will place you at the inn, where you will receive every attention, but you must give me your word not to attempt to escape."

Wild Winny gave her word willingly, and at the word of command the soldiers started off to try and take the "Sea Hawk," with what result the reader already knows.

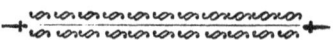

CHAPTER XXXVI.

"WELL, this here's a pretty go, this is," said Rob Rackstraw, as he took his way down to the village inn. "I thought I knew a thing or two, but these fellows have knocked me clean off my perch. To think of a low set of rascals pitching on to a quiet house like that, and causing all that destruction and loss of life. It makes me feel queer all over."

Thrusting his hands in his pockets he put his head on one side and whistled sadly.

"Miss Winny gone too!" he burst

out, suddenly. "I can't make it out at no price. Well, come what may, I'll do my best to find out the rascals, and if I succeed let them look out for squalls, that's all."

He walked into the village which stood at the foot of Hawk's Crag, and made his way straight to the inn.

Round the door of the "Goat Inn" a group of rough-looking sailors and some of the lower class farm-labourers were gathered, drinking, smoking, and talking about the attack upon the Lone

House, and the abduction of Miss Winifred.

As Rob Rackstraw walked up to them they ceased speaking.

"They are as pretty a set of scoundrels as ever I saw," thought Rackstraw.

Rob walked into the inn, ordered some breakfast, and at the same time told the ostler to get Swift, Wild Winny's pony, saddled, and to be sure to give the animal a good feed of corn, as he had a long ride before him.

"Good morning, sir," said Rob to an ugly fellow, who had looked into the parlour-door several times, and always favoured Rob with a cold, hard stare; "good morning, sir; hope I see you well. I hope that my features please you. Don't be afraid to examine them; I ain't ashamed of them. They have lasted me some years now, and I ain't likely to get any new ones just yet."

The fellow growled out something, and, turning on his heel, walked slowly away.

"Just so, sir—just so," cried Rob, who could not catch a word of what the other had said; "I am quite of your opinion, quite. You will know me again when we meet, and I shall know you anywhere."

"Why, what harm have I done?" growled the fellow, turning round as he reached the door; "a cat may look at a king, I suppose?"

"If the king likes, and the cat don't object," said Rob; "for my part, being good-looking, I don't object to be looked at."

"Blest if I know what's come to the folk about here," growled the man; "they have the rummiest kind of servants I ever seed. Pick 'em up in the hedges and ditches, and such like. I wouldn't have such things about me for the world."

With this polite remark the fellow slunk out of the room and went towards the stables.

"Now, I wonder what is up with that fellow?" said Rackstraw to himself; "he's up to no good.

"Halloa!" he muttered, as he paused in the act of finishing the last drink of his ale; "halloa! why, what on earth is the landlord speaking to that black-looking rascal who took such a liking to

my face? I don't like this. I'll keep my eyes open in case of treachery."

He was just in the act of blowing the foam off a fresh tankard of malt when a stone wrapped in a piece of paper was thrown through the open window, and fell upon the table.

"Halloa!" cried Rob, as he caught up the stone, and, placing it under the table so that no one should see it, began to unwrap it. "Halloa! here's some mystery a-going on here, and no mistake. I'm quite a hero of romance, that's what I am. Writing!—it's a letter! Perhaps a billy-dix from some young and interesting female, who, having once set eyes upon me, cannot conceal her love. Eh, what's this?—so; it can't be possible?"

The note which caused Rob Rackstraw so much surprise ran as follows—

"Be careful what you eat or drink. Enemies surround you. Look to your horse. See that she has not eaten too many oats. She will be all the better if she has not touched any of them. Look to saddle and girths, especially the latter. Be cautious, and all may yet be well. If you refuse this warning your blood be on your own head.

"A FRIEND."

"Well, that's pretty warm," said Rob, as he crumpled up the note and thrust it into his pocket.

"Don't eat and drink! Rather late to set up that cry. I've eaten and drunk up all that I could get. But about the horse! Well, that is a matter in which I can make sure of something yet."

He strolled to the bar and paid his bill.

"It might be a joke," he thought; "but it don't strike me that it is. However, joke or no joke, there is nothing like making sure, and so here goes to see what is up in the stables."

Turning round by the side of the inn Rob Rackstraw managed to reach the back gate. Passing into the stable-yard he crept up to the stable-door—which was shut—and, putting down his ear, listened.

He could hear Swift stamping his hoofs and kicking, whilst the rough voice of the fellow who had stared at him so now and then was distinguishable.

"Whoa, there! dang ye; can't you keep still?" the fellow said.

Rob Rackstraw crept round to a window, through which he could see as well as listen.

The horse had its ears thrown right back, its usually kind and affectionate eyes were glaring wildly, and were so strained that the eyeballs appeared bursting from their sockets.

Before him was a manger full of oats, which, much to Rob's delight, the animal appeared not to have touched.

"Dang me if ever I saw such a creature!" grumbled the fellow; "I can't make it out. Put a good dinner afore a human creature, and he'll precious soon mop it up, never axing no questions as to what may be put into it. But here's this here horse knows them beans have been doctored, and won't touch one on 'em."

"The letter did come from a friend," thought Rob Rackstraw, and he listened again.

"The beast knows as well as I do what my game is, and she won't be done no how."

"I only wish I had been as knowing," said Rob to himself; "if my dinner was doctored I'm done for."

"There's one chance of doing it; I don't like it, but I must. I'll just paint the bit for him. He must take that."

Whistling softly to himself he drew a small tin box from his pocket and opened it.

The box contained an ointment of a nasty dirty green colour.

He took some of the ointment on his finger and began to paint the bit of Swift's bridle.

As he was thus busily employed Rob Rackstraw slipped into the stable without making any noise, and cautiously closed and locked the door after him.

Then, with one fearful blow, he felled the rascal to the ground.

"You wretched creature!" cried Rob, as he danced about his prostrate foe. "I'm up to your games."

"Who are you?" growled the man, as he gathered himself up; "what do you mean by knocking me about?"

"Knocking you about!" cried Rob; "I'll knock you into the middle of next week in a minute."

But Rob had reckoned rather too much upon his own powers with the fists.

The black-looking ostler was a good boxer, and, springing forward, he landed Rob a heavy blow upon the chest, which sent him reeling back against the wall with tremendous violence.

"So that's your little game, is it?" cried Rob, as he sprang forward and seized the ostler. "Well, we'll just see who is the best man of the two at wrestling. You're a big man, but I don't think you'll get the best of me."

Backwards and forwards the men swung, now this side, now that side. The ostler tried to throw Rob under the horse's feet (for the frightened animal was kicking and prancing about in a tremendous manner), but Rackstraw clung to him tightly and kept his legs so well planted that the other, although the taller man, could not move him.

Now one would have the advantage; then the other would make a feint, and recover his lost ground.

Suddenly Rackstraw threw out his left shoulder so as to catch his adversary with it in the chest, heaved him up into the air, and then dashed him down on his back on the pavement.

"You would doctor my horse, would you?" said Rob; "hang me if I don't doctor you."

Seizing the tin box containing the ointment Rob, with a piece of stick he found, scooped out a quantity of the nasty stuff and rubbed it over the teeth of his prostrate foe, all the time addressing him in this style—

"Doctor a good and willing creature like that, you varmint! Just see how you like being doctored yourself. Oh! you spit and splutter, do you? The poor horse could not have done that. Maybe it's poison! You know best. And, if it is, I only hope it will poison as badly as it seems to taste. There, my lad, I think I have cleaned your teeth nicely, and taught you not to meddle with other folks' horses in future."

As he spoke he rose from the ostler's chest—for he had been kneeling thereon during the above dialogue—and, turning round, began carefully cleaning the bit.

Springing to his feet the ostler dashed at Rob, intending to fell him to the earth.

But Rackstraw heard him coming, and,

avoiding the blow, delivered one with such force full in the ostler's face that that gentleman reeled back and would have fallen, only an open corn-bin happened to be behind him.

On this he at first sat, then his heels flew up to his head, and, doubling up like a two-foot rule, he vanished into the bin.

" By Jingo! I've got him now," cried Rob Rackstraw, as he darted forward and slammed down the lid of the bin, fastened the staple, and thrust a stick into it so that it would not open. " You are my prisoner, old fellow."

" Let me out, let me out ! " gasped the man; " I—I feel so sick, so very sick ! "

" So you ought to feel," laughed Rob, " sick of yourself. There, spit away ; you will have plenty of time to clean your teeth in there, sir. How ill the fellow is, to be sure. If dear old Swift had had the bit painted he would have knocked up in about a mile."

Having soothed down the horse's temper Rackstraw soon saddled it, and rode it round to the front of the inn.

" Hillo ! " said the landlord, as he beheld Rob on the horse ; " why, where's Bill, the ostler? Couldn't he bring your horse round for you, eh ? I think that fellow is getting too idle for his place, that I do."

" So do I," replied Rob, with a grin. " I daresay, if you look for him, you will find him kicking his heels about somewhere."

" Ah ! " replied the landlord; " he knows horses—only he's so slow, so slow."

" He's fast enough now," thought Rob Rackstraw, as he prepared for the start.

" By the way, if you did not see him, I suppose you did not give him his ordinary fee ? You can pay me."

" Oh ! I did see him," laughed Rob, and I gave him so much that he was quite satisfied."

" All right," growled the landlord, who did not seem pleased with Rob's answer.

" I'm off ! " shouted Rob Rackstraw, as he dashed away. " I shall be back very soon."

" Ay ! " muttered the landlord to some of his friends ; " sooner nor he thinks. The horse will break down before he has covered three miles of ground, and if she lasted he would not. Both are doctored."

" That don't look much like a doctored horse," said one of the men.

" But I tell you that it is doctored," replied the landlord. " Bill had strict orders, and he never fails."

" Well, where is Bill ? " said another ; " we had better know for certain how the matter stands."

Grumbling at the incredulity of some people, the landlord led the way to the stables."

Vainly they searched everywhere, but could not discover the slightest trace of Bill the ostler.

At last, just as they were about to give up the search, a heartrending groan smote upon their ears.

" Hark ! " cried one of the party ; " that fellow Rackstraw has murdered him, and his ghost is groaning."

" It's in that bin," cried a more courageous person ; " and, ghost or no ghost, we will have him out at once. Lend a hand, lads, and let us turn over the bin."

Crash !

Down went the bin, and most dismal howls proceeded therefrom.

" By Jingo ! he is in here," cried the others. " Open the lid and let us have him out."

No sooner said than done.

The lid was opened, and Bill the ostler rolled out onto the floor, his clothes all dusty from the corn, his eyes blackened from the blow, and his face pale from the sickness.

Never in the world had a more ghastly object been seen by anyone.

" Where is he—where is the cruel wretch ? " he gasped. " Where is that horrible Rackstraw ? "

" Rackstraw ! " cried the others, " he is gone. Did not you doctor the horse ? "

" No ; but he doctored me. He rubbed my teeth with the ointment, knocked me into the corn bin, and shut me up in it."

Spite of their annoyance at Rob's escape—for the whole of them, landlord and all, were in with the smugglers, and wished to prevent the custom-house officers stopping it—they could not help bursting out into roars of laughter, whilst Bill the ostler slunk away to get himself washed and something to cure his sickness.

Meanwhile Rob was galloping on at a desperate rate.

CHAPTER XXXVII.

ROB FEELS THE EFFECT OF THE POISON—THE WAYSIDE INN AND THE STRANGERS—
ROB DISCOVERS THE PLOT—LIFE FOR LIFE—ROB A PRISONER.

"FORWARD, forward, dear Swift!" cried Rackstraw, as he urged his horse along the road. "Remember, I saved you from the poisoned bit that the rascals would have thrust in your mouth. It is for your friends that you gallop so swiftly. Onward, old horse."

Vainly did Rob try to keep his spirits in the usual flow; his head grew heavy and his eyes dim.

Now and then he started, for he fancied he could hear the tramp of horses behind him. But no one was near.

"Courage, Rob, courage!" he muttered to himself. "I must keep up. Oh! that I had received that warning in time to have refused to drink that beer. Hillo, there! Ay, boy, ay, forward, forward!" and, raising himself in his stirrups, Rob Rackstraw dashed over hedges and ditches, until he came to what in a steeplechase would be called a "water jump," and there, losing his seat, he rolled over into the water.

How long he remained there he could not say; but when he returned to consciousness he found the stars were glittering brightly in the sky, a cold, sharp wind came cutting across the moorland, making Rob shiver again as he rose from his damp couch.

"Where the deuce am I?" he said, as he rubbed his eyes and endeavoured to collect his scattered senses.

He gazed round at the dark, bleak plain, and at last caught sight of Swift, who was quietly grazing in the field.

"I know now—I know now!" he muttered; "those wretches drugged my drink, and I have been insensible. Well, at all events, I have escaped from their hands, and must be thankful for that. Hi! Swift, old boy—come, good fellow, come!"

The good horse trotted quickly up to Rob and stood ready for him to mount.

"Well, old fellow," said Rob, as he crawled on to the horse's back, for his head was still in a daze and his legs seemed as heavy as lead, "I must trust to you to take me out of this trouble, for I don't know my way at all; therefore, old horse, I shall throw the bridle on your neck and let you guide me where you will."

The horse neighed, as if he quite understood what Rob Rackstraw said, and breaking into a sharp trot, soon reached the highroad, down which it went for a couple of miles, and then reached a queer-looking inn, which stood a few yards back from the road.

"This is a quaint-looking place," thought Rob; "not much business done here, I should think. But I am in no situation to be too particular."

He drew up in front of the inn-door, and, having alighted, knocked with the butt-end of his whip on the door.

"Hillo!" cried a red-haired youth, opening the door; "do you know the value o' paint as you go damaging people's premises in this way? P'raps you're in the paint way and wants a job; if so, we does our own painting and can do without you. One would think as you was the Lord Mayor to come a hammering and a hitting at a door in that manner."

"I say, red poll," replied Rob Rackstraw, "you stood in the front row when tongues were given out. What with that tongue of yours and that red head you ought to set the world on fire; but I don't think you will."

"If I did, I don't think you would be the man to put it out," growled the fiery-headed youth.

"That being agreed upon, I'll just

walk inside," said Rob, "and have some supper. Where are your stables, for I always look to my horse first?"

The red-headed youth glanced at Rob in dismay; then growling to himself about the horse being a much better animal than the master, he led the way to the stables.

"There now, my little beauty," said Rob, when he had seen his horse put all snug and comfortable. "Now, young fiery locks, I'll go and see what I can get myself."

The red-headed youth stared at Rob, and seemed much inclined to resent this kind of language; however, he appeared to think better of it, and therefore led the way back to the inn.

"Now, young hopeful," said Rob Rackstraw, "give me something good to eat and drink. You understand me?"

"Of course I do; I didn't suppose you came here to suck your thumb. If you had you would not be welcome."

"It don't seem that I am very welcome even now," muttered Rob. "I can't make this place out."

Whatever the outside of the inn was, the interior was excessively comfortable.

"Ah!" cried Rob, as he walked up to the fire, "this is pleasant."

"You seem to have had a nasty fall, sir," said a gruff voice out of one of the darkest corners of the room.

Rob started back, and, for the first time, perceived that two men, in high boots, were seated at one of the tables.

Before them was a bottle, glasses, and two heavy hunting-whips.

They were both smoking, and what rather startled Rackstraw more than anything else was that they both had an eye covered up with a shade.

"Well," thought Rob to himself, "I don't think I ever saw two gentlemen whose personal appearance was so much against them as the two gentlemen I've the honour of seeing now; but 'politeness is everything,' as his Satanic majesty said to Dr. Faustus when he bowed him downstairs, so I'd best be civil. Ah!" he continued, as he looked up, "I came a nice 'purl' over a jump down yonder in the meadow."

"In the meadow!" said one of the men, who wore a white hat with a black band. and had a hoarse voice.

"In the meadow," replied Rob. "Begging your pardon, sir, but I think your bellows is out of order."

The man addressed appeared as if he were going to make some reply, but his companion, who wore no hat, stopped him.

"Hold your tongue," he whispered. "Do you want to spoil all?"

Then, looking up at Rob, he continued—

"You are right; my friend is greatly troubled with shortness of breath."

"Poor fellow! That's the complaint my grandmother died of," replied Rob, in sad tones. "Men of his habit of body pop off like an over-ripe gooseberry and are soon done for."

"I ain't of that sort," cried the man, who appeared to wish for a quarrel.

"No, it don't look like it," said Rob, quietly. "Is the bell near you, gentlemen?"

One of them pulled the bell, which happened to be near him, and the red-headed waiter appeared.

"I want a bottle of brandy," said Rob. "Mind, and don't you draw the cork until you have brought it in here. I like to mix my own spirits, and I don't care for other people having a finger in the pie."

"Do you think we want to p'ison you?" asked the waiter.

"Can't say, young vermilion-top," replied Rob. "Must taste the brandy first—tell you afterwards."

"You talks as if you was a hemperer," growled the waiter. "Who are you?"

"Don't be inquisitive; that red hair of yours inflames your brains. Take my advice, and go and put your head under a pump; it will cool them. When you have done that, come back and tell me what you have for supper."

"We ain't got nothing for supper," cried the waiter, in a passion. "Who are you, I should like to know?"

"Begging your pardon," replied Rob, coolly, "I should like to know who are you?"

"I'm the waiter. But I tell you, we haven't got any supper. We don't have many guests this way, and you know country inns don't keep goods for chance customers. You're a chance customer, and so it chances that you won't get anything to eat. There now."

"Nothing to eat!" cried Rob. "But I must have something to eat."

"Oh, very well," grinned the fellow; "but I don't know where you will get it; it won't be here. These two gentlemen have ordered everything we have in the house for their supper, and that ain't much neither."

"Surely, gentleman," said Rob Rackstraw, "you will not see a fellow traveller go supperless to bed? So I now ask you to allow me to share with you?"

"I don't think it reasonable," wheezed the stranger who wore no hat. "I can eat my share, and more."

"I don't doubt it," thought Rob.

"You speak too fast, Jacob," said the other man, "much too fast.. This gentleman, like ourselves, is a traveller —and, therefore, he shall join our table. That settles all disputes at once."

"Right you are," cried Rob; "and here comes our blazing boy with the brandy, so I vote we pledge each other's healths before the supper."

Both the men seemed delighted at the notion.

Rob served out the brandy.

"Here is the supper at last. Tripe and onions, I declare!" cried Rob. "Come along, and let us eat."

And eat they did; but all the time Rob kept his eyes wide open.

Once he managed to slip his foot over by the side of the white hat man's foot, and he caught the other man, who had a very rough head, treading upon it.

Then he noticed that the patch over the thin man's eye was rather a nuisance to him.

"It's all very well, my dear fellows," said Rob to himself; "but those blinkers of yours won't blind me. You can see as well as I can, and, maybe, better. You are only two to one—and I think I can do that lot pretty well."

Supper done, the men insisted upon standing a bottle of wine, and so the evening was spent until Rob made a long speech which nobody could understand. Then he managed to sit down about three inches from his chair, the consequence being that he rolled under the table, where he commenced shouting at the top of his lungs for his candle, as he wished to go to bed.

His new-found friends seemed to enjoy it. and, having pulled him up into a chair, asked him to drink more; but Rob was firm.

Vainly they filled his glass; and at last they were obliged, by the help of Sam, to carry him upstairs to bed.

The three men laughed, shrugged their shoulders, and left the room.

No sooner had they gone than Rob Rackstraw sat up in bed and listened attentively.

"Now, what's their little game?" he muttered; "they are not the regular thieves; if they were I should not be good enough game for them. No, that's not it; and yet they were on to me directly. No, no; they think I am drunk and an easy game, but it won't do."

He rose slowly from the bed and crept to the door, where he listened eagerly.

"All seems quiet enough," he said; "but now then to look at my pistols. If the worst comes I must fight for it."

He drew from his pocket two small pistols, and, having found them all ready for use, placed them at his belt.

He then cautiously opened the door of his sleeping room and crept out on to the landing.

He could see down the stairs into the room where he and his companions had supped.

The fire was burning brightly, but the room appeared to be empty.

With the greatest caution Rob drew off his boots, and, tying them together with a piece of string, slung them across his shoulder, and then, with as light a tread as he could, he crept downstairs.

"They keep up a jolly good fire here," thought Rob, as he glanced round the empty room. "Can I be mistaken, and are they honest fellows, after all? No; that I will swear they are not. Hark! what is that?"

The sound he heard was that of some men conversing in a low whisper.

He gazed in the direction from which the sound came, and perceived that a light was shining through a chink in the wall.

"So they are not in bed," thought Rob, "but are sitting in yonder room discussing their affairs. Well, I should like to know what they are speaking about, and will therefore take the liberty of listening to them."

He crept to the crack, through which

the light shone, and peeped through it.

Seated at the table Rob perceived, not only his two friends with the shades over their eyes, but some half-a-dozen other fellows gathered round a table, drinking and smoking.

"It's all very well to say that we must do this," said one of the men, "but I, for one, don't like the job."

"Bah! you are too particular," said another. "This is how the matter stands: the people down and about Hawkhouse have begun to suspect that things are rather queer down there. The last little affair we had in the wrecking way proved to be a great failure owing to someone— and no one knows who—ringing the alarm bell. Now, old Summerbell, having turned up, is hard at work against Mr. Grindwell, and he is one of those fellows that it ain't so easy to get rid of."

"I think it would be much better if we broke up the gang," growled a rough-looking sailor kind of a man. "Luck has left him."

"And so, Peter, you will be like the rats and the sinking ship, eh? Sneak off directly there is danger."

"The rats are very clever animals," replied Peter.

"Why, you don't mean to say, Peter, you would turn upon the captain after having been with him so many years?"

"But I do, though. Why should I not? The captain would make precious short work of me or you if he did not care for us. Why, I have seen him shoot down his crew like dogs for the least thing."

One or two of the other men evidently shared this opinion with Peter.

"Red Randulph is not so near his end as you would make us think," said the white-hatted man with the patch over his eye. "Now listen. This fellow that is now in this house is a police spy, and is on his way to London, or one of the large towns, to get assistance. We did all we could to stop him, but it was no go. We wanted to paint his horse's bit, but the fellow got wind of it and did us all. So we followed him; he lost the road, but before we had been here long he turned up. He's now upstairs tipsy. All we have to do is to bind him hand and foot and throw him into one of the cellars here, for if we let this fellow go he will give notice to all round the coast, and we shall be done for."

"Well, I don't mind much killing a spy," said the fellow called Peter, "and I'm in with you as far as that goes."

"If it's to be done it had better be done at once," said one of the fellows. "We will kill the fellow outright."

"Ah, that would be the best way," said another; "dead men tell no tales."

"Well, this is very pleasant," thought Rob to himself. "I wish I could find a way to escape."

He ran his eyes anxiously round the room in hopes of finding some way out of his trouble; but to his horror he found that the windows were guarded with iron bars.

Grasping his pistols Rob Rackstraw placed his back against the wall and prepared to sell his life as dearly as he could.

The men rose from their seats, and Rob saw them lean over the table as if busy at some game.

He soon found out what they were doing.

One of the men was writing the names of the others on slips of paper, which were then carefully folded up and thrown into the white hat.

This done the hat was shaken up, and one of the fellows having been carefully blindfolded, he was ordered to put his hand into the hat and draw one of the papers.

This he did, and then, before he had opened the slip he had drawn, the others were burned.

"Now open your slip," said the man with the patch on his eye, as he removed the bandage from the head of the fellow who had drawn the paper, "and read out the name."

The man unfolded the slip and read slowly the name of—

"Jabez Mercer!"

"Confound it!" muttered the man with the rough head of hair; "it's like my luck. If ever there's anything like this on hand I get in for it."

"Well, you were the one to propose it," laughed the others; "and, as far as that goes, we are all in the same boat. If the murder is found out we are one as bad as the other. The only difference is, you strike the blow."

"Well, look here," said the fellow, as he fastened a half-mask over his face, "when I whistle some of you fellows must creep upstairs and carry the body downstairs and throw it in the well."

"All right; but look here—we'd better have all the lights out. If any of the preventive men are about they will be sure to come down upon us."

"Ay, douse the glims!" growled Jabez Mercer; "and one or two of you fellows may as well go up and down the road just to see no one comes here. Remember, the password is 'Moonbeams.' Shoot down or knock down anyone who can't answer you. Do you understand that?"

"Oh, yes; we are up to the caper," replied the others. "Just you do your work well and we will do ours."

"Thank goodness, only one man is coming," thought Rob. "I have still a chance."

He crept to the fireplace and seized the poker, and then made his way noiselessly back to his bedroom.

Here he had only just time to rumple up the bedclothes, so as to make it appear as if someone was asleep in the bed, when he heard footsteps creeping up the stairs.

"Now for it," he muttered, as he hid behind the curtain of the bed; "now for it. All depends upon my coolness."

He could just see the door of his room open and the dark figure of a man steal in.

The figure approached the bed, and, leaning over it, raised a dagger on high, and then, with all his force, drove it into the heap of clothes which had been arranged to look like the sleeping Rob Rackstraw.

At the same time Rob had raised his poker, and, as the dagger descended, he brought it down with a fearful crash upon the back of the assassin's head.

With a deep groan the man rolled over motionless upon the bed.

With wonderful dexterity Rob stripped off the man's coat and mask, placing them on himself.

He then drew off the man's high boots, which he also exchanged for his own.

Having done this he lifted the man, who was quite insensible, on to the bed, and rolled him up in a sheet, so that his face was quite hidden.

He then went to the door and whistled shrilly.

In a few seconds three of the fellows crept into the room, and in low whispers asked if all was right.

"Yes; he is there. Take him down into the yard and throw him into the well," said Rob, imitating as well as he could the gruff tones of Jabez Mercer. "Who was that who whistled just now?"

"I did not hear it," said one of the men. "It must have been one of our friends who are keeping guard."

"Then you had better make haste and get rid of this fellow. Hark! there it is again."

"I did not hear anything," replied one of the men; "but you always had sharp ears, Jabez. Come, Dick, give us a hand here."

They hoisted the body upon their shoulders and bore it down into the yard, Rob following them.

"We must get his horse out of the way," growled Rob, as he walked to the stable.

Swiftly he saddled his horse and let it out into the yard.

"What the deuce are you after there, Jabez?" said one of the men; "can't you leave the horse alone?"

"Leave it alone! I should rather think not; I don't want to be found out by this animal. Why, if any of the preventive men see it, they will know at once it belonged to one of their spies, and they will precious soon be after us. No, no; you pitch that fellow down the well, whilst I just turn this horse out of the yard. You look after your business, and I'll look after mine."

As he spoke, he had been unfastening the stable-yard gate, and leading the horse out of the yard.

He heard a loud splash, and his blood grew cold as he knew that the would-be murderer had been hurled down the well.

In an instant he had sprung upon Swift's back, and, with a cry of triumph, gave the noble animal his head.

"Forward! Away, good horse!" cried Rob, excitedly.

"Treachery!" cried the men, rushing out from the stable-yard, "treachery! Stop him! stop him!"

THE BOYS OF HAWKHOUSE SCHOOL.

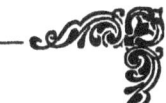

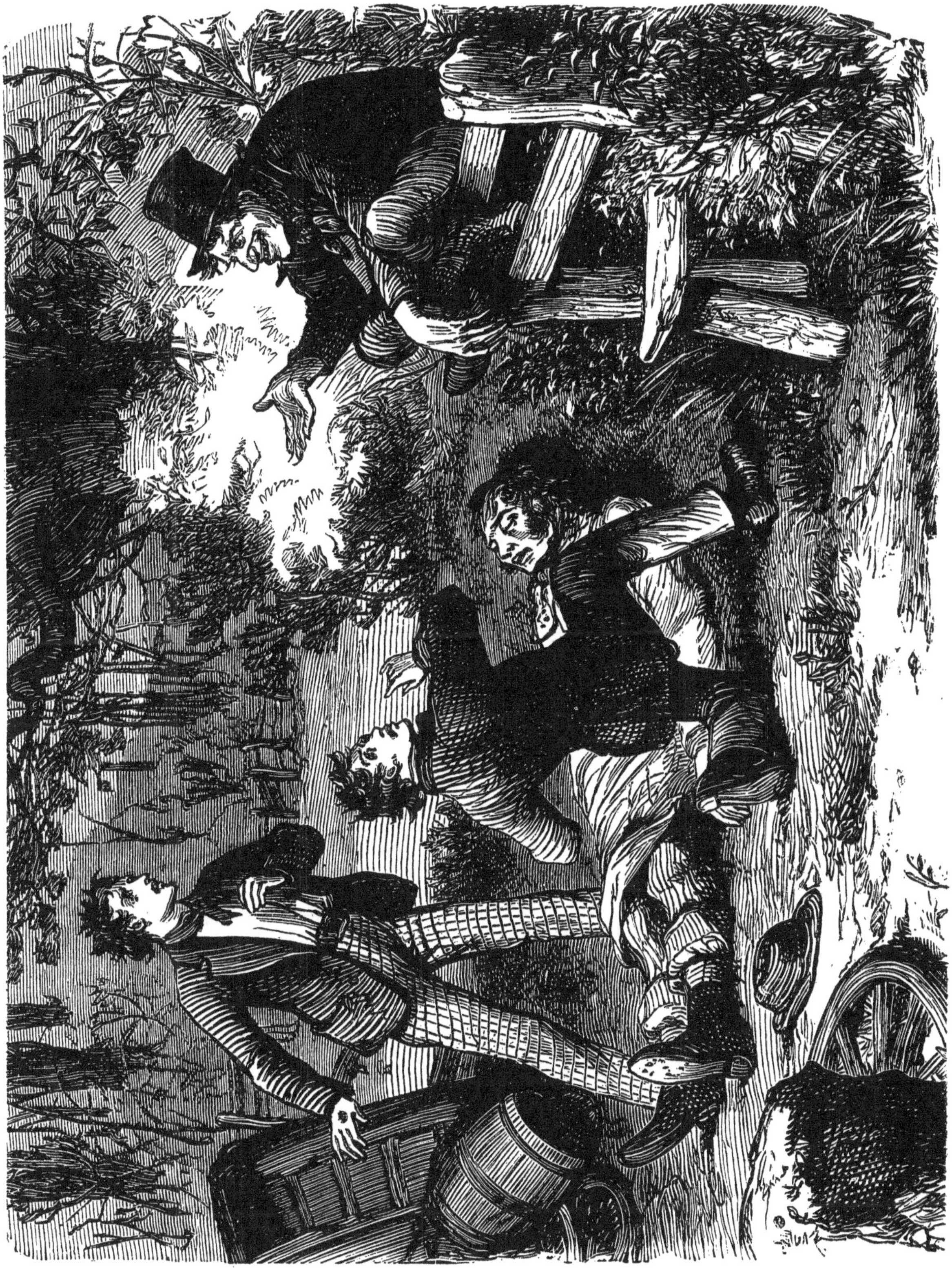

"JACK AND FLICK STARTED BACK WHEN THEY BEHELD THE HIDEOUS BEING."

No. 12.

PRICE ONE HALFPENNY.

[PUBLISHED EVERY MONDAY.]

That cry of triumph had told them all, and they knew that they had thrown their comrade into the well, and that the spy had escaped.

"Hurrah, hurrah!" shouted Rob, unable to suppress his delight at his escape. "Onward, onward, my brave horse! Onward, onward! We will bring these villains to justice yet."

"Halt, or I fire!" cried one of the men, who had been sent to guard the road.

Rob Rackstraw's answer was a merry laugh, and the next instant there was a bright flash and a loud report.

Rob reeled in his saddle, for the pistol ball had passed through his left shoulder.

He was too good a horseman to be unseated; he grasped his reins firmly, and made his horse hurry on.

For some time he heard the sound of horses in pursuit, and twice shots were fired at him, but luckily they missed each time.

At length he saw the lights of a big town before him.

He did not know what place it was.

His brain seemed on fire, and a strange red mist hung before his eyes.

The blood was flowing fast from his wound, and he reeled in his saddle.

But now the stones of the city streets rang under his horse's hoofs.

He heard people shouting for him to stop; the earth, the heavens seemed reeling round him.

A crash!

He had fallen from his horse, and was stretched insensible on the hard stones.

In an instant a crowd had gathered round him, and were pressing forward eagerly to discover who he was.

"He's been attacked by thieves!" cried out some of the people.

"He is a thief who has been pursued and shot by the constables!" shouted another set in the crowd.

"Stand back, there; stand back!" cried some of the others; "here comes Master Morgan, the head constable.

He will soon find out who the fellow is."

"Ay, that he will. Come on, Master Morgan."

"Out of the way, good people, out of the way!" cried Morgan, as he forced his way through the crowd.

"He's all safe, Mr. Morgan!" "He can't move!" "He is stunned!" "He is dead!" "He is wounded!" shouted the crowd.

"All safe! I should think he was all safe, look you. All the good folk about here are only too ready to bring a murdering thief to justice. Here is a gentleman who has shot the fellow who attacked him. Oh, but he did it well, too, look you. The fellow robbed him, and then the gentleman pursued, look you, and shot him in the shoulder. This is the man, I think?" continued Mr. Morgan, turning round and addressing a gentleman so like Griffiths Grindwell that they might have been taken for twin brothers.

"I believe he is. If it be the same man, you will find a purse upon him containing twenty-five pounds in gold and some odd silver, and a pocket-book, in which is a bill drawn upon Mr. Griffiths Grindwell, of London, for a hundred pounds."

The constable instantly plunged his hand into Rob Rackstraw's pocket—or, rather, into that of Jabez Mercer, for the reader will recollect Rob had put on that villain's coat—and, to the delight of all assembled, produced the articles mentioned.

"There can be no doubt," said the cute Mr. Morgan, "so we'll just take him off to the lock-up, and there have a surgeon to look after him. If you'll kindly come with me, sir, we will see the rascal safely locked up, sir. I warrant me he's a regular bad 'un."

And so poor Rob Rackstraw was carried off to the lock-up, much to the delight of Griffiths Grindwell's dear friend, Mr. Luke Lansner.

CHAPTER XXXVIII.

JACK OVERHEARS A CONVERSATION AMONGST THE SAILORS WHICH MAKES HIM UNEASY
—THEY SEEK NOVEL HIDING-PLACES—ONCE MORE ON SHORE—A FRESH ALARM.

"It ain't no good a-trying to close our eyes to the matter at all," growled one of the sailors on board the "Sea Hawk," as that vessel beat up the Channel. "Everything has gone against us. Here's the 'Flying Fish' burned; the soldiers at Ile de Bas come down upon us and caused a lot of the men to lose the number of their mess; and now we are going to make a run for the coast of Kent, which is about the most carefully guarded coast in all England."

"No good can come of it," growled another sailor. "It's all very well for the cappen to laugh, and to say as how it is the rats that make all the noise; but he knows it ain't the rats. If it was rats, do you think he'd go peppering the walls of his cabin with pistol-bullets, smashing the furniture and lamps in the reckless way he has been doing? Not he. Then how he swears! Why, it is awful to hear him a-calling on the dead people to come out and fight him."

"If once we gets clear of this trouble," muttered another, "I votes that we cut and run. After all, honesty is the best policy."

"It strikes me that it's rather late in life to begin to think of that," said another. "No, my lads; we must stick hard and fast to the captain. If he can't pull us through with this run no one can. If we are taken we shall be hanged; but if he is at the head of the band, at the worst we shall die fighting."

"Ay, the captain is very good where human foes are against us; but who can stand against ghosts and such like?"

"At all events, our orders are to fire at anything that may turn up, and fire I will."

"So, so," thought Jack Firebrace, who, under cover of the long-boat, had been listening to the above conversation; "so, so. The captain has given orders for any strange light or noise to be fired at. I am afraid we shall have to give up our games."

"Do you know," said one of the sailors, after a pause, "that I suspects there is someone hidden in the ship's hold?"

"Who could be hidden in the hold?" laughed another. "No, no; the noises don't come from human creatures."

"I'm none so sure of that. I believe that we have a traitor on board; so does the captain. I believe that signals are made from the ship to the coast to alarm the coastguard. Anyway, when the captain comes on deck I mean to give him my notion of the matter, and we will search the vessel right through."

"Then I think our little game is done up," said Jack to himself, "and I may as well go and give Flick this comfortable information. But I won't despair yet. We have right on our side, and will fight for it to the last."

Keeping well in the shadow of the long-boat, Jack Firebrace managed to reach the fore-hatch unperceived, and from thence crept down into the spirit-room.

"Flick, old fellow," he whispered, as he awoke his comrade, who was sleeping in a corner, "I have some bad news."

"What is up now, Jack?" demanded Flick. "I don't think we can be much worse off than we are now."

"Don't you? Well, just listen to this. The men have got it into their heads that someone is hidden in this hold. I have just overheard the sailors declare their determination to tell Grindwell of their suspicions, and to ask his permission to search the vessel. That he will grant it there can be little doubt, for even if he does not believe them, he will know that the search will satisfy the sailors and give them something to do."

"It's deuced unlucky, Jack. If they find us they will kill us."

"I don't think there is much doubt about that. What do you think is the best thing to be done?"

"Fire the ship. If we do nothing else we can destroy this nest of thieves."

"A very nice idea, and, if the worst

comes to the worst, one that I would most certainly adopt."

"Comes to the worst! Well, I should think things *have* pretty well come to the worst, when we know that in a little time we shall have all this set of cut-throats upon us. But now, let me know what you propose to do."

"Well, then, in the first place, I propose that we take two of these empty barrels—we have some tools here—and that we pierce holes in them through which we can breath and see. You get into one—when we have rolled them to the place where the full barrels are kept—and I will head in the cask. I must then get into the other and head it in the best way I can."

"It's a desperate venture, Firebrace," said old Flick, "but I suppose it must be done. I sha'n't be preserved *in spirits*, for I don't think I ever felt so dull before. Well, Jack, old fellow, as there is no other way out of this difficulty, let us set to work at once and settle the matter."

They brought two large empty casks out from a corner, and, having bored a lot of small holes in them, Flick got into one, having armed himself with a large chisel, which he determined to use should the worst come to the worst, and they were found out.

Then Jack Firebrace headed in the cask as noiselessly as he could.

But now came the great difficulty.

How was he to get into his own cask and head it in afterwards?

He crept into his cask, taking with him the head of the cask, a hammer, and some nails.

Having squatted down as well as he could, he forced the head of the cask upwards until it was well jammed into the converging staves.

He then drove some nails into the staves so that the head of the cask was well supported.

This was well done, but it cost our hero a good many raps on the fingers.

Scarcely had he finished when he heard the tramp of men coming down from the deck, and at once guessed that the search had commenced.

"If it be as you say," cried Mr. Grindwell, as he entered the spirit-room, "the stowaways shall walk the plank."

"Of course, your honour, I can't be certain," said the sailor who had proposed the search; "but I tell you what it is. I know that I have seen two Dumb Peters, and that I can swear to for I left one speaking to you in your cabin and I walked to the fore-hatch and there I saw another a-taking in the air, his head being just above the hatch."

"And why the deuce didn't you seize upon him at once?" demanded Grindwell.

"Why, you see, your honour, I was struck all of a heap like for a moment and when I looked up he had gone."

"Well, make haste, and let us get this search over," said Grindwell, "for we shall soon make the Romney Marshes, and must run this cargo on shore. I shall land here and make my way up to London, whilst you must make your way back to Hawkhouse."

The men immediately set to work overhauling everything; but of course nothing could be found.

"Stop!" thundered Grindwell, as the men were preparing to leave the spirit-room. "There has been foul play here. See! the beading has been ripped away so that this panel might be removed, and that is the way that the girl escaped from the cabin. Search the place well. Confusion! that I should be fooled in this way. Oh, I see it all now but too clearly! It was Winifred Summerbell who gave the alarm at Ile de Bas. She escaped with the French girls; no doubt one of them lent her a disguise. Perhaps she has now set the French ships on our track. Where is Dumb Peter? He must have helped her. By all that is evil he shall be thrown overboard at once! Search well, my lads. A hundred pounds to the man who finds any-one concealed in this vessel. If you discover a traitor bring him to me, for I will wring first his secret from him and then will have his life!"

"Hurrah for the brave captain!" shouted the men; and away they dashed all over the ship, sounding the decks and examining all places where a human being might be concealed; nay, they even went so far as to examine places where there was no chance of anything bigger than a cat being hidden; but, explore as they would, not a thing could they find, so the search was given up.

When all was still Jack ventured to put his mouth to one of the holes and inquire how old Flick was, for in the search the casks had been a great deal shaken about, and Jack himself was much bruised.

"Flick, old fellow," whispered Jack, "how goes it with you, old man? Are you all right?"

He waited for an answer, but could only hear a hoarse, wheezing sound.

"Flick, Flick, I say," said our hero, in a louder whisper. "What's the matter? Are you not comfortable?"

"Comfortable!" wheezed back the voice. "How the deuce can a fellow be comfortable when he's standing on his head?"

"Standing on your head!" exclaimed Jack. "Why, surely you don't mean to say—"

"But indeed I do, though," returned Flick. "One of those wretched fellows turned my cask over."

It was with the greatest difficulty Jack could help laughing when he heard this.

Much as he felt for his companion, he could not help feeling a desire to laugh at his situation.

"Oh, it's all very fine for you to laugh, Jack," grumbled Flick, for he could hear his companion chuckle; "but you would not laugh if you were in my position. Oh, it's horrible, really and truly horrible."

"But can't you turn round?" said Jack. "Of course I can't help seeing the comic side of things."

"Comic side of things? It's very kind of you to state what you call seeing the comic side, but I fail to see anything comic in the business. As for turning round, that is absurd. I feel as if I were round all over."

"What is to be done?" said Jack. "Do speak lower. If we are overheard we shall be killed."

"I'm sorry for you, Jack," sighed Flick; "but I know I shall have a fit directly. My head is as big as a pumpkin now. All the blood is on my brains, and I—I can't breathe. Oh, oh!"

Poor Flick made a fearful struggle to reverse his position, and in doing so upset the cask in which he was shut.

It fell with an awful crash upon the deck and went rolling away.

"There is someone in the hold," cried one of the men; "they are throwing the goods about."

Down poured the sailors into the hold, but all was still.

"Confound it all, it's only one of the casks fallen over," growled one of the sailors, as he righted the cask in which was old Flick. "I suppose one of you fellows did not set it up right, and the rolling of the ship upset it."

"I suppose it must be so," grumbled another. "I shall be glad when this voyage is over, for I don't like it at all. Hang me, if the very cargo don't seem haunted! I only hope we may run the goods all right to Romney."

"An hour will tell us that," replied the other, "for Dungeness is already in sight."

"How are you now, Flick?" asked Jack, when the men had gone.

"Oh, I am much relieved now. I am on my proper end. I wish we had labelled the casks 'This side up, with care.'"

"Never mind; we shall soon be ashore, and then, Flick, we must make a vigorous attempt to escape."

"I shall only be too happy to make the endeavour, even if I die in it. I never thought I should live to be thrust into a barrel like a red-herring. If once I get out of this, you won't see me shove my nose into anybody else's business in a hurry."

But now there arose a tremendous noise upon deck.

Sails were evidently being reefed and the ship brought to.

"We are close in shore," whispered Jack to Flick. "I can hear the fall of the waves on the sands and beating against the cliffs."

"I wish we were safe on shore," said Flick. "Only fancy, if they try to sink us and drag us ashore through the sea."

"Well, in that case, our sufferings will be all over in a very little time. Hush! here come the men."

And now everybody on board appeared to be hard at work, and yet they moved about almost noiselessly.

The hatches were thrown off and the barrels and bales slung up on deck.

Amongst these the barrels containing Flick and Jack.

At last these were slung upon a rope and hauled on to the top of the cliff, from whence they were conveyed to a house at some little distance from the shore, and ranged together in a room.

It is needless to say that the two lads were terribly shaken and bruised by their carriage.

But both were filled with hope that, now they had reached the shore, some chance would offer for their escape, and, therefore, they kept quite quiet, so as not to risk the slightest chance they might have.

The lads, by looking through the holes they had made in the casks, were able to see what was going on in the room, and were not a little surprised when Griffiths Grindwell entered, followed by Sidney Morrison.

"Have you the papers all correct?" demanded Grindwell, when he had closed the door.

"They are here," replied Morrison, as he placed some papers on the table.

"Good. And what news do you bring from Hawkhouse?"

"We have had the officers of justice down there. They searched the place, but could not discover anything. However, men are placed about the cliffs to watch, and everyone in the house is suspected."

"Let them suspect; nothing can be proved," replied Grindwell, with a short laugh.

He then opened one of the papers and examined it closely, comparing it now and then with the other.

"You have done this excellently!" he cried, at last, as, putting down the paper, he grasped Sidney Morrison by the hand.

"No one could tell that these signatures were not genuine. By these papers all the wealth Falkland left in my charge will become mine. Summerbell may do his best and worst now. I can defy him."

"I know not what you mean," said Morrison, passing his hand listlessly over his forehead. "All seems to me like a horrible dream since that fatal night in the cave. No sleep comes to me at night without most fearful visions. Night after night I kill in my dreams the grey-haired old man. Nothing but crimes seem around me. Do what I will, my horrid, horrid fate pursues me."

"Tut, tut! you speak like a madman. I tell you, you are safe now. No one knows of that night except ourselves," said Grindwell. "Go back to Hawkhouse. I must start for London to-night. Your horse is ready. Now go; remember, serve me well. Come, come, cheer up. Think not of the gloomy past, but only of the bright future."

Seizing the unhappy tutor by the arm Grindwell hurried him from the room.

"Jack," whispered Flick.

He stopped suddenly, for the heavy tramp of men were heard coming down the passage.

The next minute some fellows dressed like waggoners entered the room, and began examining the casks.

"These are the ones we want," said one of the fellows, giving the cask in which Jack was concealed a hearty kick; "see, here is the chalk mark all right. So give us a hand, and we will hoist it into the waggon."

Up went the cask, and Jack was carried out and thrown with so much violence into the cart, which was standing at the door of the house, that the head of the barrel—which, as the reader has been previously informed, was very badly secured—came out.

Luckily, however, the men did not perceive this, and Jack was not a little pleased to get the fresh air.

Two more barrels were brought out and placed in the covered cart or van, and then the carter cracked his whip, and the conveyance rolled slowly away.

"Are you there, Jack?" came a soft whisper, which filled our hero's heart with delight, for he knew old Flick had not been left behind, as he feared.

"Yes, Flick, I am here," he replied. "I am going to try to unhead your barrel. Keep still, and don't make a noise. I think the rumbling of the cart will prevent us from being heard."

After some little difficulty they managed to get the head of the cask out, and were able to look at each other.

"I say, Jack," said Flick, "under pleasanter circumstances we should call this a comic situation; as it is, I can't help grinning at it. Just fancy being potted in this manner."

"Look here, Flick," said Jack; "if we are found out we shall be killed for a certainty. That's not comic."

"I can't say that I think it is," said Flick.

"Supposing we creep out into the van and take the first chance that offers to make a bolt of it?"

"With pleasure, for I am cramped to death here," replied Flick, and the two lads cautiously crept out of their hiding-places.

Oh, what a treat it was to stretch their limbs again. As they breathed the nice fresh air they recovered their hopes of liberty. Liberty to shout, to run, and take their part in the world's great game of life.

"Jack," said Flick, "do let us make a bolt for it."

"We must be cautious, Flick, old fellow, very cautious. You creep out to the back of the van and I'll creep out to the front, so that we shall know how many men there are we have to fight against."

This was done, and when the boys came together again Jack announced that there were two men at the horses' heads, whilst Flick reported three men following the van.

"We must keep still, or—"

"Halt! halt! and tell me who you are, or I fire!" cried a stern voice in front of the van.

"Quick, quick!" whispered Jack, "creep into your cask. If these are preventive men we are saved. If they are smugglers we are lost."

In an instant the two lads had plunged into their casks, where we will leave them whilst we see what is taking place in the road.

In front of the van were some half-dozen men with cutlasses in their hands and pistols in their belts.

They wore straw hats, blue jackets with white metal buttons, and very broad, white trousers.

The foremost man held up a lantern, and the smugglers knew at once that these fellows were preventive men.

"Hillo!" cried the fellow who acted as carter; "who be you? If yer be footpads ye'd better be off, for we are a pretty good strong party, I can tell 'ee, and we doant mean to part wi' our maister's goods wi'out a fight."

"That's very well said indeed," replied the leader of the preventive men. "You know well enough who we are, and so that game won't do with us. Come, my lads, let us see what you have in that cart. You had better give in at once and let us do it quietly. You will be none the better off for a cracked head, and if you don't let us overhaul that cart quietly we shall do it by force."

The only reply to this was the report of a pistol, and the lantern the custom-house officer was holding up was shattered to pieces, the light extinguished, and the unfortunate man's elbow completely fractured.

The smuggler who acted as waggoner whipped up his horses, and the cart dashed down the road at full speed, causing Jack and old Flick no little pain, so much so, indeed, that Flick was unable to suppress his groans, but fortunately the noise caused by the cart drowned the unhappy youth's cries.

On they went, tearing along the road, bumping up and down, now going into a deep rut and then bouncing out again.

But above all the rattle and din the boys could hear the reports of fire-arms and the shouts of men, by which they judged that the smugglers and custom-house officers were having a fearful fight.

Crash!

"Help, help! Oh, murder!" yelled Flick.

And well might he cry, for the wheel of the cart had struck violently against a milestone, and the whole conveyance was smashed.

Jack Firebrace was the first to drag himself out of the ruin, and look around.

He had received a severe cut on the temple, and was fearfully shaken and bruised.

It was some minutes before he could recover his scattered senses, but at last he did so, and called on Flick.

"Flick—Flick, old fellow!" he cried, "where are you? I hope you are not hurt?"

"Hurt!" groaned Flick, from the depths of the cask. "Oh, dear no. I'm only killed—that's all; but it don't matter."

In spite of the pain that he had our hero could not help laughing.

"Don't be a fool, Flick, but get up.

This is our time of escape. I will go and see where the horses are."

As he spoke he rose to his feet, but soon perceived that he could scarcely stand; for what with the scant living he had had of late, and the knocking about, he was as weak as a baby.

However, he managed to stagger to the front of the van, where he found that the horses, having broken the traces, had galloped off.

He was about to return to see if he could render any assistance to old Flick, when he was startled by a deep groan, and, kneeling down, perceived by the dim light that the waggoner lay under the overturned waggon, his chest being quite crushed in.

In a moment Jack had quite forgotten about his own danger, and called aloud on Flick to hasten to him at once.

Flick came limping round very slowly, declaring that he had not a bone in his skin that was not broken.

"It's all up with me, Jack," he moaned. "I know if I were to shake myself I should fall to pieces."

"At all events, you are better off than this poor creature here," said Jack.

"I don't know that," said old Flick; "he's got the top of his chest knocked in, and my whole trunk is smashed. But I suppose we must try to do what we can for the fellow, although he deserves very little from our hands. If he had only been well I would have risked all to have given him a sound drubbing. Brutes like this should not be permitted to escape. They are enemies to mankind at large."

"We will not speak of that," said Jack, "now that calamity is so heavy upon him."

"Calamity!" growled Flick, who could not quite forget his treatment; "I think it is the cart that is heavy upon him. But come on, Jack; you say it is all right, and it shall be done."

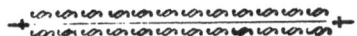

CHAPTER XXXIX.

JACK HEARS A TERRIBLE TALE—THE FATE OF HIS PARENTS—LITTLE BROWNIE—
THE GIPSY CAMP—PRISONERS AGAIN.

THE two young fellows worked away with a will, and, after a great deal of trouble, managed to prop the van up enough to draw the crushed and mangled wretch from beneath it.

"Let us place him on this bank," said Jack; "the poor fellow still breathes. Let us help him."

Jack raised the unfortunate fellow's head upon his knee, whilst Flick, under Jack's direction, poured a little brandy down his throat.

"Give him a little more brandy," said Jack. "There is plenty of it running out of that cask. I wonder what the frogs and the toads think about it?"

"I should think they will get very tipsy," replied Flick. "He's coming round, Jack."

At that moment the unhappy man opened his eyes and gazed around.

"Where am I?" he muttered. "I ain't in the power of the Johnnies, am I?"

"No; you are safe enough—quite safe at present. The waggon turned over and fell upon you."

"Phew! how hot it is! Who are you?" gasped the man, who was evidently dying. "Give me more brandy, or I shall faint. Why is it so dark? Hark! The waves are breaking on the sand. It must be near the turn of tide. Who are you, I say? Why don't you speak?"

"We are two unfortunate lads," said Jack Firebrace, calmly, "who ran away from a school where we were badly treated, and became stowaways on board the 'Sea Hawk,' which, to our horror, we found commanded by one Grindwell, whom you must know. Therefore we kept ourselves hidden, and saw the terrible murders he committed on board. But we trusted in Providence, and, by almost a miracle, we got on shore, hid ourselves in two of those casks, and so escaped."

"Ay, Griffiths Grindwell—Griffiths Grindwell!" muttered the man. "Red Randulph we call him—Randulph, the pirate. So you went to school at the Hawkhouse, I suppose? A nice nest!"

"We certainly did go to school there —if school you can call it," replied Jack. "But think now of your past sins, and pray that they may be forgiven you."

"Humph!" gasped the fellow. "Then you think I'm booked for Davy Jones's locker, eh?"

"I fear so. If I knew where I could go and get you assistance I would gladly do so."

"There's only one house near here, and that house you had better avoid," said the smuggler.

"Indeed! And why should we avoid that house?"

"Because it's one of Mr. Grindwell's, the honest London merchant—ho, ho, ho! He's a cute one, he is. Who—would—think the respectable Grindwell has been a West Indian pirate?"

"A West Indian pirate!" exclaimed Flick, who, the reader will remember, did not know so much of these affairs as Jack did. "You surely do not mean to say that is how he made his money?"

"That's it. Red Randulph we called him because of his love of blood. I remember the first time I was out with him. We had a fine crew of as fierce a set of fiends as ever were seen. Give me more brandy; my eyes grow weak and my breath comes heavily.

"Well, we sailed after a ship which belonged to a friend of this Grindwell, a Captain Falkland. When we got in sight of her Grindwell orders most of the men to keep down beneath the gunwale to leeward, so they could not be seen. Then some of the others put on women's shawls and hats, and one fellow plays a violin, whilst some of the others danced.

"So—so, give me some more drink! my heart grows cold. How cold my feet are!"

"Tell us more," cried Jack, looking eagerly at the man.

"Stay, where was I?" continued the pirate. "Oh, I know. The people on board Captain Falkland's ship took us for some sort of an emigrant ship, and fancied that we were having a jollification."

"The treacherous scoundrels!" muttered Jack, between his teeth.

The man, with deep gasps, which it would be too painful to try to describe, continued—

"Ay, treacherous it was, sure enough. But I pays for all now. Well, the crew of Falkland's ship jumps up in the shrouds when we are ranging up close on her quarter to give us a cheer as we went past.

"Then Randulph, sword in hand, sprang onto the bulwarks and shouted out, in tones of thunder—

"'Fire!'

"Open flew our ports, and we poured in a plunging fire, which swept away two-thirds of the crew.

"The next moment we were yardarm to yardarm. Our grappling irons were flung out, and we passed on to her decks like a swarm of bees.

"'Cut them down! show no quarter! cut them down! Remember, dead men tell no tales!' shouted Randulph; and cut them down we did, right and left, until the decks were so slippery with blood that we could not keep from slipping about.

"At last all were dead but the captain and his young wife—at least, we thought all the people were dead, but I have heard that an old sailor escaped.

"Phew! how cold it is!

"I don't know whether that was true or whether it was false. However, there stood Captain Falkland, his left arm round his young wife, who was clasping her babe to her breast, and his right arm stretched out, a sword in his hand, to keep off Randulph.

"Randulph made quick work of Falkland, who, in making a blow, slipped upon the deck.

"The next instant Randulph had cleft his skull in two.

"Then, with a fiendish laugh, our skipper sprang forward to seize the young wife, but quick as lightning she sprang into the sea.

"The skipper had missed catching her dress in time, but had caught the baby's frock; so the child was saved, though the mother was drowned.

"Lift my head up higher; I feel faint."

Jack lifted the fellow's head up, and poured a little brandy down his throat.

"Do you wish me to tell you more?" asked the man of Jack.

"Go on—go on," said Jack, who somehow felt that he was connected with this strange and terrible story.

"At first the captain swore he would kill the child, but old Firebrace—Jack Firebrace, the mate—he swore that he wouldn't have the kid hurt, seeing that it was only a little child. So the captain let Jack keep the boy, and we made much of the lad, and it was the only thing on board that Red Randulph dare not kill.

"Well, we set the 'Queen of the Ocean' on fire and left her, and when the flames were rushing up we saw a sailor spring into the shrouds—a fellow named Sidecraft, I think—and he called out—

"'I know you, Randulph; you are Grindwell. If I escape from this ship I will follow you about until I bring you to justice!'

"We were about to go back and finish him when the 'Queen of the Ocean' blew up, and as we saw the topmasts of what appeared to be a ship of war just showing above the horizon we made all sail.

"Here an accident happened to old Jack Firebrace.

"We were lying in a bay when he tumbled overboard, and before you could say 'Jack Robinson' the sea was all alive with sharks, and snapping at Jack.

"One went off with a foot, another had a leg, this an arm, that his head, until there was only his trunk left.

"I never saw such a horrible sight; but Randulph, he liked it, and declared that it was all because Jack was so tender-hearted.

"Then he proposed that we should stick the child upon a hook and try to catch the sharks with it.

"But he pretty soon gave that game up, for the men were nearer to mutiny then than ever I saw them.

"So the child was spared, and we sailed to England, and there Mr. Grindwell took it under his charge, promising the men that no harm should come to it, and—"

The man paused, and his gasping drew heavier and heavier.

"D'ye think—d'ye think, sirs, that I may hope for mercy?"

Jack could scarcely answer for sobs.

He knew that the terrible story he had heard was the history of his parents' murder.

"I trust so—I hope so," he murmured. "Surely it must be so, or I should not be here to hold your head, hear this horrible history, and bear, as I hope I do, a message of forgiveness to you."

"You!" cried the man, springing half into a sitting posture—"you!"

"Yes; for I was the child saved by old Firebrace, called Jack Firebrace. Now you know why I say that the hand of Providence has been in this. I, the son of the people whom you have helped to kill, I am here to pray for your forgiveness. Come," said Jack, quietly, "pray for forgiveness with me."

"You little — Jack — Fire—brace!" gasped the man, "and you—don't—curse me?"

"No. Come, we will pray with you."

The two lads knelt down by the dying man, and in bated breath poured forth prayers for his pardon.

A dull rattle in the throat, a convulsive gasp for breath, one shudder, and the pirate, murderer, and smuggler's soul had fled to that "undiscovered bourne from whence no traveller returns."

"May Heaven forgive him!" said Jack.

"Amen! Jack," said old Flick. "After all, this life is very dreadful. What shall we do now?"

"What can we do but one thing?" said Jack, as he composed the dead man's limbs.

"My dear Jack, you know I will do what you like, so speak out at once."

"Well, I have this to do: I shall make my way to the nearest house I can, and ask for the address of a magistrate; go to him, and there relate all that this dead man has told us. We will then cause Mr. Grindwell to be arrested, and perhaps at the foot of the gallows he may be made to confess his numerous crimes."

"A good idea—a capital idea! an idea that does credit to your head and heart."

The two lads started back in amazement, for the voice was a grating wretched one, such as they had never heard before.

"You did not know there was a third party listening to that pretty story, did you—eh?" shrieked the voice.

The lads looked up and beheld a broad-shouldered, hideous-looking little dwarf seated upon a stile by the roadside.

As well as they could make out in the darkness he had a long face, a long nose, a long chin, and wide mouth; long arms, long, claw-like fingers, a short body, and short legs, and was sitting on the stile with crossed legs, after the manner in which tailors sit upon their boards.

Jack and Flick started back when they beheld this hideous piece of deformity, for at first they could not help fancying that it was some evil goblin who had come to bear off the soul of the dead pirate.

"Ha, ha! my pretty lads," cried the monster, as he leaped with surprising agility from the stile to the ground; "I rather thought I should surprise you. Ho, ho, ho! I respect you, my young friends, really I do; so good, so kind, so charitable! When are you going to hang this Mr. Grindwell? I should like to be there to hear him relate all his sins. Why, it would take him a year to do it. Ho, ho, ho, ho!"

As he laughed the little wretch placed his hands upon his sides and stamped about with glee.

"Come away, Jack, come away," whispered Flick; "this creature is evidently a lunatic."

"Lunatic!" cried the little man, who had heard the words. "Yes, I'm a lunatic—a real live lunatic."

"If you are not I must say you are the nearest approach to one I ever saw," said Jack.

"You should not judge people by their looks, my young friends. Oh, no; that is not right. Who would think that the kind and generous Griffiths Grindwell could be the same as Richard Randulph, the cruel, the tyrant, the bloodthirsty, the scourge of the seas? None; no one."

"Heaven knows I would not judge you by your appearance," said Jack, hotly, "or I should put you very low down in the scale of creation."

"And why, my young friend? Am I not beautiful? I think I am, you think you are—both matters of taste, both matters of taste. You think you are clever; you may be—I know I am. You have had no experience. I have risen from a workhouse boy to be a justice of the peace. Oh, you stare! It is true, though, quite true. What do you think of that? You wanted a magistrate just now; well, here I am. Come along. Ho, ho, ho, ho!"

"You a justice of the peace!" cried Jack. "I don't believe you."

"I say, that is rude, very rude; you should not speak like that," laughed the little man. "I think you had better come with me—much better come with me. You see, I heard half that this poor smashed fellow said, so that I am sure you had better come with me."

"I tell you that we will not go with you," cried Jack, passionately. "Come, Flick, let us make a start."

Jack made a dash to cross the hedge, but was immediately collared by a man who had remained hidden in the field; whilst the dwarf threw his arms round Flick in such a way that he could not move.

Vainly the boys struggled.

"Ho, ho, ho!" laughed the dwarf; "this is real good fun. Come along; I want you to stop at my house."

"I won't go! Help, help, help!" shouted Jack, as loudly as he could.

"Silence that young hound," growled the dwarf.

And in an instant the man had felled Jack to the earth.

"Now, younker, you will submit quietly, or I shall serve you the same way," said the dwarf to old Flick.

"You can do with me what you will," said Flick, who seemed quite broken down.

"That is spoken like a sensible lad," laughed the dwarf; "so you will give me your word you will not run away?"

"I certainly will; for truth to tell I am not able to walk fast, let alone run, I am so knocked about."

"Ah! that comes of playing at hide-and-seek. Well, I'll just put this little gag in your mouth, and then we shall all be snug and comfortable."

Before old Flick could make the slightest resistance the gag was placed in his mouth and his hands and feet bound.

He was then thrust into a sack, the mouth of which was tied beneath his feet, carried into a field, and thrown across a donkey, so that he looked like a sack of flour.

Jack Firebrace was treated in the same way, and then the dwarf, followed by the donkeys and two men, led the way across the fields.

Away they went at a rapid rate.

At last the donkeys stopped, and the dwarf conversed for a few moments with the men in low whispers.

Whether it was the cessation of the jolting caused by the ride, or the natural effect of time, it is impossible to say, but certain it is that at this very moment Jack came to his senses, and not a little surprised was he to find himself in a sack hanging across a donkey.

He had no idea how he could have managed to get in such a position, but he guessed pretty correctly that it was the work of his old enemies.

He therefore remained quite quiet, with the exception that he managed to get a knife out of his pocket, with which he cut a slight slit in the sack as a peep-hole, and through which he obtained more air.

He then turned all his attention to listening to a conversation which some people were holding near him.

"I tell you it's a dangerous game," said a gruff voice.

"And why?" replied another, which Jack recognised as the dwarf's; "there can be no danger."

"But I tell you there is danger. All along the south coast the people are on the look-out. You know how we tried to give your skipper notice, but it was no good."

"But these boys are not brandy. Who cares for boys?"

"Did I not tell you that the Double has been here?"

"No; you never said a word to me about it," cried the dwarf, grinding his teeth.

"Well, I hadn't too much time. He is here, though. Rackstraw, the young detective, has been after him, but the Double so well managed it that Rackstraw is now in prison for something or other."

"What!" grinned the dwarf, "Rack straw in prison? Why did you not te me that before—eh?"

"How could I? I set out to war you not to go down to meet the 'Se Hawk'; you were on your way, and w only stopped you in time by riding. was a wonder we overtook you at al Well, he is here, and he says that th officers of justice have been to Hawl house, and that notice is given to all th coastguard to keep on the watch."

"So Luke, or the Double, as you ca him, is down in the wood, eh? Sohe then. Who will think a lot of travellin gipsies have anything to do with smug glers? But there; we will not speak this now. Come, let's into the fores Soho, lads, and off we go."

With that the artful little dwarf gav the donkeys two awful cracks, and ser them galloping off down a narrow pat which led to a thick wood at the botto of a valley.

On dashed the donkeys, evidentl knowing that rest awaited them, and i a few moments they were in the middl of the gipsy encampment.

"Hillo!" cried a tall, dark gips starting up from the ground, "what h the Black Dog brought home t night?"

And he clapped his hands upon on of the sacks in a manner which mad poor old Flick yell and vainly try to ru the roundest portion of his body.

But even that luxury was denied hin for his hands were bound, and even th kick he gave was of the faintest, for h feet were in the same state.

"By Jove!" laughed the man, "the are alive, I wonder what they be?"

"Pigs, of course," growled one of th other gipsies. "Didn't you hear ou squeak?"

"He's a precious lean one, then, an that is all I know about it," replied th other.

"Hi, you fellows!" cried the dwar coming up at the moment, "don't touc those sacks; they are my property."

The men, who evidently knew th dwarf very well, and had a wholesom dread of him, drew back.

"Pitch them onto the ground. Ther that will do, that will do."

The two sacks were at once put upo the ground, and Jack took the oppo tunity of enlarging the slit in his sack so that he might view the scene better, and also grasped his knife firmly, determined to strike, if need be, for his own life and that of old Flick's.

By the side of the fire the dwarf had taken his seat, with two or three of the gipsies, with whom he was in deep conversation; so Jack managed, in the shadow caused by the fire, to wriggle close to them, and thus heard their discourse.

"I tell you they must go back," said the dwarf; "it would be madness to take them to London."

"Why not knock them on the head at once, and have done with them?" urged one of the gipsies.

"My good friend," laughed the dwarf, "why are you in such a hurry for a halter? It will come soon enough."

"Thank you for nothing," Mr. Brown."

"Hush, you fool!" cried the dwarf, raising his hand and shaking it in the man's face. "What do you mean by mentioning names? If you do it again I will half kill you."

"You!—you half kill me?" cried the man, springing up and throwing out his brawny chest.

"Yes, yes, yes," shrieked the dwarf, starting up and dancing about. "I'll half kill you, that's what I'll do."

This scene so amused the gipsies that they gathered round the quarrellers in a ring.

"Look here," said one of the men, quietly; "do you mean a fight or don't you?"

"Fight!" cried the gipsy, who was a regular giant. "Who could fight a thing like that? Why, I would take it up between my finger and thumb and crack it like a flea. That's what I would do."

The little dwarf suddenly stopped his capers, thrust his hands into his breeches pockets, and, putting his tongue into his cheek, made a most hideous grimace as he advanced close up to the fellow.

"Look here," he said, quietly; "just you look here. Do you think that I am afraid of you?"

The giant looked startled at this horrible little goblin, and answered, hesitatingly—

"I don't know if you are frightened. I know that you ought to be, and, what's more, I know I could thrash you."

"Well, then, I am not frightened," grinned the dwarf; "and what is more, I can beat you. Look here, look here, look here!"

As he spoke he placed five sovereigns on the ground between the man and himself.

There were the five shining pieces of gold all of a row—tempting sight to the gipsies.

"Now," cried the little man, "now I will tell you what I will do. I will fight you for those five yellow boys."

"Oh, that's fine, very fine; but I haven't got any money to stake against you."

"I don't want any money. There are the sovereigns. If you win, you put them into your pocket; if I win, I put them into mine. Only we fight without weapons; we fight alone, and in any way we can with our hands, feet, and teeth. Now, is it a bargain, or are you afraid?" shrieked the dwarf.

"It's a bargain," cried the man, as he rolled back his sleeves. "Are you ready?"

"Yes," chuckled the dwarf, as he hung down his long arms by his sides and began to dance about.

The man dashed at the dwarf, aiming a blow at his head, which would certainly have smashed it had it reached it; but the dwarf, or "Little Brownie," as he was called, jumped swiftly on one side, dashed in, caught the giant by the legs, lifted him off the ground, and pitched him head foremost into the fire.

As the man fell he caught hold of the edge of the caldron and overturned it.

The men shouted with laughter, whilst the dwarf, Little Brownie, coolly picked up his golden coins and thrust them into his pocket.

With a fearful oath the gipsy sprang from the fire, and might have done the dwarf some mischief; but the other gipsies held him back, reminding him of his promise to fight fair, and so forth.

Taking advantage of this disturbance Jack cut the sack in which he was confined right open, and crept out.

Now was his time to escape.

He had only to plunge into the woods and make a rush for it, and then he would be safe; but he could not leave old Flick.

He felt that would be cowardly.

Therefore he crept back to the other sack, and silently began ripping it open.

"Flick, old fellow, Flick!" he cried, in a whisper, "I am free. I will cut open your sack. Do you hear?"

Flick tried to speak, but the effect of the gag was such that he really did grunt like a pig.

Jack started back.

That moment of hesitation deprived them of all chance to escape.

As Jack started back he placed his foot upon a sleeping gipsy boy, whom he had not perceived.

The boy started up and grasped Jack's leg, upsetting him, and they both rolled upon the ground.

In an instant the whole of the gipsies were round them, and Jack found himself a prisoner again.

"Ho, ho, ho!" roared the dwarf, "you would run away, would you, Mr. Falkland?—I mean, Firebrace. But you don't get out of my clutches so soon. You are a runaway schoolboy—d'ye hear? You have run away from your friends. So you shall go back to them, and they will cane you, birch you, thrash you until you are cut into little strips. You won't be ruled, won't you? Ho, ho, ho, ho! you shall be ruled all over your body in pretty lines of black and blue. Ho, ho, ho!"

And the little fiend danced round our hero, who, seeing that all resistance was vain, permitted himself to be bound hand and foot.

CHAPTER XL.

ROB RACKSTRAW IN PRISON—HE RELATES HIS STORY TO THE GAOLER AND PROCURES AN INTERVIEW WITH THE MAGISTRATES—A SEARCH FOR TRUTH—IN THE BOTTOM OF A WELL.

WE left Rob Rackstraw safely lodged in Newport Prison.

Sick and faint did he feel when he came to himself, but it was some time before he could call to his memory the adventures he had gone through, and how he came to be placed in prison.

"Well, this here is a pretty go," said Rackstraw, as he looked round at his dismal cell. "Only think of their locking up a constable. Upon my word, if it were anybody else's case but my own I should be tempted to laugh."

As it was, in spite of his miserable condition, Rackstraw could not help smiling.

Then he thrust his hands into his trousers' pockets and began whistling softly.

"This is very awkward, though," he said; "they've taken my coat away, and my warrant was in it."

Once more he whistled softly and plunged his hands into his trousers' pockets.

"Hillo!" he cried. "Blest if they haven't cleared me out of all my cash.

This is a pretty go. What's to be done now?"

As he spoke the room-door opened, and a thick-set man entered the cell.

"Ah! you may well ask that," said the man, who had evidently heard Rob Rackstraw's last words. "You may well say that, for it strikes me you have been and gone and done for yourself."

"You are a nice chap to bring consolation to a fellow, you are," replied Rob Rackstraw, quietly. "But look here. What place is this that I am in?"

"This is Newport Prison, and I'm the chief gaoler."

"Are you, though? But look here, gaffer. Since you are so obliging, perhaps you would not object to tell me why I am your guest. It ain't for nothing, I'll be bound."

And Rob Rackstraw, having put the question in a very earnest manner, waited with considerable anxiety for the man's reply.

For his detention would probably

enable the villains he was hunting down to escape.

"Can't you answer a question?" asked Rackstraw, after waiting some seconds.

The man looked hard at Rob, and commenced slowly shaking his head from side to side.

"Well, I never did see such a regular old Chinese mandarin in all my born days," said Rob.

"It's very good and very well acted," said the man; "but it won't do—it won't do."

"What won't do?" demanded Rackstraw, beginning to lose all patience.

"Why the innocent dodge; pretending you don't know what you are here for."

"Just you look here, old fellow. You tell me what I am in for, and I'll be much obliged."

"Why, you know what you are in for," replied the gaoler. "Didn't you go and attack a gentleman, taking from him twenty-five pounds in gold and silver, and a pocket-book containing a bill on Mr. Griffiths Grindwell, of London, for one hundred pounds? Ho, ho, ho! You never heard of it before, eh? Quite a fresh bit of news!"

"Quite," replied Rob—who, as the reader will remember, did not know anything of the matter, he having been insensible all the time—"perhaps you will be kind enough to tell me when the trial came off; what proof there was against me; who was the prosecutor?— if there were any witnesses, and if I have been found guilty, what was the sentence?"

"Well, you do do it cool, I declare. You are only here until the magistrate wishes to see you again, you know. He saw you yesterday, but you were quite cracked, so he won't see you now until to-morrow. As for proofs, the articles were found in your coat-pocket; so the case is clear enough, and I don't think you will miss the gallows."

"The cash and the pocket-book found on my person?" exclaimed Rob. "Impossible; it can't be true."

"Can't it? It strikes me you will find it quite strong enough to hang you. What do you think of that?"

"Stay a moment," said Rob. "Let me think a little. There is some foul plot in this, and I'll find it out."

He sat for a few minutes lost in deep thought, and then said—

"Look here, gaoler; I am Robert Nippit, of Bow Street, London, a police officer. You know the name?"

"Ray-ther; but that tale may do well for greenhorns; but it won't wash here."

"I tell you it is true; my warrant is in the breast pocket of my coat!" cried Rob, impatiently.

"Oh, very well, if it is true, it is true," said the gaoler, preparing to depart; "I won't argue the matter with you."

"Stay," cried Rob; "I recollect all now. Believe me or not as you will, but listen to my story, and I will explain how that coat came into my possession, and will tell you of a terrible crime which has been committed."

"Well, as I have a few moments to spare I don't mind listening to your story," said the gaoler; "only make haste."

In as few words as he could Rackstraw related the adventures which he had passed through when journeying from Hawkhouse to London, and he told the story so well that even the gaoler was impressed with it, and came to the conclusion that the tale might be true.

"If your tale is correct," said the gaoler, scratching his head, "I must say that you are in a nasty position—that's all."

"Confound it, man!" cried Rackstraw, "do you not see that I am the victim of a foul plot? You must see it!"

"I don't see it altogether; although the chances are six on one side and half a dozen on the other," replied the gaoler.

"At all events, go to a magistrate and tell him what I have told you. Let the body of the man be searched for in the well; do not let these rascals have a chance of escape. If they are innocent and you can prove my story false, then you will have good reasons to believe the accusations against me; if it be true, then you will arrest a gang of villains and will doubtlessly be well rewarded. Do not lose a moment, but go at once to the magistrate."

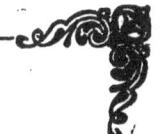

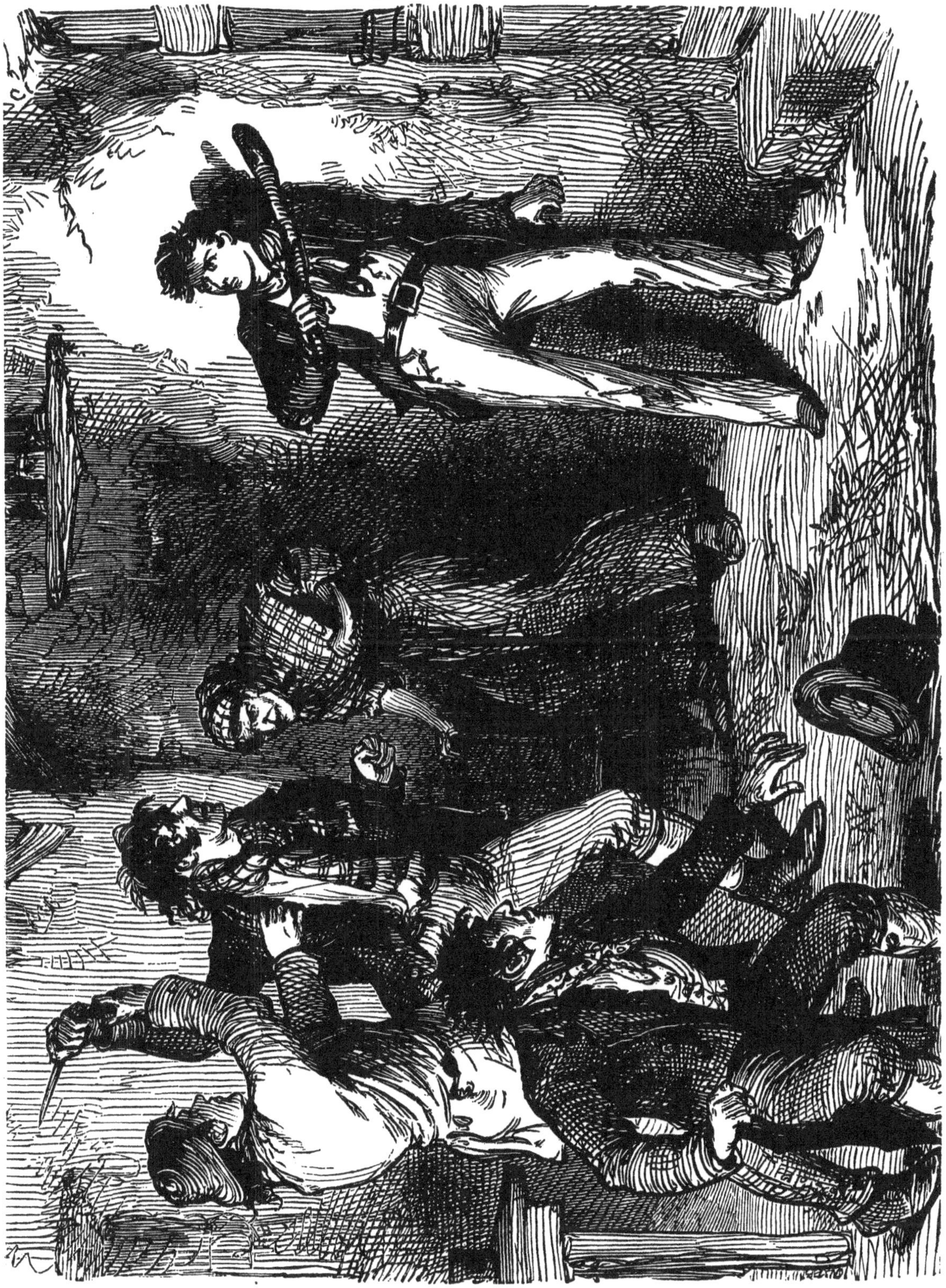

"'STAND BACK!' CRIED JACK. 'I WILL KILL THE FIRST WHO TOUCHES ME!'"

No. 13.

PRICE ONE HALFPENNY.

[PUBLISHED EVERY MONDAY.]

"Well, there can be no harm in that," said the man. "I'll go and tell Mr. Podzus what you say. Mind, I don't pledge myself to anything, you know. If Mr. Podzus says we will go and search, well and good; if he don't say so, but expresses his opinion that it is only a bit of your humbug, why then you will not be any the better off, but rather the worser; for magistrates don't like being played with."

"If my story does not prove true—well, you may hang me as soon as you like. Only go now."

Half grumbling that he was making a fool of himself, the gaoler marched slowly away, leaving Rob to his thoughts.

They were not the pleasantest of thoughts by any means, as Rob himself confessed.

Here had he—one of the cutest officers in the force—been drugged, nearly murdered, arrested, and thrown into prison on a false charge.

He felt that his reputation for cleverness was gone.

The bruises and hurts he had received made him ache all over, but he could not keep still.

He paced up and down the room, waiting anxiously for the return of the gaoler.

To him it seemed that the man had been gone hours instead of half-an-hour, and when he heard the key turn in the lock, he sprang forward eagerly, and was not a little surprised when he discovered that he had knocked off the hat and gold spectacles of a little, stout old gentleman whom he had caught in his arms, and who proved to be no other than Mr. Podzus, the magistrate.

"'Pon my word!" exclaimed the worthy Mr. Podzus, directly he had managed to release himself from Rob's clutches, "upon my word, I never was treated so in all my life before. I don't understand it—indeed, I do not! Never saw such behaviour in my life. Here, Bolt," he called, getting behind the gaoler, "I think this a most desperate fellow. He would like to send for every magistrate and judge in the land that he might throttle them."

"I really beg your pardon, sir," said Rob Rackstraw; "but I did not know who it was, and I am so impatient."

"So it would seem, so it would seem," said Mr. Podzus, as he wiped his spectacles and readjusted them on his nose. "Just go to the farther end of the cell, or I shall leave you. Remember, I am not obliged to give you this hearing; but the story you told Bolt is so very strange that I have come to see you. Bolt, stand between me and the prisoner—good. If he should attempt to move knock him down. Now make your statement."

Rackstraw and the gaoler placed themselves in the positions indicated, and then the former, who had been thinking over the matter, related his story in a much clearer manner than he had done before.

He remembered now how he had got the wrong coat—in fact, he remembered almost everything but his being locked up.

"This is strange, very strange," said the magistrate; "I must say that it is very remarkable—very!"

"That's just what I said, your honour," said Bolt. "If it hadn't have been I would not have troubled you."

"You did quite right, Bolt, quite right. Wait here a little, and I will go and see what can be done."

And the little man bustled away to consult with a brother magistrate, with whom he returned in a very little time, accompanied by a number of constables.

Under Mr. Podzus's directions Rob's face was cleansed and his clothes made as tidy as could be, considering the circumstances; then Rackstraw was carefully handcuffed and a thick cloak wrapped round him.

"Now I will tell you what we have decided to do," said Mr. Podzus, taking snuff with such rapidity that Rob was perfectly astonished; "we have made up our minds to take you to the inn and search the place, especially the well.

"If my story does not prove true," said Rob Rackstraw, "you can hang me as soon as you like."

"Oh, no, we can't," said Mr. Podzus, chuckling, "we cannot hang you half as soon as we should like, but we will do it as soon as we can. The legal forms will have to be gone through, you know; but, ha, ha, ha! they shall not take up more time than we can help, and that we promise you."

At this wonderful bit of wit all the constables laughed aloud, as was their duty when the chief magistrate made a joke.

Rob was taken out of the prison and forced into a close coach; two constables were placed on the front seat, and one at each side of him, whilst two more were mounted on the box of another, in which the two magistrates followed.

They arrived at the wayside inn, and Rob noticed that, gloomy as it had looked in the nighttime, it appeared even more so in the daylight.

They drew up at the inn door, and the red-headed youth who had been so surly to Rob came sauntering out, his hair so full of bits of straw that he had evidently been asleep in the stables.

"Hallo!" he growled, "what's up now? This ain't a place to keep a picnic. We ain't got nothing to eat."

"That's just what I told you when I came here before," said Rob; "but that story won't do now, you know."

"What did I ever tell you? Why, I never saw you until now," replied the red-headed youth, coolly.

"We will see about that," said Rob, quietly. "Now, gentlemen, if you will kindly place some men to watch the back and the front of the house, and also the stable-yard, I will show you the room where they wanted to murder me."

This was soon done, but although Rob knew the place well, no sign could be seen of any trace of the violence he had spoken about.

"I don't see a thing to warrant our believing your statement," said the magistrate.

"You are right, sir," said Rob Rackstraw; "they have had a good start of me, and that's the truth. Now, let us go and have a look at the well."

"I don't know what you are up to," said the red-headed youth; "but there ain't no water there."

"Maybe there is not. It's not water we are looking after," replied Rob, and, pushing the youth on one side, he led the way out into the stable-yard straight to the well.

The magistrates peeped down the well, but as it was, like most other wells, quite dark, they could not see if the body of a man were in it or not.

"Somebody—somebody had better go down it, I think," said Mr. Podzus, looking at the other magistrate.

"Certainly—certainly; that is very important, indeed," replied the second gentleman, who was a red-faced, pompous man, with a great idea of his own value and a very little idea of anything else.

"Just so; and the person who goes down ought to be a man of standing—in authority, you know."

"Most decidedly, most decidedly," said number two. "Whom do you propose, brother Podzus?"

"Why, I was just thinking that, if you were to go down, it would save a great deal of trouble. If there should be anything very frightful at the bottom of the well, we ought to have a responsible witness, one whose word we cannot doubt. Now, your word will be taken directly."

"Maybe it would," said the second magistrate, very sharply, "and maybe it would not. But if so special a witness is wanted, I think it would be your place to go. For my own part, I said from the first I did not believe a word of this fellow's story—not a single word. You chose to credit his statement, and therefore I shall leave this matter in your hands."

"Very well, sir—very well, sir," said Mr. Podzus, "I believe this man's statement. But that is neither here nor there. I received my commission in the peace to do justice, and it shall never be said that I punished an innocent man because I would not take a little trouble."

"Bravely said," sneered the other magistrate. "I suppose by that you intend going down the well yourself?"

"Yes, sir; I do intend going down the well. No man shall call me a coward! There, sir—there!"

With that the little man bounded away and commenced scrambling over the wall of the well, down which he most certainly would have disappeared, headforemost, had he not been held back by Rob Rackstraw.

"Heart alive, sir! don't go that way to work," said Rob. "You would be dashed to pieces at once."

"Never mind!" cried Mr. Podzus, struggling, as if anxious to get away, but taking good care to keep from the well; "never mind. I will do my duty in spite of all dangers. I am a justice of the peace."

"You will be a justice *in pieces* if you do that, sir," said Rob. "We will get a rope and lower you down."

At last Mr. Podzus consented to wait until a rope was procured, which was not done for some time, for not only had the proper well-rope disappeared, but every other piece as well.

In fact, there was not as much as a clothes-line in the whole place.

At last a rope was brought, and Rob directed the men to make a loop in one end of it and to pass the other end twice round the drum of the winch, so as to prevent any sudden slip whilst the person was descending.

"Now, sir," said Rob to Mr. Podzus, "put your feet in that loop, and with one hand hold on to the rope, whilst in the other hand you can hold this torch, so as to examine the well, sir. Please inspect it closely, as I know that you will find a man in there. Shake the rope when you wish us to pull up."

Mr. Podzus took up his position as requested, and, with a hand that shook from excitement, grasped the torch.

The next minute he was slowly descending into the well.

Just as his head was disappearing his brother magistrate, with mock anxiousness, exclaimed—

"Take care, Mr. Podzus—do take care of yourself, for my sake. Think of the poisonous air which is always in a well."

Mr. Podzus turned pale, and called out something that sounded very much like—

"Stop!"

But the men did not understand it so, for they paid the rope out quicker and quicker, so that the torch Mr. Podzus carried was seen sinking like a Will-o'-the-wisp far down in the well.

"That was a shake of the rope," said Rob, anxiously. "He has seen something, and wishes to return. Pull up!"

"No, no, no," grinned the magistrate number two. "I rule here, in the absence of my friend and colleague. If anything should befall him I should never forgive myself. Give him a turn or two more of the rope, my men."

The men, who seemed really to enjoy the fun, let out some more, but stopped as Rob, glancing down the well, exclaimed—

"Stop, stop—in Heaven's name, stop! The light has gone out! There must be foul air down that well!"

At the same moment the rope jerked violently.

"Haul up—haul up!" cried the second magistrate, who was now most seriously alarmed.

The men bent to their work with a will; but the weight seemed greatly increased at first, as if something held the magistrate back.

"He has found the dead body—he has found the murdered man!" shrieked Rob Rackstraw, dancing with delight. "He is a plucky little fellow. Haul away, my lads. Remember, he has a heavy weight to bear. Here he comes—here he—"

Rackstraw paused in horror, while a shout of laughter rose from the men, who were so tickled that they would certainly have let go of the windlass and so precipitated Mr. Podzus into the well again, had not Rob, handcuffed as he was, seized the handle.

Lo! from out the well came two little boots, soles uppermost, the ankles caught firmly round by the loop in the rope; then a pair of fat little legs, followed by Mr. Podzus's podgy little body, his coat-tails falling over his head, exposing the back of his white waistcoat.

Mr. Podzus had slipped, and would have fallen had not his feet caught in the loop.

Quickly they had him from the well, and once more he was seated on the wheelbarrow.

But, oh! what a figure he presented to the gaze of his fellow magistrate and the constables!

His hat, his wig, his gold spectacles had gone, and he looked as if he had been taking a cast of his bust in thick black mud.

They brought pails of water, and, after a great deal of rubbing and scrubbing, they managed to get him so far cleaner that he was able to see and to speak.

"You are better now, sir, I hope," said Rob.

"Oh, yes, I am better now; much

better, thank you. But, oh! that horrid, horrid well," replied Mr. Podzus.

"I knew you would find it," cried Rob Rackstraw, eagerly; "sure of it. It must have been a horrible sight."

"I don't know much about a horrible sight, but I do know that it is a horrible place. I thought I was killed."

"But how did it all happen?" demanded the other magistrate. "How did you come in that position?"

"Oh, I scarcely know. But I have had a terrible turn. I never had such a turn before."

"I should think not," replied the other, with a sour grin; "it turned you upside-down."

"The fact is," said Mr. Podzus, "I had got nearly to the bottom of the well when my feet slipped through the noose. Of course I was very anxious to get it all right under my feet again, but in trying to manage this I dropped the torch. Then I let go of the rope and fell head-downwards through about a foot of water and a foot of thick mud, where I stuck until you pulled me out. I thought you would have pulled my feet off before I came out of the mud."

"But did you not see anything?" demanded Rob, impatiently.

"See anything?" cried Mr. Podzus, snappishly. "How the deuce could I see in the dark, my body some sixty feet below the surface of the earth, and my head a foot deep in mud? Of course I did not see anything."

"Look here, sir," said Rob Rackstraw, quickly, "you are not up to this sort of thing. Just tell these fellows to take these handcuffs off, and I'll go down the well."

"If you take my advice, you will leave well alone," laughed magistrate number two.

This was a lucky speech for Rob.

Mr. Podzus hated his colleague, and, therefore, he determined at once to favour the prisoner.

"I believe, after all, that you are an honest man, and you must be a brave one to wish to undergo the perils and dangers which I have just undergone. I believe your search will be fruitless, but in the interest of justice I cannot refuse you. Take off his handcuffs, and let him descend into the well."

In less time than it takes to tell, Rob's hands were free, and having procured a fresh torch, he placed his feet safely in the loop, and was lowered down into the well.

The people waited anxiously for the signal to draw him back to the surface.

They could see the light gleaming far down in the bottom of the well, and knew that he was all right.

Suddenly there were three well marked jerks.

The men flew to the windlass, and in a few minutes Rob was standing in safety in the stable-yard.

"There are your hat and gold spectacles, sir," he cried, handing those articles to Mr. Podzus.

"Thank'ee, my lad. Did you happen to see anything like a wig in that wretched hole?" asked Mr. Podzus.

"No, sir, I did not. The truth is, I did not know you wore one," replied Rob.

"Never mind, my good fellow," said Mr. Podzus, smiling at the compliment. "I will remember your kindness."

"Never mind the wig," growled the other magistrate, who was vexed that the property had been recovered; "never mind that. But can you tell me anything about the body of the murdered man? Did you find that?"

"No, sir, I did not, and I have but little doubt the body was removed. Nay, I have some proof that that must have been the case. Here," he cried, holding up a soaking wet pocket-book, "here is my pocket-book. I have not opened it, as you see; but I can tell you what it contains. Amongst other papers, which I shall ask you to keep private, you will find my warrant, which will prove me to be a policeman. I place it, sir, in your hands," he continued, turning to Mr. Podzus, and giving him the pocket-book. "In some measure these rascals have got the better of us; but the body can and will be found. They feared this place would be searched, and had the body removed. That I am innocent of crime I can prove by witnesses from London and Hawkhouse; only I must have time, and—and—"

He paused, waved his hands before his face, as if to clear away a mist, reeled back, and fell on the ground in a fit.

"The poor fellow has overworked

himself. Over - excitement after his wounds. He is in a fit," said Mr. Podzus.

"You are lucky in fits, Mr. Podzus," said the other magistrate, sarcastically. "Ha, ha, ha! the wig did not fit! How deep did you say the well was, and the water, and the mud? Ho, ho, ho, ho!"

This last taunt was too much for Mr. Podzus to stand from his hated rival.

Casting aside his hat and his magisterial dignity at the same time, he charged his colleague full butt in his white waistcoat (much in the manner that a bull is said to rush at a gate), sending that gentleman splashing into a bed of wet manure.

Having accomplished this, Mr. Podzus calmly resumed his hat, and declaring his intention of having nothing more to do with "that man," got into the coach with poor Rob Rackstraw, and drove back to Newport, leaving the other magistrate to follow as best he could in the other coach.

CHAPTER XLI.

WHAT HAPPENED TO JACK FIREBRACE AMONGST THE GIPSIES.

JACK and his companion were marched off before daybreak to a deep wood, where they were hidden until nightfall, when the gipsies renewed their march, taking care that the boys should not know which way they were going, whilst the dwarf called the Brownie had orders to keep his eyes always on the prisoners so that they should not escape.

On the third night of their march some of the scouts came hurrying up to the main body, with which Jack and Old Flick marched, and conversed hurriedly and in low tones with the leaders.

Suddenly Jack was ordered to march forward to the front.

There he was gagged and bound, once more thrust into a sack, and thrown over a donkey.

Poor Jack suffered torture in that horrible ride—not only bodily but mental agony.

He did not know where he was going, whether his faithful companion was with him or not.

He prayed that they might not be separated as long as his senses lasted, but the horrible position he was in drove the blood to his head, and, after a short space of delirium, he was relieved from pain by insensibility.

How long and how far he travelled he did not know; but when he came to himself he was stripped stark naked, and was stretched on the grass, whilst two men were rubbing his body down with wet sponges, and little Brownie stood by, laughing with delight.

"Where am I?" gasped Jack, glancing round at the woodland scenery.

"Hold your tongue, or I will cut it out!" growled the Brownie. "You like freedom; you shall have it. Nobody is so free as the gipsy, and a gipsy you shall be. Ho, ho! it will be fine sport to see you a true gipsy."

"Hold your tongue, you imp!" one of the men growled. "If you are not quiet, I'll split your tongue like a starling's. Do you think we want to hear your fiendish clatter?"

The men suddenly jerked Jack up into a sitting posture, so that he was able to look round him.

But Jack could not perceive any sign of old Flick or of the other gipsies.

It was evident that for some reason the tribe of gipsies had separated—old Flick being carried off by some of the band, whilst Jack Firebrace was the prisoner of these two fellows and the dwarf.

"It is no good fretting," thought Jack. "I must make the best I can of the matter. I only trust Flick will escape."

"Hist!" said one of the men, pausing suddenly in his work; "that was Zarah's cry. Come, dress in these clothes."

And he threw Jack a bundle of rags, which, bad as they were, our hero gladly put on.

The men listened for some time in silence, and then they heard a soft whistle.

"That is her," cried Brownie; "that is my Zarah—my heart's delight—my princess of darkness. Here she comes."

The second title she certainly well deserved.

She was old and withered, being bent with age.

Her nose and chin nearly touched, and she was swarthy as a Hindoo.

She was dressed in a red-hooded cloak (the hood being drawn over her head), a coarse, blue cotton petticoat that scarcely reached the ground.

As she tottered along she leaned upon an oaken staff, on the crook of which she kept her bony hands crossed, so that they looked like the claws of a bird of prey.

"Ha, ha! my little fiend," cried this horrible old woman, as she noticed the dwarf's capers; "still merry?"

"Ay, grandam; why should I not be merry when mischief is abroad? Ho, ho, ho!"

"Curse you both!" growled one of the men. "Do you think that we have nothing else to do but listen to your mag?"

"Steady, steady, good Carli," laughed the woman; "it is ill with us when we are unable to laugh," said Zarah.

The man muttered a fearful oath, and then demanded fiercely whether she had the dye.

"Yes, good Carli; I have it here," laughed the old crone. "Ay, and it is a good dye, such as many a fair lady has given me a golden piece for after I had told them their fortunes. Ah! those were good old times, rare old times—rare old times," mumbled the old woman.

"Leave off that jargon, and just put on the dye whilst I hold down the lad," cried the man called Carli.

Before Jack could offer the least resistance the two men had caught and held him firmly between them, whilst the old woman, mumbling and mouthing all the time, produced a bottle from beneath her cloak.

From this bottle she poured a liquid into the palm of her hand, and then, with more energy than Jack considered either necessary or pleasant, commenced rubbing the stuff all over our hero's hair.

"Keep still, you young wretch, or I will kill you!" growled the man, as Jack struggled.

The dame, to enforce the order, twined the skeleton fingers of her left hand in Jack's long brown hair, and with the other rubbed with renewed spirit, causing Jack to twist about in such a manner that, old and ragged as his garments were, he contrived to add fresh rents to them.

"There," said the old woman, giving Jack a smack on each ear to relieve her feelings, and to wipe her fingers at the same time; "now you are a complete gipsy."

In a moment Jack knew what they had done with him.

They had dyed his skin a rich brown by the aid of the juice of walnut-shells, carefully prepared, and his hair jet black by some dye known to the brutal old woman.

"He'll do now, mother," laughed the man Carli, as he viewed his work with an air of satisfaction.

"Let's go," said the other man, with a grunt; "now we can go in safety to the hut. If anyone sees the lad they will take him for a gipsy; not even his own mother would know him now."

Jack controlled his passion as well as he could; but in his heart he swore to avenge that dear, dear mother.

"Come along, my beauty," said the men; and placing themselves one on each side of our hero, they seized his arms, dragging him along at a tremendous rate.

"Look here, younker," said Carli, shaking Jack roughly to enforce attention; "if you so much as move any way but the way we want, or to breathe a word, I will kill you. So you had better be still."

Jack saw that there was not the slightest good in resisting, and therefore yielded quietly.

They were now on a barren moorland, and soon reached a kind of hut, built half in the earth, with just a turf roof and a low wall cropping up, as it were, out of the ground.

They descended several steps cut in the ground, pushed open the door, and entered.

This hut was divided into two compartments; the farthest from the outer door having no opening, except the door which led to it, and the one in which they now stood, having a hole cut in the roof as a chimney.

When they were all in the hut, Carli closed the door, and bolted and barred it.

"Will he be here to-night?" asked the old crone, "or shall we only have the pleasure of our young friend's company?"

"How should I know?" cried the fellow, savagely. "When Randulph or his Double come, they come; when they go, they go. It is not our place to ask questions. Strike a light, and get us something to eat."

The old woman made no reply, but with a flint and steel soon managed to get a light.

She then threw on some more turf from a heap in the corner, and, kneeling down, blew the fire up.

Some cold meat was placed on the ground, together with a stone jar of spirits, and the feast began.

The man cut off a few slices of meat, and flung them to Jack as he would have done to a dog; but our hero bore the indignity quietly, thinking it better to eat the food, which he sorely needed.

As Carli drank, his temper grew more violent, and all of it was vented on Jack.

"To think that I should have to leave my fellows, when they were off to the Midland fairs. Get up, you little beast, and take my boots off. I'll make you work for a living, that I will. Get up; do you hear?"

"I hear," replied Jack, quietly, as he leaned his back against the wall, but did not move.

"Then if you hear, why do you not come at once?" shouted the bully.

"Because I will pull no man's boots off!" replied Jack, quietly, although his limbs trembled with passion.

Carli sprang to his feet, and seizing a stick, struck Jack a blow across the arms.

With a shrill cry of rage Firebrace sprang upon the fellow, and, wresting the stick from his hands, cut him across the face with it.

So violent was the blow, that the fellow staggered back with a howl of pain, and a deep purple and livid mark sprang up in an instant.

"Stand back!" cried Jack, putting his back against the wall and flourishing the stick in such a manner as to make the rest of the people who were about to rush upon him beat a hasty retreat. "Stand back, I say; my blood is up now, and I will kill the first one who touches me!"

He was only a lad, before two men, a woman, and the dwarf—who might have been any age, from sixteen to sixty—and yet they shrank back.

"By all that is evil," cried Carli, "I will have your blood! Stand back, Zarah, and let me get a fling at him."

The old woman hobbled away with the greatest pleasure, and Carli hurled his knife.

But just at that moment the other gipsy stepped forward and knocked Carli's arm up.

The weapon sped on its rapid flight, but the gipsy's aim was spoilt, and it buried itself in the wall some feet above Jack's head, where it remained trembling, and showing with what force it had been sent.

"Hold, Carli!" cried the other gipsy; "we have no need to kill the boy for nothing. If we do it now Red Randulph will thank us. Oh, he will thank us very much! But if we ask for a reward he will laugh in our faces. What then shall we do? We cannot complain, or we shall swing for it. No, no good can be done, for it will then be over. We will take this boy prisoner. We can do it. We will bind him and throw him into yonder room. Brownie shall watch over him. If Randulph wishes the lad dead, we will ask him how much he will give us. He gives us gold, and we—"

Here the fellow paused, and grinned until his white teeth glittered in the firelight.

"Ha, ha!" shrieked the old woman. "Ben is right, Ben is right. He always looks after the gold, always. Yes, yes; Carli, you must leave the lad a prisoner. Brownie will mind him."

"But if he escape?" growled Carli. "Think you that I will live with this mark unavenged?"

"If he escape, everyone will take him for a gipsy. Look at his black hair and brown face. Who will know him? Who will believe that he is not a gipsy? They will say, 'Show us your bosom—if you are English, that will be white; they would not stain that.' But he is stained all over."

At this they all burst out into a most hearty laugh, in which Jack Firebrace did not join.

"Bind him!" cried Carli.

But Jack declined to be bound, and fought with all his might and main.

Standing with his back planted firmly to the wall, our hero used all his skill to ward off the blows.

But they came showering down so fast that the stick was dashed out of his hand; and then, with a scream of delight, Brownie sprang forward, and, with a violent blow, sent Jack stunned to the earth.

He was bound hand and foot, and then thrown into the back room.

Brownie, chuckling with delight at seeing Jack's pain, stretched himself on a mat at a little distance from where his prisoner lay, in such a position that our hero could not get out without passing over him.

"What shall I do to escape from these fellows?" thought Jack, when he had lain there an hour or more. "If I make the attempt I risk my life, and I would not die if I could help it until I have brought the wretch who killed my father and mother to justice. Still, if I remain here, and Randulph sees me, my fate will be sealed. He will never spare me. Indeed, he dare not do so, for he knows that if I once gain my liberty I hold his life in my hands. Liberty! Come what may, I will do my best to escape."

No sooner had Jack come to this determination than he managed to raise himself in a sitting posture, and listen.

Every person in the hut was fast asleep—even the dwarf, believing our hero so safely bound, had dropped into a heavy slumber.

Straining every muscle, Jack sought to burst his bonds. The ropes cut into the flesh, and held firmly.

"That won't do at all," said Jack to himself; "I must try some other way."

The next way was to get upon his knees, and then, screwing his body back, he managed to reach the rope that had bound his feet.

Patiently he worked away until he had loosened the knot, and at last succeeded in undoing it, although his fingers bled.

At this moment a slight noise startled Jack, and, on looking round, he beheld to his delight that the dwarf had dropped the knife.

"Providence is with me!" he muttered, and creeping up to the place he gently moved it away from Brownie.

Seating himself down by the knife, he managed to grasp its handle and force about half the blade into the earth, so that it was held in an upright position very firmly.

He then commenced rubbing the cord, which held his hands, against the edge of the knife.

Now and then, not being able to see, it missed the rope and caught the flesh, making some nasty cuts; but he went steadily on, and soon, to his great joy, found that he was free.

In a minute Jack was on his feet and stretching his aching limbs with all the joy of sudden liberty.

He could scarcely repress the wish to shout; but, knowing that it would cost him his life, was silent. He stole gently to the door, and, pulling it open a few inches, peered out.

To his horror he discovered that both the gipsies were awake, and were conversing in low tones.

It would be impossible to describe the feelings which shot through our hero's heart as he saw this.

After all the patience he had shown, the pain he had suffered, when the possibility of escape seemed so near, the chance was snatched from him.

He ground his teeth with rage, a strange fire burned in his eyes, and he felt inclined to rush forth and fight his way to the door, or meet death in the attempt.

Better, he thought, to perish than to be treated as he had been.

Doubtless he would have made a rush had not he, happening to glance upwards, beheld the pale light of the moon shining through a crack in the roof.

To swing himself up to one of the beams was the work of an instant, and he then began as rapidly and as stealthily as he could to cut away the turf roof, taking great care that the turf did not fall inside.

Oh! how his heart beat as the work progressed—and at last he saw that the hole was large enough to creep through.

He thrust through both his arms and drew himself up.

But on this occasion everything seemed to go against our hero.

Scarcely had he drawn his head and shoulders through the opening than part of the roof, being very rotten, and therefore unable to bear his weight, gave way with a crash, sending Jack back on the beam and part of it falling on the top of Brownie.

With a fierce yell of triumph the dwarf sprang up, and, seeing Jack about to spring through the roof, caught him by the leg.

With all the force our hero could muster he drew up his foot that was free and dashed it into the dwarf's face, sending him sprawling on the floor, his nose and mouth pouring with blood.

With a bound Jack managed to spring through the roof as the gipsies hurried into the room.

But our hero was not to escape from his enemies.

He had scarcely made three bounds over the roof when he fell through the hole which formed the chimney, right on the turf fire beneath.

He scrambled up as quickly as he could and made for the door; but Zarah flew after him and clutched him by the throat with her long, skinny hands, at the same time shouting aloud for help.

"Hurrah!" cried Carli, as he bounded into the room, and, with one blow, knocked Jack down; "we have got him now. Oh, but this is really a treat! So, my fine fellow, you thought to escape us, eh? I'll take care that you shall never get loose again, so I can tell you. Do you mark this scar in my face? You may thank that for preventing your escape. I could not sleep for the pain, and, therefore, was ready to pounce on you at once. Now, are you sorry you struck me?"

"No, I am not, and I only hope that I have marked you for life, so that, if I ever regain my freedom, I may point you out and deliver you over to justice."

"You will, eh?" roared the gipsy.

"Then I will make pretty certain that you do not escape."

"Hark!" cried the old hag, suddenly; "I hear the sound of horses coming across the moor. Quick, my lads, quick! Get the fellow hidden away.

"Hold your tongue, you blubbering hound!" she continued, turning to Brownie, who was yelling with pain, plainly showing that, whatever pleasure he took in another's torture, he did not care to be hurt himself. "If you are hurt it serves you right. Had you kept a proper watch he would never have got free of his bonds—you, who boasted how you would guard him."

Whilst the old woman had been speaking poor Jack had again been safely bound, and this time gagged with such severity that he could scarcely breathe.

He was then dragged into the adjoining room and concealed under a quantity of loose straw, on which the gipsies threw themselves—without the least regard to Jack's comfort—as if upon a bed.

Having warned our hero that, if he attempted to make the slightest noise or movement they would kill him instantly, they pretended to be sound asleep.

Scarcely had they done so when three horsemen pulled up by the hut and called out lustily for the owner of the place.

"Dearee — dearee me, good gentlemen," said the old crone, as she tottered to the door. "What can you want at such a humble place as mine? If you have lost your way, maybe I can direct you; but if you need food and drink I have none. I eat only roots and scraps, such as a few kind neighbours give me, whilst my drink is from yonder spring, which is free to all. Alas, alas! I am very poor—very poor!"

"Silence, you old witch!" cried one of the men, swinging himself from his horse and descending the steps leading to the door of the hut; "silence! You must have lost your senses if you do not know me. Where is Carli, Ben, and the prisoner?"

"As I live, it is Red Randulph!" screamed Zarah, in delight.

"Then you are deceived—it is not Red Randulph," said the man, fiercely. "Keep your screech-owl tongue between your teeth—or, rather, your gums, for teeth you have none. Do you not know that it is ill to trifle with me?"

The old hag's eyes glistened with hate, and her claws moved nervously, as if wishing to tear the speaker.

"Where is Carli and Ben, I say?" cried the speaker, stamping with rage. "I have gone from one meeting place to another, and traced the red rags* in the bushes which marked their path, and they have led me here. Now, where are they?"

"Here we are, master!" cried Carli and Ben, springing up and hurrying into the room. "We did not know it was you, and there has been such queer work going on all along the south that we had to be very cautious."

"You are right, my lads. The 'Flying Fish' has been burned. Spies and coastguardsmen have been placed everywhere. One of the fellows I managed to put out of the way, and he is now under lock and key. Ha, ha! it was a rare joke to see them lock up their own detective. 'Sblood! how I did laugh when I got free of the old fool of a magistrate. You gipsies must take care. Some of your men have been shot, I hear, and some made prisoners. The latter may turn upon us, and betray our secrets."

"Not they," said Carli; "a gipsy never betrays his friends—that you may swear."

"Tut! a gipsy, like all other vagabonds, would hang his own father to save his own neck," replied the man.

"You wrong us. We are true to each other," cried Carli, fiercely. "And our women are virtuous!"

"Yes — when they are as old and ugly as Zarah here; not when they are as pretty as your lost love, Miriam."

"Dare you to—"

The gipsy paused, for the new-comer, with the greatest coolness, drew a pistol from his pocket and pointed it at the gipsy.

"Don't try that on with me. I never miss aim—and I do not want to rob the gallows. Now, where is this boy?"

"He is here. There were two of them, as you know—one went with

* Some gipsies mark their course by pieces of red wool tied to sprigs of trees, so that their friends may know how to follow them.

Joseph, and the other came with me," replied Carli.

"I know; I have seen them. The other boy is an escaped pupil of Hawkhouse School. He is of no value. He might as well have died. Where is the other? From what I have heard he is also an escaped pupil."

At a sign from Carli, Ben dragged forth Jack Firebrace.

"This is not the other boy," cried the man, stamping with rage. "What fool's game is this? This is some gipsy lad. I see it all! You have permitted the prisoner to escape, and think to palm this tawny idiot on me. Now, mark me —from the news I have heard I believe, nay, I am sure, as I said when first I saw them, that the other lad you had was the one Red Randulph wanted; the only creature who ever baulked his plans or of whom he had a dread. Had you kept him, Randulph would have given you five hundred pounds at least."

"Then," roared Ben, with delight, "this must be the young devil who has caused so much mischief. I don't believe that any dozen boys could do more than he has done in twenty-four hours, if they were to try their hardest, in twenty-four weeks, that I don't. He has—"

"Never mind what the lad has done," cried the man, sharply. "What I want to know is, where is the white lad? The one, I mean, of pure English blood, not brown, like this one; and he had lightish brown hair."

"So had this one until we dyed him all over. You see, we knew that it had somehow got talked about that two white lads were amongst the gipsies—how, I can't tell; so, to prevent our being stopped, I had this young chap made to look like one of us. That is how it is."

"Soho! not a bad idea," said the man, who was the image of Griffiths Grindwell, both in person and voice.

Jack sat there as quiet as a mouse, showing neither anger nor fear.

"Did you hear me speak?" cried Luke the Double, as the gipsies called him.

"I did; but that is no reason why I should answer you," replied Jack, as one of the gipsies removed the gag. "I am not your servant."

"Ho, ho! my young gentleman, we will see about that at some future time.

But I guess by his tones that he is the one we want."

"And we shall have the five hundred pounds?" demanded Ben, quickly.

"To be sure you shall. Mr. Grindwell always keeps his word," said Luke.

"If he will make it six hundred, we will soon rid him of this youth," said Ben, with a significant gesture.

Luke Lansner stood for a moment musing, as if undecided what he should do.

"No," he said at last; "that must not be until I know Grindwell's wish. But how are we to take this fellow across the country? Such a dare-devil fellow as that might rouse up the whole country round."

"Gag him again, gag him! and bind him!" cried Brownie; "or, better still, pull his tongue out, as they did the other lad's."

A shudder ran through Jack Firebrace's frame as he heard this, for he remembered poor Dumb Peter.

"Tut! you speak nonsense," said Luke, sharply; then, turning to Lansner, he said: "Do I not tell you that there are spies out everywhere? If we could only get him down to the coast, we might put off in a fishing-boat, and get him round the coast."

"Round the coast? Why, where do you mean to take him?" demanded the men.

"Back to the school from whence he escaped. Back to Hawkhouse and the tender mercies of his master."

Old Zarah appproached Luke, and, placing her shrivelled finger on her lip, whispered in his ear—

"If you will do what I tell you I will manage it for you. Only you must pay me."

"Well here are a couple of guineas for you. What am I to do, old Mother Beelzebub?"

"Do? Why, drink and eat. Talk kind to the lad; and make him eat, too. I'll give him a drug that will make him sleep for over twenty-four hours. By that time you will be well away to sea, and he will be safe."

"Good!" whispered Luke Lansner.

And then he said aloud—

"But it is bad thinking over an empty stomach. Call in my two companions, and let us have something to eat and drink; and give the lad some, for he seems to require something. You have knocked him about pretty well amongst you."

"It would have been better to have killed him at once," growled the old woman. "He has smashed my pet Brownie's nose flat to his face. But there, we poor gipsies are always being commanded to do what others think best, not what we think. So the little demon who would have murdered us must eat our meat and bread, and drink our spirits?"

She continued grumbling as she placed some meat before the people, and then placed a cup of brandy and water before each one.

Jack was too ill to eat, but he had a fever coming on him, and, therefore, he caught at the cup and drank off the contents.

He had hardly put the cup down, when he sank back into a deep sleep, closely resembling death.

CHAPTER XLII.

JACK IS TAKEN TO THE COAST—THE GIPSIES DISCOVER A RUNAWAY—THE GIPSIES' MEETING—OLD FLICK'S DEVOTION—BROWNIE'S PUNISHMENT—ZARAH'S BRAVERY —HAWKHOUSE AGAIN.

"HE sleeps soundly enough now," Carli growled. "One would almost think that he was dead."

"Dead!" cried the old crone; "do you think I do not know how to manage things better than that? No, no; old Zarah knows how to treat those she wishes to kill, and those she wishes to sleep. This lad will sleep well—oh, so well, that many would think him dead!

but he will awake, and feel as if he had been in a dream, a deep dream, and nothing more."

"Will it injure his health?" Luke demanded, out of curiosity—he had no love for Jack Firebrace.

"No; he will wake, I tell you, as from a sleep—refreshed, and stronger than before."

"I wish that he would never wake!" muttered the Brownie; "and it shall go hard if I do not cause that sleep to last till the crack of doom."

"Quick, Carli—and you, Ben, get out the donkey-cart and throw the lad into it. We must make our way to the Hawk's Nest. Methinks that there will be some rare doings there before long. Our game is one of great danger."

The two gipsies brought out a queer, rickety kind of cart, to which the donkey was harnessed—or, more properly speaking, tied, for traces, reins, and collar were all composed of rope.

Then Jack was placed at the bottom of the cart upon some straw, and a piece of canvas thrown over him, so that, should inquiries be made as they went along, they might declare that the boy was sick of a fever.

Away went Luke and his followers at full speed across the plain, whilst the gipsies with the donkey-cart crawled slowly behind.

Across fields and through woods went the gipsies, always taking care to avoid villages and towns, for they well knew that the constables objected to such strolling vagabonds, had a nasty way of clapping them into the gaol or the stocks, and, therefore, wisely kept out of their power.

They were passing down a long, dark lane, leading to the sea, when they met a troop of scarlet-coated gentlemen, who had evidently enjoyed a good day's run with the hounds, for they were splashed with mud from head to foot, and their horses were flecked with foam, and travel-stained.

"Halloa! you children of Satan!" cried one of the gentlemen. "What devil's game are you up to now?"

"Oh, kind gentlemen—good Christian gentlemen!" sobbed Zarah, stepping forward.

"Christian!" cried the squire. "What have you and such as you to do with that word? I know you well. You worship the Evil One, and learn to read the stars, and such like wicked things."

"Better learn that than learn nothing," replied the woman, with sudden anger flashing in her eyes.

"There!" cried the squire, in delight, as he pointed his whip at the woman; "did I not tell thee that she had the devil in her? You cannot get over me. I know them, and if I catch them, to prison say I. And such as the likes of her talk of Christianity—bah!"

As he finished he made a cut at the old woman with his whip.

Scarcely had he done so than Carli and Ben sprang forward and placed their hands on the hafts of their knives.

"What, dogs!" cried the squire, "dare you threaten me because I choose to flick an old woman with my whip? Why, I am a justice of the peace, and I'll have you all whipped if I like—there!"*

"Quiet, quiet, squire," said a young man, placing his hand upon the squire's arm; "remember, these poor people are taught differently from their birth than we are. They do but little harm."

"Better be taught to read the stars than live in brutal ignorance!" cried Zarah, stamping with rage. "Call you it Christianity to lash an old woman with your whip?—a poor old grandmother, who is mourning for her dying grandchild. See!" she continued, as she snatched the canvas under which Jack was hidden from the cart, "see there, at my dying child; he has the most deadly, the most catching of diseases."

The squire, who, in spite of his friend's interruption, was about to advance and strike the old woman again, fell back and turned very pale when he heard the announcement of the dread presence of disease, for, ignorant and self-conceited as he was, he knew full well that illness is no respecter of persons or of rank.

"Ha, ha! you draw back, do you?" shrieked the old woman. "Soho! you can strike at an old woman, but you fear—yes, you fear King Death. Ho, ho, ho, ho! he is a monarch to whom all men bow!"

---

*This scene must not be considered overdrawn. At the period in which the plot of this story is laid the gipsies were fearfully persecuted, especially by the country squires, many of whom were as ignorant as they were prejudiced.

"You old hag!" cried the squire, "I wish the old laws were in force; I would have thee burned as a witch. But ride on, and if you choose to look in at a shed farther down the road maybe you will find one of your own breed who is ill, too—ill from a skin disease that he won't get rid of in a hurry."

And here all the huntsmen burst into a laugh, and galloped away as fast as they could.

"What do they mean by that, mother?" asked Carli. "None of our tribe are on this road."

"I know that, unless Melchior has sent us some message, and the messenger has fallen ill."

"We must push on and see, for, if he be one of us, he must not perish," said Ben, quickly.

The old woman growled her assent, and, throwing the canvas over Jack, they resumed their journey until they came to a shed, a dismal place, which had once been a smith's shop.

"This must be the place," growled Carli. "See! the door has been opened lately."

But there was no doubt about it being so, for there came from the lonesome shed low groans of pain.

Pushing open the door the two gipsies entered the house, and discovered a human creature, clad in the most filthy rags, crouched down in the corner of the hut.

"Hillo!" cried Carli, "what's up here? Who are you—what are you? Can't you speak?"

"I am a miserable wretch," groaned the lad, for the poor creature was only a youth, "who has been ill-treated from a child, and now, because my garments have been exchanged for rags, I have been cruelly horsewhipped by those who should have protected me. Oh! how I wish for death, if I could only see my old friend Jack Firebrace again."

"Jack Firebrace!" shouted Carli, in joy. "Jack Firebrace, did you say? Well, so you shall, I warrant."

"Ho, ho! we have stopped you, have we, my nice little runaway?" laughed Ben.

The lad looked up in horror.

The light from the open door was not much, but it sufficed to show him he was with the gipsies.

"The gipsies — the gipsies — the gipsies!" he cried. "Oh! have I fallen into their treacherous hands again?"

"So, so; I see what it is," laughed Carli. "You have cut and run from our band, eh? Well, you will have to go back again, that is all. Come, none of your sneaking ways to me. Tell me what you have been up to?"

"I have nothing to tell; they forced me from my friend, Jack Firebrace, and I ran away as soon as I had a chance."

"Well, you shall be soon with him, my young friend. Come, get up, you young rsscal, and walk. Get up, I say, and walk!"

Terrified and frightened, the poor lad tried to get upon his feet, but fell back with a cry of pain.

"He can't walk," said Ben; "we must take him out to the cart. By Jove! I think we are in luck this time. If this lad is worth only a quarter of the other, our fortunes will be made indeed."

They lifted the lad up, and found that his body had been deeply lashed with a hunting-whip.

"That is the squire's work," said Carli. "A nice Christian, indeed—he worships only gold."

"Lift him into the cart," said Zarah; "yonder is the bay, and, if my old eyes do not deceive me, Luke the Double is waiting down there for us."

"Two!" cried Brownie. "I only asked for one, and now I have two."

Scarcely had they thrown the canvas back and disclosed Jack Firebrace, when the other lad threw himself upon him, and, in heartrending tones, exclaimed—

"Oh, Jack, Jack, Jack! Don't you know me? Look up, Jack; do look up. I am your friend, your favourite old Flick!"

"He's got sharp eyes, anyhow," whispered Carli.

"He sees through the disguise."

"Yes; rather too much," replied Ben.

And then, with an oath, he turned to old Flick, bidding him hold his tongue, unless he wanted to be cut to pieces and pitched into the road.

Onward jolted the wretched old cart down a steep road, full of ruts, which led from the cliff to the seashore.

Only about a mile from the hut where they had discovered old Flick, the sea was beating on the yellow sands, but the track they had to take twisted about a good deal, so that it was quite dark when the gipsies approached the cloaked figure which Zarah had seen when by the hut.

"I was right," muttered the crone, "I was right. It is the Double. Where is the boat?"

"It will be round here in half-an-hour. You have used great despatch. How is the lad? Sleeps he still?"

"He sleeps still; but we have caught the other lad—he who went with the other band. He had run away, and we were sent to him by one of his own people. Yes, his own people had cut his flesh with whips, and then left him for us."

"Enough of this," said Carli; "we have the two lads here. If the second one had not bolted, he would have been away up north by now with our people. As it is, you have only to stick them both in the boat, and take them back to the school from which they have run away. So I suppose you will double the reward?"

"Not so fast, not so fast," said Luke Lansner; "I have nought to do with the reward except that there is gold in earnest, and you shall receive it from the captain. As to this second boy, I know nothing of him."

"You know that he had escaped from the school," cried Carli, fiercely. "I tell you, that if one boy escapes from that school you are lost. It only needs for the smallest of those lads cooped up there to regain his liberty, and you will be crushed for ever. Now, Master Luke, we must have your note of hand that this money will be paid, or neither lad will you have from us."

"Go to—go to—you are mad, Carli," cried Luke. "Why do you doubt my word? Have I not kept faith before?"

"Ay; but it is different now," laughed Ben. "Luke the Double has been true to us because the game was good, but let things change and Luke will disappear, leaving us to find our way about as best we can. We have talked this over as we came along, myself and Carli, and we do not part with the boys unless you give us a written agreement to pay us the amount you promised."

"And you refuse to take the money I have offered you on account?" demanded Luke.

"We do. We are four to one. Zarah is as good as any man, and therefore we will have our way."

"Give me but time to consider what I shall do," demanded Luke. "Remember, I act only for another."

"That will not do. In a little time your friends will be here, and then the fight will be equal. We must have your answer now, or we at once set forth to the nearest town, give up the boys, and turn evidence against you."

Whilst Luke Lansner had been talking to the men his quick ears had caught the sound of oars.

"As you will," he said, at last. "I see that fortune must be against us. The ship is sinking when the rats leave it. I must pay you in full. Step within, that I may count the money on this rock."

"You pay for both boys?" cried Carli, stepping forward, anxiously.

"Of course, of course," said Luke, as he stood on one side of the boulder of rock, the gipsies being on the other; "if I pay for one I may as well pay for both—and thus do I settle the account in full."

He drew a brace of pistols from his coat pocket, and discharged them in the faces of the men, mortally wounding both of them.

At the same moment a boat dashed up to the shore, and three or four armed smugglers leaped on the strand.

"Seize the old witch yonder, and the dwarf," cried Luke Lansner to his men. "They have dared to threaten to peach upon us, and hand us over to justice. Shoot them down if they do not yield at once!"

So rapid had Luke's movements been, that Zarah and the Brownie had not time to fly.

"We are caught!" yelled the dwarf; "caught, and we shall be killed! But I will not die without revenge!"

Drawing his knife, he sprang forward; not at the men, but to the cart, and aimed a blow at the motionless form of our hero.

The blow was well aimed at the heart, and given with all the vindictive Brownie's strength, so that there can be little doubt but that it would have been mortal had it struck as intended.

THE BOYS OF HAWKHOUSE SCHOOL.

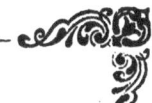

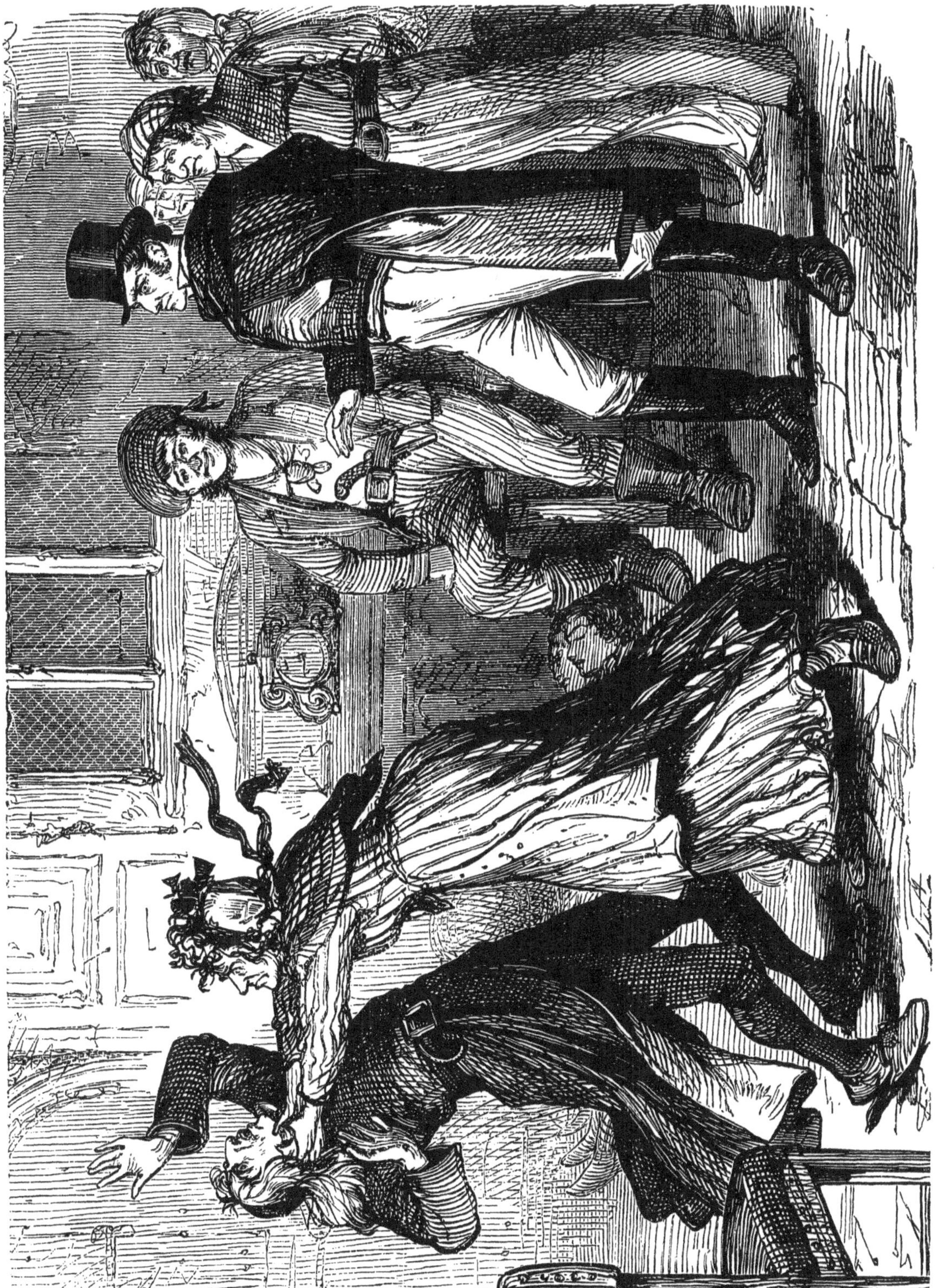

"THE OLD WOMAN LEAPED AT GRUESOME AND CLUTCHED HIM BY THE THROAT."

o. 14.

PRICE ONE HALFPENNY.

[PUBLISHED EVERY MONDAY.]

Flick, weak and ill as he was, had been watching the whole scene, and, with a swiftness which only his great love for our hero could have given him, he threw himself before Jack, receiving the blade in his back.

"Jack, dear Jack!" he cried, as he clasped our hero in his arms; "good-bye, dear fellow! I die for you!"

"Curses on you all!" yelled the dwarf, as the men seized him and wrenched the knife out of his grasp; "curses on you all! Oh, that I could only tear and rend you all into little pieces; I should die happy then!"

"Bind the hounds and and foot," said Luke, "and if he still continues yelling, hit him over the head with the butt-end of one of your pistols; silence him somehow. Here, some of you fellows, pitch these two dead gipsies into the boat. The tide is running up, and it will soon remove all traces of blood from the sands. Now, in with the old woman on top of the dwarf, and then in with the two lads."

These orders were quickly obeyed; the boat shoved from the shore, the oars put out, a lug sail set, and in a few moments they were swiftly gliding over the sea.

The first thing Luke did was to see that old Flick's wound was properly dressed, for the heroic conduct of the lad had called up, even in his cruel breast, a kind of admiration.

He admired the only thing a scoundrel, such as he was, could admire—the lad's courage.

He had just finished dressing the wound when a dismal howl arose from Zarah.

"Oh, oh!" she yelled; "take him off, take him off! He has his teeth fixed in me! Oh, oh, oh, oh!"

"What's the matter now, mother?" said one of the sailors, as he pulled the old woman up.

A roar of laughter burst from the men when they perceived the cause of all this outcry.

The sailors had, in the most literal sense of the word, carried out their commander's orders, and the consequence was that they had pitched the old woman on top of the dwarf, and he had bitten furiously at the old lady, as a slight hint that her weight was, to say the least of it, oppressive.

"We have had enough of this," said Luke Lansner; "bring that imp here."

The dwarf was dragged aft and thrust before Luke Lansner.

"Now, you little whelp!" he said, "you would have turned traitor and denounced me, would you, eh?"

"No, no, no, sir; indeed I would not have done so!" cried Brownie. "It was all that old hag there, who wished to do it. She was put up to it by the other boy. He said his friends would reward him well, and that he would see she had plenty of the money. I tried to persuade her and Carli and Ben to have nothing to say to them, but it was all of no use, she would—she would!"

"Is this true or false?" demanded Luke Lansner of Zarah. "Speak, and be careful you speak truly."

"It is false!" cried the old woman. "Have I not treated him as if he were my own son? Have I not been to him more than a mother?—and now he turns upon me thus. Carli and Brownie were the two first who proposed the insisting upon the money. It was not me, although I afterwards agreed to it."

"Oh, you wicked old woman!" cried Brownie. "Did I not ask you to leave those wicked men—"

"Silence!" cried Lansner. "Do you think I believe your lies? If, as you say, you had not joined with those men, you would not have been here. The boy whom you have wounded has no friends on whom he could rely for help. So, out of your own mouth you are convicted. Seize him and bind him between the two corpses, tie a couple of bags of ballast to their feet, and overboard with them."

"Mercy—mercy—mercy!" shrieked the dwarf. "Spare my life, and I will do anything, everything you wish. Oh, do not hurt me. I am not ready to die. Oh, oh, oh, oh!"

"Over with him!" cried Luke; "show him the same mercy as he has shown others."

There was a deep splash.

The waters circled round and round.

In the calm sea the circles spread larger and larger, but no body rose. Living and dead had found one grave.

"Now, mother Zarah, what have you to say for yourself?" demanded Luke.

"I am a gipsy," replied the old woman, sternly. "I care not what you do to me, for I have had my revenge."

"If we spare your life will you promise me that you will be silent about what has been done to-day?"

"No," replied the old woman; "I am true to my tribe. You have killed two of them—I do not count the vile dwarf as anyone. If I escape out of your hands your death is certain. So now do with me what you will."

"Why, how now, you hag, dare you threaten me?" cried Luke. "Do you forget your life is in my hands?"

"I do not forget it!" laughed the old woman. "All the days of my life I have spent in the fields, free as the birds --free as the air. That is the only life for a gipsy to live. Think you that I wish to exist for a moment in captivity? No; I would scorn such a life. Look at the rolling ocean. There is freedom— true freedom. Death is but freedom, and thus do I seek it."

Before anyone could prevent her she threw herself across the gunwale of the boat, toppled over, and fell headlong into the sea.

This movement was so violent that it nearly upset the boat, so that for some moments the men were in a state of alarm for their own safety. When once the boat had righted, all signs of the old hag were lost.

"Let the old witch go!" growled Luke Lansner. "I doubt not but her friend, the Evil One, will save her. I have heard it said that witches cannot drown, so maybe she is swimming fast ashore. See, yonder is the Hawk's Crag. Give way, my men; we shall soon be there, and then good grog and a long rest is before you."

The men bent to their oars, and, as if the weather was anxious that they should reach their destination, quickly a nice fresh wind sprang up, and in a very little time the boat shot into the creek at the back of old Peter Pigwellan's hut.

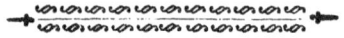

CHAPTER XLIII.

THE RETURN TO HAWKHOUSE—DRUSILLA DRYSDALE HEARS THE FATE OF GOBLIN JIM.

LUKE LANSNER leaped on shore and knocked gently at Peter Pigwellan's door.

"Who knocks at this time of night?" demanded Pigwellan, in his usual grating noise.

"Open the door at once!" demanded Luke Lansner, angrily.

Slowly Peter Pigwellan drew back the bolts of the door, and opened it.

More hideous than ever showed the face of the old boatman under the lamp, which he held over his head.

"What is the news up at the house?" demanded Luke Lansner, sharply.

"The ferrets are in the rats' hole. None will escape."

"Tut! you are mad," cried Lansner, sharply. "Help to bring the lads I have brought with me in."

Peter Pigwellan stepped forward to obey the order; but the men had already lifted Jack and Flick out of the boat, and carried them into the hut.

Scarcely had the light fallen upon Jack Firebrace than Peter Pigwellan started violently.

"You recognise old friends, eh?" laughed Luke Lansner; "they nearly escaped, but we caught them."

"Fool!" cried Peter Pigwellan; "you have brought back ruin and destruction. You know not that the lad is doomed to end the accursed doings of this house. Fate has willed it to be so."

"You are mad!" snarled Luke Lansner, pushing the old man violently from him.

"Yes, I am mad. But mad people oft have dreams which come true. I tell you, Luke Lansner, that I have in my visions seen you a mangled corpse, whilst I have also seen that lad strong and happy, rich, loved, and respected."

To try Peter Pigwellan's power of prophecy Lansner pointed to the still motionless form of Jack, and said—

"You drivelling idiot; do you not see that the lad is dead?" he cried, with a contemptuous laugh.

"He is not dead," replied Pigwellan, "but his companion will die, mark that, to-morrow," he continued, in a deep, stern voice; "to-morrow the pale lad will be a corpse; but the lad who sleeps will live to pay back the cruelty of all. Go, seek the Hawk's Nest; but, mark me, death awaits you!"

"Enough, enough!" said Lansner; "is it safe to take these young cubs up the road?"

"No. The house is closely watched. Spies are everywhere, and people do not hesitate to declare that the people who attacked Summerbell's house came from Hawkhouse. The only safe way is up the secret passage cut in the cliff."

"Come, my men," cried Lansner; "we must carry these lads up the passage. It is no use stopping to listen to this evil old raven's croaking."

Pigwellan held up the light and showed them the way to the secret passage, the one by which he had let our hero creep back to Hawkhouse; and the sailors carrying Jack and Flick were soon at the door which led into the interior of Hawkhouse.

This they found securely fastened.

The inhabitants evidently knew that danger threatened them.

But by some secret means the inmates of the house were made to know that friends were at the door.

They were soon admitted, and at once bore Jack and Flick to the great hall, where they found Mr. Ebenezer Gruesome and Mrs. Drysdale.

"What have we here — what have we here?" cried Gruesome, as he held up the candle and leant over the boys. "More pupils—why bring them here now? It is rash, it is reckless, very reckless. Griffiths Grindwell must know that it is dangerous. Why, it is Jack Firebrace and Felix Flitter."

"Ay; we have caught the two runaways for you," laughed Luke; "you ought to be thankful."

The old man passed his hands over his brow, and muttered, in a low voice—

"He told me that the boy was dead—drowned! and I dreamt that I saw him at the bottom of the sea. There is fate in this."

"Have all of you gone mad?" cried Luke Lansner, stamping with rage; "first old Pigwellan and then you commence talking of your visions, and of fate, and such trash."

"Pigwellan!" exclaimed Gruesome, clutching Lansner by the arm; "he was the man who had orders to drown the lad Firebrace; he and Sidney Morrison were to do it, and both declared that they had done so. We are betrayed!"

"Betrayed by whom?" shouted Luke, as he clutched the old man by the shoulder and shook him. "Speak, or I will shake the life out of you. Do you think that my brave fellows and myself will stand here whilst you rave about danger, and do not tell us from whence it may come? Out with it, or, by Heaven, I will strangle you!"

"I know not whence the danger may come," gasped the old man. "All I can see is this, that the clouds of misfortune are getting round us swiftly. That boy is the only living thing Griffiths Grindwell dreads. He has done all in his power to kill the lad, but his hand has failed. The captain of the 'Flying Fish' was to have taken him on board and ill-treated him until he committed suicide; but he escaped."

"Nay, master, there you are wrong," said one of the sailors. "I was one of the men who took away the lad as brought the letter down to the sands. As for torture, he had enough of it. You won't see him again, for he first of all set himself alight and then the ship, and then leaped overboard. So what with fire and water he was settled, and so were all the rest but me, for the matter of that. I clung on to a piece of the wreck and drifted about until a fishing-smack picked me up, when I pitched them a long yarn and got back to my old friends on the South coast."

"What sort of a boy was he?" demanded Mrs. Drusilla Drysdale, sharply.

"Oh! a queer-looking little chap, with a shock head of hair, a long chin—why, dash me, but he had something of the cut of your jib about him. If he had been your son he could not have been more like you."

"If he had been!" howled the old woman. "He was my son; my only son. My beauty, my darling boy!"

"Well, there ain't no accounting for taste," said the fellow, with a coarse laugh. "All I can say is, that I should not have called him a beauty. But there, what does it matter, he was good enough to feed the fishes upon, and so the matter ends."

"Wretches! murderers! traitors!" yelled the woman, springing up and flying like an enraged cat at the sailor who had told the fate of Goblin Jim, and burying her nails in his face. "I will be revenged on you all. Not one of you shall escape—no, not one! Every secret is known to me, and I will let it be known to all the neighbourhood. Oh, but my poor dear son's blood shall be well avenged. You shall all swing for it!"

"She is mad!" cried the sailor.

"Mad!" yelled the unhappy mother. "Would that I were mad, that I might forget this. No; I have been too guilty in my life to be blessed with madness. Look you, Ebenezer Gruesome, and mark my words. Listen all of you, for what I speak now is truth. I have plotted, planned, and sinned to gain wealth for my child. That child you have snatched from me. All hope in life has gone with him. From this time forward I'll devote my life to your ruin."

"Have a care what you say," cried Luke Lansner, fiercely.

"I fear you not!" yelled the old woman. "I defy you all, and will drag you to the scaffold, even if I have to die with you. Death will be welcome to me, come when and how it will."

"Hush, hush, good Drusilla," cried old Gruesome, wringing his hands; "you must not speak in that horrid manner. I am sure I was sorry when I heard before of this—this mistake about poor Jim."

"Then you knew of it before?" shrieked the old woman. "You knew of it?"

"Well, I can't quite say I did not know of it. You see, I heard Mr. Grindwell say, that is, I—"

He paused and turned deathly pale when he saw the change in Drusilla Drysdale's face.

"You—you knew this? Look at that man," she cried, as she pointed to the trembling form of the old man. "He has killed his own child! Ah! see how he starts. I am that man's wife; but he dared not own the marriage for fear of Griffiths Grindwell. He is a miser; he loved his gold alone, and he knew, if our marriage was known, a small income I had would go from me. So he hid the marriage and helped to slay his own child."

"Do not believe her!" shrieked the old man; "she raves, indeed she does. I am very poor, very poor indeed!"

"He lies! he lies!" shrieked the old woman, seeming to take a great delight in the misery of her husband. "Search Hawkhouse well, my lads, and you will find gold enough and to spare. Take the gold; I give it to you. It is accursed, and will bring curses upon all who touch it; so I give it unto you."

"No, no, you witch, you hag, you miserable wretch! Do not believe her; I have not any gold. It is false—quite false. What I have is my own—all my own—all that I have worked honestly for. If the boy is killed, good gentlemen, I did not do it—she cannot say that. Do not mind her, good gentlemen; she is mad—raving mad!"

"Yes, I am mad!" cried the woman. "My brain is on fire. Death is near, but I will not die alone."

With the spring of a tiger the old woman leaped upon Gruesome, and grasped his throat with her bony fingers.

"Help, help, help!" gasped Gruesome, as he fell backwards to the floor.

"Look, look!" yelled the woman. "See, see; he laughs, he laughs! Ho, ho, you make game of me! You thrust your tongue out and make faces at me, imitating my poor Jim. Ha, ha, ha!"

"Save the unhappy wretch!" cried Luke Lansner, who, with the others, had stood watching this fearful scene, unable to move. "She will strangle him!"

The men sprang forward, but it was too late.

Mr. Gruesome had ceased to breathe; the old woman had had her revenge.

When they tore her away from the

body they found she was only a gibbering idiot.

"Take the old woman upstairs and lock her in a room," Luke Lansner said; "we will search for the gold to-morrow. Carry these boys to bed also. I wish that Griffiths Grindwell were here," he muttered, as he turned away. "The hand of the avenger seems upon us all."

CHAPTER XLIV.

DEATH OF OLD FLICK—JACK FIREBRACE'S OATH—JACK'S PLOT.

JACK FIREBRACE awoke and found himself in a dark room, and in bed.

"Can it all be a dream?" exclaimed Jack, as he passed his hand over his forehead.

For some time he lay musing on the events of his captivity amongst the gipsies.

He remembered all about Carli, the Brownie, Ben, and Zarah; the arrival of Luke and the meal, but beyond that he had no remembrance of anything.

"I am not with the gipsies," he said; "that cannot be, for I have a nice bed. I am well — very well — stronger than I have been for some time, yet I have no recollection of coming here."

At this moment a painful cry—half sob, half groan — rang through the room.

"Who is that?" demanded Jack, sitting up in bed. "If anyone is near me and in pain let him speak. I will, if I can, help him. At all events, as a companion in misfortune, I may be able to offer some consolation."

"Jack, dear Jack, is that you?" whispered a hollow voice. "Oh! I am so glad; I have so longed to hear your voice once more before I died."

"Great Heaven! is it old Flick?" cried Jack, leaping out of his bed. "Dear old Flick, I have found you at last."

"Yes, Jack, but it is only to part again," said Flick, as our hero took his hand, having, by the faint light from the window, discovered the narrow bed in which his old and faithful companion was placed. "Yes, Jack," said Flick, sorrowfully, "we meet again. Heaven is very kind to grant me that prayer; but, Jack, old fellow, we only meet to part. I am dying, dear Jack—dying from a wound through the lungs."

"Flick, Flick, Flick! dear old Flick, do not say so! You must not die! You shall not leave me!"

"Hush, Jack, hush! I am not sorry to go. But you, Jack, are left in danger—great danger. Sit on the bedside, and I will tell you all I can remember. We must not lose time, Jack, for I have none to spare."

"Flick, Flick, darling old Flick!" cried Jack, as he threw himself by the side of his old and trusted friend, "you must not leave me, dear, dear old fellow. I can bear anything rather than that."

"Ah, Jack, it is not as we like; but listen to me. Hush! how strangely the sea roars to-night! I could fancy—I suppose it is only fancy—that I can hear strange voices—kindly voices calling, calling me far away."

Jack could make no reply, for his voice was choked with sobs.

"Hush, hush! Jack; you will wake the other fellows in the dormitory. Ah! I forgot you did not know that we were back at Hawkhouse School."

"Hawkhouse School!" exclaimed Jack, starting back in surprise. "Why, how on earth did we come here?"

Then, in a weak voice, Felix Flitter —or old Flick, as we prefer calling him —told Jack all that he could remember of what had happened after the gipsies had found him in the hut, only not mentioning how the Brownie had stabbed him with the dagger.

"But how did you escape from the gipsies?" asked Jack. "Did they let you go?"

"No; they would willingly have kept me a close prisoner, but I fancy that they were pursued. At all events, they were frightened, and hid themselves in a wood. In the darkness I slipped away.

"They had clothed me in rags, Jack, and stained my skin so that I looked like a gipsy. Well, I met a gentleman and some of his friends, and they had been out hunting; so I thought they would at least be kind to me; but they took me for a gipsy, and beat me. Oh, Jack, I think I should have died then had it not been that I wanted to see you once more."

"But you will soon recover your strength now," said Jack, trying to speak cheerfully. "The treatment at this school is certainly most brutal, but to do them justice they do not starve us, so that you will soon be well."

"Don't—don't speak like that, Jack. I shall never be well again, old fellow. I—I did not like to tell you at first, Jack; but one of the gipsies stabbed me through the lungs. I am bleeding inwardly."

"Great Heavens! why did you not tell me this before?" cried Jack. "I will seek for assistance."

"No, no, not for the world, Jack; besides, it being impossible for anyone to do me any good, I wish to spend my last moments on earth with you, Jack, and to die in your arms. You will hold me in your arms, Jack, as I die!"

Jack's heart was too full to reply.

"This is a beautiful world, Jack! Ah, how often I have dreamed of wandering with you across the fields, hearing the lark singing, watching the white sails of the ships as they glide over the sunlit ocean—being free to wander wherever we liked. Oh, what happiness that would have been!

"I shall never wander amongst the woods again; but you will, dear Jack; I know—I feel that; and when you do, you will think of me, will you not, dear old boy? and you and Winny will talk about me, and laugh—not cry. I would not have you sad over my memory; but let it live in your hearts like a bright and cheerful light. Does not the room grow darker?"

"No, no, Felix; the room is somewhat lighter. I think the moon is rising, and—"

"Ah, I understand; it is the veil—

the shadow which Death casts before him. Pray with me, Jack."

Jack knelt down by the side of the bed, and there those two young hearts —one so full of life, the other so slowly beating out its young existence—prayed eagerly and earnestly to Him who hears both great and small.

"Jack—Jack, are you still near me?" whispered old Flick; and Firebrace felt his hands grow chill.

"Yes, dear Flick; I am here," replied Firebrace, softly, as he squeezed the dying boy's hand.

"You spoke just now about the moon —is she up in the sky now, sailing amongst the clouds?"

"Yes, dear Flick; I can see the gleam of her light between the window-curtains."

"Draw the curtains back, that I may see her once more before I die," said Flick.

With trembling hands Jack Firebrace pulled back the heavy window-curtains, letting in a glorious flood of silver light, for the moon was at the full, and had just emerged from a dark bank of cloud, over which she was now sailing.

"Jack," whispered Flick, "is not that beautiful—is it not wonderful? and yet, in a few minutes, I shall know more about it. I can feel the light enter into my soul. Farewell, Jack—fare—"

A hollow rattle sounded in the lad's throat, and his head fell heavily back on the pillow.

Jack sprang forward and raised him gently.

Once the eyes of the dying lad opened and were fixed upon Jack, and then they closed for ever!

Jack Firebrace stood alone in the room, and, for a few moments, in an agony of grief, gazed down upon the corpse of his dear old friend.

But his first passion of grief over, Jack, with a coolness that almost startled himself, composed the body of his poor friend.

He then knelt down and prayed fervently for some minutes by the bed-side.

This done, he slowly rose to his feet, and, placing one hand on Flick's fore-head, said, in a low, distinct voice—

"Dear old comrade, if you can hear me—as I believe you can and do—listen to my vow—never to rest until I have brought to justice the wretches who have caused you a life of sadness and a violent death. Heaven knows that at such a solemn time the heart, in its weakness, would be pardoned if it called aloud for vengeance; but knowing your gentle nature I will not do that. I but ask for justice. It is the duty of every honest person to expose brutality, robbery, and fraud wherever they find it. I now swear to devote the whole of my life to the destruction of this nest of murderers and thieves. Sleep on, dear friend. Be near me always—nay, that you must be, for though your body is dead, your love still dwells in my heart."

He bent over the body and kissed its cold lips, and then gently and reverently placed the sheet over the face.

"And now to work," said Jack, firmly. "If it were not for the poor lads in the school I would fire the place and burn the rats out. I wish I could obtain weapons somewhere. What are in these chests?"

Jack tried to open some old sea-chests which stood in the room, but found them securely locked.

Nothing daunted by this, Jack turned them round and examined the hinges, which, to his great delight, he found to be of the common clamp sort, and eaten through with rust.

"If I could only get a crowbar," he cried, "I could wrench that lock open with ease."

He examined the door and the windows, and, to his joy, discovered an old iron bar, hanging by the side of the latter, which had evidently been used to bar the shutters.

Jack seized upon it at once and wrenched it backwards and forwards, twisting it round and round, and using all his strength until the perspiration rolled off his forehead—still the bar seemed to resist all his efforts.

But Jack continued his labour, and at last succeeded in wrenching the staple, which held the bar, out of the wall.

To wrench off the hinges of one of the boxes was the work of no time, and, to his joy, Jack found that the box was an old arm-chest, and was filled with cutlasses like those used on shipboard.

He hastily selected a sword and belt, which he strapped round his own waist, and put the others under his arm.

He next crept to the door, but, to his disappointment, found that it was locked on the outside.

Many a lad would have given way before such obstacles; but not so Jack Firebrace.

Using the heavy cutlass as a lever, he managed soon to force back the bolt of the lock.

Now he was free, and he rested a few moments to take breath and recover his strength.

Then he crept stealthily out of the room, casting but one look back at the cold, still figure on the bed.

He knew at one glance the part of the house he was in, and had no difficulty in making his way to the long dormitory where slept all the other boys.

He stood for an instant watching the sleeping lads, and thought of all the misery they had borne, and how happy they would all be if released.

"They may be severely treated if I fail," he muttered; "but even death would be better for them than this life amongst thieves and cut-throats. It must be done; and I will not fail. Oh! how I wish old Flick were with me now. I could have relied upon him, but these lads I fear. But, come what may, it must be done."

He took the key from the outside of the dormitory door, and having inserted it in the inside of the lock doubled-locked the door, and put the key in his pocket.

"That is well. Now, in ten minutes, I shall know what chances I have of success."

He stole up to the bed of the nearest lad (who happened to be our old friend Tomkins, the ghost-seer), and shook him gently by the shoulder.

The lad snorted, growled, yawned, rubbed his eyes, and sat up in bed.

"It's not time to get up yet, Mr. Pliant; it is not daylight yet, it's—"

He paused suddenly, and his jaw fell; for his eyes were now opened, and he saw Jack Firebrace, whom all the boys firmly believed to be dead long ago.

Then Tomkins, with a faint cry of "Oh, Lor'!" attempted to slip out of bed on the opposite side to that on which our hero stood.

"Don't be a fool, Tomkins," said Jack, in a whisper. "I am not a ghost; I am Jack Firebrace in the flesh. Creep out of bed, and wake the other fellows. I have much to say to them. Don't let them make the slightest noise, or we shall be lost."

Tomkins saw that something was wrong, and that, let it be what it might, Jack was not in a temper to be trifled with; so he crept from bed to bed awakening the boys, and whispering to them that Jack Firebrace had come back wishing to speak to them.

Silently the lads tumbled out of bed, and stood before Jack, looking in their night-shirts like a regiment of ghosts, but newly risen from their graves.

"Keep silence, lads," said Jack, in a whisper; "slip on your trousers and stockings."

This was soon done, and once more they gathered round Jack, anxious to hear what he had to say.

"My lads," said Jack, in low, but earnest tones, "you have suffered much in this terrible place, wherein such crimes have been enacted that, if you knew them, would make your flesh creep. I am determined to free myself from this den of infamy or die! Will you follow me? Will you work with me? Answer, but answer in a whisper, all of you."

"Providence," he added, "has guarded me through all, and I feel certain that I am doomed to revenge those who have suffered at the hands of Griffiths Grindwell; but, remember, there is no going back. If you throw your lot in with me, you must stand or fall by my fortunes."

"We will stand by you!" shouted the boys, in a chorus.

"Silence, silence!" exclaimed Jack; "we must not let anybody hear us yet."

"There's no one to hear us except old Pliant," cried one of the boys, for Jack Firebrace had instilled some of his courage into them; "and he's not a bad sort if he would only wake up and look at things in a proper sort of way; only he's always dreaming."

"I had forgotten him," said Jack, glancing at a large partition at the farther corner of the room, behind which was a place about ten feet by six,

designated Mr. Pliant's bedroom; "we must make secure of him."

He crept behind the screen, and shook Mr. Pliant violently by the shoulder.

"Up, up, Mr. Pliant," whispered Jack. "Know you not that this house is a house of crime?"

"Bless my soul, what is this?" cried Mr. Pliant, sitting up in bed, rubbing first his eyes and then his nose.

"It means this, Mr. Pliant: that I, Jack Firebrace, having been brought back to this school by violence, mean to liberate my fellow prisoners and myself."

"Firebrace, I don't understand you," said Mr. Pliant, quietly; "have you been dreaming?"

"No; I wish to awaken you to a sense of wrong that has been going on in this house. Up, and dress yourself quickly, for we have no time to waste."

"I don't quite understand what you mean, Mr. Firebrace," said Mr. Pliant, as he arose slowly and dressed himself; "it seems to me that I am still dreaming —I ought to say very much dreaming."

Whilst Mr. Pliant was dressing Jack demanded of the boys if they had any candle-ends, for he knew that the lads had a habit of appropiating all the candle-ends that they could, for Mrs. Drusilla Drysdale was so parsimonious that sometimes the candle she gave the boys was so small that they had to finish their disrobing in the dark.

A goodly stock was at once brought forward, much to our hero's delight.

"Now, lads," whispered Jack, "do you know where there are any weapons?"

"I know there are some in the other room," said Tomkins; "the room where there are old chests. I saw some guns and pistols in a kind of secret cupboard, and there are two small barrels which look as if they held gunpowder."

"You are right," said Jack. "Wait one moment."

Jack Firebrace wanted to see if the bedroom was more fitted for defence than the one in which he had left the body of poor old Flick, and was rather disappointed to find it was.

"It cannot be helped," he muttered; "we must stay here. We must carry the powder and guns into this room."

"Powder and guns!" exclaimed Mr. Pliant, who came forth from behind the screen, all dressed ; "powder and guns ! —who spoke those disagreeable words ? I hope it was not you, Mr. Firebrace. Why, bless my soul ! you have some swords there. Put the nasty things down, or you may cut yourself."

"Do not trouble yourself about us, Mr. Pliant," said Jack Firebrace. "We will take care of ourselves. Now, lads, does anyone amongst you know the way to the kitchen, pantry, and wine-cellar?"

"I do," cried each boy, with a readiness that was quite surprising.

"Do not be too energetic. Mr. Pliant, you must come with us, sir. Believe me, we intend you no harm ; but, at the same time, I must warn you that, if you try to alarm the household, it will be my painful duty to kill you."

"My dear Mr. Firebrace," cried Mr. Pliant, "I have not the slightest wish to alarm the household."

Downstairs went all the lads, and were soon busily at work clearing the larder of all the edibles and the cellar of the wine.

When they were all well loaded, Jack led the way back to the dormitory, and there stowed all the provender safely on one side, though not without some remonstrances from the boys.

"Silence !" said Jack, sternly. "You must now follow me ; but you must not only creep softly, but bow the head reverently, for I take you into the presence of a grand but terrible monarch— King Death !"

Awe-stricken, the boys and Mr. Pliant followed our hero into the room where Felix Flitter slept his last sleep.

"Look at this," said Jack, stifling his sobs, as he threw the sheet from off old old Flick's face ; "this—my dear—my dear old friend, murdered—murdered ! and by whom ? By those who hold this place.

"Boys, I have found out that this school is kept only as a blind—that this place is a nest for smugglers and pirates. Oh, my dear schoolmates ! since I have left this place I have witnessed scenes which would make your hearts grow cold. Murder, torture—all that the basest of mankind have done have I been forced to witness.

"This—my own dear friend, was killed by some of the people who are in the pay of that fiend in human shape—

Griffiths Grindwell. All this I swear to you is true—nay, you cannot doubt me, for here is a terrible proof."

As he finished speaking, he pointed to the cold, dead features of old Flick.

"Can this be possible ?" ejaculated Mr. Pliant, as he passed his hand over his brow. "Have I been duped ? Sometimes I have thought that these ghost stories were not real ghosts, and wondered why Mr. Grindwell and Mr. Gruesome did not try to discover who caused the noises."

"You need not have wondered, Mr. Pliant," said Jack. "I can tell you. The school is the warehouse for the smugglers, and is connected with the old mill by a secret passage. To keep the people round out of the way whilst they run their cargo, the villains acted the ghosts, and made believe that the house was haunted."

"Ah, I remember now. Mr. Willet, the night before he so suddenly disappeared—you remember Mr. Willet, boys —the head assistant who came before Mr. Morrison?"

"Yes, yes," said the boys ; "he disappeared suddenly. Old Gruesome said that he turned him out of doors.'"

"Yes. Well, the night before he disappeared, I remember that he told Mr. Grindwell that he did not believe in the ghosts, and that he had pursued one who fled—a ghost with a sheet on. Yes, that was it—I know he said a sheet, because it caught in a nail and was torn, a piece being left on the nail. That was what Mr. Willet said. I know I laughed at the idea of tearing up a ghost.

"However, Mr. Grindwell was very angry, and next night, when Mr. Willet began the subject, Mr. Grindwell got quite in a passion, and declared that he was very drunk—and I daresay he was, although I must confess I never saw Mr. Willet at all the worse for liquor.

"I know things got unpleasant, and I so feared a disturbance, that I crept off to bed. I never met Mr. Willet again —never. I think he ran away."

"He was most likely murdered," said Jack Firebrace, in a low voice.

"Gracious me, Mr. Firebrace, don't say that."

"I tell you there is no depth of guilt they would not stoop to—no deed so dark that they would shrink from it. I was with them when they attacked Mr. Summerbell's house, and carried off his daughter, Winnifred. The very first night I was here I saw Mr. Sidney Morrison shot at on the beach. I knew not, then, what to think about it—now I know that he is in the power of these men, and compelled to aid them in their evil work. But come, lads, we must to business," continued Jack, as he covered over the face of the corpse. "We know that Grindwell and his creatures have caused the death of our dear old schoolfellow. I know that he has caused the death of many others. Swear, then, upon this, our dear friend's body, never to rest until we are free from this fearful place, and have avenged those we love."

"We swear it!" cried the boys.

"So do I," said Mr. Pliant. "But I am so confused that I really don't know what we are to do."

"Then I will show you. Now, Tomkins, where are the guns and the powder?" demanded Jack Firebrace.

Tomkins hurried to a panel in the wall, slipped it back, and discovered a stand of arms.

"Quick, my lads, we have not a moment to lose!" cried Jack. "Carry all these into the dormitory. Mr. Pliant, you must help me to roll in the barrels of gunpowder. Don't be afraid; they will not go off and kill you. Some of you lads carry in those chests of arms. If we cannot use them ourselves, we will deprive the enemy of them. Quick, lads, and bear a hand."

In a very short time all the arms and ammunition had been conveyed into the dormitory.

Then, at Jack's orders, each boy dragged his bed from off his bedstead, and the latter were silently but strongly wedged against the door so as to make it almost impossible to open it from the outside.

After this, Jack had one candle-end lit and distributed the arms to the boys.

"Now," said Jack, "we will have something to keep our strength up. But we must be cautious."

Then he mixed some weak brandy and water in one of the jugs from the washing-stand, and divided it amongst them.

Jack Firebrace then blew out the candle, declaring that they might need

it to see how to load their guns should they have a night attack, and as they gathered round Mr. Pliant—and the grog—our hero told them all the adventures he had passed through from the time he left the school until he held up the head of his dying friend.

As he listened to Jack's story, and drank the brandy, Mr. Pliant's indignation at the wickedness of the inhabitants of Hawkhouse increased, and as our hero finished his story, Mr. Pliant sprang up, exclaiming—

"The wretches—the brutes—the vile murderers! Oh, I know where Mr. Willet—my dear old friend, Mr. Willet, went to. He was murdered by these villains. Give me some more brandy and water, Jack Firebrace. We will fight them all. Let them come here, and we will show them what honest men and true will do. Oh, the wretches—oh, the brutes!"

"Pray, be quiet, Mr. Pliant," said Jack. "We all agree with you that we will fight to the last, and, if necessary, die, but never surrender. Still, we must do all we can to ensure a victory to our side, and for that purpose it behoves us to be extremely cautious."

"True, Jack, true. You speak as a general should. Providence and bravery combined must carry the day. Phew! what a fever your dreadful history has thrown me into. Made me quite thirsty —quite. I must have another drink. There!" he continued, as he set down the glass he had just emptied; "now I feel that—hic—I could—hic—stand up before a thousand men."

Whatever Mr. Pliant's feelings might have been, his capability of acting up to them was of the smallest.

So far from being able to stand up before a thousand men, he was unable to stand up at all.

His knees gave way under him, and when he attempted to walk his legs crossed each other in a most peculiar style, so that he found it necessary to lean against the wall for support.

Having secured himself from the chances of falling, Mr. Pliant drew his sword and began making furious cuts and passes as if hacking a hundred enemies to pieces.

At each cut, or thrust, he exclaimed, sternly—

"Die, wretch!"—until at last his foot slid quietly from under him, and he slipped in a sitting posture on the floor.

Suddenly his feelings underwent a change, and he laughed heartily, bade them all good-night, and soon fell asleep.

CHAPTER XLV.

ROB RACKSTRAW'S ADVENTURES ON THE WAY TO LONDON—WILD WINNY ONCE MORE—A COACHING ADVENTURE.

ROB RACKSTRAW was kindly treated by everybody in Newport prison. Mr. Podzus, out of really a grateful feeling, as well as to spite his brother magistrate, saw to Rob's comfort, and promised him that someone should be sent to London to discover the truth of the story which the unfortunate policeman had told.

This was done, and when Rob was well enough to attend before the magistrate again a fellow constable from London was in attendance to prove that Rob was not a thief.

But what puzzled everybody the most was that the gentleman who had declared that he had been robbed was not in attendance.

Therefore, Rob was discharged at once, and after a short consultation with Mr. Podzus took his road to London in company with Thomas Trout, the constable who had come from London to recognise Rackstraw, and Mr. Bolt.

It was a fine evening as Rob and his companions pulled up their horses at a comfortable hotel between Reading and Windsor, and consulted together whether they should proceed on their journey or remain for the night at the inn.

Rob was for pushing on at once, whilst his comrades were for staying.

So Rackstraw, having ordered the ostler to look well after the horses, threw himself on a seat between his two friends.

"This has been a queer go altogether, Mr. Rob," said Bolt, as he filled his pipe. "I can't make it all out."

"The thing is easy enough, Mr. Bolt," replied Rob. "Those fellows belong to a regular organised band, headed, I say, by one Griffiths Grindwell."

"But Mr. Grindwell holds such a high name for honesty," said Tom Trout; "it's a ticklish thing to meddle with a man like that."

"Tut! I know it was him who attacked the Lone House," said Rob, mentioning the date. "I stood by Mr. Summerbell's side all the time, and saw Grindwell leading on the attack."

"Hold hard there, Rob!" cried Tom Trout, "you must be wrong about Mr. Grindwell, because on that evening I can swear he was not there."

"Why, how can you swear that?" demanded Rob, opening his eyes with astonishment.

"On the very date you mention, I went with Mrs. Trout to a hall in the Goswell Road, to a meeting held by the Society for Providing Pincushions to the Patagonians, and Mr. Grindwell, he took the chair. Oh, you should have heard him speak. He made all the women cry."

For a moment Rob looked quite upset, and then, stamping his foot, said—

"Dash it all, I can't be mistaken! It was Grindwell, and I can swear to it!"

At that moment they saw a mail-coach, drawn by four magnificent horses, pulled up at the door.

"What coach is that, my lad?" asked Rob of the man who brought the ale.

"That be the Southampton coach," said the man. "She do go along, she do!"

Now all the bustle and confusion attendant upon the stoppage of the mail-coach took place.

Rob, with his hands stuck in his pockets, and his hat tilted a little on one side of his head, sauntered quietly up to the coach to have a better view of the horses.

He was standing thus engaged when he heard his name called.

"Rob—Rob Rackstraw, don't keep staring there, but come here at once."

Rob started as if he had been shot, and then darted to the window of the coach.

"Miss Winny! Heart alive, miss! how did you come here? Who would a-thought o' this now?" exclaimed Rob.

As he spoke the honest fellow caught hold of Wild Winny's hand, which was stretched to him out of the coach window, and kissed it rapturously.

"Why, Rob," said Winny, "how did you come here? How is my father?"

"As well as he can be, considering he don't know where you have been all this long time; he will be all right when he knows that you are all safe, miss. But tell me how you came here—tell me all."

"Now, then, young fellow, don't block up the way," said the guard, as he shoved Rob on one side. "Don't you see that the coach has to start, and the passengers want to get to their places? I beg pardon, ma'am," he continued, as he touched his hat politely to Miss Summerbell; "but we carry the mails, you know."

"Stop one moment," cried Rob. "Have you room for one?"

"No; full inside and out," said the guard, eyeing Rob Rackstraw with no very friendly air; for he was a surly man, and had a great idea of the dignity and importance of the guard of a mail-coach, and it really was in those days a responsible post. "No room at all."

"You are going right on to London, Miss Winny?" cried Rob, as the coachman gathered up the reins, and the ostlers began to draw the horse-cloths off the team.

"Yes; we go to the 'Black Bull,' Holborn," cried Winny. "I will wait or leave word for you."

"Give 'em their heads, Bill," shouted the coachman.

The horses reared, the guard struck up a merry tune, and away dashed the coach at full speed, so that Rob could not catch Wild Winny's words.

"Stand on one side," he cried, as he elbowed his way through the crowd. "Here, ostler, get out those horses and saddle them at once. Here, Bolt, Trout, look alive, old fellows; we must be off at once—at once, lads! I have another witness now—one who can't be mistaken. Come along, lads; I think I can do for old Grindwell now."

Scarcely had he said the words than he repented having done so, for he noticed that a man in a long cloak and a slouched hat was leaning anxiously forward as if to catch the words.

No sooner had Rob spoken than the man hurried into the stable, and came forth leading a beautiful horse already saddled, and looking as fresh as a daisy.

"Hillo, my friend, that is a fine horse," said Rob, who would have admired a fine horse had he been dying.

The man gave a surly grunt by way of reply, and sprang into the saddle.

As he did so his hat slipped a little on one side, so that Rob Rackstraw was enabled to catch a glimpse of his face for a moment.

But the man instantly pulled his hat down again.

"Stop a moment," said Rob, as he placed his hand upon the bridle; "we have met before, I think."

"Perhaps we have, perhaps we have not," replied the man, roughly. "I don't know you, and do not want to know you. Let go my bridle—do you hear?"

Rackstraw loosened his hold, and with a dexterous twist the fellow jerked his reins quite free, dashed his spurs in his horse's flanks, and sped like an arrow down the road.

"Where the deuce have I met him before?" muttered Rob, as he helped the stable boys to saddle the horses. "Where could it have been? Confound you for a set of fools. What are you after? Oh, I see what your little game is. You want to hinder me, do you? You have been bribed to stop us, have you? Now, if you don't hurry, I'll knock your heads off your shoulders."

Thus encouraged, the boys worked with a little more energy; but it was evident that Rob was correct in his surmise that they had been bribed.

At last they were mounted and speeding on their way after the coach, which they could see crawling up a distant hill, with the strange horseman not half-a-mile behind it.

Suddenly the idea seized upon Rob,

and, with a shout of triumph, he exclaimed—

"I know who it is. It is Bill the ostler, who tried to doctor my horse. Oh, if I had only recognised him before, he should not have escaped me so easily."

The stranger had by this time overtaken the coach, and was riding by the side of it.

"What do you want?" demanded the guard, in a very abrupt manner.

"I only wish to know if you have a passenger with you called Miss Summerbell," replied the man.

"For what purpose do you wish to know that?" asked the guard.

"I have a message for her from her father. I do not wish to come near your coach. Only tell her that her father is very ill, that she must remain at the hotel where the coach stops, and that he will send a proper escort to take her home. But you must let me know at what house the coach stops."

"At the 'Black Bull,' Holborn," said the guard. "Is that all you want?"

"Yes; deliver the message carefully. Her father is dangerously ill; she may be wanted at a moment's notice. By-the-way, there are three queer-looking fellows following; they look like some of the men with whom the young lady eloped. They may attack you to carry her off again; they are bad enough for anything. Good night."

The man wheeled his horse round, and, leaping it over the low hedge, rode away across country.

"Phew!" said the guard, "this here is a pretty caper, and no mistake. I don't like it. Drive on, coachman, as fast as you can. Blest if I can make this world out. I'll give the gal the message when we get to the inn."

But poor Winny had heard the news and had fainted away.

"There," cried the spinster lady, "did I not say that she was a wicked creature? Elope, indeed, at her age!"

"They are more likely to do it at that age than at yours, ma'am," said a crusty old gentleman; whereupon the spinster lady declared herself insulted, and threatened the rest of the passengers with a fit of hysterics.

Winny soon came to herself, and wept in bitterness of feeling as she thought of her father's severe illness, and prayed fervently for his recovery.

She had not heard about the other three men following, and, therefore, came to the conclusion that the man who had delivered the message for her was a friend of Rob's, who, being better mounted, had overtaken the coach and become the breaker of bad news.

The trees grew more scarce after a time, and the houses more plentiful; then lights shone brightly, and the coach was rattling over the stones of London until they reached the stableyard of the old "Black Bull."

Poor Winifred, who was still regarded as a suspicious character, looked vacantly about her.

She had not been in London for some years, and only knew the "Black Bull" hotel by hearing her father speak of it; and so, when the French authorities had managed to place her on board an English man-of-war, to be conveyed to England (we being at war with France at the time) the captain of the man-of-war had landed her at Southampton, and paid her expenses up to London, where he told her to remain at the hotel until she could communicate with her father and ask him to fetch her.

She timidly approached the young lady at the bar, and requested to know whether she could have a room until her friends came to fetch her, adding that she would most probably have to stay at the hotel for several days.

The barmaid was a good-natured girl, but she was not jealous of Winny's beauty, which, being rather a pretty girl herself, was very strange.

She took pity upon the young girl, and told her she could have whatever she wanted, at the same time asking her what was her name, so that she, the barmaid, might know when Winny's friends came.

"Winifred Summerbell," answered Winny.

"Summerbell—Summerbell? Why, we have a Summerbell staying with us now," said the barmaid, as she referred to a kind of ledger, wherein the names of the lodgers at the hotel were entered. "Yes, here is the name — Captain Edward Summerbell."

"That is my father!" cried Winny,

in delight. "Oh, take me to him—pray do. I hope he is not very ill."

"I can't say he looks very ill or very well," said the barmaid. "He seemed down-hearted and sad. But he is out at present. Come into the bar and warm yourself at the fire until he comes in. You will see him as he passes. He only came up yesterday, with another gentleman, a Dr. Lamberhurst."

"Oh, he is a dear old fellow!" cried Winny, clapping her hands for joy. "Hark! there is someone coming in now."

"Miss Winny—Miss Winny!" cried Rob, bursting into the room, all hot and breathless with his hard ride. "Thank Heaven, you are safe! When I saw that wretched Bill, the ostler, who tried to poison me, riding after you, I feared he meant mischief, and our horses were so tired that we could not overtake you, and—"

"Then you did not send me a message from my father?" inquired Winny, in surprise.

"No, miss; I came—or, rather, was coming—up to town, and he was to follow in a day or so; only I've had one or two little adventures that hindered me on the road. But who gave you a message?"

Then Winny related all that had passed in the coach, only leaving out the sneers of the spinster lady.

"By Jove! we've caught them now!" cried Rob, smacking his leg. "Look here, Miss Winny—this is a plan to carry you off again. I see it all. They will come here and talk as smoothly as you please, and say your father has sent them—the villains!"

Winifred gave a little shriek.

"I and my chums will hide behind the curtains of the room. You hear all they have to say and pretend to agree with them. They didn't know your father lives here when he is in London.

"Just as they think they have got you all right, out we come, slip on the handcuffs, and there we are, all cool and comfortable—as the boy said when he fell through the ice."

At first Winny did not like to agree to this.

But Rob took the landlady and the barmaid into his confidence, and both these ladies advised Winny to consent, which she ultimately did; so a room fit for the purpose was selected, and there Winifred waited the course of events.

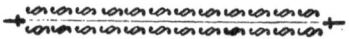

CHAPTER XLVI.

GRIFFITHS GRINDWELL AT HOME—HE RECEIVES SOME VISITORS—THE SWEETS OF REVENGE—GRINDWELL TAKES ADVICE.

BESIDES his fine offices in Austin Friars, where Grindwell conducted his large shipping business, he had another place of a very different kind which he much frequented.

This office, warehouse, ship chandler's store, or whatever it might be—for it partook of all these characters—was filled with all manner of stores.

Cans of oil, varnish, and turpentine were ranged round the walls.

Ship blocks, ropes, lamps, and compasses were all over the place.

Here was a binnacle—there a ship stove.

At one end of the room was a large roll of canvas.

Pistols, swords, coffee-pots, drinking-cans—indeed, all that was needed to fit out a ship could be had at Griffiths Grindwell's warehouse by the Thames.

Seated in his armchair, poring over some papers by the aid of a naphtha lamp, sat Griffiths Grindwell.

Now and then he stamped his foot with impatience, and listened, as if he expected someone.

"When will this be over?" he cried, suddenly starting from his chair, and pacing up and down the room. "Oh, how I wish that I had remained Richard Randulph, the pirate, and never played this game of the respectable London merchant! And yet it pays—pays well.

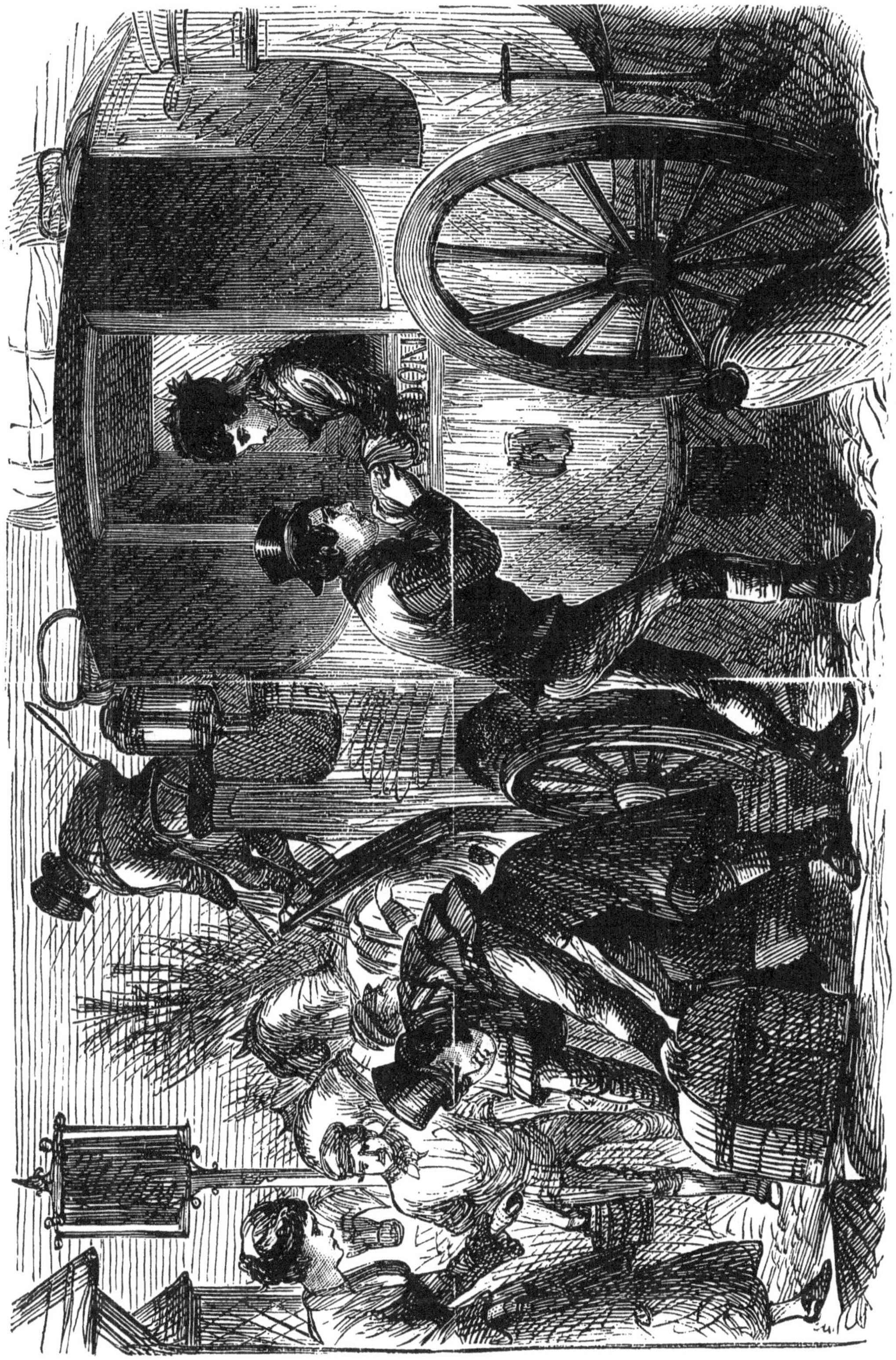

"ROB CAUGHT HOLD OF WILD WINNY'S HAND AND KISSED IT."

PRICE ONE HALFPENNY.

[PUBLISHED EVERY MONDAY.]

"They were fools who said 'Honesty is the best policy,'" continued Grindwell. "No, no; the knave who wears the mask of honesty has the best policy.

"Humph!" he muttered, as he paused before a bill, wherein he was mentioned as taking the chair at the meeting described by Tommy Trout; "that is a good *alibi*. The papers, too, all mention my name and speech.

"Luke Lansner's likeness to me is wonderful. The voice, the face, the height, the action—all the same, so we have only to keep apart, and each can prove an *alibi* for the other. Thus, when I pulled that obstinate fool's house about his ears and set fire to his household gods, I, impersonated by Luke, was praying for and preaching on the Patagonians. Ha, ha, ha! I shall weather this storm even now."

He threw himself into his chair, and turned to some of the letters on the table.

"I like not this letter," he continued, as he took up a short note written on foreign paper. "Jacques says that I must not think of going to Ile de Bas again, for we are betrayed. Betrayed by whom? Bah! my fate seems to be ruin at last. I, who used to swear that I could seek my fortune as I pleased. Well, well, come what will, I will die fighting to the last."

He crumpled up the letter and put it in his pocket, and then took up another.

"Hawkhouse quiet. That is very good. Mr. Sidney Morrison uneasy in his mind. That fool, will he never learn that I am not to be played with. I cannot make this out from Luke. Two boys escaped from Hawkhouse found with the gipsies. Who can they be? Now, if Jack Firebrace had been alive, I should have been frightened; but he is dead. Phew! what makes me start when I mention his name? I must have been drunk on board the 'Sea Hawk' when I fancied I heard him speak and saw his face. Bah! he is out of the way.

"It must have been Firebrace whom I saw on the cliff when I shot at that fool, Sidney Morrison, when he was raving down by the sea the night old Silas Sidecraft got his dismissal from this world. Well, it matters not now. There is no witness against me. Once this disturbance is over I seize old Falkland's property. That girl of Summerbell's — how could she have escaped? I walk upon a hidden volcano, which may at any moment swallow me —hark! someone comes up the steps. It must be Lansner's messenger."

There was a ring at the bell, and Griffiths Grindwell at once hurried to the door to admit him, but was not a little disconcerted when, upon opening it, he found himself face to face with Dr. Lamberhurst and Captain Summerbell.

"You do me much honour, gentlemen," said Grindwell, quickly recovering himself; "but I thought that when we had the pleasure of meeting at Hawkhouse it would be for the last time. Will you walk in?"

Mr. Grindwell stepped on one side, expecting his polite invitation would be refused, but, much to his astonishment, the gentlemen bowed, and at once accepted the invitation by walking into the office.

Grindwell closed the door, and then, throwing himself into his office chair, requested them to be seated, a courtesy they acknowledged with a bow, but did not accept.

"And now, gentlemen, may I ask your business? But perhaps before I do so, Mr. Summerbell, you will permit me to condole with you about that cowardly attack upon your house. You have a rough but honest tongue, Mr. Summerbell. You mean well, but other folks do not like it. I knew the men about that coast would one day have revenge on you. They are smugglers—all smugglers."

"Some are wreckers," replied Mr. Summerbell, meaningly.

"Ah! I should not wonder. A rough set; but why provoke them? It's so much better to live in peace."

"Have you always thought so?" demanded Dr. Lamberhurst, fixing his eyes upon Grindwell.

"I have always thought so," replied Griffiths Grindwell, coolly; "but people may go too far, and then, you know, prudence becomes cowardice. Now, we are not cowards. Oh, no! we are not cowards. Oh, no!"

Captain Summerbell shrugged his shoulders contemptuously, and said—

"Enough of this; let us come now to

business. I tell you at once, Mr. Griffiths Grindwell, that I am certain it was you in person who led the attack on my house. Dr. Lamberhurst is ready to swear the same."

"Some people are ready to swear at anything or to anything," said Grindwell, with a soft laugh.

"In a word, Mr. Grindwell, day by day, hour by hour, the evidence of your guilt is thickening. The police are even now positive of being able to bring home crimes to your door which will make your life a forfeit to the country."

"Those are bold words, Mr. Summerbell; but I told you your fault before. Pray go on."

"In the attack upon my house, my daughter—my only child—was carried off. You know where she is. If you will restore her to me I will promise not to proceed further in this matter. Give me my child back, pure and unsullied as when she was torn from my arms."

Griffiths Grindwell looked with the eyes of keen enjoyment at the father's agony.

He loved to see it.

It was to him the happiest moment of his life—the crowning victory of all his cruel triumphs.

Here was the man who had dared to threaten him—who had for years been his foe—asking, praying, and begging for mercy.

Oh! but it was a proud moment; one which his bitter heart enjoyed exceedingly.

"You have had your say," he said, quietly, as he rose from his chair; "now listen to me. You have accused me of being mixed up with the villains who attacked your house. At the time you accuse me of burning your house and carrying away your daughter I was preaching in London for savages. You do not believe the bill? Look at these papers. Here you will find the meeting noticed, and my address in full. You see how they compliment me on my speech. Well, I admit I am clever, but not so clever as to be in two places at once. No; I am not so clever as that. Have you anything else to observe?"

The two gentlemen looked blankly at each other, and had not a word to say.

"Ah! you men with hot tempers should keep quiet. You will get into all kinds of trouble."

"One word more," exclaimed Captain Summerbell.

"I am willing to let you say a hundred words more if you like—and they will pay me as well as those you have already spoken. Pray go on."

"You had a boy named Firebrace at your school," commenced Summerbell, when Grindwell stopped him.

"Pardon me; not my school. Mr. Gruesome's school. I am a kind of patron, that is all."

"I care not whose school it is. He was at that school. Where is he now?"

"I really do not know what became of him. He was a very wild boy. No training him at all. He ran away."

"I do not believe it," cried Dr. Lamberhurst. "Sir, you are a thorough-paced villain!"

"Thank you. I pray you go on; but I think if I were to ask you to-morrow to repeat what you have said to-night before a couple of witnesses you would refuse. Ha, ha! I had you there."

"No, you had not!" shouted Dr. Lamberhurst. "I'll come down here purposely to do it at twelve to-morrow, and you may have whatever witnesses and as many as you like. Why, I'll say it before the whole world. You are a scoundrel, and the man's a scoundrel who does not tell you so. There!"

What more Dr. Lamberhurst would have said no one can tell, for Captain Summerbell dragged him away, and Grindwell, having closed the door, threw himself in a chair and laughed until the tears ran down his cheeks.

"So, so, Edward Summerbell, you thought to ruin me, did you? Ah! I have you beneath my heel now, and I will crush you in the dust. You, at all events, are in my power. The girl, no doubt, sprang overboard and was drowned. She was a perfect little vixen, capable of anything and everything. Therefore, Master Summerbell, I have given you another object to search for. One that will take you off all other business, and thus leave me more free to work."

As he spoke he chuckled at his own cleverness, and rubbed his hands with delight as he thought how fortune seemed to play into his hands.

"Let me see," he muttered, at last. "I must not attempt to run any more cargoes. The Government are getting up to all my tricks. No; I will apply for a letter of marque and sail as a privateer. Go to America, sell my ship, and retire down South. I shall make a fine slave-owner. Ha, ha, ha, ha!"

He paused as he heard a hasty footstep sound on the paved forecourt of the house. Then the bell rang very violently.

"This must be Lansner's messenger," said Grindwell, as he seized the lamp. "May he bring news of success. It would be good news if that wretched old Hawkhouse were in flames, and every soul in it burned. It is well insured in my name. Well, well, we will see; all in good time—all in good time."

He walked leisurely to the door, and as slowly as possible unfastened it, for it was one of Grindwell's habits always to be slow when other people were in a hurry, and impatient when others were slow.

He had scarcely withdrawn the latch when the door was thrust open, and Bill the ostler rushed past Grindwell into the office, and, throwing himself into a chair, called for brandy.

Grindwell hastily closed the door, taking great care to bolt and bar it.

He then entered the office, poured out a tumbler of brandy, and handed it to the fellow, who drank it like water.

"Well," said Grindwell, sternly; "perhaps, now, you will tell me the meaning of this?"

"The meaning is ruin!" gasped Bill—"utter ruin—everything is lost."

"Tut! you talk like a fool!" laughed Grindwell. "Thinkest you I am so easily overthrown? No; I crush my enemies."

"Crush them?—yes; but they crop up again stronger than ever. The boy Firebrace is still alive!"

"Ah!" exclaimed Grindwell, staggering back; "who dares say that? You lie—you lie!"

"It is no lie. He was on board your ship, the 'Sea Hawk,' during your last cruise—he and another lad. They were hidden as stowaways, and you landed them as some of the cargo."

Griffiths Grindwell's face turned perfectly livid with rage when he heard this.

He ground his teeth, his eyes flashed with fire, and, as he struck the table a heavy blow with his fist, he exclaimed—

"Fool, fool, fool! I might have known that it was that boy in person. Oh, what an ass I have been to credit any such idle fancies as ghosts. I can hardly believe that my imagination could play me such a trick. To have had him in my power—to have been able, in fact, to grasp his throat in my hands and watch his death struggles, and to have missed it! Oh! I could tear my own flesh with rage at being so befooled."

As he spoke he rapidly paced up and down the room.

"Well, the lads are in your power now, as far as that goes," said Bill. "Mr. Lansner caught them and brought them safely back to Hawkhouse. So the job can be done cool and comfortably, as everyone knows that they ran away, and nobody knows that they have come back."

"Yes; he shall die! But how he slips through my fingers. I have tried to poison him, but he escapes. I have shot at him, but always missed my aim—I, who never miss my mark at any other time. He has been thrown into the sea, but has escaped. But what mean you by coming here and saying that all is lost? The boys are found, so we are safe."

"Not so. The man, Rob Rackstraw, whom I tried to overthrow, is a police constable. He and two others are now in London with great evidence against you. I followed them, disguised like this, and listened to their talk at a wayside inn, hoping to be able to overthrow their schemes. While they were doing this the Southampton coach arrived, and in it was Miss Summerbell."

With a roar like that of a wild beast Grindwell sprang upon the fellow, and, grasping him by the throat, shook him.

"Hilloa! I say, hands off!" cried the man. Do you know what you are doing? You will strangle me!"

"Then tell me you lie. Swear that she was not there; that you have been set on to this by Lansner to try me."

"I tell you the truth," growled Bill the ostler, as he shook Grindwell off.

"It is no fault of mine she has escaped."

Grindwell poured out a large glass of brandy and drank it off, and then commanded the man to proceed.

"I hindered Rackstraw following the coach by bribing the stable boys not to saddle his horse in a hurry. Then I galloped after it at full speed and gave the young lady a message that she was to wait at the hotel where the coach stopped until her father, who was dangerously ill, sent for her. Then I cut across the country and reached London, went off straight to Greenwich, and got Clement Bulstrode and his men to go with me as friends sent by old Summerbell to fetch his daughter away."

"Well, well. Ha, ha! a capital scheme. You shall be rewarded for this. Go on. You took her?"

"No; that's just it. We went to the hotel and were shown up to the young lady's sitting-room. She received us all right and polite, and seemed willing enough to go, when all of a sudden out comes that devil, Rob Rackstraw, and he slips a pair of handcuffs on to Clement Bulstrode like a shot, and then another constable made a dash at me, but I toppled him over and flew out of the room, flooring several waiters and women who were waiting outside to see some of the fun. Ecod! they saw a great deal more of the fun than they expected, for they went down like ninepins. So I got clear off and bolted here at the double quick."

As he finished he stared in horror at Grindwell's face.

Never had he seen a human being's features so distorted by rage and agony.

Every muscle twitched, the skin was drawn and livid, the lips pulled tightly back in a kind of tiger-like grin, so as to show his fang-like teeth, and he breathed so heavily that he seemed snarling.

"Baffled! baffled by that fellow! What hotel did you go to? Speak! we have no time to lose!"

"The 'Black Bull' in Holborn was where the coach stopped."

The man paused and sprang back in terror, for at the mention of the hotel Grindwell had burst out into a fearful shriek of fiend-like laughter, and, raising his clenched fists over his head, shook them with rage.

"Ha, ha, ha! the hotel where her father always stays. The Fates have declared against me. Nay, do not fear me, my good fellow; it was no fault of yours—neither will I do you any harm. As you say, danger is near, and we have no time to lose. The 'Sea Hawk' lies below Woolwich; we will be on board of her within an hour. Oh, I have been too merciful, too merciful!"

"Ay, that you have, master. I never let anyone that I was to kill slip through my fingers. Self first, say I, and anybody who doesn't look out for number one deserves anything that may happen to him."

As the fellow spoke Grindwell had been busily engaged filling a bag with some papers and other things.

But as these words fell upon his ears he suddenly paused, and a fiendish look came into his face, which, had Bill the ostler seen, would have convinced him that there was a soul in that room quite as black as his own.

"You are right, Bill, quite right," he said, as he unlocked a cupboard and drew therefrom a case-bottle. "Yourself number one, everybody else number two. Come, here is some true Dutch Golden Water; it would be a pity to leave such good stuff behind. Your glass, Bill; we will drink success to our journey."

The fellow, who was now three-parts drunk from the brandy, laughed aloud as he stretched forth his tumbler.

Griffiths Grindwell filled it to the brim, at the same time calling out.

"Drink it up, Bill. No heel taps; drink it up, and see the wondrous effect it has upon your nerves."

The fellow tossed off the liquid, staggered back, and dropped the glass upon the floor, where it shattered to pieces.

He pressed his hands upon his throbbing temples and stared in horror at Grindwell, who leaned over the table, his eyes fixed on the ostler, watching the effects of the poison.

The dying man grasped at his throat.

The room grew dark, dark, darker.

But still he could see Grindwell's eyes shining out like two evil stars.

At last even those evil lights disappeared, and Bill the ostler reeled forward, and fell dead on the floor.

"Dead!" laughed Grindwell; "that

is good. I took your advice, my friend
—each for himself; but I have no time
to lose."

With wonderful rapidity he stripped
the dead man.

Then he took off his own garments
and put them on the corpse.

He then, with the greatest celerity,
put on the dead man's garb, taking care
to remove from the corpse all articles of
jewellery—it was but poor, common
stuff—whilst his own gold watch, massive chain and rings, he placed in the
dead man's pockets, and on his fingers.

"Now I am safe," he cried, with a
laugh of scorn; "I defy fate, and will
conquer it."

Drawing out the corks from the large
cans of turpentine, he poured the contents
over the dead man until the clothes were
soaked through.

He then uncorked the cans of varnish,
paint, and such stuff, and upset them
over some bales of oakum, canvas, and
rope, until the place was one large stack
of inflammable matter.

He had scarcely done this when he
heard the sound of many feet in the
paved yard.

"I am in time, only just in time," he
chuckled; "they will find these burnt
remains and fancy I am dead."

He retreated, lamp in hand, to a
small room beyond his office, and softly
opened a window which looked out on
the Thames.

Putting his hand out, he caught a rope
which was fastened to a staple in the
wall, and, kneeling on it, pulled a boat
close up to the window.

"It is all right," he laughed; "that
is the beauty of being prepared for all
difficulties."

At this moment he heard the office-
bell ring violently.

"Now is the time," he muttered, and
taking the naphtha lamp hurled it into
the corner, where it fell, crash!

There was a flicker of light, as if the
lamp would go out.

Then a bright blaze shot up, and the
office was one mass of flames.

Then Grindwell slipped down the
rope into the boat, pulled it close in so
that he might shut the window, undid
the rope from the staple, pushed off
quietly, and let the boat drift into the
middle of the stream.

Shouts, screams, and yells were heard,
and high amongst the din came the cry
of—

"Fire, fire, fire!"

A bright glare showed Grindwell that
the ground floor of his premises were
burning well, and he rubbed his hands
with glee.

Now he could see the flames burst
out of all the windows at the back, and
he knew all must be destroyed.

He wanted to see the roof fall in,
which it very soon did, and then, seizing
the oars, pulled swiftly down the
river.

Grindwell pulled with all his might,
so as to get out of the light caused by
the conflagration.

The tide and the wind were all in his
favour, so that it did not take him long
to reach his ship.

She was anchored in the stream, and
Grindwell could see that all the men
were on deck watching the fire.

"Ship ahoy!" he shouted. "Throw
me out a rope, will you?"

"By Jove! it's the captain," he heard
one of the men say, and then there came
the answer, "Ay, ay, sir!"

And in a few moments Grindwell
stood upon his own deck.

"There's been a terrible fire up yonder, sir," said the mate, as he assisted
Grindwell to take off his cloak.

"It is my wharf and ship-chandler's
place. I have set them on fire. No
more questions, but give the orders to
set sail at once."

"Ay, ay, sir; is it to be all sail, sir?
The wind is coming up pretty fresh with
the tide, and the night is dark."

"All sails. We must be far on our
way before morning."

The lieutenant knew Grindwell too
well to disobey his commands, and soon
the sailors were hard at work, and in a
very little time the "Sea Hawk" was
running before a fresh breeze out of the
mouth of the Thames.

Then Grindwell began to examine the
vessel, and soon discovered where Jack
had been hidden, and how Wild Winny
must have been taken through the panel.

The discovery only made him more
wild than ever, and he determined to
have revenge, let it cost what it might.

He gave orders to his lieutenant to
make all sail for Hawk's Crag, and then

calling the men to him, gave them this short address—

"My lads, I have done all I can to keep you out of danger; but the time has now come when we must stick to one another. Traitors are at work. Men whom we have trusted have sold us to our enemies.

"A traitor to-night has perished in the flames. I have lost thousands by that fire; but I hold that as nothing to my revenge. Now, you know what to expect if you are false to me.

"Be true to me, and I will tell you what we will do. I shall sail to Hawkhouse. There I have vast treasures, which we will put on board this ship.

Then we will sail to the South Pacific, land on one of the beautifnl islands, where labour is folly—a land of plenty, where he who is hungry can stretch forth his hand and eat. Now, my lads, will you follow me to this paradise—follow me through all dangers?"

"We will, we will!" cried the men.

"Well said, my brave fellows. From this time forward I will never leave you. Serve the lads some brandy — they deserve it; and those who stick by me will always find Red Randulph true to them."

"Hurrah, hurrah! for our captain, and we will stick to him to the last!" shouted the men.

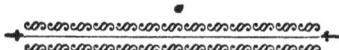

CHAPTER XLVII.

MR. PLIANT COMES OUT IN A NEW CHARACTER—THE ATTACK ON THE DORMITORY—
DEFEATED—THE HORRORS OF WAR.

WHEN Mr. Pliant fell asleep Jack assisted the others in loading their pistols and preparing the defence of the place.

Having done this, he gathered the fellows together, and related his adventures on board the "Sea Hawk" more fully, and also told them all he knew of the crimes that had been perpetrated at Hawkhouse.

The grey dawn of morning came glancing over the land, and fell cold and chilly on the lads.

Each one shivered in the cold morning air, but no one felt fear.

They were cold and haggard, it is true, and looked very woebegone, but all declared themselves ready to follow Jack Firebrace, and stick to him through thick and thin.

In whispers Jack appointed a quartermaster, who took care of the provisions, and ordered him to serve out breakfast and a little weak brandy and water, which was partaken of in silence.

Unfortunately, the word "brandy" caught Mr. Pliant's ears, and he at once awoke, but still under the influence of drink.

"Brandy!" he cried; "who said brandy? Dear me, how parched I am.

My tongue is like a rasp. Halloa! what is this?"

Here he looked, with undisguised horror, at his sword, and threw it away.

"Who gave me that? Have I been dreaming? No, there is Firebrace with another sword, and, as I live, he has a gun."

"Have you forgotten, sir, what I told you last night?" asked Jack; "have you forgotten poor Felix's death?"

"Dear, dear me!" exclaimed Mr. Pliant; "I did hope that it was all a dream, but I see now that it was not."

"I trust that you have no intention of deserting us," said Jack; "you will never go over to those murderers?"

"Jack Firebrace, what do you think me? I have been a dreamer. Whilst studying my favourite classic authors I have walked with my eyes shut to all that was going on around me. But now I am awake and—thirsty. Give me a little brandy and water, Jack."

Our hero then mixed another small jug of grog, and Mr. Pliant drank it off hurriedly.

The effects of this on the remains of his last night's excess was that Mr. Pliant became at once tipsy.

Once more he grasped his sword; but,

not content with that weapon, he also seized a gun, and striking the butt of it on the floor, he exclaimed, in loud tones—

"Boys, brothers, and fellow-citizens—hic—unaccustomed as I am to public speaking—hic—on this 'casion I feel called upon to get upon my legs—and very unsteady legs they've grown suddenly. In this house we have been treated like slaves. Shall we be—hic—slaves? No! 'Britons never—never shall be slaves!'—quotation—hic—we will draw the—hic—sword! We will pull the trigger!"

Bang!

Here Mr. Pliant dropped first his gun and then himself; for, in knocking the butt-end of it upon the floor he had managed to discharge it—luckily doing no mischief, as the bullet lodged in the ceiling. But so alarmed was Mr. Pliant that he fell backwards into a large chest that chanced to be open, and, having bruised himself a little, commenced bellowing "Murder!" as lustily as he could.

"For Heaven's sake do not make that noise!" said Jack, as he helped the others to pull him out of the box. "We wished to put off the attack as long as we could, but you have betrayed us."

"Dear Firebrace," cried Mr. Pliant, "I am wounded. I feel the blood trickling."

Mr. Pliant paused suddenly, and his cheeks turned pale, for at that moment a loud knocking was heard at the door.

"Boys, boys," cried Mr. Sidney Morrison, "open the door at once. What is the meaning of this disturbance?"

"It means that we have revolted at last against crime and cruelty—that we intend to fight for our liberty. Hurrah for Jack Firebrace!" shouted the boys. "Down with old Gruesome and Hawkhouse School!"

"Are you there, Firebrace?" inquired Sidney Morrison, anxiously. "If so, I call upon you to make those boys open the door at once. Remember, what you are doing will bring you within the reach of the law."

"And dare you talk to me about the law?" cried Jack, indignantly. "You, who have broken it in every way—you, who have linked yourself with murderers and thieves! Think you, Mr. Sidney Morrison, that I have forgotten that had it not been for the old boatman and Flick you would have hurled me into the sea?"

"Hush, hush, Firebrace! For mercy's sake hold your tongue!" cried Morrison. "You know not what you say—indeed, indeed, you do not. I was compelled to do it by that dreadful man, Mr. Griffiths Grindwell."

"Compelled to do it," cried Jack, scornfully. "Would any honest man be compelled to commit murder?"

"No, no, no!" shouted the lads. "If we surrender they will murder us all. Down with them all!"

"Hark to that, Mr. Morrison, and tell Mr. Grindwell, if he be here, that, boys as we are, we defy him. I, and my dear friend Felix (who now lies in the next room murdered by one of your friends), on the first night I came here, crept down some steps leading from the chapel to a cave. We heard cries of murder in the cave, and, stopping half-way down the steps, crawled out of an opening cut in the wall onto a ledge of the cliff. Then we saw you, Mr. Sidney Morrison, standing down by the sea, gesticulating violently. Someone shot at you and you fell. Heaven alone knows what dreadful scene of bloodshed had been enacted that night; but that you had a share in it your after conduct has proved."

"What!" yelled Mr. Sidney Morrison, "you a witness against me? Then, come what may, I will throw my fortunes in with those of Mr. Grindwell. Up, up, up, all of you," he shouted, to the people of the house. "The boys have mutinied and barricaded themselves in the dormitory. Up, up, up!"

"I think that we are in for it now," laughed Jack, for he saw that some of the boys seemed to shake.

"Wash the odds s' long ash you're happy?" said a voice, and, looking round, Jack beheld Mr. Pliant seated in a corner enjoying a glass of grog, which, in the confusion, he had mixed for himself from the general stores, wisely keeping the full jug, which he had mixed on the sly, untouched in the cupboard. "Let'sh be jolly."

"Is that the way you mean to fight

for your life and liberty, Mr. Pliant?" asked Jack, laughing.

"Don't want fight at all. Let them all go out; we stay here, an' all be sholly."

"I think you had better look after yourself, for here come the foe in all their strength and power."

A violent knocking was now heard at the door, and a voice, which sounded like Grindwell's, but which really came from Luke Lansner, demanded admission instantly.

"I think you had better not threaten us," replied Jack, quietly. "We are desperate, and will fight to the last."

"My men!" cried Luke Lansner, turning round to his followers, "get your swords and muskets ready. We will give these young gentlemen and this drunken usher such a treat as they never had."

"You had better not attempt it!" cried Jack. "We have firearms."

"'Sblood! Are we to be talked to by a set of boys?" cried Luke the Double. "Burst open the door!"

"Kneel down behind the barricade, lads!" shouted Jack. "Present your muskets at the door, and, directly it gives way, fire. Those lads who have pistols stand here, so as to be able to shoot down any who enter the room."

"Curse the whelp!" cried Luke Lansner. "Why did I not let the gipsies kill him?"

"Because fate was against you," laughed Jack. "I am destined to bring you to the gallows. I know you are Luke Lansner—not Griffiths Grindwell—Luke the Double. You are the image of each other, and have by that means carried on your cruel work. But I will expose you both, and the hangman shall have his due!"

"That's one for you, old Grindwell!" shouted Mr. Pliant.

And then he began to sing—

"'Britons never, never shall be slaves!'"

Jack saw that, badly as the song—or, rather, the chorus of the song—had been sung, it inspired the boys.

At once he took it up, and in rich tones led the lads in singing England's proud song of the sea.

"Burst open the door. By Heaven! I'll hang all these young whelps, and strangle the usher with my own hand!"

cried Luke Lansner; and directly a fearful shower of blows were delivered on the door.

But the stout old oak resisted all their efforts, and each time the men rested to regain their strength the boys cheered.

"To think that we should be shut out like this by a few stupid boys!" said Sidney Morrison.

"Stupid boys!" sneered Luke the Double; "there is one boy there, who, if he lives to be a man, will be a general or admiral."

"You mean Jack Firebrace?" said Sidney Morrison. "If it be in my power he shall not live."

Luke Lansner replied not, but he examined the door, and found that, save for a number of dents, it was none the worse for the beating it had received.

"Here, one of you fellows," he said, "put your musket through the keyhole and blow the lock of the door off."

"Stand on one side—all of you stand on one side directly!" cried Jack, in a low voice.

Scarcely had Jack given the order when there was a fearful crash.

The first thing that Jack did was to rush to the door and examine it carefully.

The lock had been blown off, but the door, supported by a bolt under the lock and the bedsteads, stood firm.

He then turned to find out who had been wounded, for he heard a yell, evidently one of pain.

No one appeared wounded.

The boys were all there—somewhat pale, but well.

"The door will give way soon," laughed Luke Lansner. "Rush at it, lads, with your shoulders."

Jack heard the order, and stepping quickly up to the side of the door, waited patiently its being carried out.

Crash! came the men against the door, and as they did so Jack slipped a pistol to where the door was broken, through the lock having been blown off, and fired.

A groan, a deep curse, and the fall of a heavy body, proved that the shot had told.

"Stand back, stand back!" Jack heard Luke Lansner cry. "The young brutes have firearms. Who is it that is shot?"

"It's the usher cove," one of the men replied. "His hip is shattered to pieces. Bear a hand, Bill, to lift him away."

"This is dangerous work, sir," said one of the men to Luke Lansner. "They have the best of it, you see. Don't you think that we might starve them out? They are boys, and are sure to be hungry, and I suppose they have not any provisions with them."

"How can I tell what provisions they may have? Go, one of you, and search the larder," said Lansner.

One of them started on the errand, and soon returned with the unpleasant news that the larder was empty.

"Well, there is no chance of starving them out," said Lansner. "Here, one of you fellows go down to the village and collect whatever of our men you can find, and send them up here."

"Bravo, my lads!" whispered Jack. "We have beaten them off; we shall have a little rest now. One of you fellows look after Mr. Pliant—he is groaning so. The rest come very quietly and help me to strengthen the defences of the door."

"The window—the window—the window!" shouted all the lads.

Jack sprang forward, and, to his horror, beheld a man slowly raising the window sash.

"Back, scoundrel, back!" cried our hero.

"I am your friend, governor," said the fellow, assuming an oily tone. "Just you let me come in and see what I will do to help you."

Bang!

A bullet, which one of the rascals in the courtyard had aimed at Jack, sped on its way, but instead of striking our hero it struck the wrist of the hand by which the man was clinging to the ivy.

He uttered a fearful yell and fell backwards, a shapeless mass, upon the paved court below.

Jack hastily closed the window.

The boys were all pale and sick at the terrible sight which they had just witnessed.

But Jack soon rallied their drooping spirits, and having placed one lad, armed with a musket, to guard the window, and two more to guard the door, he began a minute examination of the room, sounding the walls and floor to ascertain if there were any secret passages by which they might be suddenly attacked.

CHAPTER XLVIII.

WHICH SHOWS THAT MR. GRINDWELL'S PLOT FAILED THROUGH HIS OWN FAULT.

"There, my beauty," said Rob Rackstraw, slapping Clement Bulstrode on the shoulder, "I think that was as neatly done as a thing could be. See you've got company; you're not alone: here is one—and where is the other?"

"Bolted!" said Tommy Trout, wiping his nose. "I tried to catch him, but I caught it myself."

"Confound you for an idiot!" cried Rackstraw. "He was the most particular one of them all. That was the wretch who delivered the message to this young lady. If we had only got hold of him, we would soon have had Mr. Grindwell by the heels."

"Why, what is the meaning of all this noise, my good people?" said a voice on the landing.

Wild Winny sprang to her feet, and in a moment was clasped to her father's bosom.

"Winny," cried the overjoyed parent; "my own darling Winny. How in the name of fortune did you come here? But there, there, this is no place to ask for explanations. I am only too thankful that you are here and all safe."

"Why, here is Rob Rackstraw!" exclaimed Dr. Lamberhurst, after he had saluted the daughter of his old friend.

"Yes, sir; here I am, after a lot of adventure," replied Rob. "Been a little unlucky, sir, sometimes, and fortunate at others. If you please, sir, we'll just clear the room, and then I'll tell you all I know in as few words as I can, for we have no time to lose."

Bulstrode and his companion were led from the room.

Then, in as few words as she could, Wild Winny related what had happened, and Dr. Lamberhurst and Captain Summerbell came to the conclusion that they had abundant evidence to apply for a warrant to search Hawk-house and to arrest Griffiths Grind-well.

A coach was procured, and Rob Rackstraw conducted the whole party to a magistrate, who at once granted the warrants desired, and committed the two prisoners to gaol.

Having procured some other constables, Captain Summerbell, Dr. Lamberhurst, Rob, and his men proceeded to Griffiths Grindwell's store down by the Thames.

Rob rang the bell, and signed for the others to remain silent, whilst he listened attentively.

As the reader knows, Grindwell did not answer the door, but Rob's quick ears were not to be deceived.

"He's in there, sure enough," he said, as he gave another pull at the bell; "I can hear him moving about."

The constables beat loudly on the door, demanding entrance in the king's name.

"That's fetched him!" cried Rob; "I see a light in the window. No; the house is on fire!"

Before assistance could come, the house of Griffiths Grindwell was one mass of flames.

"The place has been set on fire," said Rob Rackstraw. "He was in it when I first rang the bell. I wonder how he managed to escape."

"Do you think he has escaped?" asked Captain Summerbell.

"He's not in there," said Rob; "he's not the man to kill himself unless he could kill fifty or sixty people at the same time. Griffiths Grindwell ain't the man for that game."

"Grindwell, Grindwell!" said a sailor, who was standing near them; "why, he's the chap as owns the 'Sea Hawk,' with as nasty a looking crew as ever I clapped eyes on. As for escaping from that there house, that would be easy enough. The Thames runs close behind it. He jumps into a boat, and the tide will take him down to Woolwich, where the 'Sea Hawk' is."

"Come along, sir, come along," said Rob, excitedly, as he drew Captain Summerbell through the crowd which had assembled. "There's not a moment to be lost."

CHAPTER XLIX.

THE "SEA HAWK" MAKES HER LAST VOYAGE.

THE "Sea Hawk" sped on her way on the wings of the wind.

Gloomily Grindwell paced the deck of his vessel.

As the sun set the storm-clouds gathered thick and fast, the wind grew fiercer and colder, whilst the waves leaped up, showing their white crests, and glaring angrily in the light of the setting sun.

"Sail upon the weather bow!" cried one of the watch.

Scarcely had he said the words, when another man shouted out—

"Sail upon the lee-bow!"

The mate sprang up the rigging, and, after examining the vessels with his tele-scope carefully, he hurried down to Grindwell.

"They are two cruisers with all sail set, making down upon us as fast as they can," he announced. "What are we to do, sir?"

"Hold on our course," replied Grindwell, savagely. "We can beat them in sailing, and in the night we will double, and show them a clean pair of heels."

Darker and darker grew the night, until it was impossible for the watch to see many yards before the bows of the vessel.

The moon presently rose, and by its light they perceived a small revenue cutter bearing down upon them, whilst the two, which they had seen just as the darkness had closed in, were not more than a mile astern.

Seizing the wheel, Grindwell steered the vessel, and gave his commands at the same time.

The Government ship made an attempt to run right alongside the "Sea Hawk"; but Grindwell threw her up on the wind, and directly the guns came to bear, he gave the word to fire, cutting away the enemy's gaff.

He wore round at the same moment, and managed to send another heavy broadside into the enemy.

Again and again did he do this, so managing his ship, that after about thirty minutes' fighting, the man-of-war had a good deal of her rigging cut about, whilst, owing to Grindwell's clever manœuvring, but little damage was done to that of the "Sea Hawk."

Every inch of canvas that could be clapped on to the vessel was spread, and she staggered through the heaving sea, the masts threatening every moment to go by the board.

Nearer and nearer they drew to the Hawk's Crag. They could even see the lights in the windows, when one of the men rushed aft to Grindwell, and in hurried tones informed him that the ship was sinking.

"Umph!" said Grindwell, quietly, "I thought she did not answer her helm as well as she used. Can the leak be stopped?"

His coolness gave courage to the man —who was the ship's carpenter—and he answered—

"I doubt if it could be stopped at the best of times; but with such a chase as this there would not be the slightest chance. In truth, I think we have but a short half-hour to float."

"A short half-hour!" cried Grindwell, with a scornful laugh. "Why, that is a world of time for us in such a position as this."

With carefulness he guided the ship onto a small strip of sand, which, as we have before mentioned, ran behind old Peter Pigwellan's hut.

Swiftly sped the "Sea Hawk"; then came a fearful crash, and the next moment she was firmly fixed on the shore.

"Now, my lads!" cried Grindwell.

"Keep your pistols dry; lower yourselves from the bowsprit—follow me to the Hawkhouse. Hurrah! we shall outwit them yet."

As he spoke he sprang forward, and in two seconds had lowered himself onto the sands.

"Yield, or we fire!" rang out a clear voice, and up from the rocks sprang a party of preventive men, headed by Captain Firbank and Lieutenant Purvis.

"There is the 'Sea Hawk,' take her —she is at your service," said the smuggler. "Here stands her crew— take them if you can. Forward, my lads, and show these fellows the stuff you are made of!"

With a ringing cheer, Grindwell and his followers dashed at the preventive men, who met them with a deadly fire, which sent many to their last account.

Then they rushed furiously at each other, and a terrific hand-to-hand combat ensued, during which Grindwell and about twenty of his men managed to reach the cave, and from the secret passage the hall of Hawkhouse, where they were met by Luke Lansner, Sidney Morrison, and the servants.

When Grindwell learned what had happened, he rushed off with some of his followers to the dormitory, and hammered loudly at the door, demanding admission.

A cry from the dormitory made him start and gasp for breath.

"Jack, Jack! Jack Firebrace, come here," shouted Tomkins. "The outer yard is filled with soldiers, sailors, and all kinds of people. They are going to force the door open, I think."

"Why, they must have crept round the road unobserved," said Grindwell. Quick—quick! One of you tell the servants not to open the gate for a few moments. We will go down the secret passage to the well, and so on to the old mill. Wait, you fellows, here! We will fasten these little rats in their own trap, and should Hawkhouse catch fire —why, my merry little mice will have to squeak for it."

Seizing what, to an ordinary observer, would look only like a ring screwed into the door-post, he dragged forth a thick iron shutter, which completely closed the dormitory in.

It closed with a clash, and fastened with a spring.

Jack rushing to the window, threw it open, and, in a loud voice, called out—

"Help, help, help! Griffiths Grindwell, the murderer, smuggler, and pirate, is here with his men. He is the same as Red Randulph. He it was who murdered the crew of the 'Ocean Queen.' We, the boys of the school, have risen against the crimes which we have witnessed in this house, and we are now in the dormitory. Some of you go to the old mill, up by Farmer Jenkins's. There is a secret passage from that place to this, and the pirates intend to escape by it, if possible. Break open the doors. We are armed, and will help you."

The noise of the bursting in of the doors became almost deafening.

At this sound even Grindwell turned pale, but his courage never left him.

"Quick!" he cried, "follow me. We must escape to the mill at once. The doors will resist for at least half-an-hour; by that time Hawkhouse and Jack Firebrace will have ceased to exist."

Jack, who had crept to the door, and listened to all this, waited until he heard the pirates in full retreat, and then, jumping to his feet, said, in a low voice—

"Now, my lads, off with your boots. The time has come when we must either do or die. I know what Grindwell intends to do. He will blow this house up, and kill all in it—himself included, if he cannot escape. Those lads who have muskets, to the front. The others must follow close upon us."

Silently the lads caught up their weapons, and then Jack raised a trap under one of the bedsteads.

From this trap there was a flight of stone steps, which descended to a narrow passage.

Along this Jack went, followed by the others, only pausing now and then to listen, for at certain parts of the passage he could just catch the sound of hastening feet in another, which seemed to run nearly over the one they were in. And he knew by this that the pirates were making the best of their way to the mill.

Suddenly Jack caught the glimmer of a light, and at once whispered to the lads to stop, and remain quiet.

Then they heard Grindwell's voice speaking to the other men.

"Keep on in this passage; it will take you to the well—I mean this passage to the right; the one to the left is where the powder is kept, and only those who know the way down that can avoid the pitfalls purposely dug there. You understand your work — haste to the mill. If all goes well, I will join you soon—if not, I shall be buried beneath the ruins of Hawkhouse!"

With his musket kept at the "ready," Jack stalked after Grindwell, followed by the others.

Presently they saw the smuggler stoop down by the side of a deep pit, and taking a broad plank, which had been placed against the wall, put it over the chasm, so as to form a kind of bridge, which he crossed.

Jack motioned his companions to remain where they were, and stole after Grindwell.

Onward the latter marched until he came to a large vaulted chamber, in which were a number of barrels.

Here he fixed the torch, which he had carried, in the wall, and then produced a long, slow match.

"Now," said he, chuckling with glee, "I fix this slow match in one of these casks, and knock in the heads of a few others, and then, after I have lit the match, I make off by the passage to Peter Pigwellan's hut, and so off in the boat. Up goes this old house, killing all in it, or nearly so. My men are sure to be killed at the mill, and so I get clear off alone. Oh, oh, oh, oh!" he laughed, "that will be a glorious revenge on them all."

He lifted his ponderous sword to strike in the head of one of the barrels, when Jack raised his gun, and fired.

One yell of baffled rage and agony, and the sword fell from his grasp.

The bullet from Jack's musket had shattered his right wrist.

"Yield!" cried Jack; "yield at once; you are my prisoner."

"Your prisoner?" roared Grindwell, drawing a pistol from his belt—"die!"

Whether the agony of his shattered wrist spoiled his aim, or whether it was the dim light in which Jack was standing, it is hard to say; but certain it is the shot did not touch our hero, whilst

Jack, who also drew a pistol and fired at the same time, aimed so well that he shattered one of Grindwell's knees, bringing him to the ground in an instant.

"Forward, my lads, forward!" cried Jack. "Grindwell is my prisoner."

"Where is he—where?—let me look at the monster!" shouted Mr. Pliant, dashing forward.

His foot caught in a stone, and the unhappy usher fell flat on Grindwell.

In an instant Griffiths Grindwell seized the poor wretch by the throat.

"Unhand him, villain!" cried Jack, raising his musket-butt.

"Ho, ho, ho, ho!" roared Grindwell. "I can kill even now. No one shall save this fellow!"

Gathering all his strength, Jack swung his musket over his head and brought down the butt-end of it with terrible force upon Grindwell's shoulder, shattering the collar-bone and dislocating the arm.

"Quick, my lads," cried our hero, "here are some ropes. Bind the fellow's legs and arms together. Mr. Pliant, I will leave you, with one or two of the fellows here, to guard our prisoner."

Jack caught up a tarred rope's end, and, lighting it at the torch, led the way back across the chasm. Presently he heard the sound of fighting, and, turning down the passage whence the sound came, discovered that the sailors who had tried to escape to the mill had been driven back by the soldiers.

"Quick, my lads!" shouted Jack, to his followers. "Give them a volley in the rear."

The boys, with a loud hurrah, levelled their pieces, and certainly did great execution amongst the pirates, who, finding themselves between two fires, laid down their arms and surrendered.

CHAPTER L.

A TERRIBLE TALE—CONCLUSION.

ALL the prisoners who were not seriously wounded were removed the next day to the prison.

Griffiths Grindwell, Luke Lansner, and Sidney Morrison were left at Hawkhouse.

Luke Lansner was dying from a shot wound in his breast; Sidney Morrison was greatly weakened by his wound, and Dr. Lamberhurst had great doubts of his recovery. But, strange to say, the one who was most injured bore up the best, and would—at least so the doctors declared—recover.

That was Grindwell.

About two days after the Hawkhouse School had been stormed, Captain Summerbell, Lieutenant Purvis, Captain Firbank, Dr. Lamberhurst, Jack Firebrace, and Miss Winifred visited the prisoners, who were under the immediate charge of Rob Rackstraw.

"Soho, Summerbell!" cried Grindwell, directly he saw the captain. "Have you come to gloat over me?"

"No, that I have not," said Summerbell; "far be it from me to delight in anyone's misery. I have come here to ask you one or two questions about the boy, Jack Firebrace. Who and what is he?"

"Ha, ha!" laughed Grindwell, "that secret will die with me. I would not sell it to purchase my life."

At this moment Mr. Pliant pushed into the room, and said—

"Mr. Grindwell, here is a letter which has just been sent to you—"

"Hold hard, there, sir, if you please," said Rob. "No letters must go to the prisoners before I read them."

Rob took the letter and opened it.

"Shall I read it, sir?" he asked of Lieutenant Purvis, who, as head of the coastguard station, was in command.

The lieutenant nodded assent, and Rob read as follows—

"LOUIS,—Confess all, or I shall have to. Beware!

"A VOICE FROM THE TOMB."

As Grindwell heard the name, he started violently, but quickly recovering himself, said, jeeringly—

"A very pretty trick, indeed; but it won't do for me. I have played ghost and warnings too much in my time to care one pin about such matters. Luke and I refuse to speak."

"Yes; we will die as we have lived," gasped Luke; " true to each other."

"And you will not tell me where that boy came from?" asked Summerbell, pointing to Jack.

"No; I have told you that that secret dies with me."

"False—false as ever!" cried a rough, grating voice.

All started round, and beheld Peter Pigwellan, the deformed boatman.

"Hullo! you there, Peter," laughed Grindwell. "I had wished you dead long ago."

"Alas—alas! that is but too true!" moaned Peter. "Gentlemen, that lad is the son of Captain John Falkland, and is entitled to large properties held by Griffiths Grindwell. Mr. Sidney Morrison forged the deeds, so he can and must bear witness to the truth of what I say."

"'Tis false!" cried Grindwell, passionately. "Take care, Sidney Morrison; you are in no danger at present. Open your lips and—"

Here Grindwell made a threatening motion, and the tutor, who was about to speak, sank back with a moan of despair.

"Fear not, Sidney Morrison," said Peter; "you did not kill Silas Sidecraft. I can bear witness to that!"

"You?"

"Yes. I saw Griffiths Grindwell strike the blow that killed him. I had heard a cry for help previous, and was hurrying towards the spot hoping to prevent evil, as I had often done before, but I was too late. I saw you, Sidney Morrison, fall in a fit. I heard the lie he told persuading you that you killed the old sailor. I knew it was false."

"Heaven be praised that I am free from blood guilt!" cried Morrison. "I confess to having forged the deeds, and that the papers proving Mr. Firebrace's right are to be found in the box in my bedroom."

"Cowardly hound," laughed Grindwell, in contemptuous tones; "you free from blood guilt? You would have killed this boy if—"

"I had not stopped him," said old Peter, "it is true; but I prevented that crime, as I have done many another."

"And your proof that this is the brat?" laughed Grindwell.

"Here," replied Peter, "in this log book, in your own handwriting, is the account of the murder of John Falkland, his wife, and all the crew.

"Listen, gentlemen—listen to my story: Many years ago, there was no happier man in all Falmouth than Peter Suttlebury. He had a wife on whom he doted, and twin children—boys, as fine, strong lads as could be found in all the world.

"He had been away on a long voyage, and on returning home he found his wife had died. He was heart-broken, and for some time remained at home with his boys, who were nigh upon eighteen.

"The Falmouth people called the lads bad young fellows; but old Peter loved them, and saw not their faults. At last the lads persuaded him to sell his house and invest all his money in a cargo to trade with America.

"He did so, and made a prosperous voyage to America, trading along the coast right down to the South. Here Louis and Luke persuaded the old man to become a slaver.

"They made many prosperous voyages, but old Peter could not bear it, and took to drink. At last when they were in Guinea, in a swamp far from the shore, Peter saw one of his sons shoot down a woman who had tried to escape, and the old man took a solemn oath that not only would he give up the trade, but that he would release all the slaves on board his ship when he got back to the coast.

"That night the young fellows plied their father with drink, and in the morning when he awoke he was alone. They had left him.

"Illness came on; ague shook his nerves; rheumatics twisted his bones as if they had been made of india-rubber. From being once a fine, handsome man, he became the hideous, grotesque object you see him now. Look, Louis! look, Luke! Behold your work!

"I have little more to add. I traced them out, and discovered the sad crimes they had done. I could not betray my own children to the scaffold, and so I did my best to prevent crime. This poor creature, Sidney Morrison, is my grandson. His father Louis—or Grindwell, as you call him—deserted mother and child. The mother died; I could not keep the child. I sent it to Louis, but hid whose child it was; and warned him that one who knew his past history would expose it if he did not treat the child well.

"I have done now, Louis—Luke!" he cried, stretching forth his hands. "Look at me. I forgive you all that you have done to me—all! But for your own sakes—for my sake—confess your sins."

* * * *

Luke confessed all, and died shortly afterwards in his father's arms.

Grindwell remained obstinate to the last, and underwent the full penalty of the law.

On the night of his execution a terrible storm raged over the sea.

Old Peter sailed forth in his boat, and was never seen again; neither was any part of his boat ever found.

Sidney Morrison lived, but was an idiot.

Mrs. Drusilla Drysdale was not discovered until Hawkhouse was being pulled down, when she was found in one of the secret passages.

It is believed that when Hawkhouse was being attacked, she had entered the passage, closed the spring panel, and could not open it again, and consequently died.

Jack came into his property, and eventually married Winny.

Mr. Summerbell has retired, and is as jolly as can be; he smokes his pipe with Dr. Lamberhurst and Captain Firbank, and very often strolls down to the village school to see the master—one Percy Pliant.

On these occasions they always adjourn to the alehouse kept by our old friend Rob, who, having made a lot of money by the taking of Hawkhouse, retired from the force, took a wife and a public-house, and has never regretted either since.

Every summer Jack and Winny pay a visit to Hawk's Crag for a few hours, when they go to the churchyard to see that the flowers round a certain grave have been attended to.

The inscription on the stone shows that it is erected to dear, faithful old Flick.

And thus ends the history of the "Boys of Hawkhouse School."

Printed by ALFRED BRADLEY, at the London and County Printing Works, Drury Lane, London, W.C.